Alba

Rachel King was born in Surrey in 1953. She now lives in the West Country with her partner, dog and her collection of modern jazz, Indian classical music and the poetry of Rumi. *Alba* is her first novel.

ALBA

Rachel King

Anchor

TRANSWORLD PUBLISHERS LTD
61-63 Uxbridge Road, London W5 5SA

TRANSWORLD PUBLISHERS (AUSTRALIA) PTY LTD
15–25 Helles Avenue, Moorebank, NSW 2170

TRANSWORLD PUBLISHERS (NZ) LTD
3 William Pickering Drive, Albany, Auckland

First published in 1997 by Anchor – a division of Transworld Publishers Ltd

This paperback edition published 1998 by Anchor

Copyright © Rachel King 1997

The right of Rachel King to be identified as the author of this work has been asserted in accordance with the Copyright Designs and Patents Act 1988

The publishers have made every effort to identify the copyright holders of the quoted material, where they have been unsuccessful they invite the copyright holder to write to them directly

A catalogue record for this book is available from the British Library

ISBN 1862 30018 6

Typeset in 11/13.5pt Adobe Caslon by Kestrel Data, Exeter
Printed in Great Britain by Mackays of Chatham PLC, Chatham, Kent

For Kevin H.

1

It's late April, too hot and dry for the time of year, and Alba senses autumn in its breath. As she parks the little Citroën on the hill and gets out, a hot wind funnels up the road from the peat moors out at Godley, and lifts the pleats of her skirt, puffing it up like a mushroom. Hastily, her hands fly to it. Helen is most likely watching from the window of the big white house above. Helen, her mother.

Alba takes a breath and plunges into the hot car for her sun-hat and the pile of children's exercise books on the back seat. Her skirt floats up from behind. She pretends not to notice.

Some of the books have slid across the seat and fallen on the floor. Long strips of paper have come out of them. She sighs. C2's spelling tests. Most will have no names on the top to identify their owners. When she comes to mark them she'll have to go through the books to match up the handwriting. To match scrawl with scrawl. Or maybe, this time, she won't. That'll teach the little darlings.

The car needs to be moved, needs to be tucked in closer to the kerb. It's slewed, the front wheels are too far in, the rear wheels stick out in the road. She'll have to watch her driving, she thinks. She's getting too fast. Taking the bend out of school like that . . . whatever next? Dr Kirkwood saw her roar away today – he's always there in the background waiting for her to slip up, waiting for her to make the sackable mistake. But she's been impeccable since last September – she's been sensible Miss Farson again, taking the younger staff through the public school ropes. He cannot find fault with her now.

Spring wakes the blood. Memories put to sleep over winter push up through the dull consciousness like sharp green sap. The years are slipping by. Late last summer she had a taste of . . . sweetness – only once – and then it was all over. Better to be blind, better never to have known, than to have to slam the door on the light of the soul, as she's done since.

She picks up the books and catches the smell of spit-rubbed feltpen which muzzes the children's names into fat, distorted, unreadable shapes – pregnant letters – on the covers. She doesn't like the smell, nor that of the sucked-pencil pages inside either. Children taste and confirm life through the mouth. Their sticky, sicky fingers palp and worry everything. Nose-pick, satchel strap, school meatballs and gravy . . . all grey. Smelling of grey. No schoolchild smells of anything less than the pilled grey pullover on which every sensory schoolday experience gets wiped. The germs from last week's virus are still on the paper. Better not bring them into the house or let them near Helen. Helen can't stand being sick. She's got a thing about germs and throwing up. And she hasn't been too well of late.

Alba stands up and the wind blows from the levels to whip the long, fine, white hair over her face. Irritably she thrusts it back, twists it into a coil, and stuffs it under the hat.

She goes to the garage door at the foot of the garden and leans against the hot metal, the books clasped to her chest. Here she can't be seen from the house above. She closes her eyes while the wind swirls her skirt. It's like Marilyn Monroe, she thinks, imagining, hidden behind her tinted glasses.

And there it is again – the wistful note of autumn on an April day. Perhaps it's the robin which makes her jump season. He knows something she doesn't. In one season is always the seed of the other. So what's to come? It may be spring but she feels she's seen summer already and been desiccated by a fierce August. Now she is an ash leaf, last to come, first to fall, the abscission layer and the horseshoe-shaped scar already formed, the nutrients now all sucked back into the branch. The leaf, the colour and texture of spent tea, is now the unwanted by-product of a past life. What is there now except a gust of wind to whip her off?

She slides a little down the hot garage-door metal. Above her a door opens. Sound carries so down the hill. You have to be so mindful. A small country town with no privacy at all. Everything on view. Your washing scrutinized by your opposite neighbours. Out of the question to dry underwear outside unless it's well hidden and rucked together on the small inner lines of a rotary drier . . .

Underwear isn't worn in towns. White bloomers, pneumatically inflated by the wind, hung out by the don't-cares or the daring – they're noted and laughed about – while the greyed and faded sprigged cotton cringes on mean drying racks in forever-damp bathrooms . . . White has to be neighbour-proof to be flying bold out here. Are the cotton knickers bleached or boiled white enough? White begs to be searched for stains, doesn't it? Alba shivers as she walks away from the hot metal door. The nets of the grey stone terrace on the other side of the road don't move, but they watch. They're the sort to look for stains on white knickers.

She leaves the car unlocked and begins to walk slowly, a slow tide in her feet, up the path to the house. Half way up she stops, leaning back, and gasps as if she's climbing a mountain. The sound of next-door's finches, alien twitterings among British birdsong, reaches her. The woman next door keeps them in a large cage in her garden. She's got to be twenty stone – keeping these snap-legged birds whose thready chirpings are like the envious thin woman inside her, caged, accustomed to prison. She watches Alba too, a motionless mountain behind nets, her envy locked behind set smiles.

Helen Farson sits under the shade of a large pink parasol on the sun terrace. The pink stands out against the white walls behind her like a tongue on ice cream. The parasol has a deep frill of white gone yellow and is angled so the sun does not directly strike her face. The sun ages down on everyone. Helen has spent her life cheating it.

She sits with tightly crossed legs, ankles together, red and pink dress just above her knees. A light shawl is around her shoulders. It, too, is pink, matching the parasol. It is important to present a total look. The parasol smells strongly of garaged canvas, of last year's summer which has been soured by the cold and damp winter. Every so often Helen wrinkles her nose. It reminds her of the smell of Harold's old wartime hammock, of the memories she didn't want to hear about from his time in Egypt. All of it stuffed in a canvas kit bag where it lay for years undisturbed under the garage bench. It still had the same smell when Clive took it to the dump after Harold died.

Now she tries to interest herself in the view. And what a view. Visitors love it and want to sit out on her sun terrace all the time in summer. They're always saying how much they envy her, how lucky she is. And yes, she does feel she's got just that little bit more than anyone else. A view like this is a desirable acquisition, a kind of free kingdom thrown in with the castle. A useful ice-breaker, a perennial talking-point like the English weather.

Carefully shading her eyes, she looks down. The old town slips away beneath her into a flat, green, fertile landscape that goes for miles until it hits the hills. The land was all claimed from the sea many centuries ago and the landscape is still all water, its fields divided by deep canals called rhynes. Helen can see the boundaries marked out even more clearly from where she sits on the patio, by the lines of pollarded willows which lie along the edge of each one.

Such a feeling of space! You can see the squat body of the cathedral, too, in the small city that sits at the base of the limestone hills on the near horizon. Not quite the west front, it's true, but on a clear day you can make out the nave roof and the spire which Clive quipped looked like a cigar butt. And the magnificent air! So soft you could drink it like wine. Not like the old guest house she ran by the sea where all Helen got was windblown hair and recurring tonsillitis. No, this is comfortable, bounded space, lovely countryside with no raw edges at all.

Helen sees and does not see. Out there does not belong to her. She'd like it to, so there's always a vague irritation present. She's never happy with what she's got. She un-crosses her legs and shifts in the chair as if to jump out of it. But whatever the view, it's irrelevant at present because Alba, her strange pure-white flower, is flicking in and out of sight between the white rhododendrons as she comes up to the terrace. Helen taps her chin. The bushes have grown too large and need pruning. She must mention it later. But Alba never works fast enough for her. She's always busy with her marking. Alba's supposed to be the dutiful stay-at-home daughter now Helen's getting old.

Alba is wearing *that* skirt. Helen cranes forward and notices the hem of the petticoat underneath it. She waits for the pleats to fall against Alba's legs as she stops on the corner by the *Albertine*. As the pleats collapse the sun shines through them. Alba takes a step forward and Helen sees the outline of her underwear, the bump of her suspender buttons, the darker welt of her stocking tops. Briskly she rises from the chair and goes into the house through the open front door, tossing her shawl on a chair. Her hands ball into fists, her nails dig into her palms. She takes a deep breath and straightens her shoulders, turning to go.

There is a tall mirror by the door, wrinkle-free throughout its length. She stops and looks at herself. Her hair is swept up and back, the grey hidden by the colour of her own remarkable strawberry blond, and by careful dyeing. Nothing is out of place. Hairspray makes it glisten like the spun sugar threads on a croquembouche. She pats it and makes a quick lipstick kiss to the glass. In the corners of her mouth the amber-red colour bleeds a little into the wrinkled skin. With the tip of her fourth finger she deftly wipes it off.

'The garden's looking lovely today,' Alba says in a flat voice, aiming for brightness, as she usually does.

Helen comes out into the sun, shielding her eyes with her hand, and hiding from her daughter the blaze of emotion in them. 'Sun's too fierce. All my new plants are getting scorched. You can't count on a proper spring anymore.' She drops her hand from her eyes and moves about the terrace, arms folded, hands clasping her elbows. An old woman not giving in, rage fizzing in her chest.

'Wish I could sit out here on the terrace all day,' Alba says, smiling, not at Helen, but into the space past her, somewhere into mid-air.

Helen snorts and waves the comment briskly away. 'Will you spray the conifers for me, Alba? They're going brown. Clive bought those for me, you know.'

Alba puts the exercise books down on a plastic table next to Helen's chair. Immediately the top two flutter open and the spelling tests flip up and whirl about like grubby butterflies, falling onto the garden below. Clive *could* choose plants which need less looking after, next time he buys presents for mother, she thinks. But then he knows who'll be looking after them – me. For a long moment she looks at her open-toed shoes, considering how deep her feet would sink into the soft peat earth if she tried to retrieve C2's homework. She stays where she is.

Helen sighs loudly. 'I can't manage this garden, you know,' she says staring into the distance. 'It's too large. I'm getting a lodger. Someone who'll give me a bit of help.'

'Oh. Are you? Good.' There is no surprise in Alba's voice. She's past that point these days. Better not to react. 'I'd love a cup of tea.'

'Yes . . . We don't have proper springs anymore. It's bang right into summer. What will happen to all the blossom if there's a late frost? I'm glad I haven't got cherries like next door.' Helen frowns again, looking at the sky as if her daughter were floating somewhere in it and she should talk to her up there. 'I'll put the hose on for you,' she says, addressing the air. 'You can do it now. Won't take you a minute. I'll bring your tea out to you.'

Why not tea first, Alba thinks. Tea now. I work all day in a hot classroom. It's not much to ask. Ah, but it's part of keeping me in my place now I'm living here again.

Helen's red paisley dress bears down on her in the heat. Alba answers, 'All right,' giddy for a moment. The exercise books are flapping. Misspelt words are diving into the rhododendrons like paper darts, needing to be rescued.

Helen puts the hose-pipe in Alba's hand. 'Here, take the end,' she says.

Alba stoops and the water comes out unexpectedly fast, warm like the first wave over hot sand, spurting over her shoes, soaking them. She loses control for a moment and the thick spray wets her skirt. Helen, who is on her way to the door, turns and marches back, her green eyes aslant, her lips thinned into a line.

'Alba.' They are just feet apart, Helen coming towards her, yet she raises her finger, crooks it and beckons in an obscene crone-like gesture. Her eyes are fixed on the wet skirt. The water has soaked through the petticoat. The pale grey stockings and white line of her suspenders are raised in wet relief. 'Leave that.'

Helen's voice is low and prurient. She looks around and speaks as though someone might be hiding behind the hedge, might be listening to her perhaps. 'Get my shawl, and . . .' her voice hisses, 'change that skirt! You can see all you've got.'

There is a pause. Both women look at each other. Helen's small eyes alight, Alba's wide and unseeing behind her glasses, almost dumb, the shock locked away deep behind them.

'I'll get your shawl.' Alba drops the hose onto the garden and the water runs down over the surface of the dry crust of peat like a silver snake. The palest pink-wash of colour spreads from the hollows of her cheeks, up and away across her cheekbones to her temples. It has the effect of porcelaining her skin like an expressionless doll. Helen catches her arm as she moves past.

'Didn't you know? Weren't you aware of it?'

'Know what?'

'You must have done, that's all I can say. At school all day. Men there. What would Dr Kirkwood think? You must have known.'

'I wasn't messing about with hose-pipes there, soaking myself to the skin.'

'I noticed well before that,' Helen dismisses her.

'Why didn't you say so this morning then? Before I went off?'

The muscles above Helen's jaw go tight, turning the corners of her mouth down. 'I had a headache.' She avoids Alba's glare and picks some of the wet material from her daughter's legs, holding it up. 'See – transparent,' she says in triumphant fussiness. 'You can see all you've got.'

Inside the house Alba is greeted by cool scentless air. White everywhere. Helen's favourite colour, a backdrop, a foil, like a white stage permanently set with dummies. White. Order. Tastefully done. County magazine stuff. New furniture bought before the old begins to look worn. White-leather spines of Chaucer's complete works. Never opened. Never read. Chunks of red Swedish glass on display behind locked lead-paned doors. And there are the large white porcelain bowls in every room. Bowls full of water, cleaned and changed regularly, each scattered with scentless, dried rose petals. These sit on the water's skin, unable to absorb and rehydrate, sallow and colour-parched. Too far gone, like ageing skin.

Helen's large gilded bedroom is at the front of the house. Alba's much smaller one faces north at the back. Although there are two other rooms upstairs, both these bedrooms are set aside in readiness for visitors and in particular for

Clive and his family on one of their rare visits. It is very much Helen's house. Alba feels like a non-paying lodger. There's no place for her. She has come to hate the brilliant white everywhere. And she hates her own name.

Alba – never allowed to escape. Her name a cruel curse. Wanting to be different, to be normal . . .

School – a whitemare. The catty curiosity of children – little goose-steppers, every one of them. The whole playground one large gang advancing, poking, chanting . . . pushed up against the wall, the teacher's rescue coming too late . . . 'poor little white thing . . .'

And later, in her teens, the odd one, the girl with glass eyes. Cruelty. Ostracism. Contempt. Albino rabbits, one for each girl in the class, waiting for dissection. Poor white fluffy mounds snuffed out where they crouched. The sixth form peeping through the tiny classroom window one at a time. The hush . . . the bravado. Rabbit mortuary.

The door opening . . . the smell of formalin and clean frozen death. Poke, and they aren't full of guts and organs waiting to slide out on the silver blades. No, they feel like sawdust, stuffed already, children's toys over-stuffed, the sort they like to bash and bash . . . 'When you've skinned them we can treat the skins . . . you can have them as trophies . . .'

Alba, her scalpel poised. Tears dripping from her chin onto the white fur, spoiling it. Eighteen pink-eyed white blobs. Bred for the cull, to be poked, ripped. Bred for the purpose of quack-scientific curiosity.

Alba, running from the room, the scalpel skidding along the corridor, clean-bladed, pure unsullied silver still . . .

Helen has been through her drawers again, she knows it. The air is too quiet. It holds something. What took place earlier in the day has been frozen like a negative on an unexposed film. When Alba enters the room, the negative floods into life and a picture develops. The room has been too carefully left. One of Helen's faults, tidiness. A giveaway.

Alba eases open one of the white drawers of the chest. Her underwear lies there in immaculate white piles, all the hems tight and level like pages in a new book. Alba handwashes daily almost as soon as she takes off her clothes. She wants to keep everything from Helen. Soiled laundry – the soul sweats into the fabric. There's a machine, of course, which Helen uses once a week for economy. But Alba won't use it. Helen would say, any washing? No, Alba would say. I've done mine.

You want to look at my laundry, for signs that I have been with a man. *That* man. Now, Alba picks up a pair of briefs and puts them to her nose. There. The unmistakable scent of Helen's jasmine handcream. Carefully she puts them back on the pile so as not to disturb Helen's work. But this is neither sensible nor rational.

The whole thing has gone too far. She's an adult now, for God's sake. Helen holds no sway. She could get out. Find her own place. She's always fighting old ghosts here. Ghosts from her past she can't seem to lose, summoned so easily by the little things. She sits on the edge of the bed, feeling one coming, pulling her back . . .

. . . She's back in her teens. Thirteen-teen. Wanting then to shiver back into those recent, but somehow so old, pre-pubescent photographs of herself. Naked then, running about with streamers of seaweed. Grit in her knickers, taking them off, grit in the white bread sandwiches with warm squashed tomato and sticky seed pips dropping onto her bare legs. Legs that were always plastered in creams and lotions to lessen the bite of the sun. Legs nipped now and wind-smooth . . .

. . . Thirteen, everything changing. Jumpers not loose or long enough to cover the body underneath which has eyes all over its skin now. Eyes, not innocence. Eyes up the back, running touchily down either side of the spine. Waiting for looks. Eyes looking at her back. Male eyes. Eyes made of tentacles that could pry anywhere, around a waist that did not exist photographs ago. Helen's eyes. Boring into Alba's own, knowing they were not protected anymore by juvenile unconsciousness. The time of delicacy. The time of adjustment. The embarrassment of menstruation . . .

. . . Alba remembers . . . The battle to keep her periods from Helen's knowledge. The used sanitary towels folded in half, stuck together, stuffed into a plastic bag hidden under her bed. Poked far in with a ruler, fished out with the same. The shame of it. The terror of odour, the waning smell of herself she could not stomach. And then the bleeding over, and the attempt to dispose of the clutch inside the bag without being noticed. Always Helen. Always knowing. That horrid smile on her face like a smirk. Nothing bonding there. No woman-woman stuff. Nothing conspiratorial. And then if Alba was quiet, or cheeky, or any behaviour Helen found wanting, Helen would say in front of guests, 'Oh, Alba's got her period.' And Alba would want to die.

. . . Alba, lighting a bonfire outdoors, burning garden rubbish, sneaking the parcel of sanitary towels out under her jacket, tucking and squashing them inside the waistband of her jeans. Going to the fire to feed her blood to the flames. Helen, appearing from nowhere, standing, seeing. Standing behind Alba talking about the weather and pulling a bean-pole from a pile by the hedge. Moving in, poking about in the smoking privet and the smashed brussels stems, crushed cardboard boxes and eggshells, poking the flames. Alba, stricken, red, humiliated. The sanitary towels uncurling like a shave of dark chocolate from a peeler, her blood catching fire, impaled on a stick, charring and burning never fast enough, the dark plummy red becoming the heart of the flame before it consummates, and the black char-dust falling from the end of the stick in a puff of sparks.

Alba sits on the bed and shakes the memory away with a toss of her head. It's nonsense now. A long time ago. She was a sensitive girl, easily embarrassed then. With little regard for the wet clothes, she undresses quickly and treads the skirt and stockings into a heap on the carpet. She takes a pair of jeans from the wardrobe. Large jeans, men's jeans bought at Helen's suggestion, after she came back. Fitting around the hips but loose at the waist. Like a blue bucket in which her body slops.

Adding the over-sized T-shirt the class had given her last Christmas, and yanking back her long white hair into a rubber-band pony-tail, she sits down at the dressing table, takes off her glasses. Vivid blue eyes look back at her from the mirror. Stolen blue eyes. Blue contact lenses she wears all the time at work to mask the fact that underneath them her eyes have no colour at all.

She goes to the bathroom, takes the lenses out, comes back and dumps herself on the stool again. The long hard look. For a moment she peers at the strange clear iris, its network of tiny pink exposed blood vessels. Then she puts on her glasses, and goes out of the room.

The carpet pile on the landing oozes between her toes. At the top of the stairs she stops, seeing Helen down at the bottom in the hallway. Her toes fan out, twisting into the wool, and encounter all the old dirt the cleaner has failed to suck up.

Helen is at the hall mirror, her fingers pulling at the skin below one eye. Without turning she calls out, 'Everything all right,' a statement, not a question.

Alba comes downstairs heavily. She's neither big-boned nor heavy, but right now she wants to be. She wants to be big and aggressive, thundering downstairs with the kind of centred aggressiveness men always seem to have. The da dum, da dum, da dum of their syncopated charge, like young stallions. And they say women dominate by their voices, she thinks. It's not so. We are just thin, soft-bodied reeds. Try filling a room with a reed-voice. I know, she thinks, I try it every day at school. I watch my voice go thin in the space, not fill it. But a man – oh, for him it's different. They eat up space with their stallion bodies, their braying voices. And they squash reeds.

Alba attempts to thunder down the stairs.

'Damn,' Helen says. She never swears, and this, her only curse, manages to sound cute. 'Eyelash in my eye. Get my hankie, will you?'

Alba takes the small white square from under her mother's watch-strap and rolls one corner into a point. She is about to moisten it with her tongue but Helen stops her.

'I'll do it,' she says with a little laugh and the sharp point of her own tongue stabs the hankie.

'You shouldn't wear mascara,' Alba says. 'You always tell me not to.'

'It wouldn't help you very much if you did.'

'Maybe not,' Alba says slowly, stepping back while Helen pulls faces. Foundation and powder sit so thickly on her mother's skin. Where is her real face? Layers of make-up – she even sleeps with it on. And Alba notices how large the pores are around Helen's nose and eyes, how the foundation and powder have sunk into each other. There, in front of her is the grimness of old age patched up, the embalming of skin which ought to be allowed to sag with dignity.

Helen deludes herself into thinking she looks OK. Alba colludes with her. She always compliments her mother. It gives her power over Helen, but it's not the kind from which she can ever gain any satisfaction. It wouldn't be fair.

'I think I've got it,' Helen says, going to the mirror and patting the over-stretched skin underneath her red eye which is beginning to weep. 'Are you going to do the conifers or not?'

Alba goes out, rolls up her jeans, and strides barefoot into the garden. Immediately her feet sink through the cold wet layer of peat to the dry stuff beneath. The tops of her feet, so white, are swallowed by black. She shuffles her feet through it, the first wilful thing she has done all day, watching the dry dust mix with the wet crust to form great untidy lumps that will not rake smooth. They'll hold the impression made by her feet for several days . . . for Helen's benefit of course.

She makes her way down the slope between the shrubs, collects soggy strips of paper as she goes, stuffs them into her pocket. The eager private-school children she teaches will need an excuse for the lost or torn papers. They expect, they demand, so much of her. The truth would be very much out of bounds – humiliated by children . . . It would be just her luck for Kirkwood, the new Headmaster, to inspect C2's books. She's already under review, under his watchful eye.

Her mind wanders on. What was Helen talking about – getting a lodger? She'd never mentioned it before. She disliked strangers in the house. What was going on?

Alba suddenly feels the weight of her own paralysis. There is so much of Helen, and so little of her. Helen has always possessed her. Helen is in her veins with Alba's own blood. Helen had overshadowed her even before conception, before birth, when Alba was still a floating soul. Helen thrums through Alba's life as a continual calling-note. And why? What is there to learn from this? She hates me. What is there to learn from that? This unconscious power of Helen's had been a black caul which had engulfed and overwhelmed her since birth, horrible and aweful and mystifying, in the way the winter-black sky with its fierce bright stars subdues the earth – hanging there, so present. This is the power mothers have.

Alba looks up from the watering, thumbs the end of the hose hard and fans the spray up into an arc where it makes a rainbow. *I am a fallen star, substance no longer existing, but my light reaches the earth nevertheless.*

Helen comes down the path, elbows clasped, having put a mug of tea on the terrace table where Alba would have to climb back up to get it. She notices the shuffling trail of Alba's feet through the tidy peat mulch, and the little brown rivers that seep across the stone paving where she walks. Wet crumbs sit there, difficult to brush up, sweeping only into an unsightly smear. They would have to wait.

'Aren't your feet in a state?' she calls out irritably.

'Of course.' Alba wrestles with the stiff hose, sending loops and coils of water over the retaining wall at the base of the garden and into the road beneath it. 'They're really mucky,' she continues. 'I wish I'd put my boots on.'

Helen clears her throat. 'I should think so.' She smooths the strawberry blond hair with a light touch. 'How is Dr Kirkwood these days?'

Alba looks up. 'I don't know,' she says ungraciously. 'He doesn't wear his personal life taped to his sleeve. He's only the headmaster, you know.'

Helen waves Alba's truculence away. 'Such a charming man,' she breezes. 'A quality men lack these days – charm. When I came to help at the concert evening he was . . .' Her voice drifts, face pinkens with pleasure at the memory, 'so chivalrous.'

'He'd just been appointed. He was only trying to make an impression.'

Helen purses her lips. 'You shouldn't bite the hand that feeds you,' she says snappishly. 'You were very lucky not to get the sack last July. *That* says a lot about the kind of man he is.'

Alba falls silent, turns the water into a spray with her thumb. Helen will never let last year drop. Never.

'What's this about a lodger, then?' Alba's voice comes back to her, distant, studiedly nonchalant. She is making holes with the jet of water into the soft soil between two ornamental conifers.

'A what? A lodger?'

'You said so earlier.'

'Ah, a lodger.' Helen laughs, a trill lacking innocence, and meant to imply that Alba must be absurd to have believed her. 'Oh, that. I was only joking, you silly thing. Do you ever think I would? Oh, come on!'

'How do I know? You might. It doesn't make much sense to me, though. You always said the guest house was too much work and you don't like visitors – even Clive . . .'

Helen frowns and her lips purse. 'It's not *him*,' she says emphatically. 'It's those children.' She waves her hands in front of her face. 'All this rubbish about grandchildren . . . They wear you out, that's all. Wear out the old ones first . . .,' she mutters, as she looks down at the peat rivers running across the garden. Then she laughs, aware that the nets of the nearest cottage down the hill are moving. 'I only say these things. It's pie in the sky stuff.' She shrugs. 'You know what I mean.'

Alba comes back up the slope, her feet deep in peat slurry. 'It was only an idea, then?' She tucks the hose end into the lower branches of a white cytisus.

'Silly.' Helen's voice is playful.

But Alba can't give up. 'Where would you put someone else anyway? Someone you don't know? You'd have them around you at breakfast time . . . and using your bathroom . . . You said you'd never share your house with a stranger again.'

Helen rubs her elbows briskly. 'Oh, stop exaggerating, Alba! It wasn't as bad as all that. I rather used to like all the new faces coming and going.' She flashes Alba a look. 'And it relieved some of the boredom,' she adds. 'Besides, if I didn't like them I'd make it very plain. They'd have to go.'

'And what about me?' Alba looks down at her mother's beige chisel-toed shoes, held so tight together not even a slip of paper can pass between them. 'I hope you'd say something to me before you go ahead with whatever you're planning. I mean . . . I live here too.'

'Alba!' Helen teases. 'Of course I would. But don't pay any attention to me. It was just a silly little idea, that's all. You ought to know me by now.' She turns her head, sniffs, whips out the handkerchief from under her watch-strap and wipes her nose. 'The idea's only fantasy,' she says, muffling into the cotton. 'Stop worrying.'

Alba steps onto the cold stone path and goes up to the terrace to get her cold tea. Tea with a dull film of limescale on the surface.

Next week Leon arrives and moves into the largest spare room.

2

Alba is having an affair with a bird: a buzzard. On the levels near the nature reserve the bird's been at the same spot at the same time for two days running. She takes a third lunch hour there and risks being late back for the first lesson of the afternoon.

Ten past twelve. She's driven like a madwoman to get there. Now she crawls along the single-track road in low gear, her heart thumping, the binoculars at the ready on her lap.

Almost on time the bird flies over the car, going up the road in front of her before veering off to the left where it lands on the broken stub of a fence post in a field. She can't believe it. Three times. Three days in a row. An omen.

She stops the car level with the bird. It's settling itself. The great wings rear up and back like a huge cloak split down the middle, before they fold back down on the body again. It looks about, looks at Alba's little Citroën parked a hundred yards away. The dark brindled bird is on its way to the bird circus. It's the predator in the pack. The ringmaster.

Her hands are sweaty on the binoculars as she tries to get the bird in focus. The glass in the eye piece fogs up twice and she scrubs at it feverishly with a tissue. She can't focus through the passenger window either, so, slowly, carefully, she leans across to wind it down. The bird doesn't move, though it sees her every move. A crazy thought strikes her – what would happen if she opened the window and it flew in? A wild thing, that keeps time as this bird does, could be full of surprises. She wouldn't want that. It would be like coming face to face with an eye. An eye who sees far too much.

The hawk watches her as she brings the glasses to her eyes again. It could fly off at the least movement she makes. She's aware of that. It knows what she's going to do before her brain gets the message to her cells. This one allows her to look only for as long as *it* permits.

Through the magnification of the lens the naked ferocity of its eye meets hers. She drops the glasses. It's shocking. It zooms in right up to her face, like a man trying to pick a fight just because she dares look. Boldly, she raises the glasses again. Terror lurks all the time in the natural world, and she's oblivious to it all – so why should this worry her? It's only her fright at seeing creatures normally smaller than herself, magnified, larger than life.

When Helen wore thick prescription lenses for the first time Alba had a similar shock. Helen's eyes had a bigger say in her face. Eyes are the windows of the soul, her mother would tell her often – except that in Helen's case Alba couldn't see very much soul coming out of them at all. Helen's eyes appeared larger, but whatever might have been in them had been lost in their magnification. It was like taking a thimbleful of dye and throwing it into a lake, where, diluted, it couldn't be detected at all, and could never be enough to make its mark. Helen's eyes, though larger, spread her too thin, dissolved her out until she was nowhere to be found.

The yellow iris through Alba's binoculars is made of different stuff altogether. Everything about the raptor is pushed into that round half inch. Helen could survive without her eyes – without his, the raptor would be dead in hours.

Birds have no souls. The yellow eye is alien. There's no window to see through. Alien eyes living by another consciousness from some other non-human universe. Yellow iris . . . pink iris . . . Alba feels an affinity.

And there are birds in churches, Alba thinks. Lecterns made into eagles. The bird a symbol of the spiritual. Or, perhaps, of the alien nature of the spiritual.

The buzzard suddenly swivels its head with small, ball-bearing clockwork precision, doubly shocking through the intimacy of the glasses. Alba's breath seizes at the full-frontal exposure of such a raw unconscious driving force displayed with so much arrogant totality. But the bird doesn't care for her sensibilities. He just wears his inside on his outside, on his face, all the time. He's as shocking as a man dropping his pants in the street.

The head swivels once more to see what it already sees, to know what it already knows – the world in synchrony with itself, the world flowing through every one of its cells all the time, streaming through like the wind and the water.

The bird gets all this from the grey sky, so large down here on the moors it's like the other half of the world. All sky, a great grey cup upturned. It's where bird knowledge is born. It knows from the subtle air currents tickling crooked ash branches, from the willows aburst with pewter-green catkins, from the bleached mats of last year's grass. It knows from the black peat pools, from the duck's linear wake from bank to bank, from the rooks crowding in the sky, from their rising and falling. It knows from the scurrying of voles, and from the quick-winged panic of small birds in the copse. Its consciousness straddles not only bird-dom, but, with predatory dismissiveness, the rest of creation too.

Alba looks steadily at the bird, and he looks back, holding her gaze over-long. Her glasses start to shake.

She drops them in her lap. She's seen enough. She's full up. She's got indigestion from staring at an eye with no two-way communication.

Altering the angle of the seat, she sinks back. A sandwich snatched from the newsagents in town lies next to her on the passenger seat. She's not hungry. Instead she closes her eyes. The sun shines red behind her eyelids, heats the inside of the car. She sinks into a place between consciousness and sleep while her mind throws up image after image.

She dreams of an owl in gossamer cloak. A red ruff circles its neck, choirboy innocence utterly out of place on this bird. The cloak is thin, silvery, with the insubstantiality of spider's silk, and is made up of many small coloured tesserae whose boundaries shift, shimmer, and melt into one another. The colours come and go *ignis fatuus*, like hot breath breathed into cold fog.

The owl is gliding through the circus tunnel into the main tent. Owl-man. Man or owl, the body beneath the gossamer cloak is the shape of a fat heart. The head is ruff and smooth feathers, and the eyes watch.

She sinks deeper in dream. The owl changes. The ruff puffs out to stretching point. It grows stiff as the life goes. It's now a Christmas decoration of tissue paper, a caricature owl, harmless. The tissue layers over its breast, cut and patterned into honeycomb, lie flat between two card covers and open out creakily, leaf by paper leaf to a small pompous decoration, tilted backwards out of balance. The eyes are wide open, yet they have affable spectacles – they have to do that to the owl, Alba thinks in her daydream – you have to make fun of a threat.

Dutch's house on the rhynes is not far away. For a vivid minute he floods into her thoughts. He ought not to be there, but he has owl-eyes. She's tried so hard to shut him out since last year. But she sees the inside of the house, the rough plaster walls hung with Nain rugs, the unswept floors, the dirty stone muddied with boot prints. She sees the hooks by the back door hung with jesses and leashes, and, on the shelf above, the tiny soft calfskin hoods, some decorated with plumes of feathers, lying amongst a dozen small bells of different sizes. Dutch, there, squatting near the back door tying flies . . . the cigarette staining on his moustache and the beard he had last time she saw him . . . Dutch's thigh muscles . . . Dutch's fingers, hard and dextrous gripping her arm . . . Bloody Dutch. He never goes away.

She opens her eyes, squinting at the fence post. The buzzard is still there. It has been fixed on her, a cold passion in its staring yellow iris. Watching her dreams. 'Go away,' she says, sitting up and waving her arms about. It doesn't move. 'How dare you!'

'Everything is watching me,' she says, 'and I won't have it.' And, yes, it all does, all the time. Trees watch her. On the other side of the road the cut stumps of alder branches bleed orange, and watch her.

Dutch isn't frightened of such things. He doesn't mind being known. Very deep, she envies him.

'I'll just drive past his place,' she says to the bird on the fence post, 'but I won't stop.' The car starts, and, as she pulls away, the buzzard rears up with slow heavy wings that cloak the ground beneath, and heads towards the peat diggings.

Dutch's isolated red brick cottage fronts a thin snake of a road, where grass has seeded itself in tussocks all the way along its crest. Despite its wooden piles the house tilts noticeably backwards into the peat. Opposite runs the Sheppey, a small fast-flowing river. Flat fields of wild flowers, copses of birch, sallow and alder surround the house, and all along the road, as in every road in this landscape, are willows. Their red-brown roots suck water from the rhynes, their leaves transpire thousands of gallons continuously into the atmosphere. River . . . sky – what does it matter? All is water here.

Some willows have been pollarded recently and lean out over the water like great fists, top-heavy and silent, surprised, mutinous. Others, like the row along the river bank opposite, are third or fourth-year pollards, and cast thin shade with their whippy branches.

The house is half-way through renovation. Junk is everywhere – planks, old bike frames, broken flower pots, logs, roof-racks, burst bales of hay. It spills over the road across onto the river bank. There, old floorboards holed with woodworm are stacked up teepee-fashion against thick willow trunks, and brambles grow through a stack of car tyres.

The place is quiet. She drives past very nervous, looking for a sign of him. But he's never been an easy person to find. He could be anywhere – on the coast loading up seaweed after a storm, laying a patio, searching through a breakers' yard, or down on one of the Reserves where he is warden. His Land Rover isn't parked by the side of the house, so he can't be in. So she can stop, check things out, settle her memories. She doesn't want to see him anyway. It would be the first time, after all, in months. First times are always hard.

She parks on the soft verge a hundred yards or so past the house, and gets out of the car, grabbing the sun-hat from the passenger seat. Immediately the heat swallows her up. Willows sweat. The grass in the fields grows on a black sponge. The rhynes take the run-off: choked with vegetation like blocked veins, they feed the water slowly back to the rivers. And the sun lips it all. It's the kind of sodden heat where her body feels it could turn inside out. She stretches, and stops herself.

Slowly she walks back towards the cottage, aware of the tight bun on her head, the long pink pleated skirt and matching cardigan, the white blouse and the sling-back shoes. School clothes. Schoolmarm clothes. The straw hat and sunglasses incongruous, giving her the air of a self-conscious unwilling film-star. And she should be there now, at school, marking in the quiet room, drinking too many coffees after a quickly-taken school lunch.

No-one turns inside out at school. It's the teacher's lot, and a teacher is what Alba is – it's how she walks, how she dresses, how she thinks. She espouses the role like some people assume they know what is happening in the world merely from reading newspapers. She teaches what she doesn't know. She teaches because she needs to know, but with all the normal idiosyncrasy of human nature, she unwittingly succeeds only in reinforcing her ignorance. Since she met Dutch, a little of the arcane, a little of the disturbing, bubbled up from the deep. But, inured in the teaching life, she's still looking for knowledge in answers instead of in questions. No-one turns inside out at school.

Surplus gravel has swept to the roadsides, so Alba clicks her little sling-backs along in the centre, not on tip-toe, but almost. As she reaches the hedge marking the boundary of Dutch's overgrown garden, she stops, listens hard, senses suddenly sharp and animal-like. Not Alba – but only for a second. A bit of buzzard – but only for a second.

Her eyes dart about because she's seen something out of the corner of her eye. All her senses shoot forward. Her breath stops. Her heart bangs. Her awareness tunnels in.

A shape like a woman disappears around the far edge of the building. A dark woman with a long black skirt roiling . . . The form comes out of the air like gnats do when they are not there in front of you, and then suddenly they are, mizzing about your face, put there by a shaft of sunlight, dancing in a slow frenzy with the light switched on.

Alba shivers. It's a convincing trick of the light, that's all. But it adds an anxious flavour to her thoughts. There's only the bow-cambered road now, the wild willows bending a little in the wind, and the red brick edge of the house in front of her where the figure had slipped behind. But her imagination has been fired.

Perhaps Dutch does have a woman – a wild gypsy woman with black hair, loose blouse embroidered with mirrors, and teeth filed sharp to eat raw flesh. Alba sighs and feels utterly flat. But then she clenches her teeth. What if he does?, she says to herself, what if he does?

As she draws level with the house her anxiety turns to momentary panic. How would she feel if she met the gypsy woman? – Alba, in her knitted clothes, long skirt, old-fashioned shoes. Small. Very small indeed.

She's still standing there in the middle of the road wondering what to do when Dutch calls her. 'Hello! What are you doing here?'

She looks around for the voice. Muffled, it's coming from the direction of the river. She steps back. She doesn't want to intrude on his picnic with the gypsy. She doesn't want to see his head buried in her skirts.

'Hey, Alba! Over here.'

Alba starts, and walks slowly towards him. There, at the end of a narrow path stamped through the lush under-growth, he sits half hidden on the edge of the river bank. He's looking down into the water, utterly absorbed by it. Just like him. And the woman is nowhere to be seen.

'Are you off school?' He squints, trying to penetrate her dark glasses.

'No. I've got lessons at two.'

'Ah-ha.' There's a pause. Dutch does not look up. He's as aware as she of the time-gap between them. 'Kirkwood misses me, I hope?' he mutters after a minute.

'Oh, yes. You're his alter ego,' she says with faint sarcasm. 'He misses you a lot.'

'That's truer than you know, Alba. Truer than you know.' His voice is far away as he looks into the water.

Alba stares at the back of his head. Thick, greying hair, a plait some six inches down his back, a beard – no wonder the school wanted to get rid of him. 'You're a taboo subject,' she adds. 'And I shouldn't be here either. I was just taking some time out.'

He shuffles his boots in the peat and, still crouching, turns to look up at her for the first time. He nods. 'You were just passing then?'

Alba blushes, and he catches it.

'Yes.'

'Well – how are you?'

Alba doesn't know how to answer him. The question is huge. What part of her does he want to know about? He doesn't want the meaningless minutiae of her life, she knows that. He can do without the social oil that wastes hours and saps the energy. He wants something else.

She forces a laugh, tries a compromise. 'I keep seeing buzzards all the time,' she says. 'I'm even dreaming about them.'

Dutch gets up, wincing as the bones in his knees crack loudly. 'You see plenty down here,' he says.

'Have you got another hawk?' Alba asks, making conversation.

'Nope. Can't afford one.'

Alba hesitates. 'She never came back then?'

He looks at her quizzically, making her blush again. 'No. The day before you came,' he says, 'she flew away when I took her out. Now I call that prophetic.'

'What do you mean?'

His eyes glint. 'She knew she had a rival. Another female.'

Alba steps back onto the verge, hurriedly smoothing her skirt.

'Mother has a lodger,' she says, the first thing that comes into her head.

Dutch yawns and smiles. 'You've got a rival then, too.' He stamps the nettles flat, making a path through the greenery to the very edge of the river where he creates space enough for them both to sit. Taking an oilskin jacket from where he had dropped it, he gives it a shake, spreads it out on the trampled stems, and beckons to Alba.

'I can't. I'll get my skirt dirty.'

In answer he pulls his thick shirt over his head, baring a holed T-shirt underneath. It's slightly too small for him, emphasizing his broad back and the coarse muscles of his neck and shoulders. With over-elaborate carefulness he lays the shirt and the jacket next to each other until they are spread over a large area. He's making an effort for her. He's not going in with the gouge. He's quite content to make conversation for the while.

'Come on. No excuse now.' He sweeps his arm wide.

Alba hesitates, then treads gingerly over the flattened nettles. One stings her through her stocking and she bends down to rub her leg.

Dutch turns back to the river. 'There are even more fish than last year,' he says. 'I spend hours watching them.'

Alba fusses with her skirt, wraps it around her legs, and sits down woodenly on his jacket. The smell of him is melded into the oiled cloth, and it smothers her. He glances at the shape of her thighs under the tightly-pulled pink and turns back to the river.

'You're sitting on my tobacco, I think.'

'Oh.' Having arranged herself on his clothes Alba gets up again, teetering on the bank while he leans across and takes the cigarette papers and tobacco from his jacket pocket. Already there is a trace of perfume on the fabric.

The angle of the sun off the water is such that it suddenly shines directly through her skirt and petticoat beneath to give a tantalizing glimpse of the gap between her thighs. Behind her, Dutch rests on his elbow for a moment, mesmerized by the hint of flesh above the stocking-top through her clothes. It would embarrass her if she knew. She'd leave immediately.

'OK, you can sit down now.' He pulls back, and sweeps his hands slowly up over his face and hair, wiping away the pang her innocent exposure had given him.

Alba is unaware of it all.

Casually he rolls a cigarette, his face thoughtful. Alba watches him, startled how the utter proficiency of a simple act could be so unwittingly sexual. She blushes at the thought and studies his hands. Large hands with rather spatulate fingers that remind her of amphibian's feet. Nothing delicate, nothing refined about them at all – rather like the rest of him. Hands not washed very often, as she can see, and the creases in his knuckles are browner than

35

the rest of his hands, with dirt. In seconds he coaxes the tobacco into a thin wisp, lays it in the paper, licks the edge, twists the end – in a sequence so deft she'd miss it if she weren't studying him.

'So, it's the seaside landlady bit again, is it?' he says, striking a match several times before it flares. 'How very genteel.'

Alba shrugs, the tension in her body going. It feels oddly pleasing to hear Dutch criticize her mother. 'The lodger – he's got epilepsy.'

Dutch raises his eyebrows. 'What a funny thing for your mother to do – take on somebody with no control over themselves. I'd have thought she'd have gone for the quiet life at her age.'

'Apparently he only has fits in the night. And my father had fits, so it's not new to her.' She scratches her leg irritably. 'They stopped when I was born, so I'm told.'

'So Helen's picked up her cross again,' he says, coughing violently all of a sudden on the smoke.

Alba leans forward and frowns. 'What does that mean?'

He turns to her, clearing his throat, and lobbing the cigarette into the water at the same time. 'You told me she didn't like your father.'

'She didn't.'

'Well, then, your lodger's fits are her cross.' He smiles at Alba's dawning comprehension. 'Ever heard of guilt?'

'Oh.' Alba looks at her lap, her cheeks pinkening because she'd missed the point. She flicks her fingers at a cluster of long, red-bodied insects on the head of a large white flower that leans over her, scattering them like pepper from a shaker. Some fall on her skirt, and, in her attempts to pick them off, she squashes some of their chitinous shells, and they exude a tiny drop of bloody liquid which stains the pale pink.

'Damn,' she says, and, scratching her calf vigorously, adds, 'a nettle got me. God, they're vicious now.'

'They're not so bad later on when they're in flower,' he says. 'They're so overcome with sex, then, they don't sting so much.'

Alba edges a little further away from him. Although they share the shirt and jacket, they haven't touched. And, as if Dutch picks up her thought at that moment, he gets up and settles back down on his haunches on the soft black earth at the edge of the bank.

Alba, scratching and scratching, retorts irritably, 'You would say that. But look at my leg. It's swelling up like a balloon. I must be allergic to nettles. I didn't know I was. But I'm allergic to everything else, aren't I? Can't even sit out in the sun. Oh, God, I'm making it bleed now.'

Red insect-dye on her skirt, now blood on her stockings. She shouldn't have sat down with him. The hat falls off and she snatches at it. She isn't wearing the right clothes. She'll have to go back to school in half an hour, and her usual schoolmarm neatness is slipping.

He looks over his shoulder and grins at her, watching as the pins that strangle her strange beautiful hair into its corkscrew loosen and drop out on her lap. He'd like to pull out the remainder, one by one . . . and take it from there.

'I like it when you get in a mess. It reminds me of that poem by Herrick . . . remember?'

She's ungracious. 'No, I don't. Poetry was more your thing than mine.'

'Yes, seventeenth-century Herrick . . .' he talks half to her, half to the clear-glass current in front of him.

> ' "A sweet disorder in the dress
> Kindles in clothes a wantonness"

—I forget the middle lines, but the end—

> "A careless shoe-string,
> in whose tie I see a wild civility:
> Do more bewitch me than when art
> Is too precise in every part,"

—says it all.'

Pleased with himself he takes his attention from the river, and, crossing his legs awkwardly, turns to face her. Her leg is now considerably swollen and she's made it worse with her nails. He leans over into the tall vegetation around them. After some hefty tugging he pulls out a leaf with a thick fleshy stem. Tearing off the leaf part he runs his thumbnail through the base and splits it open to reveal a sticky white sap. 'Here – try this. It might help.' He offers it to her.

'This would happen. Just look at me. Can't you do something instead of recite poetry and give me old dock leaves?' she says.

Dutch takes her ankle and peers down at the soft inside of her calf which is a deep pink colour. She's right about her skin – it overreacts to everything. Plucking at the nylon he says, 'Fine – but you'll have to take these off. It's useless till you do.'

As long as it will help, Alba does as she's told. She feels for the suspender button through her skirt on the front of her thigh, twisting on her hip to reach the one at the back. Still through her skirt she undoes the button and slides the stocking down to her knees.

'Alba – what's the matter with you,' chides Dutch. 'I've just watched the way you did that. I can't believe it . . . I know every inch of your body better than you do. Don't be such a prude.' He reaches up and carefully removes her glasses, disappointed to find the blue fake lenses behind them.

Alba looks away, embarrassed. Yes, he did know her. Well enough to make her body sing. But no longer. She stopped all that. Prudish she may be but she hates to hear him say it – it makes her feel old, spinsterly, boring. She flaps about looking at her watch, feeling her breath come and go in short little gasps.

'Get on with it. I have to go in a minute. Don't make fun of me.'

He rests both his hands on her leg below the knee, spreading his fingers out so the leg is almost totally embraced in his grasp. It has the instant effect of stilling her.

'That's better.'

Looking into her eyes with a smile which she doesn't return, he lifts the bottom of her skirt, and pushes the pleats up until they are modestly just above her knee, enough to expose the wrinkled top of her rolled-down stocking. From his face all thought is banned.

Gently he puts his thumbs inside the nylon and slides it down. It sticks to her calf over the wound because blood there has congealed and the nylon is glued to it. He tugs and she winces.

He lifts her leg up under knee and ankle and goes on his hands and knees, cursing his bones.

'God, what a fuss you make,' he says softly, as he lowers his mouth to the sore patch and calmly begins to wet the stocking there with his tongue.

The warmth of his mouth, his wet lips, makes the air rush out from her lungs in shock. No, she'll deny the memory that's instantly reborn in her head. She'll not let it get any bigger. But there's nothing she can do as all awareness of her surroundings change . . .

The tall willows on the opposite bank, the small noise of the river, the sun flashing through the branches as the spring wind shifts them, the air – wine-like today – all shrink as if her perception of the world has suddenly become two-dimensional, like a flat watercolour. And she can't help it because all her senses have shot down to just one place – her leg and his mouth on it, his tongue slipping over the irritated skin, like the most sensuous balm in the world. And the memory of his mouth elsewhere comes back like a floodtide.

He kneels back, licking his lips, and eases the now-moist stocking over the wound to roll it down neatly to her ankle. Retrieving the dock stem he mashes the viscous innards with his thumb, spitting on it as he does so. Then he lays leaf and spit on her leg, sliding the juice around.

'This should do the trick,' he says, looking up into her eyes. 'As long as you don't meddle with it anymore.'

There's a buzzard in his eyes, Alba thinks, or an owl. That's a cold iris. There's passion in it, oh yes, she knows about that. But it's not on the surface, that's for sure. It's like looking into a frozen river, where the ice is a foot thick, knowing there's a heavy surge beneath, going deep, far deeper than is comfortable to think about. What god pulls his strings?

The vitreous humour reflects everything. Sunlight flashes off the water, hits the surface and bounces off again, crystal-sharp. She looks into his eyes, forgetting herself. There is so much eye-light dancing on their wetness. Fractal skatings cross them, born continuously from the dark pit of his pupil. It's like being mesmerized by the patterns of a kaleidoscope.

Dutch slides his hands slowly over the rest of her leg, stopping at the knee. Without really thinking he begins to insinuate his thumbs and fingers together as if weighing the flesh between them – with each squeeze he wants more of her. He looks up into her eyes, each outbreath faint but audible through lips that are slightly parted and streaked with her blood.

She doesn't give an inch. Not one damn inch.

He looks down at his fingers and feels energy impulsively stream out from their tips, luring them, just begging them, to go further up. Her skin is delicate and very smooth, like white petals, with the threads of blue veins at her ankles and wrists a curious contrast, fine calligraphy on fine white paper. So familiar, so intimate, yet so denied to him. It's been a long time since he's touched it.

A sad laugh more like a sigh breaks jerkily from his lips. 'I want you too much, Alba,' he says. 'And right now I want you in the way you . . . don't . . . want . . . me. Ah, well . . .'

He gets up arching his back, flings his arms wide, and holds out his hand to pull her to her feet. Helping her through the trampled grass and onto the road, he walks away from her into the brilliant green canopy of a willow in new leaf.

Alba hops on one foot and takes off her stocking completely, rolls it tight, and wraps it carefully inside a tissue before placing it in her pocket.

It's proving incredibly hard for her, this first time. It's an incompatible mix – skating on the surface talking about trivialities one minute, quick to fall into open war the next. The old feelings haven't died, they've merely slid to the mid point on the see-saw while the opposite ends scream at one another. And what can break the deadlock? How do you shift the stuff glued up in the centre ground? Nothing but a ton weight dropped on the fulcrum itself, smashing the lot to pieces – a nervous breakdown. That's why so many people crack up after a relationship ends, she thinks. Because that frees them up. It ought to be viewed as a good thing.

Only out of the chaos of destruction can sprout new life, freedom. She looks at Dutch standing erect and silent under the tree. If that had happened to me, she thinks, he would have been blasted from my system.

Her thoughts depress, and she stares at his back, turned away from her, noticing for the first time he's lost weight. Going towards thick-set rather than tall, the loss makes his body more muscularly defined. It suits him.

Minutes later he comes back to her. His face is dark, hurt. 'I still don't understand why you left,' he says, shaking his head slowly. 'For the life of me I don't. There was no need . . .'

She holds up her hand like a policeman. 'I don't want to get into this,' she says in a small, flat voice. 'You know why I did. You promised not to talk about it again.'

'What did you expect, Alba? That I'd forget, just like that? That I wouldn't try? Oh, come on. I'm only human.'

'Well, don't try. Or I won't come again.'

'So it's best behaviour, is it?' he says, sardonic now.

'Yes. Please.'

He walks away from her and into the house, returning almost immediately with a packet of cigarettes. He lights one up before he reaches her, and draws on it heavily.

'OK, I'll tone it down if that's what you want.'

'I do,' she says primly.

'Right.' He straightens up, looks at the sky and blows into space. 'Tea? Got time for a cup?'

Alba looks at her watch and realizes now she has an extra hour because today her class are booked in at the school's uniform shop. She nods. 'I could do with one.'

Leaving Alba to hobble around outside in the sun, Dutch goes into the cottage.

She walks past the open door, looks in. It's dark in there

and has the same smell as always. But she won't go in, and he doesn't ask her to, either.

When he comes back with the tea his face has changed – it's more resigned. 'Tell me about the lodger,' he says. 'He's got under your skin, hasn't he?'

'It doesn't take much to work that out,' Alba says, a snap to her voice.

'Is he young?' Dutch swings his legs exaggeratedly as he walks around her. 'Your sort?'

'Oh, shut up. He's not my sort, as you put it, at all.' And, glad to have something other than them both to talk about, she seizes the subject over-eagerly. 'In fact he's the ugliest, most unprepossessing male I've ever come across . . . like a Breughel . . . you know, one of those big heads and funny jaws. He's actually been given the guest room. *I've* still got the back one. And he's all over my mother – it makes me want to throw up. She's only got him because he's useful to her – he's a gardener . . . you know, that's his job . . .'

She shakes her head, spilling tea on the tufts of grass in the middle of the narrow road, dislodging her hat. Until now she hadn't thought much about her feelings for the newcomer. Now Dutch has given her the opportunity. Without thinking she releases the emotions as though he has smartly punctured a boil . . .

'He's always twitching, Dutch. He's got these awful bug eyes . . . they flicker all the time. I keep waiting for him to have a fit in front of me. You know, they used to think that epileptics were possessed by devils in the middle ages. Well . . . I can believe it. There's something really unsettling, really nasty about this chap. And I'm not sorry for him, why should I be? And . . . guess what . . . my mother doesn't mind. I mean, he could throw up on her carpet . . . they do, you know . . . or, even worse, he could have one of these fits and . . . and . . . pee on her carpet. He could go bananas at any moment. Thank God he takes medication, so he has fits only in his sleep . . . ' Her breath runs out and she stops, horribly aware that words have escaped her lips that she never intended.

What on earth has happened? Why does it all come pouring out so easily? Where does it come from? That low-voiced criticism, the prurient gossiping tone. Of course – it's Helen. She can blame Helen. Helen brought her up.

'Well, well, well. Very much the acid little schoolmarm, still,' Dutch says. He puts his cup down on the window sill and comes towards her, looking up briefly as the shadow of a buzzard being mobbed by crows flits over the road.

'That's not fair,' she says, surprised at his reaction, and instantly defensive. 'You always have an effect on me I don't like.' Her voice thins. 'It's like you dig around for all the . . . shit. You want to pull the worst bits out of me. You muckrake. You don't see any good in me.'

He shakes his head. 'You do your own digging, Alba.'

'I do not!'

'I couldn't give a damn what you say,' he scorns. 'As long as you don't blame me for your feelings. As long as you're honest. But you come here all sweet and light, upholding all your bloody middle-class mores. So bloody respectable at that school, aren't you? Miss butter-wouldn't-melt-up-your-arse. And Kirkwood and his ilk have you by the neck and you're too fucking dumb to see it.'

He uses abuse to express something deeper – aware of the dishonesty he stops himself in mid-flight. The rage is wasted in words that can never approximate his feelings. His shoulders slump with the knowledge of it. With a huge sigh he turns away from her, wiping his face.

'I'm hurt,' he says. 'Jesus, but I let you hurt me.' And instantly his anger dies. 'And that shit you talk about – it's where you'll also find your diamonds. You have got to look at it,' he adds grimly.

Alba has a thistle in her chest. She can't speak because she'll be scratched and torn on the inside. And when she does she can't find the appropriate emotion to fit the words. How can she mask her shame? By pretending anger.

'Homilies. Preaching,' she hisses. 'That's precisely what landed you in trouble with Kirkwood. If you'd toed the line you'd still have your job. You're blacklisted now. No other school will even touch you.'

'The headmaster is an arsehole,' Dutch snorts, 'not my arbiter.'

Tears spring to her eyes. 'I have to tread very carefully now because of you.'

He laughs incredulously. 'Well, Alba.' He does a little mocking circle in the road around her. 'I'm surprised at that. You must be the most conventional person in the whole fucking school.' He pops up in front of her, his face malicious. 'Or are you beginning to break out at last? Are the cracks starting to show?'

Conventional. Yes. That's right. She *is* conventional, and proud of it, too. It's easy to become a rebel, she thinks. That's just a clever way of getting attention. The conventional ones have to plod on, unnoticed. But they do the backbone of the work, the unglamorous stuff, while the showmen take all the credit.

Dutch has been her only blip in a sea of placidity, in a lifetime of acquiescence. Until she met him she knew no other way of living. And when the middle of her life was approaching, just when she was beginning to feel herself rooted in a role that was slowly bearing fruit, he had sneaked in with his Trojan Horse and completely undermined all her values.

Now she is no longer considered reliable at school.

Colleagues have pulled away from her because of him. She is watched now. And she feels her power, which had never been a very big power, crumble overnight.

Yes, Dutch had been her only blip. The time she tasted life – and found it too much for her.

These thoughts rush through her head as tears prickle in her eyes. His words have a horrible ring to them. She had been happy before she met him. Now, not only does everyone question her stability, but she herself also questions it. And she's been fighting oh-so-hard in the last few months to get her old self back again, to win the respect of her colleagues, the headmaster, her mother – everyone.

But something *has* changed and she won't flow with it. She has as much ability to control her life as does the caterpillar evolving into a butterfly. Now the hard chrysalis surrounds her – she thinks it's security – but it's no such thing. For inside the brown case is the butterfly all right, but as soup. And that's where she is – stuck in the soup. Resisting like crazy the change which must come.

'I've had enough of you,' she shouts. 'I wish I'd never been so stupid as to come here. You can keep your ego. You can be unemployed for life. I couldn't give a damn.' And she storms off along the road to her car, leaving Dutch standing there, hands in his pockets.

He watches her go, looking at the one smooth bare leg and the other stockinged one. He's already forgotten what the row was about.

She hasn't.

Alba opens the car door and the heat rushes out to stifle her. She gets inside regardless, tosses the sun-hat in the back, and glances in her rear-view mirror. He's standing where she left him. Good. She's floored him. Good. He deserves it.

Dutch moves quickly the moment her attention is

diverted to fastening her seat-belt. He takes a pen-knife from his pocket and opens it out. The blade catches the sun as he slices it through the air and neatly cuts a willow branch overhanging the road.

Alba starts the car, tries to pull away but the front wheels sink into the soft verge. Dutch gains ground, coming up the road behind her, stripping leaves from the willow wand as he does, a trail of them blowing about the road. He reaches her, and bends so his eyes level with hers through the driver's window.

'You know what I ought to do with you,' he says, 'don't you?' with wicked, hot eyes.

She revs the engine, gaining and losing traction on the soft grass. The willow branch lashes over and over on the windscreen, the end fraying with the force behind it. Then at last the wheels bite. Dutch jumps out of the way, and she's off down the road, choking on short breaths, as excitement, fear and life jump in her throat again.

3

Bug-eyes has been at work. A one-man locust swarm has cut and slashed Helen's garden to pieces. The slope which had begun to green up so nicely, giving a welcome edge of maturity, now sports shrubs with no leaves. Sheer 45-degree secateur cuts leave woody stems naked to the open sky. The purpose of the exercise – to improve plant vigour.

Alba, of course, did it all wrong. She encouraged weak sappy growth by too many applications of deodorized chicken manure. She didn't read the instructions on the tub. She let plants self-seed all over the place. She didn't prune anything – she didn't appreciate that you have to say a firm 'no' to the natural world if you're a gardener.

Weary at the end of a tedious afternoon at school, Alba notes each change as she walks up the path to the house. Now it's like someone else's garden. She doesn't recognize it. Before, the shrubs grew tall enough to seclude the patio from eyes in the street. Now, every passer-by can see right up. The slope has lost its height. All the shrubs and trees which were big enough to hide behind have been tidied up. The soul of the garden she had created has fled.

And the earth. The earth has gone. The earth which Alba had worked on with Helen for years until it was soft, crumbly, peaty, thirsty for rain and sweet-smelling afterwards – all gone. Instead, a slick of pale yellow low-maintenance gravel flows down through the mutilated plants from the patio, sucking right up to every stem. No weeds in this lot. Strategy has gone into this neat outrage.

Seeds germinate easily in grit, Alba knows that. But these bright yellow stones here aren't gravel – they're just too large to be that accommodating. Wandering seeds might burst open if they land on gravel after a shower, but the size of these stones would stop any root making it into the earth beneath. So here they'll shrivel and die, a biblical parable right on her doorstep. And the colour – to Alba it reminds her of sick on the school playground. She hopes Helen finds it pleasing.

Why not concrete the garden, she thinks, her anger on a par with her incredulity at every step on the path. That would look nice. How about a concrete soul? A city soul?

She thinks of the city trees which line roads and give such grateful shade . . . rewarded by a mere square of earth, scarcely bigger than the base of their trunks. In some areas the city's just dying to nestle right up to those trunks. Every time the roads are done, a bit more tarmac finds its way closer to the trees. Over the years this acts like a cancerous fungus, depriving the roots of air and water, embalming them in a sea of grey. In years to come all that will be left will be naked stumps, like these shrubs here. With no leaves to clear the air, the atmosphere will be as thick as porridge.

Alba continues slowly up the path, keeping her shoes on

– normally she takes them off at this point, signifying the end of her formal day of work. But bare feet are too intimate for this ground. It would be like throwing herself at a man who didn't want her. So she walks on her two-inch heels, and for the first time all day she notices the ankle strap cutting into her Achilles tendon.

Helen comes out onto the terrace. With an audible sigh she sits down underneath the parasol in her plastic chair – idle, and being a martyr to it.

'Oh dear,' she says as Alba gets within earshot.

Alba looks up directly into Helen's eyes – there's no barrier of lush garden to forestall it.

'I can see now why heels never suited you,' Helen says, shading her eyes with one hand. 'You haven't the calves for them.'

Alba turns, stopping at the top, and tips her hat back on her head. 'What on earth's happened here?' she says, almost in tears with rage.

Helen smiles sweetly at her. 'It's looking much better, don't you think?'

Alba juts her chin out. 'You don't believe that – you can't,' she says tempestuously. Throwing her bag down beside the other chair, she stands with hands on hips, looking down at the damage. Her throat is so dry, the words hardly come out. 'It's disgusting. Hideous. How could you have let this happen? It's like a city park. What possessed you to agree to it?'

'Leon's the gardener,' Helen says peremptorily, folding her arms neatly on her lap. 'He knows what he's talking about. He had to cut so many things back hard because you had let them go.'

'Most things,' Alba says hotly, 'look just fine if they're left to grow naturally. You don't go into the country to see everything hacked to death – and this was a country garden.'

She catches sight of the nets twitching on the houses opposite at the bottom of the garden. 'And what about the neighbours?' she says spitefully. 'They can see right up here now. They must think you've gone mad.'

Helen blinks. 'I'm having trellis half way down,' she says. 'This is very temporary. And as for the neighbours,' she adds quickly, unable to let anything go, 'Leon has made some friends there with his no-nonsense approach. In fact, he's landed himself a bit of work with the Misses Stantons, doing their garden at weekends.' She smiles up at Alba, and pats the chair next to her.

'No,' Alba says hotly. 'I've got marking to do. I haven't the time to sit down. I couldn't anyway, not in front of this . . .'

'You're a bit touchy.' Helen's voice is neutral. 'Is it time for your you-know-what?'

'No it is not.' Alba's guts squirm. 'Why do you always think my hormones rule my emotions.'

'Because they do,' Helen responds with the confidence of someone well past all that, and able to pass judgement with no threat to herself. 'It's the same for all women.'

'No,' Alba says firmly. 'It's not. It's not like that for me at all.'

But it is like that for her, and she doesn't want to think about it. To have this body, to have it taken over by a part of her she cannot control, is mortifying. She can't see the gold in it at all. Helen may be right, but Helen is her mother. And Alba must fight her still, even if only in her mind.

And how would you know, Alba thinks now? Can you remember that far back? You're past all that. Out of touch. Out of woman. Be smug now and humiliate me. I'll just laugh at your attempts. You're all dried up inside. Menstruation is the juice of a woman's life, oiling her cells, keeping her in touch with creation. You have no such juice in your body. At least I have sap in my bones.

On the river-bank opposite the cottage, Dutch sits, his feet dangling down, his bare toes dipping in and out of the cold water. Around him is such lushness, such green abandon, he could happily lay down and die in it were it not for Alba. He has to wait. And that's something he's good at. Very good at.

He'll sit still for such a long time on the bank, the fish get used to his shadow. He'll breathe long and slow, much as a willow might do in a breeze. He'll sit long enough so the fish won't know the difference. In moments like these he can slide into the water and seize the fish in his bare hands.

There's something about him . . . so much of the tall river-grass, the dropwort, campion and garlic . . . so much of the fat willow trunks, their great bosses and fissures gouged deep into the heartwood, splitting there like the dry crease in a child's knee . . . There's something of the eggshell-blue sky and the shine, like overwaxed metal, of the slow river flowing in him. There's something about his eyes which catch the sun off the water, and glint it back. Eyes like the river, the opalescence of fish skin, glinting, gone. There's something about Dutch – he merges.

Alba blinks and feels her throat go tight. She looks down at the garden, at the white plastic table with Helen's hand resting on it. It's all changing. She can't keep up.

Helen's hand is pampered by hand cream and a daily dose of evening primrose oil, and has perfect pink nails. The coquette is there still in the self-conscious pose of her fingers. But the skin on the back of her hand is a loose brown bag. Such vanity in the old does not sit well, Alba thinks. But that's where I'm going. That's what I'm moving towards. And what will stop *me* living a life of useless vanity?

She looks across at her mother, recoiling. There sits the ghost-to-come of herself . . . unless she does something about it. What are the guidelines for growing old? There are none. None. Except living each moment now as fully as she can.

'I'll check my diary,' Alba mutters, the fight all gone from her.

Helen looks at her, the same smile present. 'Of course.'

But Alba knows Helen is wrong. She is beginning to notice the way her body talks. Right now she's mid-cycle, ready for anything.

She leaves Helen and goes into the house. Going into her room, she takes off the carefully-laundered schoolmarm wear and puts on a large blank black T-shirt and jeans. Her so-white skin stands out dramatically against the black. She looks at herself critically in the mirror. What kind of figure does she hide under all these shapeless garments? A good one, she says to herself softly. And that's why I hide it.

Irritable, she pulls off the jeans and hauls out an old pair of denim cut-offs. Let loose with the scissors last summer she'd cut too much from the legs, and wished very much that she could have the courage to wear them like that. She hadn't then. But that was just before she met Dutch.

Now, to her surprise, they look good. Possibly even sexy, but she doesn't know about that. Only a man's eyes would make that kind of judgement – or Helen's.

She goes to the bathroom and slaps hair-removing cream on her legs. While it eats away at the hair, she goes into the sitting room, through the dead whiteness of it all, to the sliding doors which open out onto a balcony. She looks out past the barbered garden. Out of sight, but down there somewhere, is Dutch's cottage, hidden away amongst nature allowed to run riot. The recent mistake of their meeting stabs.

Helen's house is split-level, with the first floor set back. The balcony runs the whole length of the building, opening out onto the upstairs patio outside Helen's bedroom. By some quirk in the construction of the house, Helen has only a small window overlooking it. The patio has to be reached via the sitting room. So, although it's Helen's private area, she doesn't use it.

Alba decides to take a book, and hide herself away in the sun, but only in the shade of it, on a chair under the large umbrella.

Ten minutes later she lounges in a deck-chair, smooth-skinned now, her legs stretched out in front of her, her shoes discarded. She takes a while to settle. It takes some time to shut Helen out from her thoughts.

If I think about her, she'll be up here, like a dog reads his master's thoughts – Alba knows – so I won't.

She hooks her sunglasses over the chair arm and slumps back. The sun melts everything away. She sighs. The black shirt draws the heat even through the cotton fabric of the parasol. If she were alone now she'd give in to the wild thought and fling the shirt off. She's ripe, and there's no-one to eat her.

Always there is Dutch. Right now he's sneaked into her head again. She sees him stretched out in a field at the back of the cottage, surrounded by meadow flowers and tall grasses. Not working, of course, but lying concealed from the world like a hare in its form. His shirt open. His flies undone.

She sees him dig inside his trousers, hook out the swelling penis, take her hand and close it around the hot, moist skin. Never taking his eyes from her face he puts pressure on her hand, guiding her, their hands moving together. Alba is stricken lest she doesn't succeed . . .

She sees his face fill up, growing heavy, the muscles under the skin melting. And his eyes, the way they flicker . . . If she knew how to see it, she could look right through the black pupil and see what he is. See the nothingness there, the vastness . . . But she's stuck fast in the physical, in her anxiety.

She sees his face dissolve into an expression both animal and vulnerable, hears the cut of his breath as his hand slips away underneath hers, leaving her own hand filled and warm.

His seed falling from her fingers onto the earth. The earth drinks it up, the seed of seeds: warm semen spilt, moon-white in the sun.

'Having a bit of sun, are we? Sleeping on the job?'

Alba opens her eyes and shoots upright in the chair. Standing beside her, looking down, is Leon. He's drinking coffee from a mug. His thick lower lip down the china outside is almost prehensile, like malleable rubber. With each mouthful he swills the drink around his cheeks.

'D'you mind moving? You're blocking the sun,' Alba says.

'Sure. Glad to.' He moves nearer. Bug eyes, big head. Big head, bug eyes. He looks around at nothing in particular – to avoid Alba noticing his eyes are so attracted by her bare legs.

Blustering, swilling coffee, he talks rapidly at her. 'I said to Helen, I said, I'll bet Alba's doing a spot of sunbathing. I bet she's lying in her bikini somewhere. I mean, it's hot enough, isn't it? Real nice to have weather like this at this time of the year. Might as well take advantage of it, eh?'

Alba sits up in the deck-chair. It's too low to get out of

without losing her dignity. She's determined to fight for this. She's not going anywhere.

'I came here because I wanted some peace and quiet.' She stares straight ahead.

'Oh, aye.' Leon squats beside her. 'I can fully understand that. I mean, it's kids all day, isn't it? Nothing but screaming kids. I say to myself, now there's a job I wouldn't want. I mean, it's all go for the teachers, isn't it?'

Alba thins her mouth. 'Not quite as you'd imagine.'

Stuck for what to say next, Leon stares down at his thighs. His red hair, prematurely thinning, is streaked out across the top of his big skull. It's been greased in place, then combed so the hair forms a patch of strands, each one the same distance apart from the next. A lot of pink scalp shows in between.

An awkward silence falls. A red flush washes up over his neck and his face. Pressure builds in his head and pushes to get out. His face changes shape, and the veins on his neck and temple begin to stand out.

Alba, greatly alarmed, senses that something awful is about to happen. He's going to have a fit, that's what. Oh, God! How dare he put her through this!

Impulsively she jerks herself off the lounger, but she cannot get past him. He is stage-struck to the spot, struggling to find himself again, fighting to remember his lines. His face grows bull-red now, and his eyes bulge. Alba is poised to leap . . .

And then the moment is past. The blood drains away and his features sink back. The skin goes grey, like meat that's been hanging too long.

'Are you all right?' The words are spoken by a reluctant little reed.

Leon snaps back into himself as though a switch has been thrown. 'Me? Yes. Fine. Nothing to worry about.' He looks at her sidelong. 'I have these little blackouts now and then, see. Nothing to worry about, though.'

Alba is spinning like one of Dutch's little rainbow fish caught on a pin, flicked out of the water, spinning in the sun. The beat of fish-heart is her heart-beat, fast and dying for breath, waiting for fat forefinger and thumb to prise open the mouth and take the gagging hook from her throat. Her hand flies there now to her own throat. She coughs the reflex away, sits down again.

Leon edges closer. For him, nothing has happened. He lives with the monster in the closet. The last few minutes are but a small humiliation to him. Immediately he shuts them off.

'I thought I might have got your back up,' he says, obscurely changing the subject.

Alba wipes away the sweat on her forehead with the back of her hand. The sun is suddenly too much and she wants to rush inside. All kinds of things come out of the woodwork in the heat. 'How d'you mean?'

He shifts from foot to foot. 'We haven't really had much of a chance to get to know each other since I moved in.'

Alba coughs. 'Don't worry about that.'

'I thought you and I could go down the pub one evening. Do something about it.'

'I don't go to pubs,' Alba says flatly. 'I don't like the atmosphere. All the smoke . . . makes my eyes sting.'

Stumped already, he lets out a long sigh. 'I'll think of something else then . . .' He pokes his tongue in his cheek. 'I suppose pubs aren't your scene really. I mean you'd probably like something a bit classier.'

'I'm so busy at the moment I can't spare the time—' she hesitates, and then adds with faint sarcasm '—to enjoy myself.'

Leon laughs. He has a large mouth and big teeth. Alba,

with some distaste, can see right down his throat to the pink blob of his uvula.

'Oh, come on,' he says, trying to play with her in a cocky sort of way, 'I don't believe that one. Teachers have the longest holidays of all. You can do what you like then, eh? What do you get now, a third of the year off? Gives you enough time to do a bit of the old sunbathing, eh?'

He sits down now on the concrete, too close to her chair and bare legs for her liking. 'I'll see what I can come up with,' he says. And then he turns to her, his big head on one side, looking brazenly up and down the length of her body. 'Sitting where you are . . . you could lie out here in your birthday suit. Do a spot of nudey sunbathing. No-one could see you. No-one at all.'

Alba gives a short laugh. 'I don't think so. I can't sit out in the sun.'

'Not into it, eh?' He undoes the top two buttons on his shirt. 'I'd do it. It's lovely and sheltered up here.'

Alba shakes her head. 'I don't like sunbathing. I burn so easily. And you can get cancer from it, anyway.'

Leon snorts loudly. 'That's a load of rubbish, that is, Alber. Cancer? Rubbish. You don't want to believe what you read in the papers.' He rubs his hands together. The sound is like a rake scratching dry earth. He winks at her. In Alba's eyes, it is grotesque.

'I used to go to one of those sun clubs,' he says.

'What?'

He looks down, red rushing up his neck. 'You know . . . you read about 'em in the papers. In the adverts. They had one about five miles from where I lived.' He wipes his hand over his mouth. 'It's a great idea, I think. Letting the sun get to your bod.'

Alba looks at him maliciously. 'Don't you need to be a

couple to belong to one of those establishments?' she asks, all innocence.

The red goes deeper. 'Sort of. But this one,' he stumbles, 'was more of a beach thing really. Unofficial-like. I didn't have . . . a girlfriend . . . at that time.'

Alba nods gravely.

Did you ever? – Alba thinks – Did you ever? Well, bug eyes, you might have gone to a nudist beach to ogle what you'll never have, but you'll get absolutely nowhere with me.

Bug eyes. Go study insects. Go look at flies' eyes. Go get yourself a dragonfly larva like the kids have in the school tank. Fish one of them out and look at those eyes. Bug eyes, all round and half out of sockets. Eyes that have no secrets. Eyes that move without an anchor, no mind behind them. Go find yourself there.

'It's not my cup of tea,' she says.

'Oh, well, I suppose that's that then.' Leon scratches the top of his head, severing the neat streaks of greased hair into untidy waves. 'Well, p'rhaps I could rub a bit of oil on your back sometime,' he says, running his tongue over his bottom lip. 'Your legs look as if they could do with some right now.'

'No thanks.' Alba's face is blank as she gets out of the chair. 'I've got some marking to do.'

She gets up, and Leon jumps up with her.

Taking her completely by surprise, he seizes her by the arms, his thumbs reaching for her breasts, pressing her there. 'I could fancy you,' he says, half in jest, half in desperation. 'You're really something. A bit of all right.'

Too shocked to say a word, Alba twists away, pushes him hard to one side, and storms into the house.

She goes into her room – except it isn't her room at all. It's a place where any fallout from her life is examined by a jasmined hand as if she, Alba, were lying under a microscope. She can make no stain upon it.

Alba, the white flower, lives there. Hot-housed from birth, she's a plant whose roots have no earth on them. No dirt. And what happens to a plant with no roots? It withers. It dies.

Alba sits on the stool in front of the dressing table mirror and peers at her face. There is a small blemish on her chin which she squeezes, and a tiny dot of pus pops onto the mirror. There – a black mark against her – but instead of wiping it away she leaves it. Such a small mark, no-one else but she would notice it. Give her a gold star.

She takes her keys and glasses and strides down the stairs, through the soft cream carpet pile, gritty with hidden dirt.

Helen and Leon sit together on the garden patio. He blushes as Alba appears and asks Helen if he can fetch her another cup of tea, to which she agrees. Hurriedly he leaves to go inside.

'Going out, dear?' Helen ices at the too-brief shorts. 'Not like that, surely? Your legs will burn up.'

'I'm going for a drive.'

'Oh? Where?'

'On the moors.'

'You're not thinking of going anywhere near that awful man, are you?'

'You mean Dutch? Why should I do that?'

'Dressed like that he'll think you're a piece of meat come to throw yourself at him.'

Alba stamps. Helen's piggy eyes are all over her bare legs. 'He's the last thing in my mind,' she lies. 'I'm going bird-watching. I don't even need to get out of the car.' And with that she walks down the path, feeling Helen's furious disapproving eyes follow her.

The car seat is blisteringly hot and her bare legs immediately burn on contact. She swears under her breath. The nets on the opposite cottage shiver back as the engine starts. And then she's gone, leaving the angry engine note to hang on the air before it fades away.

She drives recklessly. The car bounces along the narrow roads over the peat moors. There's nowhere to go. No-one to go to. But as she drives she picks up the outer thread of a spiral, and unaware, follows it as it feeds towards its centre.

And at the centre is Dutch.

4

Alba sits and writes reports in the school quiet room. She's the only one there. She's behind with marking, report writing, everything. She can't get a grip on her life. She's going under in the heat.

The reports have to be completed by Wednesday. Today is Monday. Over two hundred lie on the desk in an untidy pile. She attempts to do some in her free lessons, but she can't concentrate. It's like being sixteen again . . . blank white exam room, flat desks in uniform rows, the sound of eighty forearms making their way caterpillar-fashion across the page. Three hours of this hell where destiny is chalked up. She can see the other girls pick up their pens and begin, like robots in a fever. But the contents of two years' study are just a mash in her head, an abstract fuzz from which the required information for each question is too far-flung for her to recall.

It didn't come easy for Alba. She always had to fight.

She has another fight on her hands right now. The reports have to be written on tissue-thin paper. Each one comes in two pieces joined together by a perforated line. The top copy, to be written in black ink, all nice and legible, is then carefully detached from the back copy, and goes to the parents. So naturally it has to be perfect. It's pass or fail for the teacher. When you pay ten thousand a year for your progeny's education you expect just that little bit more from the staff. The top sheet is added to some twenty more, written by the child's other subject teachers. They are then bound into a booklet, backed by thick embossed green card. The child's name, serifed by the school calligrapher, goes centre stage beneath the school's heraldic crest. The piece of paper underneath, the smudged carbon inferior, is shoved into a bank of grey filing cabinets where all school records live out their days.

When filling out reports, it's vital to remember many things. The child's name must be correctly spelt. No hitches here. No grammatical errors. No alterations. No smudging. Black ink, remember. The Deputy Headmistress checks each one. Less than perfect forms are sent back to the teacher to be done again. And again, if necessary.

Because it is one of the highest fee-paying schools in the country, something very nice must be said about each child. By every teacher. 'Alasdair is continuing to make progress' will not do. The parents have to have their money's worth. Each report, briefed Keith Kirkwood, in jocular staff-meeting mood before the forms were circulated, should aim for the freshness of a newspaper leader, no less. No two reports should say the same thing. There had to be literary terseness in the three or more sentences which fit neatly into the allocated rectangle for teachers' comments. There must be real meat there for the parents to get hold of.

So, after carefully checking the ink hasn't smudged, the child's name is correct, the nice bits are all there and the literary touch is evident, the parent's copy must be separated from the carbon underneath by tearing gingerly along the thin perforated line. Often a tear sneaks away from the perforation, like a hair crack in ice, and cuts into the writing. Fudging with Sellotape isn't on – it's begin all over again.

Alba finds the tissue-thin paper sticks to her fingers, the ink smudges, the pen blots, the sentences begin all wrong. And the waste basket by her side is already nearly full.

Her mind wanders, and the pen slides to the edge of the desk. She takes off her glasses, puts her palms over her eyes, erasing the present moment, disappearing somewhere else . . .

She's among the peat workings at the nature reserve where she drove last night, alone. The land there, raped and managed by man, is going back to itself again – soupy swamps and black-water ponds, some smothered in duck-weed, while long runs of bone-coloured grass and rushes mark the edges of the rectangular peat pans. There, peat, cut in blocks the length of a man's forearm, used to be stacked chequer-board fashion beside the trenches to dry. The trenches became pans as the peat was used up. Now they are filled with water, the once-industrial lineality blurred by sallow copse and thick vegetation returned. It's not a remarkable landscape in any way, but she's drawn to it often.

Aah! the water so black will soon shiver the colour of pewter in the late afternoon sunlight. It's so still, this black mirror, that perfect reflections play tricks on the eye. Rushes by the edge are calligraphy upstrokes, Japanese penscratchings teased symmetrical, green-black flickings, line after line after line of them.

The sun is low now. Thin grey clouds of peach pink are growing more intense. The sun crowds in on the far end of the lake. The air is full of water-bird cries and fast wingbeats of lapwings performing aerobatics low over the water.

There's a swan lingering at the far end of the lake where the sun is dumping its oil shine. The swan is beckoned by the peach-gold, and glides casually into it. Thick ripples fan out slowly in its wake, the texture like folds of gold mercury, an alien sea from a hot planet. The swan becomes eaten by fire – Shadrach . . . Meshach . . . Abednego . . . It's ablaze in its form, burning in the fiery furnace yet untouched as the water cooks. It will flame out like shining from shook foil . . . it gathers to a greatness, like the ooze of oil.

She could go to Dutch, sit by the river, watch him fish with string and bent pins like a boy (and still catch fish). She could drive past, stop on a pretext. Find a way back . . . but perhaps there is no way back anymore. The barrier of the said-and-done past has closed all opportunities, all chance of renegotiating the present. She'd have to admit she was wrong, that her very core was all wrong, all screwed up. She'd have to own up to wanting to be . . . split . . . wide . . . open.

Alba is in the wrong mood for writing reports. There's more rebellion in her than in a class of thirteen-year-olds. She wants to tell the truth about the children. She wants to tell on them all – how rude they are, how precious, how they assume the privileged life is going to be theirs because their parents can afford to buy them education. We pander to rich parents, she thinks. Rich parents, spoilt kids. Rich kids, spoilt parents. Nobody wants an honest yardstick. Nobody wants the truth.

All the children must be brilliant here! Brilliant children, whose handwriting is illegible, whose ideas come second-hand straight from television, whose every essay is about people with lots of money. Why not a little sourness now among all the honey? Why not sourness now, like some acid rain to cut through the too-hot weather?

She stops. It's Dutch's voice in her head. His words combing through her thoughts. See how subversive he is? How he slips in?

Alba decides to take a break, shunts the reports into a pile, and goes out of the room through the back-office door and into the early evening. The heat outside hits her.

All the children are in their classrooms and halls, labouring over prep. She walks slowly across the deserted lawns to the edge of the cricket field where there is a pool encircled by cedars. The huge horizontal branches of the trees cast deep shade, and the earth beneath them sounds like a dull dry drum under her feet. But it's cooler here.

Out of sight, with her back to the classrooms, she slumps down at the base of the largest tree. Arching her back she leans against the trunk. Around her the ground, thick with cedar needles, steams earthy and resinous in the heat. She feels a stab of pain – Dutch is enjoying this evening, somewhere else, without her.

A few mallard swim in circles on the shrinking pool. She watches them mindlessly, and sifts the decomposing needles through her fingers. Now and then she tosses a small handful up in the air. Some drift slowly down again to land on the bald black surface of the pond. It makes the surface even dirtier.

'What's that?' she can hear Dutch say. 'Call that a pond? Where's the life in it? The life . . . ?'

And, yes, Alba would agree with him. It should be full of life. A little chaos amidst the cramming. Lush edges with yellow flag and the sweet smell of meadowsweet in the air. The surface of the water simmering like a pot, as beetles and larvae pop up to breathe, only to dive again. There should be skaters and spiders, duckweed and curled plates of water-lily. And somewhere in amongst the reeds, a nest. And the children, quiet, marvelling, lying on their stomachs at the water's edge, feeling the earth throb, absorbed.

Instead the banks are naked flat grey mud, tamped dry and smooth by small feet. They don't care about it. They're not taught that it matters. They know anything can be fixed by a bit of cash. Anything can be bought, everything – except appreciation.

She stares at the dead water and once again hears Dutch's voice in her head – 'living water . . . like soup . . . like soup . . .'

. . . Dutch lying under the crust of weed in the Long Drove rhyne. In it, mind you, tasting the watery soup with his whole body. Lying there, naked . . .

. . . The day much like this . . . no wind . . . steaming . . . steaming heat . . . vast blue-china sky . . . fields spread thin . . . spreading for miles . . . breathe, it's like drinking-drowning . . . knee-high grass . . . skirting the dykes . . . the wet fences all choked with plants . . . keep going . . .

. . . Grubby cucumber sandwiches from your jeans pocket . . . joke (they had crusts on, and the cucumber was cut too thick . . . no good for royalty, you said) . . . warm cucumber . . . salt . . . a herb I don't know . . . keep going.

. . . Where shall we stop? . . . Where shall we make ourselves the compass point in the middle of the circle, the anchorage? . . . Anywhere will do . . . anywhere . . . random . . .

. . . Take off your clothes, Alba . . . NO . . . but *you* do. The great china eye above watches and you don't care . . .

. . . Unlace your wet boots . . . yank on the stiff old heels

. . . pull them off . . . leather stains on socks – as if you never take them off, and boot, sock, and foot grow together . . .

. . . Trousers wet . . . you unbelt them . . . whip out wide brown belt with fancy clasp . . . unzip . . . struggle with wet denim legs . . . lose your balance . . . hop from one foot to the other . . . laugh . . .

. . . Strip off shirt . . . roll it, neatly for you, into small sausage which you lay on top of boots . . .

. . . No pants . . . I pretend not to see, as if you wear invisible underwear . . . you're powerful like this . . . child-like naked . . . naked under the sun . . . grin at me then . . . invitation to take off my clothes . . . join you . . . can't . . . can't cope with the awful stillness in you . . .

. . . Shuffle through sweet violet and watermint . . . scents rise sharp around you . . . toes sink into water, colour of farm cider . . . stand looking down at your brown body . . . feet sinking into peat . . . you crouch . . . stubby plait, which usually sits tight on your neck, sticks rudely out between shoulder blades . . .

. . . Crouching, you lean . . . Olympic swimmer about to dive, only you don't dive, you just fall – so – like you and water lure and seduce each other . . . no resistance . . . same stuff . . . same cells . . .

. . . Tumble into rhyne . . . massed underwater stems give under your weight . . . shift to hold you . . . form cradle of bright green stems around body . . . Moses basket . . . you come up, blow duckweed from mouth . . . look at me . . . part of me crumbles in your laugh . . .

. . . Water like brown must . . . cider . . . Guinness . . . warm-brown, rich and heart . . . skin tanned by it . . . motionless . . . head out of the water . . . want to make a crown of flowers for you . . .

. . . There you are . . . there you are not . . . you try to whistle . . . tiny black beetles . . . silver air bubbles . . . dive in, dive out, of your pubic hair . . .

. . . Your eyes are open . . . sky drops into them . . .

. . . Quietly . . . you . . . draw . . . a . . . breath . . . and . . . go . . . under . . .

. . . Your body stretches out, covered with brown water, shifting with the weed, while the sun brazes you yellow . . . you break surface . . . you're not the same . . . some part has been claimed by the water. As you rise up, it clings to the skin on your face, wanting you back again, wanting a layer of you which belongs to another you . . . another life . . .

'Taking a break from reports?' The headmaster, Keith Kirkwood, is looking down at Alba's open very-white bare legs. He's come across the lawn behind the cedars without her noticing.

Startled, Alba snaps her knees together. 'I've got to get back to them,' she says, her voice cracking.

Keith, one hand in his trouser pocket, stands just feet away from her, looking at the miserable centre of the pond. He's tired, and all the staff need to be jollied along at the end of term.

'Any problems?' he says, turning back to her as she gets up and moves out from under the shadow of the trees.

Nothing but a whole stack. The strong light makes her squint conveniently, so he can't interpret her expression. 'I don't think so. Is everything all right . . . ?' Kirkwood reads minds pretty well. She wants to give him no opportunity to get any glimpse of her thoughts or mood. Perhaps he'd been observing her for some time before he approached. Maybe guessing correctly. Alba keeps her eyes focused on the distant trees.

'Oh, yes. Everything's fine. I've got no complaints,' he laughs wearily. 'I just wondered how things are now.'

Alba frowns. 'Fine, thank you.'

'Good.' He pauses. 'Home life a bit more settled I hope?'

'I'm living with my mother . . . temporarily.'

Keith laughs. 'Not ideal, is it, living with one's parents? But they have their uses in time of crisis. Provide a bit of stability.' He looks across at her, lowering his eyes as he speaks. His eyes, with remarkably long lashes for a man, have an extraordinary darkness. 'Dutch still around?' he remarks, too casually.

Why should you care, Alba thinks. You cost him his job, cautioned me too, and since last autumn you've watched me all the time.

'I've seen him around once or twice,' Alba says, without energy. 'In town. Shopping.'

'Well, I suppose he'll find his own way.' He rubs his chin. 'Shame he slipped up. Could've gone a long way with more self-control.' He looks down at Alba, blinking slowly with the long dark lashes. 'These ageing rebels, you know, ruled by their passions,' he continues smoothly. 'There's a lesson there . . . for all of us.'

Alba goes to speak, but closes her mouth instead. It's not a good idea to speak her mind here. He's the school God, master of her future. And he knows it. He is the one who reaps, the one who culls.

She gives him a quick sidelong glance. It can't be easy, she thinks, being headmaster of a public school with those looks. Who wouldn't trade on them to get what they want? Alba's seen it happen many times before with other women on the staff. She's seen the blushes behind his back, the stares at his heavy, intense body, built like a fit ex-rugby forward. The women like his slow, easy grace, the unhurried movements. They like the good listener, the curious lazy way he'll turn his head like he's somehow forgotten the point half way through the conversation . . . and then the eyes hit. Always the double message. Always someone else beneath the skin invites other games, but never breaks through. Oh, she's seen the women fall all right. He'll incline towards you, tilt his head on one side, and smile – it's almost adulatory, that smile, like he can't believe his luck talking to you, the tiny gap between two front teeth disarming – the one thing that mesmerizes, makes him boyish, trustworthy, safe.

But Alba's always been unmoved. She doesn't trust him. He's too dark, too much her opposite. She's not familiar with that quality. It should attract her, as opposites often do, but it doesn't – it scares her, makes her uneasy. She doesn't like to stand next to him. It makes her so aware of her transparency, her paleness, her no-colour. She remembers school photographs when Kirkwood didn't want to stand next to her either – no-one else noticed, but Alba did. It was the contrast – too much. The pale-skinned woman with her white hair making the headmaster look large, dark, predatory, sensual – as if he has sucked Alba of her life, sucked her soul, sucked her bone-dry. No wonder we avoid each other, she thinks.

She feels tight now in the solar plexus, as if a screwdriver is pressing her in the guts – always present when he is. It's like he's forever edging her towards another false move. Oh, she'll not deny he's a brilliant headmaster. He's the intellectual star of the public schools. A showman who plays his staff like a chess Grand Master. Such a diplomat, his manipulation is flattery. She can't gainsay this common knowledge.

But her intuition says the opposite. It says the man is a consummate actor. If, Alba wonders, his iron control cracks, what then? What side of him would seep out? His features have a kind of fullness that suggests strong emotions pump behind them . . . But nothing seeps out in school. She'll look at Keith from a safe distance, puzzled, worried. It's something she just can't put her finger on. For all his dark good looks, public-school manners and charm, there's another being lurking there beneath the immaculate conservative front. Expensive tailoring merely dissembles it.

He could have fired her months ago. He had good reason – she knows that. Not that public schools ever 'fire' anyone, of course. It's hardly the correct euphemism. Contracts are simply 'not renewed'. This means at the end of each term a certain number of staff are shed like leaves torn prematurely off trees. She wonders why it didn't happen to her. An older member of staff put a good word in for her, perhaps? Hardly likely – Kirkwood rarely heeds advice.

The headmaster looks at Alba and clears his throat. 'I think we teachers need to be more conservative. Don't you agree, Alba?'

They are approaching the banks of classrooms now. Kirkwood strolls beside her, arms behind his back, the knuckles of one hand clasped in the palm of the other. Alba quickens her pace. She wants to get away from him, quite desperately so. The smell of the wet bark and heavy resin floods the still hot air around her. It grabs at her senses, makes her sway and lose her balance.

Kirkwood, apparently looking at the Library in front of them, surprises her by reaching out viper-fast, and seizing her arm to catch her fall. The pressure is just a little too hard, the grip just a little too long.

'I'm all right,' she stumbles, her face going very pink. 'It's the heat. That's all.'

He lets go her arm. But he leaves something behind. There's an imprint on her skin, a subtle trace of meaning without words. Something has been said, laid down for the future. What, Alba does not know. She does not know how to interpret the headmaster. She dare not.

They walk further apart now, through the shrubbery in front of the library. The noise of chairs scraping across floors, the chatter in the classrooms, signify prep drawing to its end. The headmaster straightens his tie. His face lightens up, changes. He's the boys' headmaster now – affably Bunterish. Why on earth would anyone find him a threat? Not him, surely. With a mock rueful grimace at Alba, a gap-toothed smile, he makes off in the direction of the main building.

'Here they come, Alba.' Still walking away, he turns around, walking backwards a few steps, and calls out, 'If you're working late take a dip in the pool afterwards, when you're finished. There'll be no-one about. You'll want to cool off. You'll deserve it.' And with another practised smile and a wave he disappears from sight behind the library block.

The reports are finally done. Alba swans out of the Quiet Room in an orgy of release – she's just taken the most difficult exam of the whole year. She's done well. There's been more work in these reports than in preparing six months' lessons. She'll get ten out of ten, though . . . from the parents.

The night air is thick with heat. A swim in the school's outdoor pool has been on her mind since Kirkwood suggested it. She makes her way there under the floodlit walkways past the main building.

The pool is screened and sheltered from the classrooms by the high blank wall of the gymnasium on one side, and by laurel hedges on the others. Normally there'd be security lighting there, but there's a fault and it's all off. The loom from the light outside the main block reaches the poolside.

Most of it, though, is in shadow. It feels safe enough – even for Alba – though in her present mood a little rashness, a little excitement, would not go amiss.

She dips her hand in the water. Silk-warm. The odour of chlorine dispelled by the hot air. Delicious. Then she remembers she hasn't a costume with her.

In the dim light Alba hesitates. But there's no-one here. All the children are in their houses. All the staff, with the exception of the houseparents, have gone home. And the slight edge of uncertainty is what she craves right now. The damned reports are done, and Alba is right out of her head.

Hardly breathing, she strips off, throwing her clothes on a bench by the poolside. Moments later she dives in with hardly a splash.

She swims three lengths and comes to a halt in the middle of the pool where the water is just deep enough to cover her breasts. She's not a strong swimmer, in fact she's rather scared of water – she gets out of breath easily.

But look now! There she is in the middle of the lake. The water dancing with fireflies of light. Look now, Dutch, she's the Lady of the Lake. Watch now as she goes under . . . and punches her arm up, breaking the surface, uncurling her fingers to grasp Excalibur. Look Dutch! Look Kirkwood! Look Bug-eyes! You teachers, you kids! I can do it! I am! I am!

And as she comes up out of the water for the last time she finds she is centre stage, stared at by a huddle on the poolside. At the front, his arms spread wide to stop the children looking too closely, is the headmaster. He is not looking at her.

Alba swims towards them as fast as she can, splashing too much so the disturbance will hide her nudity. She reaches the bar around the edge and jams herself up against it, half crouching so that only her head is visible above water.

'Miss Farson, we have an injured child here,' Kirkwood calls down to her. 'Peter snagged his hand on some barbed wire near the sett. We need your assistance immediately.'

Of course, it's the half dozen children from the badger group who've been out late as a special end-of-term privilege to watch the sett at the edge of the school golf course. Alba had forgotten that. But they didn't need to have come back via the swimming pool. Surely Dr Kirkwood would have remembered Alba would likely be there? She looks at him questioningly . . .

He throws his hands up in the air.

'I was just having a swim,' Alba says weakly.

'I forgot about you,' he says in a sharp voice. 'We're just taking a short cut. But anyway, isn't it customary for staff to wear a swimming costume in the pool? Now, come and get dressed. I need help with this child. He's fainting.'

The boys start to snigger. 'I saw her boobs,' one of them says excitedly.

Alba feels horribly small. 'I'll need my clothes.'

'You will indeed.' He picks them from the bench and drops them in front of Alba on the pool edge. 'Hurry up and get dressed while I deal with these little spectators.'

So saying, he sweeps the boys away from the poolside and onto the main thoroughfare. As they leave, Alba can hear their little voices raised in prurient excitement. She heaves her body out of the water and throws on the clothes without any attempt to dry her skin. There will be hell to pay for this, both in terms of her reputation, and her job.

For the rest of the week Alba avoids Kirkwood. She looks in her staff pigeon-hole at least twice a day, but there's no note summoning her to his office. With just another week before the end of the summer term, and open day looming, she hopes he's put the matter to one side. Not forgotten it, though, Alba knows that – swimming naked in the school's pool has got to be a disciplinary matter. The rashness could cost her her job. Perhaps he'll see her in the holidays. He'll be more relaxed then . . . more lenient with her, perhaps?

As the week leading up to speech day wears on, the weather changes. The whole country is hit by storms. It's still hot, but there's April's mercurial edge to the ferocity of the wind and the rain. The worst storm happens the night before the big day. From five in the afternoon the pink sunset turns sombre green, and unbroken dark clouds climb up from the western horizon. Alba, home early, watches from her window as the great roll of grey advances over the moors towards the town. The evening is shut off by leaden doors as the sinister premature darkness creeps in.

The wind gets wild. It has a taste and a sound and a feel that's almost sexual. The rain closes in, the moors are wiped out. Every living thing out there is spinning in the grip of the turbulence – it's all trying to keep its head down.

Alba finds herself thinking of the sunset swan – where will it be now? What will it be doing as the rain smacks its feathers, and the wind blows it across the water? She sees it with its tall neck looped over, cowering against the weather. Not fighting, not running away, just accepting. Swimming through fire-water or being caught in a storm, what's that to the swan? . . . whatever is, the bird will embrace . . . it has no choice.

What a mess I'm in, she thinks. I have so many, too many, choices. And I never make the right move.

She hangs out of her bedroom window way into the night. The weather has passion – she does not. It gives her some, kindles a kind of mad excitement in her chest. A recklessness that's long been coming. Somewhere out there, deep in this chaotic mad play, is the answer. She opens the window wide, letting the rain fall on her head and shoulders. Maybe some of its essence will distil into her skin.

The branches of next door's willow retch and flail about, the new leaves shredding as the boughs dip and smash together. Until past midnight she watches the weather try and destroy the tree. When she eventually goes to bed she ties the window catch open with a stocking, and leaves the curtains drawn back. All night she hears the rain and thunder fight to get in through the gap.

In the morning it's stopped raining, and the fields in the near distance beyond the town slip into a thick grey wall of humidity which flows over the land like a tidal wave . . . all sky blended down grey to the sodden grass. The tiled roofs, chimney stacks and trees are all grey. The air feels solid with colourlessness.

She slips past Leon filling his flask in the kitchen and goes outside. The air is so heavy with moisture her lungs dissolve every time she takes a breath.

All the noise of the town as it starts up is held within the mist. Each sound stands out too much like an out-of-key solo in an orchestra. Suddenly a plane punches a soft path through the mist, throbbing zub-zub, zub-bbb: the sound like an insect bumbling around the inside of a cup, unable to get out. A dog barks, hearing its echo bark back, and a milk-float whines up the hill below her with a sudden ruck! as it goes over a ridge in the road.

'It's a heavy sort of day, I'll say.' Behind her Leon walks smartly out onto the patio, rubbing his hands together, the rough skin on his palms catching like a rasp. 'It's not over yet either. I bet you, Alba, by the time I get started in the garden, there'll be another bloody downpour. I'd take an umbrella if I were you.'

There can't be more rain, Alba thinks. Where would it

come from? No, today is speech day, and the weather will be fine.

He comes and stands next to her. His trainers trap the only few bits of gravel there are in the sea of swept neatness, and he scuffs them, foot to foot. She winces, half turns to look at him, and then returns to the mist. His coarse skin doesn't tan – she thinks with distaste, forgetting her own, taking in the raw red face and scalp under his thinning hair. The sun smacks him red for being so ugly.

Looking at her for a minute he goes to speak, but checks himself. He wants to say something, doesn't know how to. Whistling, he picks up his canvas bag and starts down the path. A few steps later he stops, turns, runs back up, takes a folded envelope from his jeans and thrusts it in her hands.

'It's for you,' he says, flushing at her automatic recoil. 'Go on, take it.' Then he's gone, his legs tripping down the path, the awful whistle back on his lips.

Alba turns the envelope over in her hand. The white paper is greyed, the nap in the corner worn as though a child had sucked it. Evidently the envelope has been in his pocket for quite some time.

Helen appears in the doorway behind her, peering out into the mist. She's half way through her morning make-up. Alba turns to see her mother's flour-white face, and her eyes spring open wide with the shock.

Helen makes a face at the weather and beckons Alba in. 'Don't look so surprised,' Helen says, misunderstanding Alba's expression. 'I've seen this coming for a long time. Why don't you open it instead of twiddling with it?'

Alba doesn't like the peculiar excitement in Helen's voice. Already, as of old, she is beginning to feel set up. She slips her thumb under the paper flap, and tears it untidily. Two pieces of paper fall out onto the hall doormat, and she bends to pick them up. They are theatre tickets for *Hamlet* at the

Theatre Royal. Inside the envelope is a thin thrice-folded slip of paper. 'I would be grateful of your company, Alba. Yours, Leon, xxx', it reads self-consciously.

Immediately Helen moves forward, craning her neck eagerly to read the message. 'Well, isn't that nice? You must go Alba. You must,' she says, her small eyes fierce and terrifying in the flour-white face. 'Those tickets must have cost him forty pounds each. It's the Royal Shakespeare Company, a special performance. Isn't that so nice of him.' She pauses to draw breath. 'You mustn't let him down. It would be so cruel.'

'You knew all about this.'

Helen folds her arms. 'He did mention it. I thought it was a good idea. I said as much.'

Alba snorts. 'Isn't he a little out of his depth? I bet he doesn't know the first thing about *Hamlet*.' She holds the tickets up. 'I don't want to go. Not with him. I'll make an excuse.'

'Alba!' Helen raises herself up, sticks out her chest, her voice bursting inside her. 'What a snob you are! I think that's utterly uncharitable of you. The boy needs a little culture, you know. You could tolerate him for one evening, surely?' Her voice is hot and angry. 'Not that he's anything like that odious Dutch fellow,' she spits. 'I suppose that was different. Now *he* was a cultured man, there's no doubt of that,' she ends sarcastically.

Alba shrugs. It's the only thing to do when Helen is in full flight. Then, after a few moments she says quietly, 'Why don't you go?'

Helen sniffs. 'I can't. It's my bridge night. I've never missed one yet.' Her voice drops, all the air rushing out of it. 'I think you should go. You need to get out a bit. Stop moping. Anyway, I told him you'd be keen . . .' She looks down momentarily. 'Maybe that was a bit of a liberty of me

79

to do that. But have you heard these fits he has in his sleep?' she plays for sympathy.

'No,' Alba says drily. 'You put him in the bedroom next to yours, remember.'

Irritably Helen waves the remark away. She marches to the hall table, picks up her large black patent leather handbag and opens it. Taking out a small unsealed envelope, she gives it to Alba. 'This is for you,' she says tartly. 'I want you to buy yourself something suitable for the occasion. Leon has already arranged for a dinner suit.' With that she snaps the bag shut, blanks off from Alba, and goes back into the bathroom, shutting the door behind her.

Alba stands in the doorway, her emotions hot. In her hand is a hundred pounds, far more than Helen has ever given her before. A hundred pounds to go out with a dwarf. A cocky little bastard, with as much charm and grace as a farm-hand who shovels manure. Who's bound to have ideas about her. Who – damn it – already has ideas about her.

She turns and stomps upstairs. She'll give him something to think about all right. She'll floor him. She'll eat him for breakfast. He'll find out just how far out of his depth, out of his class, Alba Farson really is.

In the old lean-to greenhouse tacked onto the west side of the house on the levels, Dutch has made a discovery. Hidden amongst the mess, the jumble of scrap iron, mouldering wooden seed boxes and weeds, there, on a corner of the rotting bench, are eight old clay pots full of earth, covered by a tent of cobwebs. And something in them is trying to grow. There had been weeds sprouting from the soil once – these have long since died, their pale forms stuck to the outside of the pots like shrivelled hair. Tubers now, not weeds, remain on the crusted surface of the earth, and small green spears are starting to push up from them.

He examines the pots, and at first decides to throw them out, but curiosity gets the better of him. Would the neglected plants grow if they were given a bit of care? They are the legacy of the previous owner, after all. A man rather like Dutch – living alone, keeping himself to himself. The locals said he was strange – he used to play with light, used to make rainbows around the house – all kinds of weird happenings were rumoured.

Dutch smiles. A kindred spirit haunts the cottage, perhaps? If the old man were a mage or crazed, what does it matter? There are too few like him these days.

So he keeps the pots. He looks after them, grows fond of them. Gives them water from a nearby spring. Every now and then he trickles the blood-red dregs from a bottle of elderberry wine down the shooting leaves and over the bellies of the tubers. And he watches over them. Sometimes he goes into the greenhouse at night when moonlight washes everything with blue-white milk. He begins to tidy up, throwing out the scrap, sweeping the hordes of woodlice from under the potting bench, and scraping all the dried green algae off the panes.

The tubers have healthy strap-like leaves now, and he moves the pots out from the corner, lining them up in the middle of the bench where he can keep an eye on them from the kitchen door. It's important not to forget about them. Very important. He's waiting for something extraordinary to happen. And he knows it will.

Now the weather is so warm he leaves all the doors open, and in the early hours he goes to sit in the greenhouse on a slatted wooden chair, his boots resting on the staging. He thinks of Alba and waters the pots with red wine. During those nights his mind, between sleep and consciousness, flits to another place. It's like falling into the night sky where occasional thoughts are stars.

What I need is her blood – comes a thought – her menstrual blood. Suck it out of her, mouth to mouth . . . and dribble it in the pots. Then it will happen . . .

He shifts a boot, crossing one ankle over the other, and for a few seconds the moonlit greenhouse comes suddenly into focus again as the door opens into his daytime mind. Then the muscles in his body relax again and his eyes slowly blink.

But how to get it . . . ? And what a sacred thing to do.

Perhaps it would be forbidden – even for him.

Leon, damn him, is right. While everyone expects the mist to clear and the day to be sunny, the opposite comes about. At eleven o'clock it starts to rain again. The mist gets swallowed up in a heavy unrelenting downpour. Day and night reverse – it's now a Cimmerian underworld, a cursed event. They should cancel it and not go through this English pretence inside the marquee. Nature is malevolent today. The whole thing feels spooked.

Alba has dressed unwisely. In her long thin dress and high-heeled shoes she reflects the formality of the occasion, but she is not suitably clad for the weather. Fairly soon the dress is wet with all the rushing in and out of the tent, and the material clings to her body with the tenacity of a swimsuit. Her sophisticated chignon falls down, pins scattering everywhere. And she has forgotten how impossible it is to walk in high-heeled shoes on grass, muddy grass at that. Even though the marquee had been erected before the storm, the ground water has seeped down through the slight slope it stands on to soak through the covered area like a sponge.

Alba is mortified. She's made the right effort, but at the wrong time. Now she looks a fool, constantly plucking at her dress to stop it sticking to her thighs, trying to pin back the long hair now all straggly and wet. Her calves ache with the effort required to balance on her toes. She lurches and totters as first one heel bores deeply into the grass, then the other. She wants to cry and run away. The day requires a composed stoicism she just hasn't got. And in her distress, embarrassingly obvious to most of the parents who talk to her, and to her colleagues, too, she catches the eye of Keith Kirkwood.

On his way to the podium for another speech he stops just feet from Alba and his eyes pierce darkly into hers. She can almost hear his contempt . . . get this woman out of here. Then he's gone, the practised joviality back as he takes his stand on the platform.

The day is over. All are happy to go home. Alba flies barefoot across the grass to the car park, high-heels in her hand. She's going to run like the devil. She's going to leave it all behind, drive home, collapse in her room. Shudder.

As she gets near her car, Kirkwood suddenly appears, shadowed by his golfing umbrella. He looks back, checking to see his wife Maria duck under the library porch with a couple of parents in tow.

'Alba,' he says ominously, 'you are in a state, aren't you? You'd better come and see me in the holidays when I get back from the Bahamas. We must have a little chat, don't you think?' He bends and catches Alba's hand on the door. 'We need to talk about the general mess you seem to be in. How does that sound?'

'Fine,' Alba says thickly. 'Fine,' as she twists her hand free and gets quickly into the car.

5

Inside the cathedral all sounds blend in the vast space, swirl into each other. Voices are dragged under water. They don't get a chance to keep their identity. They lose it, the small pipings tease out. Each goes to make up part of the huge song which bowls around the pink limestone pillars and goes right up to the roof of the nave. Every footfall, cough, laugh, whisper, is borrowed to make something bigger.

Alba is in the cathedral Sunday afternoon because she read in the local paper that a bird of prey – probably someone's falcon – had taken up residence in the building. Where builders had been repairing glass in the clerestory it had found a gap and flown in. It doesn't want to leave. It's been there four days already. Clerics are uneasy. Who's it come to check up on, eh?

It's a long time since Alba's visited. Sure, she's been here with the school for their Christmas and Easter services, but her focus was on the children then – they might as well have been in a barn, for all the notice she took of her surroundings.

No, in a cathedral you need the time to look up. You need to be alone, in a particular frame of mind. Alba rarely is.

A peregrine imprisoned here is desperately important. Something might happen to it. It might die of starvation, be poisoned by the cathedral clerics. She's filled with panic. The bird has to be rescued before wildness surrenders, before the fight goes, and it drops dead, tamed, on the cold stone altar.

She checks with a cleric that the bird is still there, and then phones Dutch – he will know what to do. He has a stack of old jesses hanging on his back door – he knows about hawks, he used to fly them. While she waits for him, she paces the building, wanting to be elsewhere. She's trapped, too.

The cathedral is not here for her. She feels absolutely nothing as she walks. Only the empty sound of her footsteps talk back. She's supposed to feel something – that's what cathedrals are for – to invoke reverence, to calm the troubled heart. But the space feels vacant to her, and only invokes guilt. She has to bring something to fill it, and she can't. She's too small. The place demands the impossible of her.

The thousands of tourists who pass through each year bring nothing either. They just take. Perhaps that's what's wrong. It's been sucked dry, plundered, so there's nothing left for her. They might pay money at the door, but they still steal. No-one brings anything to the building anymore, no gifts of heart. It's the thankless taking – the coins in the offertory columns add up to just nothing.

Centuries ago, she thinks, people had hearts. They gave themselves up to the building. The stones were laid with a vision that seeped out over the decades, calling forth the same awe in generations. The cathedral was the unity of the cosmos in stone, the vessel which held them from birth to death and beyond. Today, there are no visions. The cathedral is overshadowed by skyscraper buildings, and by supermarkets designed to be the new temples. God has discreetly moved house and lives elsewhere. Could she blame him?

She walks slowly up and down the nave. She still looks for something – old habits die hard – for support, for some kind of help, for something outside herself that will accept all her life and heal it. She's on trial by Kirkwood. She could lose her job. It is her only anchor. Instead the cathedral doesn't shrink it at all, but makes it seem worse, weightier. Is there something wrong with her, she wonders? Or does everyone feel like this? And is the serenity they speak about after praying here just fake, some sick one-upmanship?

She sighs, thinks back. If once there had been a passage between this and the world outside, then it's gone for her now. She might as well look for God outside under a cracked paving stone as find him here. Religion – it's an illusion for those with good imaginations and the ability to believe in them. She wants the truth, knows she'll not get it here.

Time is running out. She's seen through belief. She's in a vacuum, a desert with no signposts. Imagining God is not enough. But he'd better show up quick. What meaning is there in the approach of middle age? – only the slow stumbling towards death.

Yes, when she was young, when she was told what to feel, there was meaning. Going into a church or a cathedral then was like walking on tiptoe lest you trampled spring flowers underfoot. It was terrifying. The person who would be offended if you weren't quiet couldn't be seen. He could watch you all the time, clock up errant thoughts, nose picking, fidgeting.

She sits down on a seat in the empty nave. She shouldn't be here really. When she was five she did meet the unseen one. Clinging onto her mother's cashmere coat at the Easter service for parents and children, with the sun splinting through stained glass onto the mass of daffodils . . . she did meet him then. And it was too early for her. She couldn't handle it. She was a small vase into which oceans of liquid gold were poured. She didn't have the capacity to take it. It was the best day of her life, and, later, the worst day, too. The unseen one had graced her in the church. She remembers the moment it happened. Later, she had wilfully tossed the gift away . . .

Within an hour of returning home from the service Alba had gone into a nearby field, and come across an injured black crow at the foot of a hedge. She took a stick, clubbed it to death. It made no attempt to get away. Its eyes became silvered in the throes of death, and the tough black beak yawned in pain. Her mother had called her Alba. Purity. Chastity. The white one.

Abruptly Alba gets up, forces the shutter down on the past, mutters to herself in a reproachful whisper. It's done. It's dead. Just a pile of old corpses, that's what the past is. Forget it.

Now where is this damn bird . . . ?

Flirting with the boundless, that's where. And who can touch that? Who flirts with the unseen? The hawk does. The hawk cleaves through the air as man is doomed to slice butter.

Alba sits on a wooden chair next to one of the pillars in the nave, and looks up, expecting to see a great wingspan swoop across the vaulted roof. Mechanically she looks along the row of small stone arches up in the triforium, one by one, trying to see into the dark recess behind. Perhaps the bird is hiding there? Her eyes flick back and forth until they are tired of staring. Tired of willing.

There's no sign of it at present. Nobody else seems to be bothered. The tall black-frocked clerics go about their business, head-bent, as usual. After a while she begins to wonder if the story she heard is true.

Dutch has already checked where Alba's parked. He hopes to get a lift home later. Now he ambles across the grass, pausing here and there to assess the damage to the west front. It looks worse every time he sees it.

Leaving the heat outside he goes quietly through the glass entrance doors and into the grey-dark beyond. The doors are slapped with capitals, WELKOMMEN! BIEN-VENUE!, to accommodate the sight-seeing tourists who flock here by coach.

Inside, the ancient air shocks. The old ghosts still their tongues. He hasn't been here in a while. They might have trouble on their hands again.

He walks slowly up the nave, hands on hips, head tilted back, a man from the fields wearing dusty brown cords, the nap at the knees and thigh creases rubbed away, his shirt sleeves rolled up, the top button gone. He could be a mason, a carpenter, a weaver. Whatever, he's ancient today. Very old.

He doesn't fit in. He's looking his worst – old trainers, unshaven, rough dark hair thatched with grass seed, smelling of sweat. He's the kind of man most women would be ashamed to be seen with.

Alba is.

Going through the doorway into the choir stalls he continues his slow walk towards the high altar, fingering the carving on the front row of stalls. Here some of the spotlights don't work, and the dark wood sits heavily bedded-down in the gloom. Fondly he runs a finger over it all. Then he sees Alba ahead of him.

She sits on one of the tapestry kneelers at the high altar rail, her knees hugged to her chest, long skirt pulled down over her legs with only the toes of her shoes exposed.

He nods his head as a greeting, and motions her to get up.

'And how are you?' he says, walking past her.

Alba gets to her feet. She's going to make a comment about his appearance, but swallows it. It's what he intends her to do. Instead she follows him, a couple of paces behind.

He pauses at the lectern, an eagle carved in yew. It holds the Bible open on its back, on outstretched wings. The beak is hooked and long, the vicious wooden claws spread wide.

A fleeting smile crosses Dutch's face. 'Look at this dumb bird. It understands far more than anybody else who might stand here reading this book.' Yawning he pats the bird on the head, and then beckons Alba with his finger.

'Where's this other bird, then?' He turns to her.

'I haven't seen it,' she says, looking straight into his eyes. 'Apparently it was crashing around earlier. Flying into things. But I missed that.'

Dutch nods, yawns again, and waves his arm loosely around in the air. 'Then she's resting.'

He grins at her, his eyes and smile meeting in a way that's innocent, boyish, disarming. 'I haven't been inside here for years.'

Alba smiles back, cautiously. 'Neither have I, in a manner of speaking. I don't seem to be able to see what I'm supposed to.' She lets out a loud sigh.

Dutch picks up a piece of paper lying on the floor in the choir stalls. It's an order of service left behind from the morning's matins. Turning it over in his hands, he says,

'What? What do you mean by that?' Then, raising his eyebrows, he adds, 'Is there anything to see?'

'I suppose I feel there ought to be. But I'm still waiting to find it, whatever it is.'

Dutch nods. 'Let me know if you find it, won't you?'

They wander into the Lady Chapel. He sits down on a small chair and proceeds to roll himself a cigarette.

'You can't do that in here.' Alba, shocked, moves away from him.

He laughs. 'See – that's the trouble with this place. Too many shoulds. But I won't light up, lest you brand me a rebel and bring up all that stuff about irresponsibility.' He crumbles the cigarette between his fingers. 'I've had a basinful of that, remember.'

'I know.' Alba sits next to him, a chair-space between them. 'I think I might soon be for the chop, too.'

Dutch's face lights up and he twists to face her. 'What? Then we should celebrate! Christ, Alba! What have you done to bring this about?'

A blush floods her face. 'I swam without a costume in the school pool. Well, that was the beginning of it.' She ignores Dutch's deep laughter and continues, 'But I think I've been watched ever since you left. Kirkwood still links us together. I've become the scatty English teacher now, who might do something stupid or irresponsible at any moment.' She slaps her hands on her knees and looks at Dutch. 'It's funny that when people expect you to be something, you start to become it.'

'I'll store that one up.' He looks at her then, very seriously, with a great tenderness. Alba sniffs and looks up at the glittering stained glass, her eyes focused on the blue bits. The silence holds. She gets up and walks quickly away. He lets her go.

She makes off towards a door in the side wall, threading

her way through a coach party of tourists bunched together below the mediaeval clock, waiting for it to strike the hour. The door leads to the chapter house, a bolt-on bit of architecture with wonky stone steps leading steeply up to it.

She takes the steep steps slowly. Numberless feet have worn each step smooth like a trough between waves. This minute, now, she is the last person to tread them. Such visible evidence where past folk have trod. She pauses to look back down. The first two steps have been replaced by new flat lintel-like slabs – cathedral improvement. Just like them to efface the tide-marks of people like me, she thinks. Ecclesiastical rule must be felt, even as it destroys the past, and even though it will soon be dead itself.

It's noticeably colder here than in the rest of the cathedral. The stone smells damp. Late afternoon sunlight floods onto the peeling plasterwash and down onto the deep depressions in the wide steps. Apart from her shoes on the stone and the sound of her breathing, there's no noise at all. She turns the corner half-way up the steps where they slope off, feeding into the Chapter House.

It's like she's stepped into the inside of a bell.

The octagon takes her soft footfalls, amplifies them. The sound flows up the central column and along each stone ray in the vaulting. Stone fans burst from the top of the column like a flower opening. The sound trickles down them. As she cranes her neck back and looks up, the vault spins. Bright light on the pale milk-white stone makes her squint. Unsteadily she turns around. The room turns with her.

Faint sounds from her throat bounce off the walls and roof like the clapper inside a bell. She sings a note. Immediately it's taken from her, streams out from her, grows, fills the space. Hitting the stone fans it cascades down the eight sides, runs along the floor and up the centre, blossoming into echo after echo.

A little shocked, Alba retires to the small stone benching round the edge of the room and sits there, letting the sound fade, the stillness fall again.

The door at the bottom of the Chapter House steps creaks open, then closes heavily. Footsteps on the steps. Alba sits up, blanks off her expression as the visitor ascends.

Dutch comes noisily into the room, humming. The sound flies wildly about.

'Oh, it's you. Have you seen anything?'

He shakes his head. 'But she's in here though. I'll flush her out.'

'How?'

'I'll think of something.'

Alba snorts and the echo hits her. She claps her hand over her mouth. 'You mean you've no idea how to catch this bird?'

'None at the moment.'

'Did you tell them that?'

'I said it might be difficult.'

'And what did they say?'

He walks over and squats in front of her on his haunches. 'I think they were just about as impressed as you are.' He looks at her bare legs, sighing. With one finger he draws a circle on her kneecap, waiting for her to flinch before he takes his hand away. Then he's up and strutting about the column, humming louder than ever.

'I think you're nuts,' Alba says, fighting back a smile.

'True,' he shouts, and the word boxes off the walls.

'Not so loud. You're giving me a headache.'

Dutch swings round in front of her and puts his foot up against the base of the column. He leans forward, arches his head back and looks at her, flames in his eyes. The shouting dies away. He breathes and looks at her.

'Right,' he says, very softly. 'What shall I do then?'

Alba pulls a face. 'Be serious for a moment. Tell me how you're going to catch the bird.'

'OK. OK. I will – listen . . .' And he begins to sing:

> 'The soaring hawk from fist that flies,
> Her Falconer doth constraine
> Sometime to range the ground unknown,
> To find her out againe;
> And if by sight or sound of bell
> His falcon he may see:
> Wo, ho! he cries, with cheerful voice
> The gladdest man is he.
> My dear, likewise, behold thy love,
> What paines he doth indure:
> And now at length let pitie move,
> To stoup unto his Lure.
> A hood of silk, and silver belles,
> New gifts I promise thee:
> Wo ho ho! I crie; I come, then saie
> Make me as glad as hee!'

The sound is like all the bells in the tower ringing at once. It takes her utterly off guard. Before she finds she has nothing to stutter, she's crying. There are no words for this.

She sits making irreverent splashes on the heads of stone saints above the high altar. The excrement shoots out violently, the colour of cream distemper, as the bird raises its tail feathers, turning its back to the body of the cathedral. Like paint flicked from a brush by a clown in a circus, gobs and streaks of it land everywhere.

Some falls on the gentle flower pyramids made by the ladies' flower arranging group. It runs down the white daisy petals, and the open yellow trumpets of scentless lilies. It creams the white funnels of arums. And, on the sprays of fern, it sits like a spider's web holds dew.

Little cream-green flecks sink into the white front of the green and gold brocade altar cloth. Oh dear.

Shit lands on the polished altar rail, splashing the three-legged brass candlesticks, soiling the cross. Oh dear. Shit is silently absorbed through the tapestry kneelers at the altar rail, sinking into the dull cross-stitch patterns. Onto the dulled red blue and dirty-orange pattern of diamonds on the worn floor it sprays, smearing, smelling underfoot.

The bird can read music too – she adds her own notes on the organ pipes, on the gold angels blowing their trumpets above the organ.

The bird must be disposed of.

Alba has run. Run from Dutch and his singing. At the bottom of the Chapter House steps is the door which leads into the main body of the cathedral. She stops, listens. The sound follows her, chases her, threatens to engulf her. But it does not succeed. She escapes just in time.

Shutting the heavy oak door behind her she makes her way quickly through the tourists who are still waiting for the clock to strike the hour. There is a small chapel off the north transept, curtained off from the rest of the nave by a thick velvet drape of Magdalene blue. She goes in, drawing the curtain tight behind her. The blue is a protective caul. She'll hide behind it for a while. It'll give her skin back to her again.

The chapel is empty. She sits on a small chair at the back and watches the play of light from the late afternoon sun through the scarlet and mustard squares of stained glass in the stone-mullioned window behind her head. It's like the projectionist's beam dancing about in the cinema.

In front of her, an old wooden altar. A stone Messiah, supported by ministering angels, rests in the middle. The orange-red light shines onto the tableau, softening the pain and the pity. As the sun inches round, the ordinary little chapel fills up with red and yellow until the atmosphere is thick with shifting colour. A painting in motion, never making it to canvas. No need to tie it down, give it form – just enjoy the evanescence . . .

Outside the chapel another world plays on. The shuffling feet, the subdued piping from the organ, the mediaeval clock's hammers striking the quarters, the hushed coughs, the muted conversation – all the sounds are distant, teased out and softly cushioned, as though from afar.

Wherever the bird is, it's looking down on them all, and they don't know it.

She finds it hard to think. She's in shock. She doesn't know why she's here. Her sense of purpose has gone. She ought to be somewhere else, mapping out the next bit of her life, seeing the days ahead planned out. She doesn't know what she's doing anymore.

The blue velvet shivers, and Dutch slides into the chapel, his expression unreadable. He steps up to the altar and leans against it, his body blotting out the bath of light from the face of the stone Christ. The colours play upon his old clothes and his hands as he moves them about.

'I embarrassed you? Or was it something else?' He pulls out cigarette papers again and a small leather purse of rolling tobacco from his trouser pockets. Turning to the altar, he takes a paper and smooths it flat on the polished wood. Threads of tobacco spill from his fingers onto the stone-cold feet of the Messiah. He blows them away. Filling the tissue carefully, he rolls it between brown forefinger and thumb before twisting the end.

Alba says nothing. She uncrosses her legs, pulls the skirt

close to her thighs, wrapping herself up. 'It doesn't matter.'

Dutch sticks the cigarette on his lower lip, takes a box of matches from his pocket and lights up. He draws the smoke so deeply into his lungs, holding it there, so that when he breathes out again very little is exhaled. Alba's incredulity is locked away deep. She can no more react than if he suddenly took off all his clothes and ran naked around the cathedral.

'Shit! Alba – it bloody does matter! Don't give me this crap,' he sneers. 'How are you today?' – 'Fine,' he mimics in a high-pitched whine. 'What's the matter?' – 'Noth-ing.' Swinging his boot under one of the chairs he lifts it up, balancing the chair on his foot, letting it drop. It clatters to the floor. He scrapes it along the stone in front of Alba's feet. 'Don't insult me, Alba,' he says in a low voice.

'What about the bird?'

'Fuck the fucking bird!'

Alba, angry, cornered, gets up. 'I want to go.'

'Do. Go. It's what I expect from you. You did it last year. What's new? Go now before you lose face. Go on, run. I don't want you when you're like this.' His face is twisted, sour. He turns away from her, blowing a stream of smoke over the stone tableau of the altar.

'There are no words,' he says slowly, turning back to face her. 'I can't find them when I talk to you – or should I say, when I attempt to talk . . . It's just total frustration. I really think one of these days I'm going to take a bloody whip to you. That's how I feel.'

Alba squares herself up. They face each other in front of the altar, their faces red and green in the light.

'Oh. I see. I dent your fragile ego and you want to thrash me. Very adult of you. Violence is always the last resort of someone of limited vocabulary,' she snaps in her best schoolroom voice.

Dutch takes her by the shoulders, his anger vanishing as quick as it had come, a smile in his eyes.

'Shut up Alba,' he says gently. 'Do you know so very little about me?' His voice tails off. 'Maybe you do. Maybe it's impossible to get things across . . .' And he draws her close to his chest, pressing her head against his old sweater, feeling the stiffness of her body. 'Will there ever be a bridge between us again?'

She pulls away from him. The contact makes her shake. 'Not unless I become like you.'

'Then I'll work on it,' he says.

'I've got to go. I've got masses to do. I've wasted a whole afternoon here doing nothing.'

He smirks. 'I find doing nothing most valuable.'

She waves the remark away. 'And I haven't even seen this . . . this hawk. I don't think it's in here. It must have got in through some hole or other, so it can fly out again just as easily.'

The corners of his mouth turn down as he shakes his head. 'It's still here all right.'

'You know that, do you?'

The fire of wickedness flickers in his eyes. He looks around for somewhere to stub out his cigarette, and ends up squashing it under his boot. Seeing Alba's face he picks up the butt and shoves it in his pocket.

'Alba, dear, you must know by now I'm not your ordinary kind of man.'

She snorts. 'Well, I shall come back this evening – just to see you make a fool of yourself, if nothing else.'

He runs his hands down her arms, trailing his fingers over hers and off. He wants to kiss her. But he does not. Instead he puts the kiss into the air between them, where it waits in the yellow butter-light. She blushes. She feels it.

He knows it.

*   *   *

Alba returns in the evening, dressed all in black. Black jacket. Black trousers. Black shoes. Her hair, puffed by the wind, is a mess of silver threads like an overblown flower, startling above her clothes. She feels safe in black tonight. She'll blend into the dark.

The west front is floodlit at night, and it rears up as she approaches. To her it's a gingerbread house, with its soft carvings in high-up niches crumbling, the saintly noses and stone eyes sand-blasted smooth, blackened by acid time and rain. Stumps remain where fingers once beseeched.

She walks briskly to the doors, guilty as ever because she cannot appreciate it.

Expecting to find a dim light coming from inside the building, it's a shock to meet utter blackness in the covered porch. Panic rushes over her arms and scalp. It's darker than death in here. She doesn't want to blend with that. In black, she's going to her own funeral.

She pushes against the heavy glass door. Locked. No give. She thrusts again but it's futile – that second shove doesn't work for women. Helpless she waits, her dark form swallowed up by a bigger darkness. Then a small torch zips out of the dark and flashes around, and the door is unlocked. A thin young cleric with prominent Adam's apple and clay face peers down at her. Alba, no teacher in her voice now, explains the purpose of her visit.

He ushers her in. No-one meeting Dutch's description is here. Alba knows his offer of help has been discredited, disbelieved. Instead – or to make sure that the job will get done – the cathedral has brought in a professional team. They've been here some time, with no success. The bird is badly disturbed. The men are packing up. Alba can go and look if she's quick.

As she hovers in the dark, disappointment overwhelms

her. She's been stood up – that's just how it feels. All excitement vanishes. She thanks the young man and turns to go, bumping en route into a fat perspex cylinder which stands ten feet tall in the middle of the aisle, blocking her way, demanding her 'voluntary contribution.'

The outer door bangs. The inner one wheezes open. Dutch appears, his shoes scraping on the stone floor. He comes over to Alba with the exaggeratedly conscious gait of someone who has been drinking and has to think how to walk. Alba sinks deeper into her black clothes. He's doing it again. He hasn't changed. Always when she'd like him to fit in he subverts. Last year's elderberry wine breathes over her. He wears leather boots with thick grooved soles which hold dried worms of mud in their pattern, and shed them with every step. His sweater is old and smells of dog. Alba flushes with shame. It's worse than the afternoon.

'Where is it then?' he shouts at the young cleric. 'Where's our little madam, eh?'

The man's thin shoulders shimmy up in agitation. A long finger goes to his lips. He tells Dutch – in a tone kept for hospital bad news – what is happening.

'Nets and bloody lights?!' Dutch's voice booms in the womb-still nave . . . voluminous, thumping against stone. 'Christ! What a bloody performance. Just show me where . . .' He's half leaning on Alba now, and she steps back. His breath is heavy and floods her face.

The young man winces. It's how he's been taught to behave. The rote-learnt responses of ecclesiastical college – reserved for all blasphemy from men such as these – sit on his pasty features in a smug mask. For a moment a smile twitches at the corners of Alba's mouth.

Dutch is angry. He's not being taken seriously. Dress, formality, manners – what do they matter if he can do the job? What does it matter if he's had one too many? You don't need to be sober to do what he'll be attempting. In fact, the less so, the better. He slides his hand under Alba's jacket, up to the tender flesh below her armpits, painfully squeezing her with thumb and forefinger. 'Where are the buggers?'

The cleric swishes his skirts walking away. Dutch pushes Alba in front of him and follows the torch. His hand is on her trousers, pressing her there on her thigh. Too intimate. He touches the black suiting fabric, making, to her, a visible gross paw print for all to see. As if the trousers were pure white. She pushes her hips forward, shrinking from the contact.

They follow a man who makes no sound as he walks. Not a man, no, but a spectral form. No sound at all. But yes, there is. She catches it now. The sound of a door travelling across carpet, caught by the wind. Nobody at home but the door . . . goes . . . fouf-fff.

Moonlight coats all the pillars, and emphasizes their solidity, their heaviness. Gone is the space, that con-trick of ton-heavy stone soaring up with the lightness of feathers. You can't look up in the dark, you just spin, lose your sphere.

'Fuckin' usherette, isn't he? Eh?' Dutch says into Alba's hair. His mouth breathes hot on the nape of her neck. He's too close. He always is.

And Alba has no skin in the dark tonight. No boundary between the perception of herself and that outside. Nothing is real. The one flows through the other, and even her thoughts don't bring her back. They are flotsam in this expanded sea that has cunningly overtaken her. Coming into her head, or into some space . . . there . . . as little ribbons of words, DNA scrawl, snake loops, fairground spinning machines, skeins of voluptuous undulation, fripping up and down in the troughs of forms that have all the ungraspable substance of water. She feels light. Headless. She chokes on a laugh. Not her laugh – how could it be? Nothing belongs here, nothing is owned. Anything could happen.

Dutch's lips are grabbing at her ear. He pulls her back. There's no noise, no noise at all. The cleric is in front swinging the torch like a miners' lamp, and Dutch pulls Alba back as though she is a rag doll under water. There's not a trace of them. No trace.

Facing her squarely in the silence, their faces milked by the moon, his breath – which Alba realizes at that moment she has not heard for some time – comes in a long sigh, almost a moan.

'I want to fuck you Alba.'

She whips out from under his grip, the silence full of clashing pans, hissing and booing, whirlpooling around her.

'Don't be daft.'

'I want to.'

She shakes him off, dusts her sleeves. She's trembling. The teacher-voice is so out of place. Like a cockerel crowing at midnight, it zips her up again, puts her psyche back in the bag that had been so uninnocently opened. And yes, if she was game he'd have her as he wanted, up against a pillar in a black corner, she thinks. But she is not game.

'I want to fuck you, Alba,' he hisses.

But she spins and is gone, her feet skipping across the stone. The torch-eye watches her run towards it.

Three men are in the choir, their forms glued together in the dim like a triquetra. Hunched, defeated, embarrassed and annoyed at the wild thing which would not come when it was supposed to. Hooks, nets and the indistinct shapes of other equipment lie on the pews and on the floor around the lectern. The wooden eagle surveys it all with cynical detachment – so much rubbish to be gotten rid of, so much carrion.

'What's all this paraphernalia?' Dutch's voice is thick,

contemptuous. He points at the stuff on the floor and grabs handfuls of the net. 'So you've had no luck then?'

The triquetra men laugh – they're dealing with a rough drunk. They wear smooth beige anoraks and slender needle-cords. Dutch is as ungainly as an uncombed bear. They are embarrassed by him. They take the mickey.

Alba edges back and rests her thighs against a pew. She's humiliated, angry. Dutch lets himself down. He lets her down. He won't play by the rules, so won't get others to listen. He must concede something, but won't – she knows that now. He'll never concede anything.

She can hear his words in her head – it's your conditioning, Alba.

She's a wasp trapped in amber, crystallized. She flew in and shut the doors around herself. Yes that's what she did. For a while she could move in the stickiness. It was warm, it felt comfortable. She got to know it well. It protected her from the other world. Then it began to seize her, compress her chest, tighten, plaster-cast her limbs.

Then one day it had happened, and she didn't realize. There. Snap-shut. Held fast. Sure, she can see out, see through the transparent prison, but it all looks like an old sepia photo. She's not present anymore to what's going on outside. She's just trapped. Crystallized.

That's how he sees these men, Alba thinks. He sees them like me. All seized up. He doesn't want to waste his time on us, oh no. He's angry at what they're doing. Perhaps, on a deeper level, angry at who they are? And, do I imagine this, or is he also . . . hurt? Is he also . . . unsure of himself? It's the whole damn lot. Everything. All of us. The whole world. He's talking, and he shouts now because they wish he'd damn well go away. And he knows it. So he's trapped too.

Alba feels acid churn through her guts. Her breath is

tense and short. She fumes inside. Everything's all mixed up. Why can't he dress so that people will take notice of him? Why can't he look the part? He comes here drunk, filthy, swearing like he's scum and skip-rubbish. Where are your middle-class roots, she wants to scream. You can't avoid them. They're useful to you. They get you accepted. They'll make me respect you. You need an image, a respectable one.

She looks at him now, at his roughness, at his distress. She wants to dress him like royalty so that he shines and stands out. They need to see who he is. Then they'll listen. Confused emotions grate . . . she'd hate him if he was respected.

'For Christ's sake, turn all the bloody lights on!' This shouting, this raw grate in his voice now, is like nails screaming down the marble and the stone. Everything is on edge. All the singing in the stone battered.

'Will somebody please . . .' Alba says under her breath.

'I can't see a bloody thing in here! Turn them all on. Do it!'

Suddenly there is a great clunk of switches. Lights climb up the choir. Power floods through all the ugly cables that insinuate themselves around the pillars and carvings. Lights. Light.

Dutch is raving. He's almost in tears. The men unglue themselves, pick up their possessions, and move smartly away down through the choir stalls. They're laughing. Off to hide somewhere quiet and watch the fiasco unfold.

When they've gone Dutch sits down on the altar rail and rests his head heavily in his hands. He sobs, swallows, sobs, gulps great breaths. And then . . . still.

Alba has pushed all the cells of her body back into the wood she is leaning against. He hasn't seen her. He won't see her. She's invisible. She wills herself so.

Dutch gets up wearily and shambles out of the choir. His steps are slow. The energy has gone. Alba wrenches her cells back and follows him cautiously, silently, at a short distance.

He's like a man on his way to a meeting with something bigger than himself. Bigger than he can handle. She sees the effort in his steps, the resignation.

And then she hears it – the whistling. Soft. Penny-whistle under water. Sinuous. Tickling the spirit. Charming the stiffness from bones, muscles and thought. Breaking down the cage. Cracking the amber.

The sailor-gait has gone. Was the man posturing drunk? Was he doing it just to challenge her? Was he just pretending? Was he frightened of failure?

Alba follows him as he ambles around the building. He's into the swing of it now. It's like a jaunt in the sun on a warm spring day, when you feel yourself open up with the flowers.

As he walks his eyes sweep the clerestory, and then he looks down the lengths of the empty pews. He expects nothing. He's only whistling. But how the cathedral calms down with the sound. The clerics are hiding in their little snug on the north transept – probably wondering how to eject Dutch without too much fuss. They're unaware, amber-bound.

Alba listens. The sound is like a warm wind blowing now, coaxing, cosseting, restoring. Making all as it should be. Tickling the old ghosts' fancies.

At the Lady Chapel he makes his way slowly up to the star on the stone floor, a mirror image of the one in the vaulted roof above, and stops. Alba slinks into the shadows by the cope chest – an old brown box like a segment of wooden fruit, large enough to take the bishop's cape in full fan – and stops here, wrestling with her thumbs. The air prickles. Her safety is once more at risk. She's wide open, can't close herself down. She must. But, how do you do that? Suddenly, everything is changing. The rules have been blasted. Rules? What rules? There are no such things.

> 'My dear, likewise beholde thy love,
> What pains he doth endure . . .'

He's singing. This is a voice to shatter stone, not glass. Amber cracks. Her armour cracks. The air of the New World seeps in. She clasps her hands over her chest trying to press it all back. The sound is inside her head, vibrating there, smashing all the icicles . . . singing her. She claps her hands to her ears, pushes a forefinger deep into the wax. Still the singing, ringing. Coming not from out there, not from the clear rich alto standing in the centre of the immense stained-glass octagon, but from inside herself.

> 'Sometime to range the ground unknown
> To find her out againe, . . .'

She doesn't need ears, tympanum, tubes, drum, to hear this. No, the sound is in her bones, in her cells, jumping, calling, dancing. Acid, sweet acid, boiling her up, breaking all the cell walls. Making cytoplasm, cell stuff, vibrate inside cell membranes, and burst into . . . ?

Dancing.

Dutch turns in a circle now. Slow, dreamy, head on one side. He pulls from his pocket a tiny bell taken from one of the jesses which hang on the back door of his cottage. He turns, gives the bell a little ring. Such a small sound, like an old-fashioned reins' bell from an infant's harness.

'And if by sight or sound of bell
His falcon he may see
Wo,ho! he cries, with cheerful voice
The gladdest man is he.'

Alba is dizzy now, terrified. She has her hands behind her, nails digging into polished wood. She's being dragged away from it. She's going to spin, spin, until all of her is flung off. All the crap, dross and gore will spin away. Her guts, where so much is stored deep, will burst, melt, be absorbed away. And all that will be left is form, yes, Alba the body. But Alba will be gone.

Silence. Just in time. Silence.

For the last time the voice bounces around the high chapel windows. The ringing from the stained glass fades. The ensuing silence is huge, eternal.

Alba, shaking, cries in an unfamiliar, grovelly, hiccupping way that she's never done before, slides back onto the cope chest, and sits there.

She looks up.

The hawk comes from nowhere she can see, high up off in the clerestory to her right, and glides into the Lady Chapel. Dutch's arm goes out. The bird alights on his bare wrist.

Alba gets down from the cope chest and comes out of the shadows. Dutch looks at her. His eyes are terrifying – glittering snakeskin . . . or diamond. She ought not to have seen them. He smiles and comes towards her, and Alba lets her breath go in an explosion.

'Look at her . . . my beauty,' he purrs to the bird.

The peregrine swivels its head to look direct into Alba's eyes. It's such a rude stare from this wild creature. Alba daren't move. Everything she does is being catalogued, held against her.

The vicious claws clutch Dutch's wrist, pierce the skin. He bleeds.

'Let's take you out.' Moving smartly down the nave to the heavy door in the north transept, he tells Alba to go ahead and open it.

She does so, flicking her head round to take stock of the sight of the bird balancing on his arm, the tail feathers acting like a rudder to keep it upright.

It's real, all right.

He marches through the open door into the dark deep porch. Moonlight sends licks of light towards his feet. He throws his arm up to release the hawk. But the bird does not fly away as expected. It turns its head to Dutch, and in a moment Alba will never forget, it rises, opens its great powerful wings, but does not fly away. Instead it comes to rest again on Dutch's elbow, settling itself. The bird arches its feathered neck.

In Alba's lungs, there is breath held in that moment for them all. The hooked beak lashes down, rips and tears the skin on Dutch's cheek, hooking the meat from beneath it. Blood runs from the gash down his face and onto the stones. She hears a noise cheat Dutch's lips.

He takes a step towards Alba, his face lop-sided with pain. He's smiling. 'It's only a kiss from my beloved,' he says, trembling with love.

The peregrine lifts up its outstretched wings, and takes off over Alba's head. It's so close she can feel the air swept aside from beneath them. And then it's gone. Gone into the night. Flying towards the moon.

Now, nothing. The well is empty. There's nothing left.

Just Dutch, bleeding, standing in the deserted porchway as if he has been robbed of his clothes. He sniffs, wipes the wound on his cheek with his sleeve, flicking the blood away. Blood lands on Alba's black clothes – she won't see it till the morning. Then, it will have eaten into the cloth like an entry in a diary. Unerasable. Tough. It'll do her good to be reminded.

And what is she to do now? – left with this empty bucket, this empty well. The most evil anger rises through her body. It's sucked up out of the ground, through her legs, soaring up her spine, to burst like red fireworks in her head. Her arms grow taut and pull back behind her, straight, like she's going to throw a punch. She and Dutch are feet apart. It feels like miles. She steps forward until her shoes touch his boots. The gash on his cheek is bleeding profusely. He's in a lot of pain. She ignores that. Her feelings don't encompass compassion.

'You . . . !' she hisses. 'You make me sick! I hate the way you are. I was so right to leave! How could you be like . . . this . . . ? Making such an exhibition of yourself!' She sweeps her arm and gaze over his old clothes, the matted hair. The Helen in her head crows.

He laughs at her, sweeps the blood from his face, and laughs, throwing his head back. Blood runs into his mouth. He coughs, spits it out, and catches her swinging fist before it reaches his face, throws it back at her, and walks away towards the cathedral wall, to the cars beyond. He is well ahead of Alba when she starts to run after him.

'Don't you dare go . . . ! Wait . . . !'

He searches for her car. The driver's window is open. He shoulders it down until the whole thing gives. When Alba gets there he is sitting in the passenger seat, a scarf of hers palmed on the bleeding cheek.

'Take me home,' he says simply, in a voice of no energy.

6

Dutch's gypsy woman dances in the cathedral all night long.
Her ankles turn as she spins, feet following in staccato
rhythm. The black ballerina pumps skip over the centuries'
old stone like a feather sweeping the dust, leaving no mark.
Lightfoot. Magickfoot. Clovenfoot . . .

The long full skirt sits heavily on her voluptuous hips,
but as she gets up speed the weight of cloth rises and spreads
out in an undulating circle. It bellies and surges up, the
sequinned edge alive and writhing around her. Aaron's
Rod . . .

The moon filtered by the stained glass of the Lady
Chapel windows fills the octagonal space with motes of
light. And where there is no red and blue glass the light
comes through in a beam, catching tiny mirrors stitched
on the velvet skirt. She spins faster and the mirrors leave
brilliant phosphene streaks in their wake, chasing her,

always behind. Like tails of shooting-stars . . .

Dutch is there with her in the octagon, dazzled, a dumb and clumsy participant. Not dancing with her, but trying to watch as she flashes this web of lights about him. He could tear himself away, but he can't. Nothing holds him but he's a slave nonetheless, ashamed, still held by invisible bonds . . .

Hips meet hips as, by design, she bumps against him. Her pelvis presses in hard before pulling away so he feels the softness and the urgent bone beneath. Her breasts, naked under the loose drawstring tunic, flick over his chest, nipples scoring wordless script like the incoming tide blurs, then erases, footprints in the sand . . .

Long black hair hides her face except for her lips. As the night wears on they drip with blood. Blood from the open wound on Dutch's cheek she inflicted with long red dirty nails. Blood the gypsy uses to paint her mouth. She taunts Dutch with lips that are ever-so slightly parted, moving in to kiss him one minute, moving away the next, transfixing him in a tarantella of a kiss . . .

By morning Alba is convinced the woman is real. She must weave some magic, some blood magic, to get rid of her, to get Dutch back. Black magic? White magic? No. Red magic.

All by itself on the difficult slope, on the no-man's land between Helen's garden and next-doors-with-the-birds, is a *Gallica* rose. It lies low, its habit wide, febrile, with too-thin branches that cower and sneak along the boundary as though someone had stepped onto the centre of the bush deliberately with a heavy boot, and it's had to struggle ever since, unnoticed, as all survivors are.

Helen can't see the rose from the patio or the path – which is a good thing or she'd have had it ripped out. The garden has mostly white flowers – like Vita and Sissinghurst, she likes to think. Red and white flowers would make her most uneasy. Take care never to give a bouquet of red and white flowers to a sick patient in hospital. In combination they're an ill omen. Take care you never give them to friends. They're a curse – blood, accidents, bad luck. Alba will cut one red rose, take it to the cathedral, and throw it down at the gypsy's feet. That'll get her running.

Cupid gave a rose to Harpocrates, God of the silent world, as a bribe not to betray Venus's love for him . . . *sub rosa* – under the vow of secrecy. And this rose and Alba lead secret lives where each has meaning for the other. This rose won't blab. It's an ally.

Alba lies in bed this morning, her thoughts running at dangerous speed. She's at the thin end of a megaphone, but the words aren't going out, they're being sucked in instead: sentences, fragments, all a-spiral, drawn in a quickening vortex towards the thin end where there's no room for them. There they pile up like the layers of dead material in a compost heap, wormy, sinking, slowly putrefying. Demons will come soon to take her over – she knows the signs well. Time to down some codeine and hope they'll ride past.

She gets up, throws on her clothes, takes three pills and two mouthfuls of gin, before slipping quietly out the front door into the garden.

This morning the *Gallica* is open wide in full bloom. Alba sits on the bank absorbing the colour in the early light. The red sucks her in, though it isn't really red. It's a kind of heavy pink which greedily claws as much redness as it can for itself. That's where the density comes from, this greed to hold onto more than its fair share of colour, and demand yet more. This is what hooks the eye, this assertiveness in something so delicate.

The ancients knew this rose was a fighter. Each bloom spends all its waking life drawing in as much red spectrum as it can – even daring to take on the sun . . . And that is why this rose is the healer, the *officianalis*, the *chosen* one. The life force sings loud in that red cup, the cup of fimbriated tubes and uteri, the healer of women. The healer and avenger of the jealous heart. It's a hue to turn inside out for, for red to meet red, heart, muscle, blood. Red never grows up. Good thing. It's life.

Today there's a war of colour in the garden and Alba's obsessed with it. Blue: red. Red: blue. Carnal: the *other*. Fuck or pray. All these polarities – no mid-point, no fulcrum on the see-saw. But life is neither this nor that – no primaries – so what does she expect? A wrong is never black, and beauty is always flawed. You can never find the middle ground. Never by seeking it out. And if you did, how d'you think you'd like to balance, there, one foot on either side, teeter-totter, keeping it level . . . ?

No, you'd want to jump off pretty quick, you'd get so bored. You'd want to dance with the devil and pray to your God and have the freedom to lurch from one to the other. Just like Atlas with the world on his shoulders, you'd want to put the burden of balance down and run away into sin . . .

Twining up the fence on the other side of no man's land between the gardens is red's mate, a blue *Ipomoea*. In high summer it tries to set seed. Alba snaps off each pod early so it doesn't get a chance. It'll have to bloom itself to death, instead. Near autumn, as the sun begins to crisp leaves, the blue bindweed puts on a spurt, knowing it's going to succumb without progeny. These later flowers get streaked with red – sometimes the blue thin-silk petals are streaked violet, making the flower less fragile then, less looking-glass. Red streams in supplanting the blue like a broken artery, as the flower bleeds for its seed. Red eats the flower, consumes it, earths it. Red wins, blue loses. The amalgam is a colour to die for. Violet.

And what is violet? A shy flower, a love-token. Innocent, passive. Not like purple, the overbearing maiden aunt, the one with hairs on her upper lip.

God's little finger is violet. How he wipes it here and there! with all the economy and rarity of rainbows. It's a colour that brings on a faint wringing hunger. It's the ninety-nine per cent colour, the one which has the small scent of our very selves held between the red and the blue. It's not enough, never is, that we have this nearly-all. No, the one per cent, the hungry bit, is the thread through life, the calling note we chase. (He put it there and laughs, and draws on . . .) And, like the rainbow, violet's a fugitive and melts away if we stare too long, too greedily. And we want it because violet is in perfect balance – always.

Alba wants to roll in the colour, eat it, eat violet air, paint her white body violet.

Blue? I've done with blue, Alba thinks. That's the colour of empty philosophy. No power in that. Useless for magick. Always was. But violet, what was God doing when he drew that one in? By the time he thought of indigo he was fed up, a blackness in his mood. But violet, ah! that's his secret. Our secret. Our souls bed there.

Alba's eyes flick from the *Ipomoea* to the rose. At blue she loses her breath. Blue does that to you. It makes you fly away from the denseness of the body . . . before you're ready. It's not a calm bedroom colour at all. Subtle, indescribable, it's just light playing about. You look through the colour into another world.

The sky – no real colour there. Just air to dive through. Clear air with no blue dye to be found. The sea – no colour there either. And the sea and sky are so blue you can almost spoon them up. But it's a trick, a dissembling, a con. Always blue flees from the grasp, as does sea and air through the fingers, while red sits, like a full stop, the colour of earth, pigments, rocks, iron.

But, flirty blue. All the stuff about eyes being the soul's windows – if you believe that one. But that's only for blue eyes, isn't it? If you look into brown eyes you see only a muddy pool. No soul there. Brown-eyed people have no souls. (Dutch's gypsy woman must have brown eyes. Of course she does . . .)

But the devil . . . He has red eyes. Eyes that keep your feet on the ground. Eyes that keep you *here* – we should be grateful. The Virgin, and the other blue-eyed mob, ask us to equate blue for soul . . . when there's nothing really there at all.

Blue eyes. (Ah, then perhaps she has blue eyes . . .) They're just windows with borrowed tints that you can see right through. Through to the nothingness on the other side. The nothingness ....

Red sits. Red does nothing but flame . . . absorb . . . absorb and consume. The colour of attraction – children go for the bloodiest red berries every time – and they're the dangerous ones . . . bryony, honeysuckle, nightshade . . . They lure the children back into their dense greedy chubby bodies.

And who wants to dive into a doll's glass-eyed blue and escape into the never-never anyway? Not Alba. She's terrified to let go. The *Gallica* is of the earth. No Icarian flights of fancy here. A colour to hold Alba to the ground, to anchor her in her body. Red's the antidote to falling into nothingness. The antidote to the myth that there *is* something else out there. While blue sits demure in the nunnery, red fucks . . .

Alba won't pick the viola at the rose's feet. It's the wrong talisman. It would be like going into the fray with her soul as a shield. She could never risk that. Her soul's too small, too fragile, like the flower. Better leave it tucked up here where it won't get damaged. Better take the red.

Red for rape too, Alba thinks. That was how it all started . . .

Yes, Alba had gone to see Dutch when her curiosity was hot, when there was talk at school about what he'd said to the kids. She'd watched him ever since he had arrived. He was a grinning wolf thrown among sheep. The staff ran from him in all directions. He challenged, he undermined, he bit . . . She saw an outsider, and to her surprise recognized it as a place she also knew. The atmosphere around him curdled with the desire for scandal, for the opportunity to make him suffer, make him pay for his difference.

She knows it wasn't what he said that caused the complaints. It was the passion in him that hit the kids, knocked them over, split their world. They had been ignited, had stumbled upon their own passion, their enthusiasm for a life led from the core, which cramming had stifled. It was this that made them want to share it, tell their parents, and the staff. But no-one likes to see kids getting in touch with themselves way deep, when they're there to be taught and controlled. Sleepwalkers don't want passion. Parents see firelight in the children's eyes, see it mirror the absence in their own. He had to go, so they could continue to sleep.

'They're saying I'm inappropriately bringing sex into school . . . that the parents have objected . . . I'm talking about *union*, Alba, but would they understand that? This is the stuff Yeats was on about in *Leda*—'

'It was?' Alba had looked at him, puzzled. 'I thought it was about rape.'

Dutch laughed scornfully at her, and turned on his heel in the dark living-room of the cottage. 'Huh,' he said, and shook his head. 'Huh.' Then he had turned and seized her forearms, drawing her into the centre of the floor with him.

'I'm to be kicked out for talking to a group of thirteen-year-olds about where they come from. I get more interest out of that group than any before. I talk to them about *Leda*, about Yeats, about mysticism, about orgasm . . .'

'That isn't wise. In fact, it's plain stupid. You can't do that there.'

'What?!'

'It's a public school, for heaven's sake.'

'So? What difference does that make?'

Alba sighed, drawing her wrists from his grasp. 'You have to be careful. You have to pretend—'

'Pretend? What the fuck for?!' He bangs his fist on the table with grim theatricality. '*Who's* doing my job, then? Me, or some faithless caricature of myself, eh? If you fall for that one – start pretending – you know where that ends up? Yes, you do, Alba. You do. You become a teacher – full-time. And *you're* dangerously near it. You go into your teacher-mode during the day and forget to switch it off. You wake up in the night and forget who the hell you are. It should be just a coat, Alba, this teacher-bit. Yeah – put it on *if* you know what you're doing, but take it off again when the job's done. For fuck's sake, take it off.'

'Are you drunk?' Alba says, quite still.

'Sure. Sure I am. Here, have a glass of elderberry wine yourself. And why have you come anyway?'

Alba helps herself to wine in a stained white earthenware cup, and leans back stiffly against the edge of the table.

'I heard all kinds of stuff,' she says slowly, looking into the cup.

'Like what?'

'I came because I didn't believe it . . . I wanted you to know that. It seemed important.'

His face pales. 'You mean I'm the closet paedophile in the pack. After thirteen-year-olds. Is that it?'

'Some have been malicious enough to make that inference.' She pauses. 'But it's not the official line. Dr Kirkwood thinks you went too far, that's all.'

Dutch sighs long and expressively through his teeth. 'Jesus, I feel utterly crushed.'

'I know.'

He snorts. 'How would *you* know, Alba?' he says with weak contempt.

Alba laughs. 'I am an outsider of sorts, too, you know.' She holds up her long white pony-tail and takes off her glasses. 'It's as bad as being black.'

He stops, looks at the pale hair, the transparent skin, the eyes not fake-blue today, but like clear water (she's forgotten her lenses – Helen was a bitch this morning), and nods slowly. Of course she's an outsider. Daily familiarity has made him blind.

She looks up. Something connects. In that moment, the rawness of recognition as their eyes meet. Just for a second. But it's enough.

Alba watches the *No*! fill her body and run through her like a stream of fast-flowing water, trapped inside the container, in amber, as he rushes for her.

She falls back, lies back, on the table as he pushes her. Dutch ties her calves to the table-legs with a thin strip of leather. He pulls up her skirt, her best Marks & Spencer, and grabs an open pen-knife from the clutter above her head. He cuts through the white cotton of her underwear, exposing her wide.

The thrust . . . the lunge, the power . . . when will it come? No. But the tongue, the lips, the beard chafing her until the *No!* bursts from its container and sings around the room. Only then, when she's as soft as grasping butter does he dive on her and smash his rough face on her throat, his Leda . . . And the container bursts, the water swamps him. He goes under, meets her there, and their eyes meet, too, in astonishment . . .

Yes, that was how it began, Alba thinks. He nicked the skin on my thigh with his knife as he cut away my clothes. He spilt blood. It stained my best skirt, his shirt. We got up having been apart and at war with others all our lives, and saw we were blood-brothers. And we drank elderberry wine together afterwards from the stained cup.

Now, Alba, eschewing the white flowers that are her namesake, and the viola which guards her faint soul, cuts the chosen red flower, the symbol of what he did to her and of its power.

Back on the patio again, she sits on a plastic chair, the rose on the table in front of her. Her heart beats fast. There's sweat on her forehead. She looks at the view of the sweating fields and soft frothy shapes of willows, and it's like looking out over the sea. A thin dense mist, so dense it's like a piece of white cambric, lies between the trees and the rhynes, carefully cut to fit around the irregularities in the landscape. Where there's a hill it thins a little, but still hugs the contours. It begins to move as the sun rises. Trodden-down smoke.

The cathedral city was host to a mediaeval play last night. Now, this morning, Alba's come back to finish the final scene. The one where you kill the ghost.

She parks the car some way off and walks through the quiet streets, the rose wrapped in a tissue in her pocket. She stops on impulse to pick a white ox-eye as she passes by low-walled gardens with flowers spilling over. The red, and now, the white. Omen. Extra protection. Maybe she'll need to get tough with the gypsy.

The boxy towers of the cathedral suddenly come into view above the town, like giant solid exclamation marks among the low mean buildings that wriggle away from their base. As she walks closer, the stubs disappear, slipping out of sight like a galleon slowly going down.

Alba's lungs have shrunk until they tremble against the sides of the box half the size of her chest. She can't breathe air, she can only hover with it. As she walks across the cathedral green she has to tell herself to breathe, or else faint. The woman is in there waiting for her. Perhaps the hawk will be there too – her pet – her little . . . face-ripper? Will she, Alba, come out with unscathed face, or will she be disfigured, outcast? Will she lose . . . ? Near to sickness, fainting, her head pounding, she goes in.

Opening time – and the cathedral is no different from the shops that lead the way to its feet – a shop with set hours. A man and woman, both suited, both retired, stand inside the entrance doors, armed with guide books and the skippy watery-eyed enthusiasm of the elderly. Alba shies past them as the man shoots a fund-raising leaflet at her.

Quickly she walks along the nave, and sits down halfway up on one of the stick-backed chairs which fill the space between the pillars. Empty chairs, forever empty. If there were none at all it would be better. Then there would be an auditorium, a dance floor, a standing place for dipping around in circles with neck stretched back to look at the roof, the pillars speeding away, the vanishing . . . Instead, the bare seats mock, their sheer number an embarrassing arrogance . . . expect and ye shall not find . . . yes, the congregation's all split up and now gathers in the market place where it worships buying and selling.

And God, he's gone too. Sidled out under the draughty west doors like a long oil slick. Gone. Seeped down through the cracks between the pavement, to listen, feel, breathe his people walking above him. Homeless.

Alba slumps and lets out an exaggerated sigh of relief. The cathedral is full of light and unexpected ordinariness. A woman in a blue workwear-tabard, large identity badge pinned over the left breast, hoovers between the rows of seats, dragging the noisy cleaner-body after her, rasping the castors over the stone flags. Above the noise of the hoover she talks to a man, also wearing a badge, who loiters at her side. Alba can't make out what they are saying, but she knows it's gossip. It has its own stance – the intimate heads, the eyes pretending to look ahead, the kept-in flush of well-I-never. Gossip, the mundane – in the cathedral, the glory of architectural glories.

Gossip . . . Who forgot to put the brooms away in the cleaning cupboard, who didn't empty the bins, whose daughter has had an abortion, which one among the clergy isn't gay . . .

The woman's elbow saws briskly back and forth and, in synchrony, another cleaner behind her briskly polishes the already brilliant altar rail with a duster.

Cleaning. How prosaic, Alba thinks. These people, these cleaners, bash their tools irreverently against the stone, view the whole as one huge dirt trap. They only see what their job's worth. They clean toilets with the same dedication. And why not?

Reverence only tots up as the day wears on. Morning has a loose tongue. It's easy not to care and be cavalier when the light is young. There's a time every morning when there really is hope and a lightening of heart. It's that God's-in-his-Heaven-and-the-world's-all-right moment. If you're awake to these things you can almost set your watch by it.

A spring wind catches you, blows up through the boles of your legs, chest and head, cleaning, scouring, causing temporary joy and madness.

And then it's gone. Dark clouds scud over the day, and it's all downhill from then on. In late afternoon, as the energy fades from the light, we know what's coming, and our souls quake. Then you can feel reverence, all right. Then the votive candles get lit. Oh, yes, you can feel the fear and the blind hope then.

The building suddenly fills with visitors. They talk in loud voices as they poke and prod at the architecture, demanding the slice of history they feel they are owed. They don't want to work hard at it, no, they want someone to package it for them.

A group of six stand around a grey-haired tour-guide dressed in a black cape, over-enunciating (for the benefit of foreigners) the history of the stained-glass window behind. But they get too much information. They've already reached overload, and they don't listen anyway. It's what you do when you're a tourist. You stop noticing, stop experiencing, and go back to being spoon-fed. You don't mind as long as you get something *big* in the historical surprises department. You see the cathedral as a zoo of bricks.

Alba sits, idly philosophizing. She can't be alone with her thoughts – cathedrals, churches, places of worship, don't allow it. She can't have a blank mind either. Whatever's on her mind, she'll go inside those heavy doors and feel she ought to search for the profound, or be sobered into the fruitless compelling debate about life and death. Greater things are demanded of her than the ornery sin of jealousy.

The cathedral builders – they were jealous men too, they were human. They were much like us, dull and menial. They had no vision. God did not appear to them any more than he does to us. (He moved out and now lives under cracks in the pavement, remember.)

The master mason had the plans. He was the wheel: the builders, cogs. Awe was not their lot. They did as they were told, laying stone upon stone, seeing no more than was in front of their eyes – like the cleaners focused on dirt. Awe came when the building was finished, made by man who could not take himself seriously. Silly fellows to give so much of themselves away to someone who'd moved house because they couldn't see it. So what *had* they done? Created this vast edifice for man? No, no, no. To what, then? Better make it God.

We can't cope with the beauty of what we create, we feel out of step. It's unseemly, uneasy. Better to cut off an ear, or create a deliberate flaw in the carpet we're weaving. Better give it on over to something bigger. Man can't contain it, he bursts, goes mad.

Finished – they stood in the nave and looked up, saw the pillars, the way the structure floated on these vanishing verticals, and blindly wondered who could have made such a thing. And threw themselves down in worship. Truly then, man had made God, but didn't know it. As always, man was blind to the moves in the making.

Tourists think it all differently. They lose sight of the real history, the real significance. The carving on that stone – see – it was made by a man smaller than yourself with a scar on his jawbone. He had red hair. He drank too much. He had twelve children and half of them died before they were three.

So you expect to find God in here. Why should He want to dwell here? This is a place of man, to the glory of man, not God. Give credit where it's due, to the peasants, the rustic artisans, who died seven hundred years ago and slipped in between the stones.

The little group look round at the other people filling the building. History weighs heavy. It's another 'should'. Japanese shift from foot to foot, delicately impatient to move on, feeling nothing, their cameras champing at the bit.

A man with a short telephoto marches straight up the aisle to take a picture of the scissor arch. This is his first visit, it's obvious. He's greedy for the 'special features', cruising the nave with an open lens to fire at anything showy enough to take his fancy, to clobber him in the eye – like a kerb crawler after thigh.

The mechanical eye selects for him, cheerfully lies, while the subtleties, which could tell him much about the past, hover like ghosts around the edges, always out of the picture. For the rest of his walk up the aisle his head is bent, looking at the dull stone floor. If God could deliver an upper cut . . . now that would be worth recording.

Noise surges about. If she closes her eyes Alba could be in a swimming-baths or a train-station – never a building like this. She picks up the green English hymnal in the little rack above the tapestry kneeler and opens it. Ah! childhood hymns, entombed years ago, yet still sing-song now in her head the minute she reads the words. How like geese children were then, crammed with religion every morning: hymns, the little talk, the impossible goodness to live up to, the man's death that so incomprehensibly paid for the lot without being asked.

Taking the rose from her pocket she sandwiches it inside the book, and puts it back on its shelf. Bring a little blood to the bloodless, she thinks, as the pink stain from the wet petals smudges into tissue-thin paper. And a real gypsy would spice things up. If she is here, Alba thinks, let her find this rose pressed between these ancient covers. Let her find the power of religion.

Meanwhile, God's little finger moves on, unconcerned

with jealousy, unconcerned with the cup of sea and sky. Oozing out from beneath the pavement, unseen, he lays his bait, licks his finger to moisten the paint, and trails on . . . God's little finger stained violet.

Breathy, heady, freed up, Alba walks quickly around the rest of the building. She's carrying a thread with her, tying up the parcel, packing the past in it, making it neat to send to someone else so she can forget it all, and doing it as fast as she can, lest something take her unawares and spoil it.

Some twenty yards away and coming towards her, is Keith Kirkwood, the headmaster, with a woman on his arm. Alba slips through to the other side of the choir stalls until they have passed. She doesn't want to meet him.

The other woman is not his wife. So, does Mr Kirkwood have a mistress? Alba could never conceal her astonishment well enough if she were to meet them face to face.

As the couple reach the west end of the nave and move towards the exit, Alba comes out from her hiding-place to watch them. The woman is slight, delicate, blond, with a tight-fitting skirt that pinches her knees together as she walks so she can only take tiny steps. And she wears high-heeled shoes whose metal tips sound outrageously loud in the echoing building. The woman must be a prostitute, Alba thinks immediately. What else could she be? A wife or a sister would never be guided through the front door by a hand on her bottom.

The Lady Chapel is hawkless, full of Italian leather moodily chewing gum instead. The shit on the altar rail, on the organ pipes, on the brasses and the church flowers, has been whisked and polished away. And Kirkwood, like a will o' the wisp, has come and gone. It never happened.

*　　*　　*

She goes back to Helen's and to medieval hell – inside her head. Her skull is full of demons. They live there all the time, but lie low. She's not aware of them. But today, on her return, the inner world and the outer world aren't seamless any more. They don't glide over each other. The fascia glue up . . . Migraine.

Fingers, long, bony, with dirty nails, scratch and claw the bottom of her neck and base of her skull – from the inside. Somewhere just above the atlas they get a hold, and dig in to pull their obscene bodies up . . . There they are, all the minions, all the dishevelled toothless cooks and drunkards, hoisting themselves up her spine from her sacrum, following the leader, digging into her trapezius until it knots, making a series of toe-holds to climb up on. It's like naughty children trying to peep over next door's wall, clinging on with their fingernails, eyes all agape.

Except they aren't children, these demons. There's not one whit of innocence about them. They carry on hoiking themselves up her crucified back, over her stepped concrete shoulders, and into her brain-box, into her skull.

It's too small in there. They brace foul bodies against the bony plates and peer out through her eyes. She's being ousted, pushed aside.

Drugs don't help much. They don't bring her back. Instead they just wool her limbs and head until she's full of confusion, full of white fuzz. The demons are still there, suspended in whatever state they happen to be in at the time the codeine hits. And they still hold sway.

The terror of being taken over . . . In the night they creep out through her nostrils and monkey about, mocking her body, their host. They play cards on her chest in the small hours, their weight pressing her down, making her flail her arms for air in her sleep. When she wakes from a state that's neither asleep nor awake, they fold up the card-table and stools with a bang!, and leave to crawl back into the seedy warmth of her skull. Her eyes will open suddenly and her hands fly to her chest. The nightdress sticks sweatily to her skin, and to the valley between her breasts where card-sharp players have lounged all night. She can taste their presence – like burnt silver metal on her tongue – a taste of forging from the fires of hell. On her breasts the visitors have abused her, and left.

And there's a radio jam in her head. The sound, constant, is a low hum, like a ship's engines heard underwater. The rhythmic throb merges into one almost-steady note that acts as a backdrop to her heartbeat. All sounds distort, only half make it. Birdsong – each note a clank of threadlike feet stamping on a piano, the sound flat, dead, unreal, carrying portents, a harbinger of the malefic. Like birds who sing in the cage-like silence of the thick grey air before a storm, black clouds of menace surround her, pressing in, pressing down, not her friends, colluding with the enemy to frighten her. When the song stops, hell will strike. And then the silence – huge. The emptiness – over-full into a great thrum, buzz, clamour.

Flowers smell rotten. The sweeter scent of their immediate route to decay tumbles too fast into the smell of nauseating death. Food has all been spat on. It's all yellow, the colour of yesterday.

Red hurts now – it's the colour of the fierce pumping behind her eyelids, the colour of the raw insides of her face. And the ultra-vividness of red extends to all the other colours too. White Alba, unbearably sensitized to what she lacks.

Objects advance. The wooden chair legs threaten, the glistening butt ends of record sleeves are sinister. Curtain fabric has life. Cushions in a neat row wait to march and devour. Shoes on the floor could walk now! all by themselves. Clouds through the window bear down, tumbling towards the panes like shaking grey fists. Rain falling hard is no blessing – it can press you into the earth with its force.

Meanwhile the demons tweak and fiddle with the buttons inside her cerebrum, mess up the order, cause a short circuit here, rip out a wire or two there and, laughing, fling part of her memory, part of the present, against her skull wall. Her hands are not her own – they move at others' commands. Her limbs feel weak, yet her movement is made in a suit of unforgiving armour, every joint seized up in tension. Walking is difficult – a thread attached to the back of her head keeps jerking her up and back. One of the demons has her on a lead – he likes to tweak it. She's his little rag dolly – with one nip her floppy legs will fly up in front of her and she'll go down hard. She loses her balance. Objects move. Her head wobbles, swims, too much liquid swashing about inside the brain-box.

Alba, on the surface – same as always, while cracks rivel through underneath. She wears dark glasses. Not only does the world seem toned down, in a sepia fog, but they serve to hide the bloodshot eyes, the droopy lids, from the power of Helen's twisted sympathy. It's just a headache – Alba will lie to Helen if she asks – nothing serious.

And the worst part of the torture is this: deliberately, cruelly, the demons leave part of her mind untouched by their meddling. Just a small fragment of her mind still belongs to her, but it's about as much use as a telescope in the dark. She can't do a thing about it, so the little unfettered part of herself watches helpless as the rest of her is split open and thrown away.

She hates Leon even more at these times. When *he* goes his mind snaps too – but completely. He doesn't know how long he's been out for the count. In moments like those the very earth could cleave open and swallow all, and he would not know at that moment that it was *his* finger which had pressed the button.

She thinks of the kites he makes on his days off. She'd like to rip them to pieces. She sees him on the side of the hill opposite, with a giant ball of string wound around a piece of wood – more string than is legal if aircraft are to fly safely.

He stands quite still, the little tissue paper trapezium above him winking like an eye in the sky. Leon, in control of something so far away, while the string forms a great bowed shape in the nothingness beneath with the pressure of the wind.

There's Leon, unable to hold onto himself by the thinnest of threads, so he plays with control, dices with walking on the edge. The frail kite dances with blasts of air which, on the ground, would blow a man flat. The kite string is the umbilical cord. The kite is Leon – the missing bit of him, the free bit. And at the same time, the part which is bound.

The black mood, this megrim, is shame. Oh, to be pushed over the brink! Oh! for guiltless oblivion. How clever to be left with the smallest piece of the pie, the flimsiest skein to her self, and to have to hold it. Torture indeed. For whatever small consciousness exists, there goes with it a ton weight of responsibility too . . . what kind of woman is she to entertain demons, to have them party with her?

7

Clive arrives not long after Alba has come back from the cathedral. Clive. Oh, not him. Please. Not Clive. She's raw, open, her feelings scraped bare. She wants to be left alone.

Clive looks for blemishes. Always. Her legs, her weight, her hair – they're all sibling points to be notched up even now, even at his age. Ten minutes of his company and she'll be sliding into greyness, into a depression of self-dislike. It's always been this way.

She sits head in hands on the edge of the patio, and watches her brother and his family come up the path. He takes his time, pausing every step to make sweeping gestures with his arm at the garden. He likes it – of course he would. He'd really go for the peculiar deadness living forms take on when over-managed. He'll want to copy what he's seen on his return home. Nature's all battened down here, screwed firmly into place. And his mother has it all under her little fist. He'll just love the yellow gravel.

Clive looks up, sees Alba, and waves. Alba nods and gives a pretend smile. There's never been anything between them. As he reaches the patio he looks down at her, and wipes his face with a red handkerchief. His eyes squint at her. He doesn't like the dark glasses she's wearing – he can't see her eyes, so he can't even attempt to judge her mood, even if he were good at it – which he isn't. Shielding his own from the bright light with plump hairless hands he turns to hurry up Angie and the little girls who are right behind him.

'You've lost weight,' Alba says.

Clive laughs. 'And you've put it on – whatever is happening to us, Alba? Are we swopping roles?' He laughs, a sound like a steam train starting off. Not a real laugh. A learnt one. Who knows what it might conceal?

'How are you and your family? All well?'

'Just great. On holiday. The caravan. At a site. Bad weather due though. Storms, they say. Thought we'd stay here overnight. See how Mum is,' he replies, chopping sentences to fit his shortness of breath. 'You OK?'

'Bit of a headache.' Alba looks past him at the clear, clear sky. Not a hint of change in the weather. Clive must be making it up.

'Oh, well. We'll leave you in peace. Where's mother?'

'Inside.' Alba jerks her thumb at the open door. 'She'll be pleased to see you.'

Clive has a large square face. In its making his eyes were left out till last, and then squeezed in without regard for the flabby tissue that surrounds and folds in over them. They're poked too deep, like marbles in dough. Having opened them as wide as he can he quickly narrows them back to slits which look out from the safety of a deeper place behind. Recessive, that's what he is, Alba thinks, her sunglasses tilted up at him. A recessive gene, going back-wards, half-connected to Alba by blood, not wanting it so.

His cheek muscles relax, and he walks quickly across the patio. Angie and the little girls mouth at Alba as they pass, their greetings no more than sugar-whispers.

Clive will be upset he's got thinner, Alba thinks. He's one of those extremely rare people who likes the fat oodlesome plumpness of his own body, who likes to swim in eternal fatness. And he does like it. He really does. He likes being snug inside a blubber coat of Hollywood pro-portions.

And Angie – what is she but a mean shaving off his rib – all knife-sharp angles, skin and bone in expensive camel. Her neck is long, thin, a Modigliani, a cultivated stem, bondaged like the Masai women with their neck rings. To punish, the men take the rings away . . . the neck wilts, the bones give like over-stretched elastic. No wonder Angie moves with such nervous grace. Her head, her whole world, could so easily topple if Clive was having a bad day.

The girls are even thinner, mere half-echoes of their mother. Angie doesn't look robust enough to have given birth to them, and here they are, two slivers barely present, stretched too thin for their height. When they were born they must have slid from between their mother's legs like smoothed-down soap.

Identical ribbons tie back their brown hair, and identical pink dresses with wide ruffled necklines emphasize in-substantial little frames inside. Alba finds them fascinating. They are children of nine and ten like any others, but they've stepped back already from what goes on in the world. They've seen it all, they know the pitfalls, they've no desire to experiment. And Alba – she deals with children, it's her job – even she can't talk to these faint vague alien offspring of her brother. They merely look back at her through adult eyes full of patronizing toleration.

Helen gets plenty of attention being their grandmother. Her make-up drawer, her dresses, all are curiously inspected by the little girls. But even she tires of them. They wear her out, make her feel her age. They look for something to replenish a great hole inside them, two little sweeties in pink flounce, two little vampires.

Clive feeds on them every day, Alba knows it. He's linked to them by a fat umbilicus. Everything they consume gets sucked out before they can make any bodily substance from it. There's just enough blood, gristle and bone left to keep them alive. But they don't thrive.

All three follow Clive the way shadows feebly chase solidity. There's more of them in him, and they all know it. Better stay close, never stray, lest the sun get too bright and they shiver away . . . How else would he continue to grow and they not, Alba muses, unless he eats them every day for breakfast and dinner?

Helen's voice shrieks as Clive surprises her. Alba gets up and moves further down the garden to sit on the path. The day can go hang.

It's evening. The weather's changed – Clive was right. The clear sky was just a trick. The family watch the news on the television. There are reports of floods, of trees being uprooted in gales, of lightning striking houses. And the weather's coming this way. They all decide to go out for a meal at a restaurant in the cathedral city – they won't let a bit of bad weather upset *their* plans. They must celebrate Clive's visit no matter what. But Alba doesn't go. The thought of it makes her head throb. For once she's glad of being in pain, and of looking so.

Alone in the house now, with the heavy scent of departing

cologne in the air, she begins to feel irritable. She can't go to bed – she has none. Her room has been given to the two little girls for the night – Alba can make do with the sofa in the front room. She'll have to wait for the party to return, for Clive to sit up late with Helen, telling her his stories, before she can go to bed herself.

On an impulse she rings Dutch. She could pretend an enquiry about his face. The phone rings for a long time. No answer. She puts it down, hesitates, picks up the receiver, and keys in the numbers again with childlike deliberation. She wants very much for him to be there. Her willing this to be so causes the beat to intensify behind her forehead. It gets harder to focus. With every fast heartbeat blood surges through her temples, filling her head with too much, too much.

Dutch answers after the eighth ring, his voice deep and full of langour.

'Hello . . . who is it?'

People always answer the phone with their other voice, the stagey one, the one where they consider how they're going to sound to the caller, the posh act. No-one normally talks like that. It'd be comic.

Alba's breath snatches into the mouthpiece. Dutch is no actor. He sounds like himself. It's a shock. His voice is fully a part of what he's been doing. There's no break. No self-important, self-conscious alpha in his connection with the unknown caller. And it makes Alba twist. She could never be like that. Her life, as he had often mocked, was full of too many shoulds. She clears her throat and there's a prolonged silence. She does not know how to talk to him, how to talk.

And she's interrupted something, she knows it. A picture of his room comes into her mind: the room dark because of the weather, the old sofa in disarray, brown limbs spread-eagled upon it. Oh, yes, she's interrupted something: sex with his dark gypsy woman.

'It's only me . . . Alba,' she says in a minor key.

There's a long drawn-out sigh on the other end of the line. Yes, he wouldn't want to be disturbed, by her of all people, the woman who tried to hit him the night before when he was in the middle of one of his few miracles. He had seen so clearly the emotion she so hotly condemns in others: envy.

Better to be ripped herself on both cheeks, to suffer disfigurement herself, than to be a candle eclipsed by Dutch's sun, by this man who did so well and so fully what she had never done, and damnably never would – to live – to love – to risk. Judas! She had seen the veils part for just a second. It's what people dream about, what they chase. But like the sweet-sourness of Judas, she had betrayed no-one but herself. Awful, shameful, Dutch had witnessed it.

'What do you want this foul night?' He's not angry with her, no, that's only her imagination. He's tired, spent, depressed.

The line hums in the gap.

'Is it a foul night?' she says, watching her voice, aware of how artificial it sounds.

'It's pissing down here. Haven't you noticed? So damn gloomy I've lit a fire.'

She coughs, takes the phone away from her mouth and listens. Sure enough, rain is smashing against the window by the front door, and she had been unaware of it until now.

'Lit a fire? At this time of year? Well, it's not that bad here. Anyway . . . sorry I interrupted. I didn't know you had company.'

There is an irritable snort from the other end of the line. 'I haven't.'

'Are you sure?'

'Christ, Alba . . . !'

She pauses. 'Could I come down and sit beside your crazy summer-fire for a while?'

'Of course. Come right over.'

She drives in the rain. A current of energy like invisible tramlines keeps the car on the road. With such rain after heat the surface is slippery with a skin of rubber, enough to make her up-end in one of the rhynes. People have drowned like this. In places the ditches are twelve feet deep and full of black peat-water, tonight innocent under a skin of green plants. And Alba's eyes don't see right. The crew inside her skull want some sport, some danger. She drives on the edge of recklessness and fear, the battle exhausting her with every mile.

But she needn't worry. The way is mapped out for her. She could drive with her hands behind her back, and her foot pressed to the floor – it would make little difference – Dutch is at the end of the thread.

The house is lit with candles. She pulls up on the wet leaves opposite the cottage, leaves torn prematurely from the willows by the wind, and looks across at the orange-yellow haloes. Dutch opens the door and stands in the doorway as she gets out of the car and hurries across the road.

'Alba.' He almost shouts because of the noise of wind and rain. 'Have you been drinking?' That soft slur is present in his voice too.

'No. Why?' She stumbles past him into the room, stiffening, jutting her chin out in defiance of the headache.

'You bloody well look as if you have. You look awful.'

'Speak for yourself,' she snaps. 'So would you if you had a head like mine.'

He grunts, shuts the door and unglues a candle from the

unprotected bare surface of a large oval rosewood table, and comes over to her, shoving it in her face, peering down at her.

'Why didn't you ask me to pick you up?'

'You . . . you'd have picked me up . . . ? Done that for me . . . ?'

He nods, withdraws, and up-ends the candle so the wax melts in the flame and drips onto the wood. He screws the base down.

A little of Helen creeps sourly into her mind. He never looks after anything, she thinks. Nothing he owns has any meaning for him. There he is now, abusing a beautiful antique as if it was a packing crate. Candle grease curdles all over its once-polished surface. A man like him doesn't deserve such things if he can't appreciate them properly. Another good reason to have left.

'How's your face?'

Dutch sniffs. 'Sore.'

Alba presses the flat of her hand hard against her forehead. 'Was it your bird in the cathedral last night . . . the one you lost?'

He gives a short laugh. 'Nope. Mine wouldn't be so stupid as to fly into such a place.' He leans back on the heavy table leaf, making it creak, pushing the strength of the wooden bar underneath to straining point, and runs his hand over the livid flesh on his cheek, wincing a little, hoping for sympathy.

'Was it a tame hawk, then . . . ? Belonging to someone else, maybe?'

He shakes his head.

The heat searing through her head drives towards her mouth. 'Then how come it flew to you when you called . . . You whistled. I was watching, I saw it all.'

His body jerks against the table and his arm goes back,

almost, it seems to Alba in the half light, as if he is drawing a punch . . . Instead the arm comes forward and he bounds towards her, springing onto his haunches, making her shrink, terrified, as his hand swoops down. It catches her under the chin. He lifts up her face.

'I don't know the answer to that.'

'Yes you do,' Alba says defiantly. 'You're just not telling me. I want to know. I have a right to know, don't I?'

'No.' His voice is still, quiet, the kind you can hear for miles over a calm sea. 'There's nothing to tell. Now, shut up about it.' And he gets up, turns his back on her, takes a half-smoked cigarette from a saucer and lights it, breathing smoke into the fire, his back still turned.

The pain inside her head gets worse, as if it is not only hers, but in some way, a little of the world's too. She sits up, suddenly someone else. Of course – the other woman . . . where is she? Alba had forgotten about her. Dutch must have hidden her, probably in the bedroom. Crazy, she gets up, her hand on one side of her head, and looks about the room, peering into dark corners. 'Why are there no lights?' she asks, sharp, suspicious.

'Digger cut through the cable down the road.'

The room tilts. She reaches back to steady herself on the chair arm. 'I thought I heard a noise – there! – upstairs – see.'

Dutch turns, mashes the cigarette on the saucer and observes her carefully. He looks down at the floor, waiting, watching her with the rest of his senses.

'There it is!'

He shifts himself. The table creaks. 'What's the matter, Alba?' It's that soft way of his, like he's taken the clouds down and made them into words that curl round her, innocent, moist, like damp thistledown. He could unzip the world so easily. Her world.

'Are you really alone? There's really no-one here?'

His laugh cracks. 'What a question. Want to check every room?'

And yes, she does want to check. Thank God he said that. Thank God he invited her to – although she would have done it anyway, even if he hadn't, the impulse is so irresistible.

A gremlin inside her skull has jumped to the front of the pack with a banner which he spreads out the full length of her forehead, obliterating all other thoughts. Don't step on paving cracks – it drums with big hammers on a tightly-stretched drumskin. Cross your fingers when you see a black cat. Toss spilt salt over your left shoulder. Spit nine times if you see the devil.

The devil's upstairs. She knows it. She can feel it tap the cloven ballerina pump on the floor. She feels it in her muscles as it calls to her, making her body creep inch by inch ahead of her like a cat. If she doesn't heed the call, the lure, her skin will burst with the effort of containment. Upstairs, in Dutch's bedroom the woman lounges on his bed, her long mirrored skirt flung to one side, baring her legs, Alba's red rose held contemptuously between the silky grip of her thighs. In her mouth is a black cigarette holder. She plays with it in her mouth, and gazes out of the tiny window at the crescent moon.

Trembling, Alba almost runs across the room to the stairs, pausing at the foot, and then as quietly as she can, goes up.

Dutch runs his hands slowly over his hair, rearranging the lie of the plait in his neck, and sits on the edge of the sofa, swinging one foot.

Alba bursts into the bedroom through the half-open door. The room is in darkness. There's a shape on the bed. Someone curled up. Her hands scratch for the light switch. On. Off. On. Off. Of course, no power – that digger in the road. She holds her breath and lunges forward, running her hands over bedclothes which are all rolled up in a heap.

Clapping her hand to her mouth she goes to the wardrobe – the only other thing in the room big enough for someone to hide, and jabs her hand inside, sifting through the clothes. Nothing.

She pads around the bed and climbs across it before going out of the room. In the next minute she has quartered the whole of the upstairs: the other bedroom, the room full of junk. She can't just stand in the doorway, no, she has to go in, walk around, leave her scent, make her mark. Exorcize.

'Alba.' Dutch's weary voice calls to her from the sofa.

'Coming.' Breathless, excited, she runs back down the stairs into the living room.

'Whatever's the matter with you?'

'Oh. Oh.' Flushed, breath in jerks, she throws herself next to him. 'I'm sorry, I'm sorry, I'm sorry,' she hears the demons chant through her lips. 'I thought someone was there. I had to check. Don't you ever get like that . . . ? Have to go back and check you've shut all the windows . . . or something. Sometimes I'm like that. I think I've left the car door unlocked and I have to go back. Don't you ever do that?'

Dutch waves a hand in front of her face. 'Now who d'you think might have been upstairs, hmm?' he says, exasperated.

Alba, too bright, burning out, burning, looks at him, sees a feral man, a man rough with rape at every corner, sees his eyes glitter like snakeskin, knows him for Mage, for Crazed, for Shaman about to change now, yes, about to shape-shift right in front of her eyes, take a leap at her neck and suck on her blood. The fingers inside her head tap, tap faster, fiddle-de-dee, fiddle-de-dee, ta-rum-ta-tum, go on . . . do it. Go on. Tell him. Go on . . . tell him . . . go . . .

'Your girlfriend? I thought I heard her, upstairs . . .'

Despite himself, he folds up with silent mirth. 'Oh, yes,' he quips. 'I like that.'

'I'm not wrong, am I? I mean, you do have one, I've seen her,' Alba's voice wobbles, 'when I called by and you were sitting by the river. I saw her then.' She looks into the small fire with hands that have balled into clenched fists. 'Not like me. Nothing like me at all. This one looked like a gypsy. Very free. Very . . . very sexy.'

'Well, well,' he murmurs, patting her knee. 'There's hope for the English teacher yet. At least she's still got some imagination left.'

Under the pressure of his hand on her forehead, and the guide of the other one behind her shoulders, he pushes her body – it feels like wood – back into the sofa cushions. 'Stay here,' he says. 'You've gone temporarily nuts. I'll get a cold towel for your neck.' And he goes into the kitchen, comes back with a towel wrung out, a towel that smells as though it's seldom been used, but has hung there for ages. He lifts her hair and lodges the cold wet thing against the back of her neck, wrapping the ends up over her ears and the top of her head.

Leaving her, he turns his attention to the fire. A fire on a late summer's night. Not the kind of thing most people would have. A man especially. But he had lit it not for its warmth, but for its life. As he plays with the embers using a bent poker, he talks to himself, to her, to all the threads of the current streaming through the house from the roaring unseasonal visitation outside.

Raking through the wicker log basket, he pulls out different woods sawn and chopped. 'Nothing burns so brightly as a dry, rotten log,' he says. 'Look at this one: dried, sponged out, you'd think it had nothing else to give. But it's just waiting to go, to give itself up. All that energy waiting to be released.' He lays it on the flames and immediately the wood bursts into sparks.

Will I be like that, Alba thinks, from her dim prison, where his words reach her in a dream. Will I be like that when I die? Will I fly upwards in a November sky to the remembered space among the stars from where I came? I am a fallen star . . . A fallen star . . .

'. . . And green logs . . . curious how they don't burn . . . except ash . . . now that burns green . . .'

Ash, named from spent fire. Ash sap, carrying alpha and omega in its xylem and phloem, silent, strong. The thunder tree against an April sky, the leaves shimmying a mischievous yellow-green. Lighting the ground in October with yellow leaves full of stored sun. Ash – the tree that is often man's nemesis. Ash – the widow-maker.

'. . . Don't die on me Alba. Let yourself become so rotten I can plant a good seed or two in the compost . . .'

Alba cannot follow his stupid rambling sentiment. She shrugs, sighs and sinks back, her legs tucked underneath her, arms clasped tight about her, trying to hold her body together.

'Smell.' He passes her a chunk of cedarwood. She sniffs. The smell is as it is, untainted by her sickness which finds some smells repulsive. She turns the slice over in her hands. The grain is like a river stilled. Light and dark bands configure it. Where these are dark and rough the scent is strongest.

'My head's bad.'

'I know. I can see.'

'I haven't got a room. The little girls have mine. I'm to sleep on the sofa tonight.'

Dutch silently takes the log from her and lays it on the fire. The smell feeds into the room. He turns his back to her for a moment. He can hear the dam of tears.

'Clive – he's the brother, isn't he?'

'Half-brother.'

'You don't get on, of course,' Dutch grins to himself.

'I don't even know him.'

'When are you going to leave that place, Alba?'

'What? I've lived with Helen all my life. I'm quite content with it for now.'

'Exactly.' He sits on the rug and turns to look at her, his face fallen, shadowed, sad. 'You know why I didn't answer the phone?' He flips a cushion from the armchair behind him and leans against it, wedging the pad behind his back, pushing his bare feet towards the flames. Fire glow hovers about his features. He notices the long strands of Alba's hair in an untidy web on her shoulders: white hair, old before its time, but not past its best yet.

'I was lying on the sofa,' he goes on, 'where you are now, thinking of you and masturbating.' The shadowed sockets hiding his serpent eyes are hidden. 'The first time the phone rang I was coming.'

'Oh,' Alba says, her body tense as wire all of a sudden, too quick in her response, too smart, wanting to stop him saying more.

'I knew it was you,' he says, very low. 'My spunk shot in an arc in the firelight. Every streak like your name stretched out, like white words in seaside rock: A. L. B. A.'

The room falls into silence.

'What is it with you?' she whispers after a minute, tears running into her mouth. 'Everything you say scares me so. People don't just whistle wild birds out of thin air. When I'm with you I feel I have to be other than what I am. I can't come back.'

Dutch sits up abruptly. 'What do you mean, you can't come back? You're always going fuckin' backwards! Why make an exception now?'

Alba shivers, cuts herself off from his words. It isn't hard, either, to distance. Her head is a laundering place for mayhem. The silver sliver of herself is being booted around, and she has less and less control over it. There's not enough of her left to react with.

'I don't know why I came,' she says, in a voice at the far end of the tunnel. 'It was a stupid thing to do.' And her body, running ahead on its own steam now, having junked the scrambled mind, leans forward and vomits on the carpet.

Tears and sick pour out of her in one great urgent clamorous rush to be rid of the aliens tap-dancing inside her skull. Dutch is beside her in an instant, holding her head down, feeling tears and sick slip over his fingers. When she's finished Alba sits up, her body shaking. She digs her fingers into Dutch's shirt, pulling him to her, butting her face against him, craving the beat of his heart. He breathes shallow lest the slightest move will break the moment, but he knows better than that. You can't still time. It isn't there for the taking.

The room stinks. He gets up, pushes the sofa back with his knees, and it squeaks across the stone floor. Catching hold of the soiled rug by the corners he drags it to the back door. The night air rushes in, the candles sputter. Some phut! and go out. He's gone a few minutes and when he returns his hair and beard are wet. The wind grabs at the door as he goes to shut it again, and it slams. Ripping the wet shirt from his back he pushes the sofa and Alba towards the fire again. He kneels, and riddles it noisily to raise the heat.

'Are you going to be sick . . . throw up again?'

Alba shakes her head.

'Good.' He shifts to one side of the fire, his wet back shining in the light. 'That was an old Nain rug, one I took off the wall,' he smiles. 'I guess the rain'll clean it . . . with a bit of luck.'

Suddenly he's saviour, saint. In throwing up she's gotten rid of a lot of garbage, not all of it related to her migraine. She blinks at him as he goes to get her a glass of water. Right now, if he only but knew, he could have her any way he wanted. But he does not know.

'I'm not going to take you back to your mother's,' he says on his return. 'So you'll have to stay here. It must be getting on for midnight.'

'Oh, I couldn't—'

'Ring Mummy, then. Tell her you're staying somewhere else, if you have to,' he sneers. 'Go on.' And he snatches the phone from amongst the clutter on the table and throws it into her lap. 'But make it sound convincing,' he hisses, disgusted.

She dials, utterly sure that Helen and everyone else are still out, sure she will be fine in another hour when she'll be able to leave.

Helen answers the phone.

'I won't be coming home tonight,' Alba says, her voice tight with panic.

'Why on earth not?' Helen's voice clips.

'I'm staying over at a friend's. They've got a bed for me here.'

'What friend? Who are you talking about?'

'Dee . . . from school.'

The phone goes quiet. Alba moves it away a little from her ear. At the other end Helen peers down the wire, antennae everywhere, listening, listening, scanning her daughter's soul, piercing it with an ice-pick from her eyes, winkling out the weak spot. When she speaks her voice is terrible, deep, obscene – masculine in its surety.

'You're not with that man?'

'Who . . . ? Dutch . . . ? Of course not.'

'Because if you are, you can pack your bags, Alba. I'm not going through all that humiliating fiasco.again. And if you are with him, there'll be no slice of my will for you either. Not one slice.' The line goes dead. Alba, feeling weak and foolish, turns to Dutch.

'She knows.'

'Oh, come on.'

'She does. I know it.'

Dutch's face is pure joyous evil. 'That's good then.' He's got her. He's messed up the web. May the old spider shrivel without her food.

Alba stays. She doesn't feel well enough to go anywhere. And why bother to go home? There's no good reason to. To sleep, an outcast on a sofa, after enduring a late-night joke-telling session, with Clive gradually getting more and more obscene? She sighs.

'I'm carrying you to bed,' Dutch says after a while.

'Don't be daft. I can walk. I hate your chivalry.'

Nevertheless, she lets him carry her to his room. It's the same room, nothing's altered. He probably hasn't changed the sheets since she left. The bed dominates: large, with tossed sheets, and the smell of him in every fibre. He lays her down in the middle.

'Where are you going to sleep?'

He smooths her calf. 'With you,' he says, controlling a grin.

'No. I'd rather you didn't.'

The edge of the bed sags as he sits down on it. 'What the hell makes you think I'm going to sleep anywhere else?'

'You'll want to—' her voice trails off '—and I'm ill.'

He laughs. 'Of course. And your being sick wouldn't worry me in the least.' He snorts, bends low over her so she can catch the lizard, the snake – his eyes. 'Just for tonight, though, I'm not going to. OK?'

'What a martyr you are,' a weak smile crosses her pale face. 'Aren't you going to sing me to sleep?'

He looks up quickly, his face softer, pained, lost. 'No, I won't do that.' He looks towards the window, at the howling dark beyond. 'No singing. I don't want any rivals turning up. Not now.'

Her rival. The hawk who flew away the day she came. No, Alba couldn't take any more of that.

In the night Alba's head gets worse. She throws up twice. Then Dutch's body curls round her, and she sinks into its hairiness. All night long his erection weeps into her buttocks while he fights the remainder of her demons in his sleep.

In the morning there is a large bloodstain on the sheet. Dutch sees it as he pulls back the covers. In a fierce erotic half-sleep Alba catches his arm as he moves to get out of bed.

Slowly his hand runs down over her, stopping between her legs. She's not aware she is bleeding. His fingers vibrate until she is writhing for orgasm. And at that point he sinks down slyly, his lips to her lips, taking her into his mouth. And then silently he covers her up, and slides out of the room, his fingers bloodied, his mouth full.

8

Sunday . . . Leon sits on the edge of the patio making repairs to his kites. Alba watches from the doorway, spitefully engrossed in his ugliness, her tea going cold in its cup. When the mind isn't following its usual civilized trammels, when it's not being politically correct, there's always a return to spite. It pops up, the unsmacked child with a crowing voice.

She considers his body with distaste. He's small, with every extremity over-large. He's the stick-man that children crayon in – a balloon for the head, sausage ends for hands and feet.

Leon is the wild card slipped into the pack. Ugliness – even the word trips up over its own big feet – the card God held behind his back, waiting until all were drowning in the early beauty of the world before he sneaked it forward. They didn't notice his sly manoeuvre, those air-light fingers lifting up the King, the Queen and the Nave, to slip the Joker in between.

Leon has fits because he can't stand the sight of himself, Alba thinks. He'd need to live in a mirrorless waterless land to be safe. But – ah! – easy to forget eyes – and eyes don't lie. Eyes are mirrors – he couldn't look into the blue, the brown and the green, and not see the horror of himself looking back.

Leon's kite is made from orange tissue. Around the thin canes of the trapezium it's wrapped and taped neat, but from the apex a tear snags into the kite's belly. With big teeth he rips small bits of sticky tape from the roll, and dabs them over it. But the tape is wet from his mouth, and won't hold. It won't behave. It sticks to itself in a long mucus string.

Alba stares at him, at the dry rough skin on the back of his hands. Skin with the permanent appearance of sand glued on seaside legs. His throat makes little noises, little grunts of impatience as his despair increases. In a minute he'll punch a fist through the tissue, and throw the whole damn lot across the patio – Alba's waiting for it. The humiliation nursed in the hunched bow of his shoulders will break out then in tears, rage, both. At her. At Alba.

When she was very small, Alba's father used to make kites for her. Together they flew them in a field behind the house. Crude affairs, they were made from newspaper and garden canes, always gluey, lop-sided. When launched, she remembers, all they did was swoop in dramatic circles, Catherine wheels with no fire, and dive into the ground, crash after crash. Alba's job was to carry newspapers and a ball of string across the field. She'd follow Harold – he made the kites for her, he said – but when they were ready to fly she was forgotten, left behind, and had to run to keep up with him. Too fast, too eager he was, his nerves jumping in a hot fry-pan, the newspaper kite held tight to his chest.

Alba, the rescuer . . . . After the first disastrous flights she'd sit down, only her head visible above the dry meadow grass. With the serious deliberation children have, she'd tear the newspaper into strips. Neat for a child. But she had to be – Harold's world depended on her. So she would tear those strips as cleanly as possible, and stow them under her shoe. Harold hated things to go wrong. He hated having to try. Trying brought shame, brought him all out in a lather . . . and, before Alba's birth, gave him fits.

But Alba was there, his little page, all ready to take the sting out of his failure before it set in. She'd take a strip, and twist it into a bow-tie. Strip after strip she'd do, and then hand them to Harold in silence while he wrestled, sweated, fevered, and tied a long train of them onto twine. There she was, making it all right. And it was the tail that made the kite take off, fly. Harold had to be kept smooth, she had to take care of his delicate balance. He counted on Alba. From her unwanted birth she was now the five-year-old saviour who held the mystical cup of his cure.

Throwing the cold tea onto the garden, Alba goes over to Leon, no saviour in her now. 'You must be disappointed about last night,' she says in a voice learned at school for dealing with children in a tantrum.

Leon turns. His fingers jab through orange tissue, fist finishing the job. His face is red, off-key. 'Why should I be?' he says with a bullish pout. 'You were ill, weren't you? It doesn't matter that you didn't come. Helen and I had a lovely time.'

'Oh, well, that's good. At least the tickets weren't wasted.'

She looks out into the nothingness. The air is good this morning. It has a fullness, a curious substance, a buoyancy.

The birds go past in effortless flight, launched slow, like gliders. Not a day to get into an argument.

'She didn't enjoy driving all that way, though.' Leon flashes her a mutinous look. 'And back. Not in the dark, she didn't.'

'Oh?' Alba's surprised. 'She quite likes driving. It does her good to get out. And her eyesight's fine.'

Leon scowls. 'She's a bit . . . old, if you ask me.' He lowers his voice.

Alba snorts. 'Just let her hear you say that.'

'Oh, aye, she can do it all right. I mean there's nothing wrong with her faculties. But she weren't happy, all the same. She was dead when we got back.'

Alba frowns and looks at the hole in the kite. Leon wants her to feel guilt. Her face tightens as the unwelcome weight descends. She'd had another headache, it wasn't a lie. Not a bad one, true. Maybe she could have gone to the theatre with Leon, but what if she couldn't have driven back? 'Well, I'm glad you enjoyed yourselves,' she says, lamely.

Leon jumps to his feet. Surprised, Alba steps back into the doorway. He runs his hand across the thin red streaks of hair on his scalp, raking it into an angry red score. 'You didn't want to go with me, did you?' he says. 'You didn't want to be seen with me. I know. I'm not stupid.'

The air thickens like soup, no longer benign, as unseen twitterings look on. Best be honest in front of so many witnesses.

'You're not my type,' she says, immediately leaping in, her sarcasm boiling over. 'That's true.'

'You've been leading me up the garden path . . .'

'I what?'

'Helen said you were very keen to go.'

'Oh, she did, did she? Well that was Helen,' Alba shouts, 'not me.'

'I was beginning to think you did like me a bit . . . that we might have got to know each other a bit,' he stammers. His words suddenly blot out. He stops, looks around in bewilderment as if they have flown away in all directions. He snatches at some, but others don't make it. It's what children do – speak, and clap their hand off and on, off and on, over their mouths. The next minute he's lost the lot. The words go down his throat in an indigestible lump of sound. His eyes roll at the air, his body twists, lunges forward, dives upward. The demon that is his intimate shadow throws him violently onto the concrete patio.

'Oh, Christ.' Alba, horrified, stunned, leaps back into the house. The rictus demon stretches Leon's face into grotesque contortions.

'Mum! – Quick!'

Helen walks quickly out from the hall, screwing lipstick back into its cylinder before putting it in her dress pocket. Her face is set in a calm pointed way. The most unlikely people can drop into a curious serenity when they're going to meet a crisis head-on. Every feature gets thinned, keened, the jaw is set, every movement economical. They've been training in secret for years, and you never knew it.

Leon lies jerking on the concrete, the side of his head smashing up and down, while blood trickles into his eyes. Helen goes to him smartly. As his head jerks up, she shoves her chisel-toed shoe underneath. He bounces up and down on the top of her foot, bloodying and foaming her stocking and shoe. His eyes aren't there. They've gone to never-never land in the back of his skull.

Helen looks past Alba, ignoring her. Instead, she folds her arms and looks at the view – such a nice view – as Leon's shaking subsides.

'Alba,' she says, addressing the air in front of her. 'No, don't run away . . . I want you to do something for me today.' She looks briefly down at Leon. 'After we've cleared this one up.'

Alba, shaking, sick, clasps her elbows to her front, and shrinks away. What is wrong with her? There are epileptic children at school – she knows how to behave in a crisis like this. But on the rare occasions when it's happened she's never had to deal with it directly. And children, they're so pitiful, so beautiful, they can take grotesqueness – you can feel sorry for them. But Leon is pushed to the extremes of ugliness – it's difficult to look.

'You'll do what I say for once,' Helen says. 'I want you to take me to the cathedral this afternoon. I haven't been there for years.'

The words go in immediately, as if Alba knew they were the next thing Helen would say. There's no surprise. That place has it in for me, she thinks. It draws me in whether I want it or not. Did my star fall there? Did it? Why do I look, pretend not to look, but look for it all the same?

She looks at her mother. With one of God's misfits under her foot, Helen stands like a figurehead shearing through the wind, as if it is her unalloyed right to master calamity under her shoe. Helen, queenly, everything-under-control, make-up immaculate, hair coiffed. Blood on her shoe. Alba's guts twist, there's a tight punched feeling in her solar plexus. She could cry.

'What are you staring at, Alba?' Helen asks with soft scorn. 'I often used to do this for your father – put my shoe under his head when he had a fit. Stops them smashing their faces to bits if you can't get a cushion.'

Helen holds out her arm, but Leon can't move yet. His bubbling stops. The skin over his cheekbones falls back into place. He's a drunk, unsure of his bearings. Newly born, he blinks into the light. He's been somewhere else, had a vision, and this world, this nightmare, isn't real. It will take some getting used to.

Helen stares blankly at the view. Out there in the artist's landscape – the conversation-stopper – she floats so delicate, elegant, a silk chiffon scarf around her neck trailing behind her in the wind. Leon is only a minor inconvenience. She can deal with it. She pretends she's elsewhere. It's always been Helen's strategy to look away.

When Alba was born she was doing it then. She didn't look down at her splayed-out legs, at the gowned nurses with mess on their hands. No, instead she found a chink of light coming through the top inch of the open frosted-glass window, and she fixed her eyes on that. Never present to what was going on in the room, she moved house outside her body. All her dignity and gentility strained away from the birthing bed and flew in a stream towards the one exit in the room, to the elsewhere on the other side.

Alba had to be wiped clean and tidied up, wrapped in a hospital blanket, before Helen would look at her and acknowledge she'd had the child.

Now she looks down at Leon with slight reproof, distant sympathy. He is not like her – he cannot help himself. He has nothing under control. He's just like Harold was. Softly she laughs to herself. 'He stopped those damned fits the day you were born. You were such a shock to him. A daughter. He expected a son.'

Cautious, Alba comes over to look down at Leon. There he lies, foetally curled, his face bloodied, still pillowed on Helen's old foot. For a moment he goes completely still, with no breath, like death – like a dead puppy.

Years ago, a memory . . . Alba in her aunt's house, the boxer-dog having puppies . . . They'd made the creature comfortable under the stairs – a cardboard box, old blankets, a bar-heater at a safe distance, newspapers spread all around on the floor.

The distress of birth . . . The animal fighting to run away from it, curling round itself, throwing up, whining. All that stuff about birth being a natural event for animals . . . At the time, this dog would have done anything not to go through with it. She knew she was giving birth to death – what a traitorous thing to do: to birth more suffering . . . The reluctance to drop the puppies, to let go of a doomed life. The minute each sleek slimy head appeared from the body, death had it by the scruff.

And Alba had watched, stricken and dry-throated. Is this what's in store for me? God forbid!

Green liquid and blood. Green and blood, and through this mire the bitch would shiver, her teeth visible, and her eyes would roll, look, strain the other way as the next puppy was born . . .

. . . Long, thin, this one was. Nearly twice the length of all the others already safely delivered. Stretched on the way out through a mangle, all floppy now like a wet cloth. The way it lay there, curled, foetal, a grey rag. So thin, because it's proper substance was made up of what was absent – the life-force – and this had been squeezed from the body on its descent into the world. A descent, yes, a going down, a life sentence, a coming back to a lower form . . .

Alba picked up this long thin squeamish bit of flesh – now meat – and, yes, it was dead. No breath from the tiny lungs, just the density, the horrible solid density of its flesh, the life stolen for another creature in some other time, the puppy just a mockery, a born corpse.

And Alba, cramming the dead length into her hands, watching it ooze out gristly between her fingers. Holding its snout down, shaking the head like scattering drops of water from lettuce leaves in summer, shaking out all the wet, flicking the head and scrawn of a neck and chest up and down.

Imagine . . . How much will can a thirteen-year-old caught in such a drama bring to this moment? Seconds go by, and death still lies warm in her hands. Dead. Dead. Dead. How much will, how much adolescent power? (Adolescents know they have no power.) All the will she has she brings to it. All the will she doesn't know she has. All the prayers that can be prayed, drawn down into her hands. Hands which weep with the effort.

. . . Alba – the giver of life . . . The tiny nose bubbles mucus, the chest flutters, and the current snaps through its grey dead length like switching on a bulb. The energy pulsing now, making muscles twitch and relax, testing life. Life. Alba, the bringer of life, the female Jesus. Jesus . . . !

Leon uncurls as the switch throws back. He sits up unsteadily, brushing Helen's hand aside. The ugly body, for a few moments transfigured by movement not his own, but a swan's – a bird unfurling its large white wings – sitting up and blinking at the New World. Alba watches him in astonishment. There is utter innocence in his eyes.

They clean him up – Helen doing most of the work. As he comes round, the coarse brusqueness, the embarrassment at his condition comes back to him. He throws up.

Dutch drops granules of frankincense onto the rusted iron plate of his stove. Pale amber melts, steams and bubbles. The smell, the heaviness of oil, bitter-sweet. He knows a lot about frankincense. To get the resin the tree has to be incised. It bleeds white milk-like juice which hardens in the air. The slit is deepened. More juice flows out, is left to harden, and then scraped off as tears of resin.

In times past it was used for all kinds of medical

hocus-pocus. But the church uses it now. The people who sit beneath the smoke are unaware that it has another power. Why would religion exclusively use it otherwise . . . ? Think on it . . . Power.

It frees the mind from the clutter of thoughts. Like a light-beam on a penny, it hones awareness, makes a gap, allows the mind to be fooled by what it hears. Ears to be tickled by the good works of saints, the real terrors of hell . . .

But no amber cracks. No souls are won over. The censer is swung by unconscious men. Those who breathe the smoke are also asleep. So much is missed . . . missed. The smoke-blinded lead. And the smoke-blind follow. No-one's heart cracks. And this has kept clerics in power for years . . .

Dutch knows that if he breathes the vapour long and slow into his lungs his mind will slip. This is the place to ask for information, to trawl the boundless. To ask what he may do.

He takes a lump of the resin and holds it up in front of the window. It begrudges light. There's too much stored up inside already, and it's closed the door on any more. He drops the tear of amber onto the stove. Soon the still room is so thick with the resinous smoke it is like being fingered by mist. What will crack her? He cannot.

The scent cuts in deep to his heart. He cries. What a scent it is. The smell takes him on down beyond under-standing, where words, the literal, do not help. Paltry gropings, they are, for the tide of the numinous he has touched many times before. For centuries now. Alone.

Yes, the numinous is not kind, it has a razor's edge. You do nothing but cut your feet as you walk along it. Slip and cut your feet to the bloody bone. And yet you can't jump off. Once you step up and feel the edge bite you're stuck.

You just have to stay on the bloody rollerblade ride, and try and keep your balance. And all the while you do nothing but bleed, bleed, bleed. Alone.

Dutch leaves the fog in the room, goes into the little lean-to greenhouse. The blasted tubers sit in their pots. They haven't grown. He throws his head back, feels sick from dread and failure. He has meddled. Last year it was sex. That blew up in his face. It didn't pay off. Her blood was not enough. Why? Because he had stolen it. What is there to be done now? He sits down on the old chair, his boots resting on the staging for a long time. Hours pass. The smoke fills the greenhouse. The fire, still burning inside the stove — all by itself — keeping going, keeping going. Sweat like tears, like blood, runs down his face.

In his impatience he's made a mistake that will have to be paid for. He kicks the pots and they wobble. He'd like to smash them now, claw back the talismanic value they're imbued with. But he can't — it's not the kind of investment you can cash in. And they don't even belong to him, but are the legacy from a crazy man before him. What taints and spells are already stitched into their fabric, he doesn't know. It may not be good stitch-work. There might be a pile of shit to work through, a sick joke from the crazy man to teach him a lesson — only she's the one who'll pay for it. She's the one who'll have to work through that shit. How foolish, how weak he was, to try and add to his own power by borrowing from another. You cannot take unless it is freely given.

Night falls, time passes. He aches all over now, swims in a dark world. The consequences of his greed for Alba stretch out before him. He stares at the pots. It's up to her now. The plants must take their chance. If they bloom, so will she, as twins live the same life. He must let her go, he knows it. He's tried everything to make her see what she is, and it hasn't worked. If he told her, she'd laugh in that scornful way of hers, right in his face.

In the morning, stiff, exhausted, chastened, he moves from his vigil into his own bed to sleep. He has invested these plants with too much. He can't watch anymore. If she cracks, the plants will flourish all by themselves, without water, without light. They'd even grow in a cupboard – he knows that well. They don't need his attention, his longing, his meddling any more. Yet he couldn't bear to see them die. He couldn't be around to see that happen. Already, fissures run down through his own heart again.

Siddhartha had to let his offspring go over that bridge into the material wilderness. Siddhartha knew this pain. So Dutch will go – he's wanted on a Reserve in the North. But he'll meet Alba before he goes, say goodbye. She won't know any of this. That will be the hard part. The lonely part.

Helen makes Alba drive them both to the cathedral in her Citroën. In that picky way of hers, she criticizes Alba's driving. By the time they reach the city Alba feels like an abused chauffeur. But she stills her tongue, and parks in the old market place.

Helen loiters in antique shop windows. She looks with irritating fondness at the displays, points out secondhand jade jewellery which has no interest for Alba at all. Old things, time suspended. Objects which encapsulate the time when she was a girl. Links with herself, with a body that has since moved on.

When they go through the familiar cathedral doors, Alba wishes she hadn't agreed to this folly. She's brought her mother into a secret – the one belonging to herself and Dutch. But what is the name of this secret, she wonders, only now aware that there is one. Does it have a name? It's a wordless one, a wordless loyalty. Part of her own history is in here too, although Alba can't find it. But why the fuss? Alba's always felt untouched by the place. And jealous of anyone who is.

The nave is bare of chairs. Alba can't believe it. Space, sudden space, this dancing-fair among the pillars, all new. God's broom has swept away the dead wood. He doesn't want spectators, he wants dancers. Well, here it is, the empty floor, the verticals, a gift. And no-one's dancing.

Helen can't dance, she's too old. Surprises are something to be subdued, played down. Alba can't dance either, or thinks she can't – it's bad enough for her at school. And she'd be too self-conscious anyway. But Dutch would love it. He'd stamp his boots, clap his hands, sing in his deep voice. And the people would come, like the Hamelin rats to the piper, to watch and follow him.

The kids did just that at school. They'd see him in the playground and rush up. They wanted to sup the air around him, get high on the currents. He sang 'Lord Franklin' to them once, in his lunch hour, and you'd never find a quieter playground. Then he'd clapped his hands, broke the melancholy spell, and danced a sailor's jig.

'How lovely. No chairs,' Helen says, breaking into Alba's thoughts. 'They've done it all for me. It's just how I remember it all.'

'Well, the chairs were always empty,' Alba says. 'I'm not surprised they've removed them.'

Helen turns to Alba. 'I used to come here a lot. You never knew that, did you?'

Alba raises her eyebrows. She didn't know. It never occurred to her. Helen – the cathedral. How could the one entertain the other? I suppose it could, Alba thinks. Helen's just another tourist.

'Take my arm,' Helen says. 'We'll walk round together.'

What! Touch her!? It's not something Helen's ever asked

Alba to do before. Helen doesn't touch, she really doesn't. A life-long barrier is being breached. It feels wrong, embarrassing, awkward, contrived for a purpose of which Alba's unaware. It's all Alba can do to keep herself steady. There's great shame in it now. Other mothers touched, but not Alba's, not ever.

A lifetime of missed opportunities for closeness floods through her. She can never remember being cuddled by Helen at all. She fell down the stairs once, when she was five, and cut her head. Helen had dressed the wound at a distance, her arms as remote and unsuccouring as a shipyard crane – and another wound had entered through the cut.

Numbly, Alba takes Helen's arm, her fingers pinching the cloth on the sleeve. Helen chatters on while Alba wrestles with massive feelings of loss. Here – so unexpected. But she ought to know – damn this place. It's a jack-in-the-box, always about to spring the nasty surprise. Yes, she ought to know by now.

Beneath Helen's jacket is flesh, flesh that's lived and moved in another universe. Better not to try and change things at this late stage. It would be too uncomfortable for them both. Better to try and slip her fingers off without Helen being aware of it. But Helen pats Alba's hand back in place, pushes herself up against her daughter. Her body heat sears through Alba's clothes, connects with her skin, and assaults the cells beneath. It's not an innocent touch. All the time Helen talks, her body absorbs details about Alba by osmosis. She wants to find out about Dutch, Alba knows it. That's one secret door never opened to her.

And Alba would love to have been able to let her in, to have few secrets. She never thought mothers were not a daughter's best friend. She'd watched other teenagers and their mothers, and envied them, not realizing that on the inside there was always this chafe, the pull-away, the battle going on which she didn't see.

She had a false view. When you miss something in your life you imagine everyone else has it. Life becomes a myth then, built around the perceived hole in an attempt to fill it. How much of our behaviour is really just piling old junk into bottomless holes . . .

Motherhood has no sense of protocol, it makes the rules up as it goes along – that's how it is with those closest. My mother is not my friend, Alba admits bitterly. She is my pryer of secrets, my depriver of youth. She sits on my self-esteem. She is the judge of my life. I could never tell her anything.

While Alba struggles with her emotions, Helen pulls her on, unaware of Alba's turmoil. Her eyes are alight – rare for Helen.

'See, there—' she points '—the cat . . . Look, right at the top of the column. I bet you hadn't noticed that before. You see, there's a cat in the cathedral.' She giggles into her hand. 'Now you'll be able to tell all those schoolchildren next time you come . . . Now let me show you the owl hidden in this little chapel.'

So another bird's been watching Alba all these years, and she hadn't known it. A stone owl – what's the trouble in that? But these wretched birds of prey are all over the place. Their eyes don't miss a thing – even stone eyes. Owls look through bone into your thoughts. Why hadn't Dutch shown her what was here? You have to know where your rivals are. Even if they don't speak, they listen.

'I do like all the little details,' Helen goes on. 'They make the place more homely.' She turns to look up at Alba's glum face. 'But it's not something the tourists ever get to see. They only want the spectacular, I suppose.'

'I didn't know you were interested in these things.'

'Oh, yes,' Helen answers emphatically.

'Well, I've been coming here for years, and never knew they were here.'

Helen's tone rises. 'Yes, but that's because there's no magic here for you, is there? You're bored with the place. You've always said so.'

Alba's taken aback. It provokes her honesty. 'I suppose I am. I always think I ought to find something in here, but I don't. I suppose I'm just not religious, after all.'

'Neither am I. Anyway, what difference does it make?'

Alba stumbles. 'I don't know,' she says as the floor suddenly seems light.

'You don't appreciate what's on your own doorstep. I suppose that's the way of things these days. I sometimes wonder what it would take, Alba, to shift you out of your lethargy.'

Alba looks down, unable to reply.

'I used to come here such a lot.' Helen turns, her shoulders do a little shimmy, and she blinks, a coquette in the old silent films, all exaggerated emotion so Alba can't miss the point.

'I used to meet Arthur here.'

'Arthur?'

'Yes, Arthur. He was one of the cathedral guides. He taught me such a lot about the place.' She smiles, a lit-up smile, and tosses her head. 'You didn't know that, did you Alba?'

Alba looks at the stone floor, at the marble tombs, at the light coming through the stained-glass windows, but the solidity of the building has vanished. A large hand has suddenly moved everything ten inches to the left, where it wobbles like a mirage in the heat, uprooting Alba's anchor and perception, clouding her with confusion. She feels sick.

'Was this a friend? One of your bridge friends?'

'No, no, no. This was somebody else. I suppose you could say we had an . . . affair. It lasted for years – until he died.'

Affair: Helen. Helen: affair. My mother. Seeing another man. When? How? Seeing someone else behind my back. Me, innocent, unknowing all the while. Helen . . . having . . . sex? It can't be. People of her age don't have sex – they only have platonic relationships.

'I don't think you should tell me this,' Alba says.

Helen mocks her. 'How silly you are. It was a long time ago.'

'Did he love you?'

'Love . . . ? Such an over-used word. Well, of course he did, but the physical element was very . . . very strong.'

Again the cathedral takes Alba's breath from her to fill its emptiness. She goes on with measured slowness to the gloom of the south transept, up to the tier of votive candles burning in the shadows. She picks one up and rolls it in her fingers.

The feeling of let-down is palpable, an indigestible weight falling with a thud through her body. There's so much of Helen of which Alba knows nothing at all. The scales have been most unfairly tipped. Helen knows Alba. She's known every inch of her since birth. She's had the advantage. By the time you're old enough to put the sharp lens of focus on parents, they're sleeping in separate beds . . . and you look at them, wondering how they could ever have had sex.

What a hypocrite her mother was. How she had mocked and castigated her for the dalliance with Dutch. How she had torn her to shreds over it all. Yet she did not see her own behaviour as incompatible in any way.

And what an opportunity Helen had had. She could have met Alba on open ground. This knowledge would have made their relationship easier. But Helen had always wanted the balance of power. To be friends with your daughter wasn't wise – they were rivals. You could never be sure of daughters. Sons might be different. But better to ride on a daughter, keeping the heavy foot down.

The candle snaps in two between Alba's fingers, falls to the floor. Alba bends to pick it up, placing her foot over the spot where tears have fallen. Tears Helen must not see. If Helen had held an invisible noose around Alba's neck, then it was she, Alba, who had grabbed it and pulled it taut. She, Alba, who'd jerked the rope every so often to check it was in place. She, Alba, who had denied all her own impulses, and had shut the door on a normal life.

Grateful for the darkness and the sobriety the lighted candles bring, Alba looks at the many flames. For the first time she feels a kind of reverence. Yes, one can be a tourist in the rest of the building, but here, the sudden lurch of the personal calls out. All the grand architecture is left behind. What really matters isn't the congregation, the choir, the piping singing, the tables of religion, but the tiny flame of the individual soul. Souls past, present, and in hope . . .

She takes another candle from the basket and touches the wick to the nearest flame. Who was that one already burning for? Whose life do I touch there? Whose pain do I let in? Hesitating, she pushes her own candle in the emptiest quarter of the tiered display, so that it burns there alone.

'Who's that for then?' Helen pries behind her.

Alba moves away. 'Me.'

'And now I want to show you something,' Helen says. She looks at her watch. 'You'll have to hurry. Come on. Be quick.'

Helen leads the way out of the cathedral, through the cloisters, and heads towards the Bishop's Palace. Coming into daylight makes Alba sigh with relief. Things got too hot back in there. Out here though, thoughts can flow freely, they don't stick inside your skull. Out here you could be guilty and live with it. In there you'd look for someone to hear your confession. In there old ghosts chase after you as soon as you discard your thoughts, and haul you back with malice, lest you forget what a poor weak fallen creature you really are.

Swans glide on the moat around the Bishop's Palace. Near the gatehouse tourists throw flabby slices of white bread to the ducks and pigeons. Helen walks away from them in the other direction and stops close to the drawbridge leading into the Palace. Part of the building juts out into the moat. On the far side of the walls is a tall mullioned window. From the window hangs a rope. As they watch two swans swim seamlessly up. One takes the rope in its beak and pulls. A bell rings.

'See,' Helen whispers, 'they're ringing for food. Swans have been trained to do that at four o'clock for over a hundred years. Who would've thought they'd be so clever? And aren't they beautiful. So clever. So white. I love that purity.' She looks up into Alba's masked face, a watery brightness in her eyes.

'There you are,' she says, even quieter now as the window opposite opens and food is thrown out onto the water. 'Now you know where your name comes from.'

Alba starts. 'From the swans?' She blinks at Helen in disbelief. 'Surely not. It's got to be my skin . . .'

Helen looks out over the moat, her eyes wet, a faraway expression in them. 'Well . . . that's partly true, and I'm not sure I should have done it. I suppose it was unfair of me, drawing attention to your albinism like that. But I liked it, you see. I didn't think you were a freak at all. You were my little white gift.

'I was here with your father before you were born. I was standing on this very spot with him. I said how nice it would be to have a daughter and call her after the swans. He wanted a son – of course he did. You were such a surprise. He'd convinced himself you were going to be a boy. I don't think he was very keen you were a girl, but his fits stopped and I . . . I was delighted. I'd got exactly what I wanted.' She takes her handkerchief from underneath her watch-strap and wipes her nose. 'So you have a link with this place, a link with the palace and the cathedral.'

They go back through the cloisters to the cathedral teashop. Helen buys tea and cakes. 'We must do this more often,' she says. 'I'm so enjoying it.'

9

The morning dawns with a mercury greyness, the sky leaden but shiny. Rain fell overnight. There's more to come.

Lacklustre trees and bleached summer growth have been given a fresh injection of green. Each leaf shouts with 3D brightness, aggressive viridian clamouring for attention under a sky that finger-pokes. A sky that's looking for a target this morning. The eyes behind the blank mass of cloud have nothing in mind other than faint arbitrary malice. It's the kind of day to stay at home.

Alba's out early, walking the back lanes, the collar on her unseasonally heavy coat pulled up high around her neck. Especially the back, the tender nape. That's where things get in . . . She keeps herself tight together, hands pushed far down in the deep pockets, arms locked at her side. There's no solace to be found in nature today.

She should have stayed at home, and brooded in bed. It's

the luck of things, she thinks. Looking for empathy in the natural world doesn't always pay off. Especially this morning. What a mistake to come out in this! Not today is the country her lonely-as-a-cloud ally, where every leaf cries empathetic tears, and every current of air in the beech canopy carries a comforting message.

Some weekends she walks alone, like other lonely souls fallen temporarily out of love with their kin. There's a woodenness in their walk when they first go out. They hold everything in until they're past their neighbours' houses. Neighbours can read that tilt of the head, the set of the back, the footsteps of light thunder, and know there's bad blood. But an hour or two later, maybe a whole morning later, the aggrieved come back. There's a meandering river in the step, now. The country has done its bit, absorbed all the pique. A successful dump has been done. But nature can handle it. She's big enough. Times, days, like these are good. They're something you can count on.

But there has to be a pay-back, a recompense. The natural world, of which we arrogantly presume to know so much, has to have its way, has to spit back. No loitering melancholic humanity dumping its shit all over the place today, thank you! Open the door on such mornings and a huge No! slaps the face. An autocratic mother speaks now, whose No! comes out of non-negotiable choler. Said in a starched grey voice, there's no give at all. To go out is nothing short of foolhardiness.

But who listens to this? It's just a bad day, nothing more. Don't let the weather get you down. The weather – only the weather. Put up an umbrella and ignore it. There's nothing more sinister at work.

Don't you believe it. If you discount the shiver up the spine and go out as normal, angry cross-winds will whip legs and fingers, and poke grit in the eye. And at the day's end you'll feel bruised and sore, glad of your four walls.

Yes, it's never a good idea to step into the field of an argument. You get in the way, make yourself a target. The malice can suddenly re-direct. You're alone on the golf-course in a thunderstorm, every bit of metal drawing attention to how vulnerable you are. You wandered stupidly into the frame. So you'll do.

There are moments when we realize we have never led our own life. Until then we thought we had – we thought we pulled our own strings, jumped into the tide when we chose. But in reality, others pull our strings all the time. It's just a matter of degree. Babies – what little despots they are. But that's fine, we accept it. We call it nurturing. But what happens when baby grows? Don't they have a debt to pay back? Don't some people demand it? Mothers – they have a black mountain owing. If they call in the debt – well, that's most unmotherly. But it happens. It happened to Alba. Suddenly her past has no meaning – someone else had lived it for her, through her. What she's had has been mouthings, secondhand spoutings of another's script.

It's the morning after Helen dumped the bucket-load of shit on Alba, in the cathedral. Alba's left the house before Helen has even stirred. She doesn't want to see her and suffer her questioning look, her myopic surprise. What! Going out for a walk before breakfast – what's wrong with you, Alba? What are you up to?

No, Alba's trying to deal with the dump. In this case it's a slice of the truth she doesn't want. She's dug her heels in deep. Mothers have to play by the book. They have to keep that safe little pariahdom over their vulnerable daughters. They mustn't lose face. Oh, no. Play the game, Mum. Alba's been living in a house full of secrets and falsehood. It's been going on for years. And now it's out. Helen has had two lives. One, the clamp-down mother. The other, quite frankly, a tart. Alba has been deceived.

She thinks of Helen's light words of treachery – 'it was more of a physical thing' – and her innards squirm with embarrassment and humiliation. She sees Helen's face in the telling of it – a smugness, a pride, and a certain child's prinking in her mother's expression. Little girls twist and turn, clutch their dresses, look at the floor, try to control the red flooding in the cheeks, a flooding of triumph that must never be sung, never be shouted. Embarrassed at being noticed, they try to hold back the bubbles in the blood, the excitement, the hallelujah. It is a feeling deep like no other. It is when you jump out of the ordinary flatness of the human queue, punch the air, and shout, 'I am'.

Secrets. We should come in with a contract at birth that we never conceal anything from each other. Instead we spend our lives wondering what we haven't been told. We live in a world polluted by shadows and ghosts. They're always over our shoulders, tittering behind our backs. We don't tell in order to spare the other – at least, that's what we say. Is that really so? Isn't it rather different? Isn't not-telling the greatest weapon, the surprise knife, the only real power each and every one of us has . . . ?

The man on his death-bed – he's waited a life-time to tell his son the truth. Oh! dutiful son of mine, you do not come from my loins . . . your real father was an American serviceman. You were conceived during a quick fuck in a hayloft, when your unfortunate mother had drunk too much farm cider. I took you in. I kept the secret well. Your mother died before I could exact appropriate revenge on her for never giving *me* a child. So you're left. Here, I give it to you

– the truth. Now, take this knife and push it in to yourself, son of mine . . . American sonny . . .

Why then, the young man's life is but a joke. In the dying out-breath of the man he thinks has been his father, who's been his mentor and masculine role model, he's suddenly stripped of *his* life, flayed of his skin. All his former links and anchors were dream-shadows played on a giant screen. The projectionist just died. The camera stopped whirring. The figure on the screen vanished like the spectre it now is. The son stands there, holding the cold hand, and knows he has never really been . . .

We grow in secrecy, in silence. Our soft bones in the womb bend and unfurl like leaf stalks, green and wavery. Birth . . . and the mystery grows within us. And so it goes on, the secrets running, ruling our lives – although the cocky mind would have it else. All life . . . the winnowing of leaves, the dive of birds, the wake on the sea, the sap going back down the stem, happens there, right in front of our eyes, yet *how* it is remains unknown to us. And ageing, dying, dust – where we go forward into nothingness, who can say it happened? Who can say it wasn't a dream in some other mind, and we are just mist in the frosted air. Be glad there are some secrets. They keep you in control of your little world.

. . . Look at the mage, his life is one long trail of shadows. He sees behind the visible world, earns the right to manipulate the unseen currents. But it doesn't come without a price. If you were to meet God face to face, you'd never forgive your arrogance. The impact would kill you on the spot. You'd fry in the light. Shrivel. Fry. Burst into sparks . . . The mage – he can risk it.

The knowledge that Helen has kept the affair secret from her all this time fills Alba with dismay. What power in the keeping of secrets! Imagine, you pull yourself up, rein it all in. The bigger the secret, the more the powerless lonely inner chasm gets filled. The power lies locked in. Potential damage, sudden hell.

You live with a man for years, and he does not know that you are also living with another. You adopt a child, pretend it is your own. They don't know about the daily deception, they are the innocent. Every day you can play God, and watch your power grow. The arrow is always drawn back in the bow. The eyes hone in on the target, take their time, narrow it down to the width of a hair, and then at the right moment . . . the muscles hold the arrow back. They grow stronger with time, build up strength from holding on, holding back.

Secrets are cultured poison. Nursed, cultured, cultivated. A secret alchemy. Inside the alembic the lion roars, but he never gets out. And he's never transformed. He stays in prison getting stronger all the while, fed on nothing but promises. That's the poison – the promise in the future.

Bitterness is about future. So is jealousy.

They don't live *now*, they live in all the might-be's over the next horizon. Lion, one day you will be given freedom. And all that you've been denied will spew from your throat as acid.

Alba knows the power of the secret. She knows one that would flay Helen's parched skin from her bones. Thirteen . . . seeing Clive with a man . . . Helen would die if she had to give up on Clive, and this little knowledge would surely make her.

Alba's arm is strong, if she but knew it. The barb on her arrow has been through the Book of Shadows, through fire, water, air and earth. She's held it back for years. The arrowhead, the barb with its anointing poison, remains. By now it's strong enough to pierce any skin. That's why the mage is feared. The keeper of secrets is always feared. But Alba is just unaware, locked in, scared.

Helen has let go such a little secret, yet it has wormed its way into Alba's flesh and sticks there, under the skin, a bee sting still pumping its poison.

Sometimes other people's lives get in the way. You've got news you've got to tell, only to arrive on the doorstep to find a new piece of action has blown in, and you, you're just old news.

At a bend in the road Dutch crouches in front of a stone wall, bedding the last stone in place. He has his back to her, and carries on working while she makes up the fifty yards that lie between them.

'Thought I'd run into you this morning,' he says, turning round, rubbing the stone dust off the front of his shirt.

Alba blinks and gives a doll-like smile. She's surprised to see him. 'You did? Well maybe I thought I'd bump into you too.'

He laughs, sits down on the wall. 'If only you would come when I willed it – now that would be another story. But you're such a stubborn thing.'

She snorts. 'Don't patronize me, Dutch, I'm not at your – or anybody's – beck and call.'

Dutch reaches into his back pocket for tobacco and papers. He doesn't answer, but tries to roll a cigarette instead. Normally it's an unconscious ritual. Today threads of tobacco spill from his fingers and blow away on the road. He draws a great slow breath. 'I'm finishing off here before I go,' he says, screwing the fragile paper too hard between finger and thumb, watching the roll-up disintegrate.

'Go? Where? What are you talking about?' The brittleness of fear cracks into her voice. He can't go. She has something to tell him about Helen. He'd like to hear how Alba now finds her mother so treacherous. He'd like to see the final rift.

'Up north.' He jerks his thumb behind his head. 'They need some help setting up a network on the reserve.'

'You mean you're going away?'

'Yes.'

'For how long?'

He crumbles the mess of paper and tobacco between his fingers, drops it on the road, scuffs it noisily with his boot.

'Few a few months . . . maybe a bit longer.'

'Oh . . . Does this mean you won't be back at all?'

He meets her eyes then, a mixture of shame and lust in them. 'What for? There'd be little point. A relief warden'll take over for me down here.'

'What about the cottage?'

'Ah, that.' He gets off the wall and walks slowly along the road. Alba is right beside him, her mouth open, staring at his face.

'I want you to keep an eye on it for me while I'm gone.' Digging into the other pocket he pulls out a key and gives it to her. 'You won't mind doing that for me, will you?'

'No, I suppose not.'

'You can think of it as a bolt-hole if things get too bad with Helen.' There's a smirk on his face he can't disguise, but Alba doesn't notice. 'But don't screw anyone else there while I'm away.'

Alba leaps onto the grass verge. 'What do you say a thing like that for?' she shrieks. 'That's the last thing I'd do. So crass of you. So bloody typical. You're just trying to wind me up.'

He nods, gives a loud sniff. 'People change,' he says evenly. 'Even you. Who knows, in a couple of months you might have a new man. Think of that, Alba,' he mocks gently. 'And you don't want to go through another charade with Helen now, do you?'

'The problem I had with you,' she spits, 'wasn't anything to do with her. It was because you looked – and acted – like a tramp all the time. I was ashamed to take you home.'

'You weren't ashamed of me, Alba,' he says. 'It's just that you couldn't let Helen see what a little animal you'd become. Don't you remember? I do.' He grabs her behind the neck, making her spin round. 'I do.'

Alba freezes, shakes him off. Another theatrical gesture from him. Another macho divus in action. A whole load more nails in the coffin. 'It's pointless. I'm not staying to hear this. I've got better things to do.' And she walks away, her face set, her arms swinging, the key in her pocket, the desperate tale untold.

He stands and watches her go. She's not giving an inch, as usual. Not one damn inch.

Alba returns to find curtains still drawn in the living-room and Helen's bedroom. Puzzled, she goes upstairs, aware she is not alone. Ghosts glide with her, their windy fingers flexing as they crowd round. Something's wrong.

Helen lies in a twisted heap on the living-room sofa. She breathes in rasps. Her face – not her face at all – is half turned away, her features melting. Alba runs to the windows, opens the blinds. The smell of urine and the cold of the curious ghosts chase after her.

People fall, injure themselves every day, and we know it's fixable. We feel the gasp of horror and the reprieve all in one breath. It looks bad, but it's going to be all right. We know it. Once everything's cleared up and the victim's in hospital, we know it was just a temporary scare. We feel light-headed, celebratory. We open a bottle of wine, laugh hollowly. The big poking finger missed its target that time.

But there are other times, not so many in number, when we know the finger's gone home. Then we see it stuck fast in the body, and nothing will get it out. The heart gasps, and the muscle feebly embraces that celestial I've-come-for-you until it shudders to a halt, and all is lost.

It's strange, but you can see a person lying face down in the sand on a beach, yet you don't run to his assistance – you know he's shamming. In a minute he'll raise his head, you'll see the bare calves rise, the sandy feet wriggle and he'll roll over, get up bemused and happy.

And sometimes you'll see the old on their benches, lips and newspapers flopping in the heat, and you can smile, walk on past, feeling a sad warmth and a bit of fear at *your* lot. But it's not over yet.

And then you see the man asleep in his car by the sea front. Businessmen have their lunches there, hoping for a bikini or two. As you walk past something taps you on the skull. Someone calls out, and you look again to see the big one in place. Breath seems not to be lung-bound in these moments, but flows like a hot river of sand through the body, down the spine in a rush, to your feet where it earths with a jolt under the shoes. Then you're looking at someone who's a no-one, who's just said his goodbyes to the world.

Helen's been got at by the pinball finger, Alba knows it. There's no point in trying to pull it out, to prise the ghostly digit from the corporeal. The transition is already in process, the house-moving underway. How does Alba know this? How does she know there'll be no reprieve this time? How does she know Helen's not face-down in the sand, shamming?

She knows because her own innards shift. There's a pull on her own vitality like current leaking from a battery. Helen is caught in a web, her struggles bleat out like ripples in a pond. Alba has her toe poised on a filament of the web elsewhere in the matrix, some distance away – we all do. The life draining from Helen drains her, too.

Is this why we die, Alba thinks. We never get over all the little deaths of others. We are all fuelled by the same energy. Someone goes, and the bit extra we think we've stored up goes with them. There's never enough of it in any one person to keep going for ever. We're all ensnared by the web, all touched by it, drained by it.

It must be so, this connection. It's no myth. One twin will know of the other's death, though countries part them. The mother feels the finger-echo touch her body, crumples as her son collapses in the fields.

We get up at a strange hour of the night and make our way, breath held, to the door of the baby's bedroom. We know what we shall find. We dream about accidents and drownings, we miss trains, put off appointments, cancel flights . . . something on the web shivers and we feel the vibration. And we listen, not with mind, but with soul.

Helen has had a stroke. The ambulance crew are so gentle with her roly-poly body as they ease her onto a stretcher. Alba stands back as they strap her in and manoeuvre her down the stairs. She follows close behind and slips into the kitchen for the gin on the top shelf, grabbing the mail before leaving the house. It's another play. Another bloody pointless stupid play. Over in a minute, back to normal again soon.

It's Helen's last journey through her garden. It's un-believably poignant to watch her go thus . . . a mummy wrapped in stained hospital blankets, the straps tight over her thin body. The Misses Stantons' nets move. As Alba reaches the bottom of the path they move aside completely to reveal the two old ladies motionless behind the glass, still and pale as thin marble. They witness Helen's passage in silence. They know they will not see her again. They're familiar with the random hand of God, hovering on grey days, touching their friends one by one.

Helen's face is shocking. The stroke happened before she'd had a chance to put on her make-up. Now the skin has a sallow greyness, a parchment texture. Alba wants to daub rouge over her mother's cheeks, run lipstick across her lips, pretend now. She looks inside her own bag. At the bottom, buried beneath the dust and pens, is a tarnished silver lipstick stuck with fluff. The unguents have melted and run out. It's a tame pink lipstick, a conservative school colour, barely noticeable when worn. Not Helen's shade at all. Alba twists the wax up, stretches her arm out, rides the roll of the vehicle, and jabs it on Helen's mouth. Helen would kill her if she saw the mess . . .

'She'd hate to think she was like this,' Alba says, as the ambulance-man stares mildly.

'I wouldn't bother,' he says. 'They'll clean it all off in hospital.'

And there Helen is whisked away, and Alba is left in the hot dead air of the corridor. She sits down on a vinyl bench, hands tight, mind in disorder. The first of many let-downs. After a minute she sits up, digs out the letter from her pocket.

It's a note from Keith Kirkwood. He wants to see her for their 'little chat'.

Hours pass. She phones Clive, and then Leon. He'll have to leave, now that Helen's dying.

Dutch comes into her thoughts. Immediately tears for him well up and run down her face. She lets them drip. He'll have gone by now. But maybe not . . . Seized, Alba rushes for the phone kiosk, keys in the number, and prays with tears. Please . . . *Please* . . . The phone rings on and on. She can see the silent room, the silent house, empty of him now.

There's little point trying again later. She knows she's alone. As she walks slowly down the stifling corridor, wiping the tears away with her coat sleeve, she is shocked to see Leon, his straddling sailor's gait unmistakable, coming towards her. 'What on earth are you doing here?'

He grins, shy, proud. 'I got a taxi.' The grin fades. 'Thought I'd come and keep you company.'

'Oh, really, there was no need to put yourself out.'

'Oh, aye, but is there anyone else here to give you a bit of support?' Leon looks around at the empty benches. 'No. See what I mean. Good job I came.' He pauses. 'Thought I'd find you on your tod. How's Helen?'

'They're doing tests. I've been here ages. I haven't been told anything yet.'

Leon looks at her, his head on one side. 'She's on the way out, isn't she?' he says with surprising gentleness.

'Yes,' Alba says, her eyes meeting his without cynicism.

Alba sits beside the bed while Helen slips into a coma. An old woman dies in the opposite bed. Around her in stiff-backed hospital chairs sit four relatives. The bed lies like a vast water which they will not cross or touch. They are the death-watchers, looking at what they themselves walk towards, denying it with the hubris of the still-living.

The woman in the bed dies without a sound. She sinks into the bed and shrinks. The bed shrinks. The watchers stretch their arms, and look round for the nurse who knows the signs immediately and comes. The four walk out, their watch done.

Alba does not know how long she will have to sit with

Helen. Death will have its own time. For the first hour she watches Helen's every breath. She wants to control Helen's death, have no surprise. She leans across the bed and talks to Helen in whispers. It's OK to go now, she says, I love you, Mummy – waiting for the final heave. But it does not come. Helen would never listen to Alba, never believe a word she said.

Helen is dying. There's nothing for Alba to do anymore but accept it. There's just a vacuum between that and the death itself – a no-time. Waiting for death – it's what we're doing all our lives from the moment we're born, Alba thinks. We come in squalling, we go out quiet. Life sure sobers us up. We live with it every moment, and we don't believe it'll happen – to us. When someone dies, there's just a space, a nothing. One minute here, one minute later, not. How can you deal with this sudden sharp hand of nothing? You can't touch nothing, you need a person in order to grieve. You just try to make sense of this gap, this horrible gap . . .

Helen, on the way out, but still here. Alba can deal with that. She feels almost calm. She can deal with what she can see. Never before aware of the breath, she listens to her mother's as though her own life depends on it. Breaths like waves across the sea, becoming flat, calm, grey, smoothing out before the horizon. So much is in this . . .

After a while Alba gets used to the shaky rhythm. She can follow it with one part of her mind while the rest wanders. She looks out of the hospital window. Gardeners work below her, their sleeves rolled up, skin tanned. There is a swarthy life about them that leaps up to her. One is Dutch's age. There's a similarity in the way he moves, a laziness in his walk, the walk with no purpose in mind. It's not Dutch, of course, but she follows his progress around the rose bed as if he has profound significance for her. And he does . . .

Heat fills her, an on-edge heat where coldness creeps over her skin, yet her body breathes fire. The feeling runs over her cheeks, her jawbone, as if Dutch's hands had slipped past her there, making all her will and desire chase after his touch. It pours into the hungry hole below her ribs and goes down, down. It's like going up too fast in a lift – too much pressure, exaggerated sensation. Her thigh muscles twitch involuntarily, trying to clasp what she had rejected for months – Dutch, Dutch lying between her legs, rising and falling, inside her, filling her up, pushing apart her boundaries.

Helen is still breathing. Alba gets up and walks quickly out of the ward, hand on her heart. A nurse catches her arm. Yes, she's fine, it's just the heat – and the smell – of dried-out skin, the dust of it everywhere, and the disinfectant. It's all starting to break through.

Back at Helen's bedside and Alba can't help but look straight past her as though it's not her mother in the bed dying, but an impostor. Alba's got a key in her back, she's all wound up, there's got to be a set way for dealing with this, but she can't find it. Die now! Now! Blast you! The longer she sits, the more frightening the feeling she'll lose part of herself. Soon she won't be able to cope. The key will wind down. She'll stop like Leon in one of his fits when the world splits open, just a grin with nothing behind it. Her body shakes, her breath gets fainter than Helen's. Who's dying here? Alba is the one who is dying. A wall inside her head has crumbled, and now, now of all moments, the contents dammed there free up from the prison and squawk loud, claiming all her attention.

Sex. Here. Now. In hospital. By her dying mother's bedside. Helen could draw her last breath right now, Alba would hear it, the impact like a mountain falling into the sea. And at that precise moment her whole being would be ripped apart by the recall of the past . . .

. . . Filth, that's what it was, those months with Dutch. Helen did not know, nor would she ever know, what her white daughter had done in the shabby cottage on the rhynes. And not just there, either. He'd screw her anywhere, anyhow. Yeah – screw. Fuck. Let's hear all those words Alba had shouted. Dutch, Alba, in the fields, the sodden peat feeding all its wetness through her clothes, owls seamlessly flying through the dark, as she sat on him, bucked her body back and forth, bent over him, her breasts in his mouth, her nipples blinding his eyes, blotting out dark, moon, everything for him. Let her smear his semen over her white cheeks, streak it back through her white hair, lose white on white . . . Let him go between her soft, soft, thighs and she move on him until he was the *axis mundi* on which the earth spun. In the water, thigh deep in water – oh! the silk of peat-water – and him . . .

Alba dreams in her bed that night. The dream-eye pans over a country estate, all large fields with oaks on their boundaries. Inside the house it's dark drapery, heavy furniture, the stillness of elegance. Helen has just died, and lies in her open coffin in a room which has the atmosphere of the cathedral, the Lady Chapel. Helen's body lies there, waiting for someone to come . . .

Alba is looking down into the coffin when a man appears at her side – the undertaker, fat and solicitous, his small head bent forward in that wringing-hands obsequiousness when there's business about – but it's so indelicate to call it so. He cranes forward, looks at Helen with bland disinterest, and tells Alba that her mother will need to be embalmed. I can do it here – he says. I can put something in her vein and drain all the blood. She'll then be as white as you, Alba. Albino white.

Alba's horrified – she must take Helen away. The

dream-eye moves to the grand sweeping drive where the coffin is being pushed along on a trolley. Alba looks down. Helen's skin is like pale yellow clay. It shudders a little as the trolley wheels rumble slowly over the gravel. Helen moves. 'She's alive!' Alba cries. No, says the fat man, it's just her nerves twitching. 'She's alive!' Alba cries, the sound echoing in her dream-head.

And Helen sits up, swathed in cashmere blankets. 'What am I doing in this coffin?' she says, and climbs out. 'I am not dead.'

Not dead. The words wake on Alba's lips and she sits up in bed, panting. Not dead. That's not true, is it?

The phone rings. She rushes downstairs. It's the hospital, a nurse. Helen died ten minutes ago – right in the middle of Alba's dream.

10

Helen is dead, Alba numb-dead too. Only a year ago everything had been so different . . .

. . . Dutch had raped her. In her mind Alba had not called it rape. But if that was its name, she had enjoyed it – now there's shame. The white cotton underwear he'd cut from her, she'd stuffed in her pocket. The skin on her hip had been nicked by his knife. She looks at the blade still open on the table. The brown edge near the tip is her blood, dried.

There's too much astonishment for talk. Dutch slumps back in the faded corduroy arms of the old chair, and watches Alba collect her things. Will she come again? He'd tied her legs, taken her by force. He hadn't planned – it had just happened. The Albas of this world don't get treated this way. They never get the extremes. They're overlooked.

He had overlooked her too. She was always sliding into the background in her forties' floral dresses at school. The last person to have understood what he had done there, and to his surprise, the only person to believe him.

But that wasn't all. No. He had no idea what she was, until he was deep inside her . . . looking at her face, her head skidding backwards on the table as he made his thrusts. Make-up, every feature just fractionally enhanced – you'd not suspect she wore any at all unless you were this close. He'd stared into her clear eyes and her face had shifted, shivered, like heat-haze. Then those probing eyes so full of challenge, slightly hostile still, had come through. The mouth he knew so well, with its animal teeth, had smiled out at him. And he recognized her in that moment, the shock total. He came, shot into her with a cry of astonished bliss, each sperm smaller than a dot, a shower of a greeting for her, a spray of flowers . . .

Alba's face is now her own again, but pinker in the cheeks, with an easy fullness about her mouth, but her eyes move in a more watery sea, and the sharpness of her heart has gone . . . for a while.

There is *nothing* to say. Dutch sits undone, just watching her. She pours wine into the crazed china mug, takes a sip, and passes him the rest. She does not know why he looks at her the way he does. To her, it's the look all men have post-orgasm: the blood, the energy in his face, all gone. He's older, lined, splayed out, his arms are behind his head, mouth a little open, breath barely there. She passes him his Rizzla's and tobacco. It's customary, yes? He looks at her, still blank, agape, the tiny objects in his hands a temporary mystery to him.

Alba turns away, about to laugh, swings around, squeezes his knee and walks out of the cottage without a word. She knows she'll be back.

That night she's woken from sleep by a burst of light, a shoot of energy in her womb, so intense she sits up. A speck of star-dust has left its home and sped through the atmosphere, diving into her belly to explode like a firework there, into gold. She puts her hands down, feels a heat spread out. She can't be pregnant, not at this time of the month, but something has come back in. Something chthonic, precious, has returned.

On the way downstairs next morning, Alba meets Helen in the hall, about to come on up to her. In Helen's hands is a white cloth.

'Are these yours?' she says in a trap-shut snap.

'What?'

'These?' – Helen holds out Alba's white knickers, sliced through on both sides by Dutch's knife.

'Um, yes.'

'Well?'

Alba brushes past, leaving Helen holding the underwear up. She's faintly ridiculous, like a miffed old shop-girl who's being ignored.

Helen makes an exaggerated noise of impatience and marches after her, her shoes biting tightly into the hall carpet. 'Well? What's the explanation? Is this the way you normally take your knickers off these days?'

Alba, her back to her mother, slaps her fingers over her mouth. Two seconds of carefreeness for her, two seconds of triumph. But short-lived. Helen's voice venoms them out of existence.

'There's blood on them . . . here, at the top. What *have* you been up to Alba? It doesn't look very healthy at all.'

Alba tenses, her moment so fragile, now gone. Humiliation seeps through her as the glow of yesterday disappears like water spiralling down a drain. Helen is enough to clobber anything. Enough to wipe out a star.

'Let me have them . . .' Alba reaches out to snatch them from Helen's disdainful fingers. 'I had an accident.' And she runs upstairs, small Alba, found-out, wanting to hide.

School lunch-hour . . . Dutch, Alba, on playground duty together. He at one end, deep in thought, she at the other with a butterfly heart that wants to fly over to him and raise his head up. She looks at him hungrily instead, with so much intensity he feels it, looks up and grins at her, his old self flooding back.

She watches him stroll across. The way he looks today, she could eat him, although there's nothing new about his dress. But this day he shines – his maroon needlecord jacket, the jeans, the wide belt – a rebel's uniform. She's so glad he's a rebel. It makes her heart jump in its cage, it so excites her. And the plait in his neck, thick hair, black with grey, neat, oiled, immaculate – a rude gesture, but so innocent, so outrageous. Not something a man of his age should wear. She almost dances on the spot, a little crazy, as he draws near.

'And how are you?' she says, mischievous.

He looks at her very slowly, focused on her face, eyes wandering lazily round her chin, her mouth . . . 'Good.'

'You're thinking about Kirkwood.' She takes off her glasses, twisting them between thumb and finger.

Dutch leans against the wall with her, quietly looking over the small groups of children in the playground. 'I am. The man's an arsehole.' His face grows dark. 'He's been a thorn in my flesh ever since I came. I really don't know why he gave me the appointment. If he expected me to toe the line he must have been looking up his own arse when I came for the interview. I didn't keep anything under wraps when I was interviewed for the job.'

'Perhaps he thought he'd take a risk with you. Bring in some new blood.'

'Oh, yeah.' He laughs, shifts his body closer to her. Their bodies began their secret talk – both pretend otherwise.

'So why do you think he chose you for the post?'

A slow smile comes and goes. 'Curiosity? Does that sound plausible?' His hand slides up and down Alba's bare forearm before dropping back to his side. 'I doubt it though. They're not risk-takers, headmasters. To settle an old score, maybe?' His voice disappears as he clears his throat.

Alba looks up at him. 'Have you and he met before, then?' she says, surprised.

He looks sideways at her, his eyes very still for a moment. 'What I need is a fag . . . and a fuck,' he says, ignoring her question.

Alba blushes. 'That's coarse.'

'I *am* coarse.' He laughs aloud. 'If you want a man with airs and graces you should go for the likes of someone like Kirkwood.'

She lowers her head, fighting the redness, fighting the shame of thighs that quiver damp above the tops of her stockings.

'Talk of the devil,' Dutch mutters, kicking the tarmac with his boot as the headmaster comes out of the main school entrance and into the playground. He's heading in the direction of the library. He sees Dutch and Alba, nods in acknowledgement, and carries on. But something makes him change his mind, and he alters course to come back to them. He's coming for a better look . . .

Alba goes to put on her glasses again. Before she does, Keith squints up at her, trying to catch her eyes, to trawl. But she avoids his stare and looks away.

'There was something I meant to ask you, Alba,' he says, perfectly in control of himself, the long, long lashes blinking. 'But . . .' he laughs, 'for the life of me I've forgotten what it is. Must be the heat.'

'Yes,' Alba murmurs, looking out from underneath her hat. 'It must be.'

And with a rueful smile, Kirkwood turns and walks away in the direction of the library, his walk a saunter.

'He ignored you,' Alba says, when Keith is out of earshot.

Dutch looks down at her, his eyes as unsettling as a deep dark river. 'I was thinking about sex,' he says. 'All the different ways of fucking you. It must have put him off his stride.'

. . . And, yes, all those different ways . . . Alba remembers, sees it all now in her own private movie, happening to someone else, someone else . . .

. . . To begin with, there was just desire to get at each other. All day Alba in school, with this sick ache inside her. She'd be talking to a class . . . and her words would falter, she'd forget where she was. The heat, the peculiar prickling heat that dances on the skin, would eat its way through, over and over. Always slightly over-weight, now her dresses skimmed over a figure that was losing its fat, revealing a becoming roundness, evident curves.

Three weeks into the affair there is a note from Kirkwood in her staff pigeon-hole. He wants to see her in his office. Although it's probably routine, it doesn't happen very often. She wonders what the man wants.

Kirkwood is standing in front of the French windows when Alba comes into his office. A cigarette burns on the edge of an ashtray on the desk. The smoke goes up dead straight in a thin line. Alba sits down and the line fractures. Smoke buffets into the air around her.

Immediately Keith goes to the ashtray, picks up the cigarette, gives one last hungry draw before twisting it out.

'Old habit,' he says, with a sigh. 'I thought I'd managed to crack it for good.' He gives a short laugh. 'A few days ago I found a packet . . . and had this terrible craving . . . wouldn't have thought it possible after all this time. So . . .' He moves back to the windows, opening them wide. 'Apologies for the room full of smoke.'

Something ticks away inside the headmaster. He's partly here, partly not, his mind working elsewhere. He turns and looks at her, a naked stare, a calculating appraisal, and then shuts it off.

Silence. He loosens his tie, settles himself in his chair.

'Alba.' He lets her name hang in the silence for a moment as his focus comes together onto her. She looks beyond him through the French windows, down the private lawned area to the shrubbery at the bottom – an effective screen against all movements of staff, children, noise.

'I wanted to talk to you about the new dyslexic initiative we're developing next year. But . . .' He picks up a fountain-pen on the desk, takes it apart, and shunts the end on and off. 'There's a delicate matter I want to get out of the way first. That's why I asked you to come to my office.'

A worried expression flits over Alba's face out of the white composure.

He notices, smiles, leaning back in the chair, making it swivel and rock. He picks up the pen and plays with it in mid-air, screwing the top on and off, on and off. After a few moments he shunts the chair back into the desk-well, and drops the pen on the desk between them. It rolls towards Alba.

'It's about Dutch,' he says, soft, conspiratorial, velvet.

'Oh?'

'Are you two – forgive my asking – having an affair?'

Abruptly he gets up, turns his back on her and walks to the open windows where he stands, hands on hips, taking long deep breaths, his large form silhouetted in the doorway. 'It's difficult,' he says, shutting the windows and coming back to her, 'because it's none of my business, naturally, but I feel somewhat alarmed. I don't like to keep up any pretence with my staff.'

Alba nods. There's a game going on. Every gesture – the opening and closing of the windows, the playing with the pen – all is part of a crafted act. Better watch from the wings and say little.

Arching his back with a grimace, he sits on the corner of the desk, hooks his foot under the chair and pulls it towards him. 'Of course, you're aware of the problem he's causing – rumours are going round the school like wildfire. I've noticed that you and he . . . well, let's just say I've noticed.'

Sliding off the desk he moves to the chair again, and stands behind it, arms braced straight on the chair-back, looking at her intently. 'Why am I interfering, you will rightly ask? Well, Alba, you strike me as being a very innocent woman. And I'm afraid certain aspects to Dutch have come to light which are most unsavoury. Although it was my decision to employ him, it's one I've come to regret. He's actually quite a ruthless opportunist, with no regard for the ethics of what he's been doing here. You'll be cruelly used by him, of that I have little doubt, and then he'll move on.'

He stops, slaps his hands on the back of the chair. 'I'm sorry,' he says, 'I've no business to interfere. You're annoyed. Forgive me.' He smiles, brief, formal, running his tongue over the tip of his teeth.

'I don't know what to say.' Alba, her voice steady, makes a gesture with open fingers. 'I can't believe he's as bad as you say.'

'The man's a rebel,' Kirkwood smooths, keeping the heat in his voice well down, under wraps. 'He's completely out of touch with public-school life. You can't sneak your own brand of sex education into English lessons. It's just not done. The parents won't have it.'

There's a quality in Kirkwood's voice that makes Alba falter. She's come to secretly fear this voice – it's got the power to turn her right around, to make her doubt. Doubt Dutch. Doubt herself. She looks up, worried. 'Is that all that really happened?' she asks, a little quaver in her voice. 'I heard rumours.'

'My dear Alba,' Kirkwood expands, 'don't get alarmed. D'you think he'd still be here if there was the slightest hint of anything else? There's nothing more serious going on, heaven forbid. The man's a disruptor, he makes people uneasy. Makes them question too much. That's why he's not safe. He likes to knock down people's boundaries – just for sport. That's why I'm concerned about you, Alba. You're a good solid member of staff. I don't want anything upsetting you.' He seizes the pen suddenly, and shoots it into an open drawer. 'Enough of this. It's all rather unpleasant. We'll talk another time about the papers I had to show you. Come, leave by the windows, get a bit of fresh air.'

Alba gets up, her dress stuck to her thighs. She does as he tells her, for a moment standing bowed and awkward next to him in the doorway. It's been a difficult encounter for him, too. She can smell fresh sweat from under his arms.

'Don't set too much store by what I've said.' He looks down at her. 'But consider it all the same. Consider it.'

Alba nods, thanks him and walks out onto the lawn. The air is cool there. She takes a slow breath of relief. Keith's eyes follow her, she knows it. She's going to be a watched woman from now on.

*   *   *

Boundaries . . . Alba's name is a boundary. A neat white package of a name. Alba – all sewn up. But what happens if you peel the letters of her name apart, take them one by one and fling them up in the air? You get chaos, limbs spread open, eyes to heaven. When they fall to earth, they land anywhere, upside-down, drunk. They don't care if they're never put back together.

Alba listens to Kirkwood, oh yes, she worries about it for a while, but sex makes her rash. It pours oil on anxieties, hides them from self-knowledge, from view.

After school she comes face to face with Helen. Just like the head, she thinks. Controlling. Interfering. Prying. I'll have none of it anymore.

'I want to know what is going on.' Helen stamps on the patio. 'You're going off the rails, Alba.' She bars the way at the top of the path.

'The Misses Stanton will hear you if you shout.'

'*Blast* them. I couldn't give a fig. What's going on . . .? You've got to tell me . . . Never here for meals, always out. I don't know where you are. I'm alone in the house wondering what's happened to you. It's simply not fair.'

'Make me a cup of tea – and I'll tell you,' Alba says. 'I've had a hard day.'

Helen scuttles back inside the house. What price a cup of tea for a secret? She comes out, tea and biscuits on a tray, puts them on the table and takes a cup, this time pouring Alba's first.

'Now, then—'

'I don't know what all the fuss is about,' Alba says airily. 'I'm a grown woman, for God's sake. I've got a boyfriend, that's all. I've been seeing quite a lot of him lately.'

'Boyfriend! You! This is a fine turn-up for the books!'

Alba sips her tea and shrugs.

'Who is he, then?'

'A teacher. At school.'

'A colleague?' Helen scorns, her voice dropping to a knowing deepness. 'You're a fool, Alba. You *never* have a relationship with a colleague. It always ends in disaster. Then you've got to look them in the face every day afterwards. The embarrassment . . . Oh, Alba, it simply isn't worth it.'

'We're being very mature about it. Taking things slowly. Not rushing into it. There's nothing to worry about.'

Helen purses her lips. 'I think you're asking for trouble,' she says, bolt upright on the chair, pink and agitated.

'We'll see,' is Alba's response, made on the spur of the moment. 'I'm thinking about moving in with him.'

Next day Alba takes her case, leaves her past behind with Helen, and moves in with Dutch. As she pulls up in her car opposite the cottage, a hawk circles overhead on a thermal right above the roof. Dutch is outside in the road looking up, a frustrated expression on his face.

'Is that yours?' Alba looks up, follows the wingspan as it gets smaller.

'It was, I think.' Dutch comes towards her, his face soft. 'I don't think I'll see her again.' He shrugs, takes Alba to his chest and holds her there, a new hope beating in his chest. 'She came to have a last look – at you.'

'Kirkwood gave me a little lecture. He said you were dangerous.'

'Well, well, a bit of respect, eh? What next?'

'We have to be careful at school.'

'Why? It might be more fun not to be.'

'If I thought you meant that, I'd say you were an irresponsible middle-aged rebel. I'd be wary of you.'

'But that's what you rather like in me, isn't it?'

'Sometimes—' she hesitates, wrestling with prissiness '—but I don't think it's appropriate at school.'

'Too many shoulds, schoolmarm.'

'Mock me, but I've got my job to think of. Kirkwood heartily disapproves of you.'

Dutch waves her remarks away. 'Sod him. Sod the place. Come inside with me now. I want your body, schoolmarm.'

You lie, Dutch. You want Alba's soft flesh, oh yes, many would the way she is right now. But that's not all, is it? When you dive into her, each time you make a link she's not aware of. You connect, you bliss, you look down the tunnel of the past in her eyes and she's yours again. But this time round, she's Alba, a tougher nut. This time, oh, she's tough all right. You'll need a lot of dye to turn a white cloth black.

Alba moves in with Dutch, and part of her moves out. She thought she was safe. She thought it was sex, just sex. She can handle that delight. She can make up for lost time. But she's wrong. How often what we crave, what we most desire, is the very thing that trips us up.

Sex is a doorway. Few know it. Few want to. They want to keep it dirty, they want to bring in their little animal, have it satisfied, then lead it guiltily away. People screw all their lives and that's all there is. Nothing comes of it. Children . . . what are they? The compensator, that's all, and the justifier of lust.

Before Dutch, only guilty skirmishes. Now a kind of war. He takes her from the bed to the unbounded outdoors, his body pushing her into the ancient peat under a night-sky. He drives her on, the sex an echo of something else. He will break her, crack her open. He has forgotten the rules.

One night, he goes in with the gouge . . .

She's in front of the sofa, on the floor. She's fallen there – bruising doesn't matter, they'll be plenty to nurse in the morning. Tonight his fire is up, he's possessed by howling fury. He can't have enough of her. Lips drag orgasm from her once, twice, she loses count. Inside her, she loses count . . . She can't get up, can't move. There's just his big dark bear-form in the dark, just the feel of his hairy back as her fingers flutter there – nothing else. As he works on her, sweat shines on his chest, the sex-sweat of him pungent down his sides, in his groin. She feels him enter her again and again, and then . . . Nothing . . .

. . . Nothing . . . A numbness there, a floating . . . All used up, a going beyond. Some inner river flows now – there's no need of the physical. She lies, still, detached, looks out through another's eyes. Eyes not her own, strange eyes. Nothing but his dark shape bears down on her. Dark, dripping – she's being fucked by the sky – the enormity of it all distilled in his density, living within his body. He breathes in her face, not breath, but a Saharan wind, scoring, snatching at her skin, flaying its way through her, breath to burn the bone. And she hears the rhythm of his grunts, his rutting. On. On. On. An urgent pulse, it's a rhythm of desire that as she listens seizes her until she can hear nothing else. Roaring fills her head. It comes from without, from within. Roaring, stillness – one and the same. She holds them both, one in each hand – she's the scales. And she's steady, there's no wavering, no teeter-totter, no effort to stay there in this . . . space . . . of . . . perfect . . . balance. (Effort, what's that? – Something belonging to the normal world.) And, lying there, she hears her own cries, seagull cries tossed into the air, swallowed by air. She's inside a bell and it's singing.

Lying there, she leaves, looks down on herself, comes

back in, flows away . . . Out there, in *here*, a shred of perception that Alba, the letters, the name, has been thrown up in the air in a wild game of cards, the cards scattering joyfully as they come down. The player of secrets is in the room, and it so surprises her – she thought else, she thought it would be serious, heavy, full of shoulds . . . But its nature, its quality, is not what she could ever have expected – playful, playfulness, fullness.

She looks into the darkness of the room and it's not dark. It dazzles – the dazzling dark, all motes of silver and gold, dance, play, lure. The call is so light – a will-you-won't-you, a toss-the-coin, a hide-and-seek, a coaxing – so seductive.

But it's bigger than me, a little voice of fear says in her mind. It might eat me, swallow me, and I'll never come back. I'll never be in this body again. I won't be me. Just what will I be?

It saves her, the old interfering mind, and she calls out to Dutch as if he's vanishing from her, 'Where are you? Don't go away.'

Alba, at school, no longer under the school's boot. Loose, free, flowing, her eyes like coals. Teaching is suddenly effortless. The children obey her. The staff are all her equal. Mistakes – what are they? Effort – what is that? Quietly, Alba goes through the day, her blood on the boil, a different energy coursing through her.

'Alba – a word . . . ?' It's Kirkwood – he watches her now, sees the dance going on beneath her skin, sees the energy jumping like a snake in a bag. A substance, buttery, yellow-gold, oozes from Alba's whole being. He can see it on her face – there – a gold-leaf sheen, a plumpness of richly filled cells. She is one of the Wise Virgins, primed from within by a strange self-begetting unguent, alight, melting the fragrance out through her.

He walks past her in the dim green school corridors. He turns to smell the air in her wake. It's not perfume, not a blend of esters, but a pure note. It fascinates, eludes him, makes his innards shift every time he catches a strand of it. She's like a white lily sweating its scent, voluptuous and innocent at the same time, dissolving herself in the humid air. She flits past, giving off a note that comes from elsewhere. She's mediaeval, she holds a torch of light. She's come back for him.

'Alba, can we have a word?'

Alba has gone past the study door when it opens behind her and Keith steps out.

'Of course.' She comes back. He opens the door wide for her, steps aside. The mysterious scent rises to his nose, wraps him in a rush. Narcosis . . . He leans in the doorway and the room recedes. For a minute he's in a giant bath of the stuff with her, making love in the gold. There's no way he can stand aloof. He'll have to dive in, drown, if he wants it.

'You're looking well, Alba.' There's a thin crack to his friendly tone. He comes around the desk, past her, to sit in his swivel chair.

Alba sits down. This morning her white hair is loose and long, and her skin has a luminosity beneath the subtlety of her make-up. She's not wearing her glasses. Blue eyes look out at him – contact lenses – a fact that both irritates and reassures. Albinos don't have blue eyes. They have jelly there, like a camera lens, probing and clicking all the time.

Alba smiles. 'Things are going well for me at the moment.'

'Good. Jolly good.' He sits down heavily in his chair, opens one drawer after another in the desk, finally producing a folder which he slides across the desk-top. 'I want you to read this,' he says. 'I want to know what you think. It's the report on dyslexia I was telling you about. Here, get back to me some time next week.'

His face is different, thin. He looks at her, and he's being carved away from the inside. Slivers of cheek and the plump crescents under his eyes get this daily paring. Gestures, voice, are sharpened too. A cold surge, a nip in the wind on a hot day, rises and falls, scours and recedes. He tries to catch himself, re-build the old boundaries, feel the ease of moving inside familiar skin again. Alba, just by sitting there, challenges all that.

She picks up the folder and moves to go. The unsaid quickly fills the air, over-saturates, makes breath difficult.

'I take it the Dutch business is over.' The words shoot out. Words that hurt, cost. Words going two ways at once – oh! that he didn't need to say them – oh! that he must. They're like an exhale. No choice.

Alba sinks down in the chair again. 'Actually, we're living together,' she says, looking Kirkwood straight in the eye, brazening the inevitable blush.

For a few seconds he stares at her, not blinking. All he wants to say comes to the surface, like a diver running out of air on his way up, but no words come out. They're being digested as they rise. His mouth twists. He clears his throat, coughs. Fishbones lie there snagging the mucous membrane, fouling him up.

'Is this a good idea? You must know I hardly think it's wise.' He looks over her head, feeling the bars of the portcullis smash down around him. 'But it's your life, Alba.' Distaste creeps into his voice – be done with her now. 'I'm surprised at you, I must say. I thought you might have . . .' He claps his hands, squashes her between them forever as his attendants drag her out to be burnt. There – gone, banished. Good – free again. 'I hope it all works out, for your sake.'

The air between them has a sourness. Keith's face closes down. He slips a hand inside the middle drawer and takes a packet of cigarettes, shakes one out, and holds it between thumb and finger. He looks Alba up and down, in silence, quickly. It is the kind of glance with which we dismiss a jewel we can't have, yet inwardly desire. What you can't have, destroy. Remove for ever from your sight what you tried to win . . . and failed to. Stitch the rent seam together again. No-one will notice. It'll be as good as new, like it was before.

'Go out through the windows,' he says, tapping the cigarette impatiently on the box. 'Good for you, fresh air, good for you.'

Alba gets up and walks past the desk, too quick, feeling him about to swoop after her. Suddenly he jerks himself out of the chair as she passes. She trips, rights herself, and opens the casement clumsily.

He's there, right there, waiting for her to falter, waiting for her to slip up. The side of her body nearest him goes cold – the cells have run away to the other side of her. With a dip of her head she ducks past him, steps onto the lawn.

He swooped, but missed. Immediately he lights the cigarette, sucking it dry. She walks past, and the scent slaps him hard in the face. He knows what it is now. He's known all along. How could he not? She lives within him in many guises, wrapped in feminine gauze, seldom unwrapped, seldom understood . . .

Hetaira. Houri. Anima . . . *Animale*.

Alba has earned Keith's disapproval and she's got to live with it. Over the next few days she finds herself a little chilled in his presence. He's shut her out. For a while she holds up her head but a tiny fear has done its work, slipped in. Alba, her boundaries further apart.

Evening – nothing but sex in the evenings. Dutch, on heat, with the need to push her open. Going too far, too fast. Going where he should not . . .

Freeing the leashes from her legs and arms afterwards one night, Dutch lies back, while she sits, watching him drink. Ruby drops of elder wine spill like blood on his chest.

'I told Kirkwood we were living together.'

Dutch laughs. 'That'll set the cat among the pigeons.' Choking, coughing, he inches up from where he half lies to sit in front of the sofa, leaning his back against it.

'He's been really off with me ever since.' She looks down, troubled.

'In what way?'

'Really cold. Really unfriendly.' She speaks soft, slow, regret in her voice. 'I keep feeling he's very angry with me under the surface, but . . . it's more anger than the whole thing warrants. He's deliberately setting out to be as curt and sharp as possible.' She shivers and wraps herself in Dutch's shirt. 'I feel I'm being punished for something I haven't done. It's none of his business what I do outside school with you. It would be different if our being together affected my work, then he might have cause to be annoyed. But I've never felt so good about my teaching before. I *know* it's good. I just don't know what's going on with him.'

Dutch takes several mouthfuls from the bottle. 'The bastard's jealous.'

'Oh, come on. He's never shown the slightest interest in me – or any of the women there. He's married, for God's sake. He's never been interested in *me*—'

'Until now.'

'What?!'

'I tell you, he is.'

'There are scores of women at school much better looking than me.'

'Alba, dear, none of them look like you,' he mocks her. 'But it's got nothing to do with looks anyway.'

Alba snatches the bottle. 'Don't be mean. But you're wrong about him. He can't be jealous of me.'

'Look at it carefully.'

'I am.' Her face grows serious. 'And you're wrong.'

'How has he always made you feel? Be honest.'

'Uneasy – but he always has. I think he'd like me to slip up badly so he can get rid of me.'

'Possibly. You bother him. He would like you out of the way.'

Alba shakes her head. 'No, no, no. Not for the reasons you say. And what could possibly make him jealous, anyway?'

Dutch stretches his arms behind his head. He takes a deep satisfied breath and lets it out long and vocal. 'Men look for something all their lives,' he says. 'But they don't know exactly what it is they're looking for until they find it. Ah-ha! there's a mystery in this . . . You can get sex anywhere, you can screw your own hand . . .' he gives her a strange, soft look. 'But Cleopatras are rare.' He laughs, rather drunk now. 'I should bloody know.'

Alba giggles. 'But this is *me*, Dutch – Alba Farson. No-one ever notices me, other than to stare at the freak. I'm no film star. I've got nothing. And you're talking drunken rubbish. I wish you'd take me seriously.'

'If I saw you with another guy, giving off what you do now—' he straightens himself, his face aiming for seriousness '—I'd be turned inside out with envy. I'd be, uuhh, gutted. You're like a rare flower, Alba. And Kirkwood sees that . . . but he sees you're with me.'

'So this is an act of male rivalry over a near middle-aged woman,' Alba says with scorn. 'Well, of course, that explains everything.'

Dutch laughs. 'You're thick.' He waves his big hands in the air. 'You know how it is with most people . . . they try too hard, they read up on sex. All surface stuff, a waste of time. But you let me dive into you . . . right through you . . . and I come out on the other side, somewhere else.' He yawns. 'Kirkwood's like most men – thinks he's well sorted, has got everything he wants. But something's happened to you recently, Alba. And Kirkwood's seen it. He'd be a fuckin' blind-man not to.'

'Oh, for God's sake—'

Dutch pulls the shirt from her shoulders, widens his legs, pulls her over to him, sits her down, down . . . He whispers into her mouth, his voice rough-edged, his fingers digging into her upper arms. 'My dear dim Alba . . . you've come alight. Here you are – even to look at – this white, innocent, untouched woman. Yes, you do look like that . . .'

'Who's discovered sex . . . oh, very amusing.'

'Oh, absolutely. You're the virgin and the whore . . . the perfect combination, perfection itself . . . together in the same woman. Irresistible to men.'

'Especially to Kirkwood, of course.'

'I don't know what makes the man tick . . . but I'd say you're a hook for him in some way, a real hook. Just watch out, now. Don't bite it.'

'There's no chance of that.' Alba shivers. 'Uh – h . . . none whatsoever.'

Openings can happen at any time, when we least expect them. What causes you to split apart will not be the same for another. For some, it's meditation, silence, the vastness of nature. For others it's travel, where the unfamiliar unzips and demands you leave your usual self behind and play a new part, one whose identity you have to learn. Some court it, contort their bodies into fierce shapes, ram-rod their spines, lose the feel of their limbs. Some go on fasts, some crawl on their hands and knees, some become beggars. Chants, bells, music, dance – all have their place in the design of things. A few find their way through pain they invite . . . Yes, pain can push you to the edge, sometimes over it, and the one wielding the punishment-stick will never know the gift he wields . . .

In the school Quiet Room Dutch finds Alba there, alone in the silent gloom of a late evening. No lights, she's turned them off. She sits at a desk, a pile of exercise books fanned out in front of her, bronzed by a late ray of sun.

'I must have you,' he says, pulling up a chair and straddling it opposite her, scattering the books with a sweep of his hand.

'Oh, God, not now.'

'I mean it.'

'In here? Don't be crazy. What's the matter with you? Are you trying to tempt fate?'

'There's no-one about, I've had a look. We can't be seen behind the bookcases.'

'No. I don't like dares. They've always backfired on me.'

He shrugs, lowers his voice till it's deadly. 'So, what have you been thinking about sitting here all alone in the half-light?'

Alba cannot tell a white lie. She lowers her eyes. 'You.'

He takes her arms, pulls her towards him, makes her stand up.

'I knew that.' His grin is evil. 'Why d'you think I came looking for you?'

For the first time Alba feels unsafe, fearful. It's wrong. She wants Dutch to stop. He gets on his knees, flicks up her skirt and puts his mouth between her thighs, and his fingers form a cone, pushing up behind . . .

Open . . . When you least expect, when you'd least want.

When orgasm comes her spine lights up and her body goes rigid. A stream of hot-cold pain shoots up her back, up her neck, and out through the crown of her head. It snaps her mind like over-stretched rubber. Most times the thread of fear, even ever-so-tiny, keeps hold of the self. Not now, though. Not here. She's gone.

With open eyes she sees the library shudder. A gypsy woman with animal teeth and black skirt dances in front of her, a bloody skull in her hand. Black shapes dance around the gypsy, take the skull, sup, and throw it back to her, and she laughs, catching it again. Alba can see all the way down her throat, down this dark, wet, bloodied tunnel. She finds herself being sucked in by the red, red lips, swallowed against her will, the throat a great maw, pulling her down, like Jonah. And then she's inside . . .

She looks out now through gypsy eyes, sees a light so bright she curls up into it with desire. It takes her, spins her round until the black becomes white, the white black, and the colours merge and spin so fast that they go beyond themselves into nothingness . . .

Kirkwood, passing the windows on his way home, follows the last rays of sun into the Quiet Room. He sees Dutch and Alba there, Dutch with his back to him, Alba's face up-turned like a tortured saint, her white hair brilliant. He stops, stares. The seconds fizz. He throws the cigarette on the ground, grinds it with the heel of his shoe, and then almost runs through the main doors to the room. Looking through the small glass window of the Quiet Room door he sees them both, their clothes messily in place again, Dutch holding Alba by her arms. Kirkwood opens the door quietly, stands half in the shadows . . . when they catch sight of him they will think he's been there the whole time . . .

'You've finished, have you?'

Kirkwood moves out of the shadows, jubilant – they hadn't heard him come in.

Alba, still nowhere, hears his voice from a long way off, and it pierces into her with dramatic effect. Now she's suddenly full of dross, of rubbish. Someone has opened up her head and poured all that stinks and cuts and rots into the empty space there. She's forced to come back in. Forced to encounter the rapist, the burglar, in the middle of his obscene works. Forced to watch the murderer at his business. Forced.

She tries for the breath which has gone, and, feeling a great pain in her chest, falls over, crying, shaking.

Dutch shouts, 'Keep away from her!'

Kirkwood leaps at him and punches him on the chin. Dutch stumbles back with the surprise of it. Alba slumps in a chair, coughing and crying into her hands.

'You're fired,' Kirkwood says to Dutch. And to Alba he snaps, 'I want to see you tomorrow – first thing.' With a look of scathing contempt at Dutch he turns and walks out of the room.

On his way to the headmaster's house which lies beyond the tennis courts, he stops in the half-light, a smile of triumph on his face. Taking the packet of cigarettes from his jacket pocket, he tosses the box into the air. As it falls, he bats it hard with his fist. It flies over a large laurel and drops onto the road the other side. He doesn't need this addiction any more.

Distant, tremors going through her body, Alba sits in the one armchair in Kirkwood's study. He puts his jacket around her shivering shoulders, fetches a cup of tea from the staffroom. He's enjoying this. The kindly touch, the fatherly concern, before the cull. When he comes back Alba has broken down in tears.

He lets her cry, watching her.

'Alba – what made you do it, hmm?' His voice purrs.

She raises her head, wiping tears and hair from her face. 'I suppose you're going to give me the sack too.'

'No, I'm not.' The words are out, but not to plan. Why not get rid of them both? It's what he intended, isn't it? But she begs him just by being there, just by scenting the air, and he has to bow to it. The Madonna always won.

'I couldn't blame you if you did.'

'I've given it some thought, but no. I don't think you are to blame.' His face becomes serious, hiding his confusion. 'You see, Alba, the rebel in Dutch just had to have its day – at your expense this time. He knew he was going at the end of term. Having . . . having intercourse on school property was his way of getting back at me. However, this does not absolve you completely – not at all. I can't let this go without saying how incredibly naïve and stupid you were to get involved with him in the first place.'

'I know that now,' Alba says sadly, looking at her hands in her lap. 'I'm so very sorry for what happened. I'm very grateful to you for being so . . . lenient. Thank you, Keith.'

He waves her remark aside. 'Just watch yourself,' he says in a tired act of a voice. 'Don't see the fellow again. For your sake, OK?'

She leaves, so compliant now, so bruised, his loins ache and he wants to smother her, possess her, feed off her, lick the gold oil from her skin, spin and spin and spin . . . But there will come a right time – a ripe time. He knows this with all the surety of a life made up of calculated moves, opportunities taken, right moments seized. The force of will has a lot to do with it, too. He has plenty. You can whisk things out of the air, you can manifest what you want if you have a certain kind of will. There's always the ripe time, way off, when all the loose strands meet and melt into one. Will and patience, that's what you need. And the wild card – luck.

After school Alba drives slowly back to Dutch's cottage. 'I've come to collect my things,' she says.

He looks at her, his face fallen in hurt, his shoulders dropped, purpled, bruised, shielding his heart. 'Why?' he says. It's all there is to say. 'Why?'

Fury boils up in her. She feeds it. The more she feels, the easier it will be to go. 'You humiliated me,' she shouts. 'Kirkwood saw everything. Do you know what that feels like? How could you know? It's the worst kind of rape I could imagine.' She moves around the room collecting her belongings. They aren't her things. They belong to a dead woman.

'It's your job, is it?' Dutch snaps bitterly. 'Kirkwood lays down the law and you cringe, yes? What kind of person are you that you can just dump what you had here?' He looks down. 'What we had . . .'

Alba shuts him out. 'Another thing . . .' She daren't look at him. 'Something happened to me in that room. I feel terribly unsafe now. Out of balance. I don't want it to happen again. You've made fun of me so much about me being locked up inside a piece of amber – how I need cracking open – and I feel that's what you've been trying to do. Why? Why?' She looks at him now. 'It's power, I guess, isn't it? So you could have power over me.' Her voice saddens. 'Not much different from Kirkwood – or all men.'

Bars of grief press on Dutch's chest. 'Not power for me, no,' he says, very soft, appalled at her interpretation. 'Not for me. Oh God . . . no.'

'I'll be happier in my own skin again,' Alba says, crying. 'Don't . . . don't . . .'

But she's gone, her frame fills the doorway for the last time. The house and Dutch weep.

11

It's over a year since Kirkwood caught Alba and Dutch in the Quiet Room. By now he should have forgotten, but still it slips into his thoughts in unguarded moments. He needs to speak to Alba – that's been brewing for some time. He's been watching her of late. She's slipping . . .

Keith's study faces south, but the room is always dark. It's long, rather narrow for an office, with leaf-green walls and old-fashioned small-paned French windows that open onto a private sloping lawn, dense shrubbery at its base.

Many people pass through this room every day: his secretary from the adjoining room, staff, visiting parents – all flow in and out. Flotsam, leaving the essential character untouched, intimate, a monk's cell in a monastery, a closed environment, an extension of himself. Over time the fabric of the room has absorbed his thoughts, and it feeds the room, seeps into the air, colouring it red . . . black . . .

The desk straddles the middle of the room, facing the door. It's a weighty mahogany affair once belonging to Keith's father. Each drawer handle is ornately fashioned into a lion's head. On the green leather top the edge is tooled with red fleur-de-lys. The desk-top is clear except for an empty set of stacking wire trays, a desk lamp, a vase, and a photograph of his wife, Maria. No clues there. Nothing that would help you read the man.

An armchair with a tapestry seat, and another small uncomfortable straight-backed one, face his own on the other side of the desk. A row of slim built-in cupboards and recessed shelves line one wall from floor to ceiling. The cupboards all have locks. The shelves are lined with files and books on curriculum, neatly ordered, unrevealing.

If you want to read Keith's character, his office would give paltry pickings. It's only the empty stage before a performance, the heavy stage-curtain always drawn. Behind it, from the wings, the cast looks out to judge the mood of the audience, to see how they might play to it. But you're not aware of this. You think *you're* the waiting watcher.

When staff have an appointment to see him – especially Alba these days – he'll fling open the French windows just before they arrive. Fresh air rushes in, dilutes what is there. No-one astute must sniff anything out.

And he's been thinking about Alba a lot recently. If it weren't for her impeccable teaching history, her utterly conventional dress and personality, he'd have found a way to lose her long ago. But Alba's one of the school stalwarts, she was already there before he arrived to take up his own appointment. You can't shed a member of staff because she gets under your skin . . . not with her skin . . . He missed an opportunity last year. He fouled up badly. He should have sacked her along with Dutch, wiped his hands, forgotten her.

In a few days the boarders will arrive and then, a day later, the school will open for the autumn term. He feels the edginess of needing to get into gear again, the sallowness of the holiday just gone with nothing of satisfaction to show for it.

Twisting in his chair at the desk, he is deep in thought about Alba. The fact she ignored his recent communication has made up his mind. She'll have to go at the end of term. Somehow, he'll have to find an excuse.

The winter past he could have had no complaints. She'd thrown herself back into work with a fearful energy, after the tacky business with the odious Dutch. But as spring wore on he'd seen her begin to slip. Had she been seeing Dutch again? And yes, there was the swimming-pool incident, the mess at speech day – that did no-one any favours. Enough meat there, surely, but he didn't act when he had the chance – unlike him. Instead he'd hung on, he'd waited . . . for what?

Alba comes quietly into his office. Her glasses hide her eyes. She wears a simple loose blue dress – the weather's hot, another Indian summer. Her hair has less of the sleek groomed look than usual, and is tied roughly back in a long pony-tail. As she sits in the proffered chair, her hands flutter, and she smooths the skirt down several times, a nervous gesture not lost on him.

Keith goes through the pleasantries – the holidays, the weather, the imminent start of term. Alba nods, mumbles the odd word. He considers her carefully, gets up, and walks around the desk to sit on the corner facing her. There's a still almost-frozen quality about her this morning. Of course – she must be apprehensive about what he has to say to her.

She'll have been living with that all through the last nine weeks. He rubs his jaw thoughtfully, goes back to his chair, draws it up close to the desk. Clasping his hands in front of him, his eyes skate over her face. How will she take what he has to say?

'Alba—' he's about to begin.

'Keith.' Alba jumps in, takes off her glasses, and drops them in her lap. She's looking down, her words come out strange, awkward, like a child trying to play a first tune on a piano. 'Keith, I'm sorry.' She looks up. 'My mother died yesterday.'

He looks into water . . . clear still deep water. Her eyes . . . nothing but trouble for himself . . .

. . . Years ago he was a young teacher in rural Surrey. He'd gone to the Silent Pool, an eerie shivery magical lake in the middle of a tall April-green wood. It was a place you went to, soft, uneasy. You took plenty of respect along with you. Jack-in-the-Green lurked behind the trees. He could leap out at any moment and accost you – his face cunning, terrifying, primeval – and demand your business there.

The small lake lay in a clearing. Among reeds at the edge he'd looked down through twenty, maybe thirty feet of the clearest water he'd ever seen. He could see all the way down to the sand-coloured stones on the bottom. He dropped a small stone into the water, followed its descent. It shimmied slowly down, the ripples on the surface disappearing well before it reached the bottom. He'd whistled – it was deep all right. And there was another urge as he'd cast his stone – to follow it, to plunge headlong into the clear water, to sink, to drown – to look up and see water stretching on up into unbroken sky as his lungs filled.

Brilliant green weed lay teased out on the surface, and there were thick mats of it still further down – Ophelia's hair, floating, spread out, still. Held by invisible watery hands, this corpse buried in glass.

Legend told years ago of a jilted woman who'd thrown herself into the lake, and drowned. They'd found her on the bottom, thirty feet of clear water above her. Her body balletic, arms above her head, lips palely open.

Imagine . . . They'd had to go down deep to trawl up the body. They'd had to dive and see her open blue eyes, with nothing in them any more, looking at them as they made their descent. Why! a subtle current moves her, and she touches one of them, her fingers stroke his cheek in a wavering embrace. Her body, so wanton, arms falling back and forwards in a mockery of a caress . . . And her face . . . so wanton, so agape, so submissive in death . . . the glassy, crucified face of a woman in orgasm. Imagine, those men who dived down to her – and Keith had imagined it often, for years – they would have wanted to fuck her, there, under the water. He himself had fantasized it enough, such was the power of the image. Imagine . . . shooting up inside that pale utterly receptive corpse . . . going under, yes, drowning, as he, as they, came . . .

Kirkwood sits back in shock as he looks at Alba's eyes now. He's never seen them like this – she normally wears tinted glasses. Sometimes she takes them off but her eyes have always been blue. But these eyes . . . surely they're not hers, these are borrowed eyes, they must be. Glass eyes with a faint pink tinge, with the limpidity of water, not of this world. The woman in the water.

As he stares at her he holds his breath. There's absolutely nothing between him and her soul.

A memory – from the previous summer – unlocks with vivid, painful presence, spills over, fills him now with all the feelings he had not given their due at the time. The ones he'd stamped on all year. Strange how you could make trivial an event so seminal. Strange how you could laugh at it, laugh at yourself when it happened. But while these feelings are sealed away in the can they continue to cook. They grow like yeast in the warm dark. One day . . . it could be indifferent, it could be beautiful, you never know . . . a word, a look perhaps, breaks the seal, and the whole thing bursts out in a filthy rush, years of fermenting crazily expand, and the world, your world, is smothered.

Dutch . . . Alba . . . in the Quiet Room . . . walking past the window, the last slab of sun pouring into the room, focussed on them – on what they were doing. Alba's face, turned up, eyes open, oh! the naked eyes, blasted open as she'd orgasmed. He'd seen it all, and immediately denied what he'd seen.

She sits here now, not aware her eyes are unveiled. Shock, her mother's death, has made her forget the habitual routines she normally takes for granted. Yes, it's this kind of action which is always the first to go. She'll put her lenses in every morning, but she's not there when she's doing it, no, she's thinking about the first class of the day, the books she must collect, the mistake in the register . . . while her finger dabs those blue discs in place. Normally she can get away with not being present to her actions. But now shock has blown a hole in them all. This is the first day she's forgotten to plug in her artificial eyes. Today . . . and the day she was with Dutch behind the shelves.

Keith's little speech, his intentions, were ready to shoot in one clear, disciplined direction. He'd known what he was going to say, the line of it, the tone, all the gestures. He knew how to tell people they were going to be moved on. Moved on, yes, not sacked – he almost made it sound like a choice. It wouldn't come immediately, they'd still have a term to sort things out. It'd only be a pinprick. At home later, when they were alone, the force of it would hit. But Keith wouldn't see that. He'd only see the gaunt faces the next day, the pale looks of betrayal. That was the way to do it.

Now the words, the smooth-worn speech, won't come. *I shoot an arrow right. It lands left. I should be suspicious of my intentions . . .*

Sweeping his black hair back over his head he feels the breath shake in his lungs. But luckily there's time to regain composure, time enough – Alba is crying.

Tears, liquid glass, water, water, run over her bottom lid, as if the iris itself has lost its viscous nature and turned to liquid, and her soul is melting behind it. He watches her, completely thrown. It's the first time he's ever really seen a woman cry. Maria, she's cried, but never like this in front of him. The impulse is here, as it was at the Silent Pool, to take that carefree leap, launch himself, go under, drown.

He opens a drawer, finds a packet of tissues, and goes to her. Taking one, he puts it to her face. He must get close. He must look into this source, feast on it.

Alba's fingers, wet, trembling, touch his as he dabs away the wet on her chin. He crouches next to her, his long lashes unblinking, to see her look at him through shivering glass, a mirage of tears. Swallowing, he gets to his feet, yanking the tie loose around his neck. He needs air. He goes to the windows, opens them wide, stretches his arms back, trying to fill up the cavern.

There's something about her he's never seen before. The un-noticed gem, Miss-Clear-as-an-Open-Soul-Eyes. Now, he wants it.

'Do you mind if I smoke?' he asks. 'This is a shock for me, too.' Without waiting for her assent, he takes a cheroot from the middle desk drawer, lights it with a match, and saunters to the windows again, closing them. Inner calm returns as the distinctive odour fills the room. The smoke will impregnate her clothes. When she leaves she'll smell it for hours . . . in her hair . . . in the pores of her skin.

The mother has died. The ripe time has come. Why do some women stay with their parents, never leave, lie down like submissive dogs for the growing-old to feed off their youth? It's simple. They can't shake off the need for security, for authority. Freed, as Alba is now, she's ripe for an easy take-over. Out goes Helen – leaving a vacuum. Who to fill it? Keith. He'll slide into Helen's barely-cold space like the conniving understudy.

'I'm really sorry, Alba.' He sits in his chair, kicks it away from the desk on its castors, and draws on the cheroot with slow satisfaction. 'I offer you my condolences. Is there anything I can do?'

Alba shakes her head. The tears dry. She gives an unsteady sigh.

Keith allows the ensuing silence. He's comfortable with long gaps in conversation. You don't have to gun-fire people for information, for disclosures. Why waste energy? All you need do is watch, slightly quizzical, head on one side. People like to be engaged, not watched. They need a dialogue, all the superficial fillers-in . . . whereas too much focus threatens. If Keith oils the silence with prompts he'll miss the secrets that come blurting out. So he'll sit, wait, change his expression now and then, smile, look down, lace his fingers together, look sharply directly up into their eyes. And say not a word. Some people will tell anything and everything to avoid such scrutiny.

Today Alba is opened by shock and grief. She could be read oh! so easily. She could give him the key to her soul and not know it.

But Alba is not aware enough to be tripped. She's dumb

– not garrulous. She wipes her glasses, puts them on, blows her nose, and comes to herself again.

'I'm sorry about that. The shock just hit me.'

'Not at all. Don't worry,' he murmurs.

She looks up, her chin jutting out in a small gesture of bravery. 'I forgot to respond to your letter. My mother had just gone into hospital. I've forgotten a lot of things this past week. I suppose you wanted to see me about the swimming-pool incident . . . and speech day . . .'

Keith taps the desk with manicured nails, his face thoughtful. What to say now? The Madonna has wept. He's undone once again. 'I was going to suggest a few things,' he says in a rather unfocused voice, waving his hands. 'Have a chat. See what we can sort out. But it seems life's events have overtaken us.'

Alba nods. 'It's all been so sudden. A stroke. But she's not been too well this past year. I wonder if there was something I missed.' She pokes the tissue under her glasses, wipes away new tears.

Keith takes one last draw of cheroot, whips an ashtray out from a drawer, and stubs out the remainder carefully.

'Maria's had that problem,' he says. 'She's been away looking after her mother a lot, as you know. The old lady won't go into a home – is damnably independent. As soon as Maria comes back here she's worried something might have happened.' He sighs. 'You can't watch the old all the time, Alba. We have our lives too. They don't always dovetail perfectly, do they?'

'I should have been with her. I'm haunted by it.'

Keith gets up and comes round the desk to the armchair. He stands over her, one hand lightly on her shoulder. 'It's natural to feel guilt,' he says, in a slow sympathetic voice, 'and easy to be wise after the event.'

Alba looks up at him, surprised and moved by the empathy.

Without thinking he moves her pony-tail so it lies in the centre of her back, his fingers skimming over the strange too-soft texture of her hair. 'Don't forget − if there's anything I can do . . .' he says as he moves away from her.

Alba arranges the funeral all by herself. Clive does nothing to help − he goes to pieces. Angie gives him some of her tranquillizers. He can't deal with any kind of surprise. And Leon − Alba's all set to tell him to go, but, somehow, she can't and he shows no sign of wanting to leave. Since Helen's death he's given her a wide berth, but he's become a mover behind the scenes in a way Alba would never have thought possible. He follows Alba at a distance, washing the dishes, answering the telephone, replacing items of food as they run out.

To her surprise the sofa in the living room where Helen had collapsed has been taken away. The room cleaned, aired. 'I didn't think you'd want the smell,' he'd said. 'The reminder . . .'

Two days before the funeral Keith calls unexpectedly with a large wreath.

It's early evening. Alba paces the patio, gin in hand, looking at the garden, seeing Helen's last journey down it on the stretcher over and over again. Keith's sleek grey BMW pulls up in the road. He gets out, looks up, nods in greeting and climbs the path, wreath in one hand, car-keys in the other.

He's casually dressed to impress: fine black cords, charcoal-grey silk roll-neck under a black cashmere blazer, costly Italian slip-on shoes. Alba stares at him, the glass wavering in her hand, her mouth slightly open. For a second she looks beyond him to the cottages on the road at the bottom of the garden. The Misses Stantons' nets move, as well they might. Next-door's-with-the-birds stands motionless behind her vertical blinds, eating a vanilla cream-slice, seething with envy – as well she might. Kirkwood has come to see *her*, Alba.

She sees him freeze-framed against town, fields, and misted horizon. He's like a dark obelisk against an undistinguished background. His darkness suddenly attracts her so. Darkness is something she doesn't have. Oh! so much there in the black hair, the olive shadow of his skin, the black clothes . . . It's all been forged, born and purified in the most beneficent of hells. He kicks against light, boots it in, stamps on the indifference of all other colour, white included. Not Arthur who seized the re-fashioned sword from the lake, but dark, impassioned Mordred . . .

'Good evening, Alba.' He smiles. A slow, almost reluctant smile, that widens bit by bit into a quick flash of perfect teeth with the winsome gap between the front two. Lightning unzipping the night. Guaranteed to freeze her. Then the smile goes as quick as it came, and a sober expression of great gravitas supplants it. 'I won't be able to come to your mother's funeral,' he says. 'I've a meeting, unfortunately, but . . . I'd like to give you this, all the same.'

'How very kind of you, Keith,' Alba blushes, surprised.

'As I say, I would have come—'

'Oh, I wouldn't have expected that at all . . .'

'—to give you some moral support.'

'That's so considerate of you.'

Keith props the wreath by the door, and looks around him. He's only visited Alba at her home once before – during the business with Dutch the previous year. He'd met Helen – an instantly forgettable woman with a sugar-iron grip on her daughter. Gone now. An easy gap left.

'Wonderful view,' he says. 'Most pleasant indeed.'

'Can I offer you a drink?'

'Thank you. Gin and tonic? – but don't worry about the tonic if you haven't got any.'

'Oh, I have, I'm sure,' Alba breathes and goes inside the house.

Keith pulls out a plastic chair from underneath the patio table, and sits down, legs crossed, ankle circling. He takes a slim packet of cheroots from his jacket pocket, slips one out, and undoes its Cellophane wrap with studied precision.

'D'you have some matches, by any chance?' he turns to ask Alba as she comes out with the tray.

'Oh, yes. I'll get some.' She hurries back inside. Keith smiles to himself.

'Here . . .' She returns, bends down, takes a match from the box as he puts the cheroot to his lips. She used to light her father's pipe . . . it's an innocent memory that suddenly pulls at her now.

The match flares. Keith leans forward and takes hold of her wrist to steady it as she holds the flame. Gently, quite deliberately, his thumb glides over the soft skin on the pulse-spot. Skin like a palest pink petal, veins like blue stamens underneath. 'My, you've got very delicate skin, haven't you?' he says in a soft fascinated voice as he holds up her wrist, examining it. 'It reminds me of . . . what's the blue poppy? . . . Ah, Meconopsis.'

Alba eases her hand away, smooths her dress, takes a large mouthful from her glass. The musky earthy pervasive smell of the tobacco curls around her, and dissipates down the garden in the still-warm evening air.

'Will the funeral be a formal affair?' Keith asks changing the subject. 'I've seen people turn up in jeans, with dogs on bits of string, before now.'

Alba laughs, for a moment forgetting. 'It will be. My

relations are all rather old and very traditional. They'll expect it. I've had to buy some sober black clothes especially.' Helen's money, given to Alba for the theatre visit with Leon. Never spent then. Now, for her funeral.

Keith turns to her lazily and smiles, lowering his eyes to inspect Alba's bare ankles, the pale skin, the Meconopsis veins, her white doll's skin.

Unaware of his gaze, Alba pours herself another half inch of gin. She holds the bottle out to Keith. He shakes his head.

'I bought a hat with a veil,' she says. 'Purely on the advice of the assistant. I shouldn't have listened to her.' She makes a face. 'I guess that's money down the drain.'

Keith stretches, relaxes, sinks a bit in the chair. He looks into the middle-distance above the town chimneys, sipping his drink, contentedly drawing on the cheroot. 'Oh, I don't know. I like hats on women. Remember those old mafia funerals – *The Godfather* . . . ?' He laughs to himself. 'How the women looked? D'you remember that? All glamorous and . . . incredibly sexy.' He turns to Alba, laughs aloud. 'I used to rather like that at the time.'

'Did you?' Alba laughs with him. In an instant an image comes into her mind . . . the cathedral . . . Kirkwood's lady, his mistress, his whore . . . not Maria, his wife. Definitely not his wife . . .

The sudden appearance of Leon disturbs the flow of conversation. He comes out of the house onto the patio, hands on hips, his large bottom lip jutting out in disapproval. He looks at Alba, and whispers loudly, as if Keith can't hear, 'Who's this then?'

'My headmaster – Dr Kirkwood. He's been so kind . . . he's brought a wreath.'

Leon looks Keith over rudely, frowning as he picks up the wreath. 'Oh, aye. This one . . . ?' He fingers the evergreen foliage with disrespect. 'Very nice.' With a sour look in Keith's direction he goes back inside, the *nibelung* to his cave.

'I must go.' Keith gets up.

'Thank you, Keith. Thank you for coming.' Alba looks at the silk lining of the cashmere blazer as he pockets the cheroots. She can't look him in the eye. His face – so much a lure – she wants to reach out and slip her fingers down the dark shadow-stubble on his cheeks.

'I hope it won't be too distressing for you.' He takes her hand, smooths his fingers over the tendons below her wrist, and gives it a pat. 'See you at the beginning of term.'

For the twenty-mile journey to the crematorium Alba rides in the funeral limousine with an ashen-faced, visibly-shaking tearful Clive. There's no point saying anything to him. He's locked himself away beneath the fat. Next to them sits Angie, bolt-upright with tension, her lipstick a garish clash, her clothes all lines and angles. Angie's bones stick into Alba's flesh, so Alba tries to move away from her, but with every inch claimed the elbows and hips follow her and grind into her again. She's trying to escape Clive, Alba thinks. He's on the look out to fill a pretty big hole today.

The hearse waits at the crematorium gates, white wreaths of lilies on the casket, at Helen's own request. Clive sniffs and begins to cry silently as the hearse pulls slowly away in front of them, and their own limousine crawls after it. I'm still following her, Alba thinks, aware of her own black humour. Even in death I'm one step behind her.

The cars pull up and Alba gets out as quickly as she can to get away from Clive. To her astonishment, Keith Kirkwood stands elegant in an expensive black suit by the entrance to the chapel. Alba walks as fast as her new high-heeled shoes will allow.

'Keith . . . What are you doing here?'

He steps out of the doorway and comes to her, takes both her black-gloved hands in his. 'The meeting finished early,' he says smoothly, 'so I thought I'd come, if only to give you a shoulder to lean on.'

Alba's eyes fill with easy tears. 'Thank you,' she says.

She stands motionless as the coffin slides out from the hearse and onto the waiting chapel trolley. There is a rush of scent, of lilies – the narrow flutes of *longiflorum*, the slightly reflexed petals of *regale* and the wide open petals of *Imperial Silver*. All Harold's favourites. The scent hits her in a place deeper than shock, and she sways, chokes on her breath.

Keith, standing behind her, whips an arm around her back, and, seizing her elbow, holds her upright, his body against hers for support. Kirkwood, the pillar of appropriate sobriety for Alba. Gliding into every move, every space, as though the very air has given way to him, bowed out, deferred – Moses parting the sea. Yes, he can walk into any situation and know there will always be a space allotted to him, and to him alone. No-one else can share it.

Now, Alba tastes this space. It begins to wrap, to insinuate around her, pulling her after him into the security of its wake. It is a powerful taste. Exciting. New to her.

Alba smells his cologne – she's being drowned in scent – she doesn't know which way to turn – lilies, Helen's lilies – Kirkwood's *Eau Sauvage*.

More powerful than any other sense is the limbic gift of smell. It can take you back years, to the moment in a day the mind has forgotten, but which the old brain has stored. Just a chase, that's all it is, a thread on the air, an invisible unravelling. Never captured, never tied down by thoughts. Innocently abiding there, uncorrupted by the mind's influence.

The lilies . . . She remembers Harold and his lilies for the first time. How every March he'd take them out of their large clay pots, and get excited at all the little bulbils, all the free lilies of the future, which he would carefully replant. How he'd given Helen many a bunch of them, though you'd hardly call them a bunch with their four foot stems and huge white flowers – no, they were an armful. Yes, Alba remembers the scent of lilies. They were in Helen's bedroom when Alba was three, and she'd come in, shy, around the door, to see her father kneeling over the naked body of her mother, his penis in her mouth.

She starts to pant. Kirkwood's grip on her tightens. She is aware of it, of him drawing her into himself, of the strength, the surety, the unequivocal power in that grip . . . and she gives herself up to it. With the utmost grace he guides her into the sad bare chapel, following the scent to Helen's grave. The mourners file in after her – did Helen really have so many relations, so many friends? And did they all love her, love her more than Alba had done?

She stands in the front row, Keith beside her, almost touching but not quite, ever aware of where he is and where she is in relation to himself. If she stumbles when the coffin disappears into the fire, he will be there to steady her, quicker than her own thoughts.

Emotions pass through her like a searing wind. Helplessness. Guilt. Fear. Numbness. Anger. Betrayal – where is Dutch? Where is the man who called himself my soul-mate? Where is he? Not by my side, and if he was, he'd be reeking of drink, he'd have mud on his shoes, dirt under his nails, and he'd probably light a roll-up at the back of the chapel just to show his contempt for all the 'religious crap'. How childish he was!

No, beside me is what I want. What *I* am. What I feel

I deserve – Keith. Helen would have been proud to see me with him.

Alba looks at the wooden coffin, and feels nothing. She can imagine Helen laid out inside it with nothing to say for herself, and it seems all wrong. It is Helen – therefore she ought to have a say in the proceedings. She'd had a finger in all the other pies of life, Alba's in particular. Perhaps, at any moment, she'll walk into the cold room in her chisel-toed shoes, and give Alba her scornful smile. Alba is tempted to turn around and look, so intense is the thought, but there are too many faces behind her. They might read in her face something she'd rather they didn't. Resolute, stone, she looks ahead.

And whose funeral is this? Alba can't make the connection that there is no more Helen. The world is iron-grey. Her body, the room, the world, is made of scratchy grey wire that scours thoughts from her mind like an abrasive rubber. She is left with an eternal graze on her skin, the wound unable to heal – it pops up first in one place, then another, always appearing where she does not expect. Loss. The eternal shroud that dogs the living, a shroud made of wounds, bloody wounds, scoured wounds.

But a part of her psyche has a loud voice. Mischievously it functions on its own. It has no rules, no shoulds, and its voice is unseemly, and threatens to stamp out the grey. If that does happen, Alba will go crazy with shame. The funeral is not real. It is not. It can't be – there's been no rehearsal. Where is the repository of appropriate feelings to hold on to? There is none, no gauge, no yardstick, no clue. Instead the untouched mischief rears up ghoulishly, laughing at her. You don't feel grief – it says. Ha! Ha! You feel relief. Alba . . . Alba . . . Alba . . . Who stands beside you? Dr Keith Kirkwood, the headmaster of your school. It is the knife-sharp creases of his trousers which nudge the back of your knee that you feel. It is the *frisson*, like an itch, a tickle, on the tender vein behind your kneecap that you feel.

And from that fragile link there flows from him to her a fine thread, a filament carrying enough energy to light a room. She can feel it. She knows it.

Kirkwood has opened the skin in that soft crease of her knee, and is feeding her with nectar down this thread – as continuous and subtle as a drip in a vein. By degrees it warms through her whole body, filtering into her substance. She moves a quarter of an inch back on her heel, just to feel his trousers nudge against her. He is too far away from her – continents apart. Indecently her body craves the contact, and wants more.

Keith . . . Keith . . . Keith . . . The word thrums through her head as the curtains draw around the coffin, and it slips on creaky rollers out of sight. The wooden box containing the scrap that was Helen. A useless toy box, discarded. Gone now. Gone.

Alba, the child, had a small cardboard suitcase full of paper dolls. Each had a wardrobe of paper clothes which dressed the doll by a number of tabs around the edges which had to be bent over the body to hold them in place. One day, too soon, Helen told Alba she had grown out of them, and they must be discarded. They loaded the car with spring-clean rubbish and drove to the rubbish dump. Alba saw the suitcase thrown into a large skip where it burst open. The paper dolls flew up into the air, their clothes scattered. She remembered the faces that she had lovingly crayoned – they all looked at Alba with wide-eyed surprise. Alba was a traitor – she ought to have saved them. But there was no point in picking them up again. She saw death on their pale paper faces. They had no funeral.

Helen's face will be like that now, Alba thinks. As dry and lifeless as paper. No rouge. No crayoning. Tinder.

She lives on in me – Alba mimes to herself, and wishes she could feel tears. But Kirkwood's name continues to thunder, and the sincerity in her thoughts is missing.

The service over, Kirkwood steers her outside. He holds her elbow, manoeuvring her wooden body through the mourners – mourners left with nothing to do, wanting to go now and get on with their lives, temporarily stranded, cut off by the tide of death. This is Keith Kirkwood, my headmaster – Alba says to everyone – he was so kind to come today, I'm so grateful.

The headmaster murmurs his way through Alba's relatives, and walks briskly ahead to his car. Without a word he opens the door of his car, and looks away as she gets into the seat. There is a far-away expression on his face.

'I'm very grateful to you for coming,' Alba says as they drive off.

He does not look at her. 'Not at all. Not at all. It was the least I could do.'

There's silence. Kirkwood nods, then breaks it softly. 'I really had quite a shock when I arrived at the crematorium,' he says. 'I could have sworn I saw Dutch here. In fact, I was so convinced it was him, I went round the side to have a look. But it was only a gardener. Must've been his double all the same.'

Alba's hands tighten. 'It couldn't have been him,' she says, with a brittleness. 'He's left the area. Gone up north. He disappeared the day my mother was taken into hospital.'

Keith's eyes widen. 'Really?' The lashes lower, and he clears his throat. 'I suppose one could say that's not entirely untypical behaviour for him.'

'I'd agree with that.' Alba jumps in bitterly. 'I did see him a few times last term—'

'—I thought you might have done,' he interrupts her, very smooth.

'—but it was a waste of time.'

'What – if you don't mind me asking – was the attraction in the first place? You're such an . . . elegant woman. I wouldn't have thought he was your type at all.'

Alba blushes, shrugs. 'It was just one of those things,' she says. 'One of life's mistakes, I suppose.'

Ah – Keith knows now. Knows the whole story. He'd thought as much. Yes, Alba's little dalliance could be summed up in one simple word. One sordid word. Sex.

Alba takes the pins out of the hat and lays the little black pill-box on her lap.

Kirkwood, driving fast, without taking his eyes from the road, says, 'It's such a pity women wear hats with veils only to funerals.' He turns briefly to half-smile at her. 'I think they look very elegant.'

Alba blushes. 'I'm not used to this kind of dress. I've never bought clothes specially for a funeral before. But I thought it would be proper – although I do feel strange wearing them.'

He looks ahead, blinking slowly, the long, long lashes veiling and unveiling . . . 'They become you, Alba. Have no fear,' he purrs.

Something in Alba does a dance. It is the dance of the Seven Veils, the dance of Salome, the writhe of the houri. It rolls through her uncoiling like a snake, loose-limbed, sinful, free. Its eyes are dark. Pouring out of them is slow seduction. Knowledge. Power. It has a life all its own.

She glances across at the dark suit of Dr Kirkwood. 'But black is definitely a man's colour,' she says.

'It is?' he responds in a light, kindly tone. It's been an ordeal for her, and worse will come. He will make pleasant banter with Alba for as long as she needs it. 'I always think black brings out the gypsy in women . . . the *femme fatale* . . . although, of course, there's no overtone like that at a funeral.' He smiles. 'As I said, you shouldn't worry. The more formal look suits you well. Not all women have the figure for it.'

Keith drives fast, assured. Alba sits back into the seat and silence. Exhaustion descends. They arrive back at the house ahead of the mourners, all apart from Leon who'd slipped away as soon as he arrived.

Keith opens the car door for Alba, catching sight of the dark welt of her stocking-tops as she swings her legs out of the car. He is about to leave her, he's supposed to be at the school for another meeting – but that can wait. Her helplessness stops him . . . she's gone utterly quiet, she's in shock. He can't leave her like this. And there's so much to be gained by staying.

Walking behind her as she climbs the path, he notices the way her carefully-chosen funeral outfit draws attention to the curve of her hips and thighs, how the flesh sways gently beneath the black suiting, how her calf muscles contract with the effort of wearing such high-heels, and how pale – how very pale – her skin is beneath her stockings. The fact she does not know, in her innocence, how she looks, makes him sweat.

'What's your name . . . ? Leon? Good. Have we got any food in the house for the mourners?' Keith enters the house, finds Leon in the kitchen eating a sandwich.

'We've got tea. Cups of tea,' he says, uncouth, with a full mouth.

'Is that all?'

'Why?'

Keith takes out his wallet, hands over twenty pounds. 'Go out and buy some cakes and a few pints of milk,' he says, ushering and smiling Leon to the front door. 'Be as quick as you can.' And Leon departs grumbling, but at a run.

Alba leans against the table, her face grey. Keith pulls out a stool, pushes her down and searches through the bottles on top of the cupboards. He pours her a large brandy, takes off his jacket, tucks his tie in between his shirt buttons, rolls up his sleeves and, with a wry smile, seizes Helen's apron, tying it round his waist.

'Drink,' he orders. 'And don't ever say you've seen the headmaster in a pinny, will you?'

Alba gives a little weak tremulous laugh.

The mourners arrive. Keith makes tea, quietly orders Leon to distribute it, and passes round the cakes as if he's been used to waitering all his life. He doesn't invite talk. The relations don't want to stay either. After a decent interval they leave, their hugs and solicitous condolences going mainly to Clive. Clive, who has crumbled under the enormity of losing his mother, and who is clearly in greater distress than his sister.

Keith has cleverly kept Alba out of the way, fenced with elderly relatives, supported her – constantly at her side with his commanding physical presence, with the right words, the appropriate prompts at the correct moment.

The house is empty now apart from Kirkwood and Alba. He washes up at the kitchen sink, the floral apron in place again. From the stool Alba watches him closely. He works fast, efficiently, with no self-consciousness at all about his chosen temporary role.

Alba has been holding his jacket. While he works she squeezes the cloth, examines the tailoring, feels shapes, intimate only to him, in the pockets. He turns once to catch her, far-away, smoothing the fine quality worsted.

She brings the jacket to her nose. She smells the collar, where the scent of him is strong, along with the faded scent of cologne. As the material moves she catches the underarm smell – not coarse at all, but refined, and very, very sensual.

Keith dries the last cup and shoots all the crockery into a cupboard. He takes off the apron, picks the jacket from her lap. 'Done,' he says.

The blue lenses gaze half shy, half in admiration into his black pupils. 'I don't know what to say. I don't know how to thank you. You've been wonderful.'

'I must go,' he sighs. His face set, he looks at his watch. 'Get some rest,' he says pointedly, opening the front door to go.

'I'll do as you say,' Alba responds, a curious emphasis coming into each word as she speaks.

Kirkwood catches it, smiles, and bends to kiss her with the lightest of kisses, a sheer feather of a kiss, in the middle of her forehead.

12

Helen gone, the house is massively empty in the days after the funeral. Alba prepares for the new term, and spends hours in the school library, hours in her classroom. Home she has no longer.

Keith sees her from a distance but they don't meet: he's on his way to meetings, irksome meetings, reassuring Nigerian diplomats about security, checking on the new staff arriving to take up house-parent duties. Time for Alba he will have, but not yet. Even though at the moment he is its runaround, time will serve him eventually.

For Alba there are other dilemmas. Leon – what to do about him? The question churns in her mind – the answer not. He comes and goes, watches Alba from the wings, saying little, behaving with uncharacteristic tact. After three days Alba knows he will stay, and that, oddly, she will be glad of it.

The weekend after the first day of term, Clive arrives. There is the matter of Helen's will to be dealt with, the effects to be shared out. Clive wants to stay for the two days, and Alba can't disallow it – it's not her house any more: it's a half-way stage to somewhere else. She's merely camping out. But his presence irritates. He's a giant insect bumbling around in empty, dusty rooms, unable to get out, bashing, buzzing, in a fat white heat.

Alba comes home on Friday evening to find him in the dining room rooting through Helen's Wedgwood gravy-boat. He's already been through the napkin drawer and the stone vases from Land's End, where Helen had hidden some of her savings . . . and then promptly forgotten the money was there. Alba catches him in the middle of stuffing bank notes into his trouser pocket. She's shocked. It's the beginning of a war. She backs out of the room as if she hasn't seen the thief at work, coughs loudly to let him know she's there, giving him time to push the wodge of notes deep into his pocket – and notices, shamefacedly, she can't confront him.

Leon passes her on his way out, gives a shrivelling glance at Clive's fat back. 'I'm going to the pub, Alba. Want to come?'

Alba hesitates. Suddenly she'd really like to go. The company of workmen in the public bar appeals. They have a rough honesty, she thinks. Leon hasn't rifled through Helen's drawers for money – she knows it. But she's discovered Clive in the act. She can't leave. It's not only Helen's memory she's protecting. It's her future.

Clive comes out of the dining room. His back pocket bulges. He takes Helen's will from his other pocket, teasing it out carefully. Alba hadn't even thought to look for it. How did he find it . . . and when . . . ? After the funeral? So he managed to root it out despite all those blubbing tears, Alba thinks. And it must have been inside Helen's bureau, the key to which was hidden in a small pewter jug on the living room mantelpiece. Clive must've searched his fat arse off to find that.

'We've got to . . . sort . . . this out,' Clive says in his jerky out-of-breath way.

'D'you mean she hasn't left anything to me?' Alba says with sarcasm.

Clive puffs a laugh. 'Oh, no. But there's nothing to say who'll get what.'

This feels like Helen's work, she thinks. She wanted us to fight over her things when she was gone. She didn't care a damn one way or the other.

'I want to put the house on the market. Sell up fast.'

Alba looks at him. His face is ruddier than usual. Of coure he wants it settled. He wants the money. 'What about me? Aren't you bothered about me at all? This is my house, too, at least for the moment. I would like to have a say in what happens.'

'What about the dwarf?' Clive wipes his face with a red handkerchief.

'Dwarf . . . ? Oh, you mean Leon?' The words catch in her throat. There's anger, and defence. 'Mother told me before she died she wanted Leon to be looked after,' Alba lies. 'He's got severe epilepsy. So he stays as long as he wants. He hasn't anywhere else to go.'

'I think you're making that up.' Clive laughs without mirth, the sound a faded wheeze. It reminds her of steam trains opening their valves in the station – going nowhere but making a lot of noise about it.

Alba folds her arms, leans back. 'Think what you like. *You* weren't there at her bedside. *I* was. And Leon stays.' She turns, walks out of the kitchen and goes upstairs.

In the dead beige-carpeted acreage of the living room Alba notices that some furniture has been moved into a corner: two leather chairs, a small rosewood coffee table and matching bookcases, and all the ivory from Harold's expedition to the Congo in the 'thirties. A small Persian runner is rolled neatly, and laid on one of the chairs, along with a valuable antique edition of Longfellow's poems. She moves closer. Each item is marked with a small rectangular peel-off sticker – 'Clive's'.

On a suspicious impulse she lifts up a chair cushion to find a framed pencil sketch of a little lost boy sitting on a step in the garden: 'I'm going into the garden to eat worms', it says. 'Yesterday I ate two smooth ones and one woolly one.'

That's mine, Alba thinks in a hot rush. I want that. How dare he. She picks it up, hugs it to her chest fiercely, walking about the room. Seizing the last volume of *Homes and Gardens* she puts it on the chair base, and lets the cushion drop back into place. She'll need to get a few stickers of her own.

Clive is in Helen's bedroom going through her clothes . . . he's not interested in clothes, Alba knows that . . . only what women hide beneath them. She hesitates before going into the room. She hasn't been able to go past the door since Helen was taken into hospital. Now, Clive is sifting through Helen's underwear, an expression of distaste on his face. He takes each item out individually, giving it a little shake in case there's something stuck inside. Pink corsets . . . he opens them out. Vulgar, they remind Alba of the flesh-pink dress dummies you see in shop windows. Naked, everything on show, but nothing there – squeamish. Clive throws the corsets behind him, and they land on top of a pile of Helen's other clothes on the bed.

'I don't think you should do that,' Alba says. 'You should leave the sorting of her clothes to me.'

'Why? She's dead and gone. What's it to you? It's only clothes.'

Alba opens her eyes wide, shocked by his dismissiveness. Where is the grief so openly displayed at the funeral? Was it all fake? Is this the real Clive . . . ? Grabbing, pillaging, holding up Helen's knickers as though they'd been tainted by the wearer, freeing their scent of jasmine handcream into the room – the scent of Helen.

'I think I should look through her personal things.'

Clive throws half-empty perfume bottles on the bed. He takes out the red handkerchief again and wipes his small, fierce eyes. 'Look Alba, we've never been close,' he says, trying to soften his sneer, but failing. 'Let's just keep this to a business arrangement, shall we? Let's get it all done as soon as possible.'

Alba steps back, stung. Why should she care about the uneasy under-the-table relationship she's endured with Clive for years? But she does care. Tears fill her eyes. Clive sees them, and gloats.

'All right, you do it,' he snaps. 'But I want the silver-backed hairbrush for Angie, OK? She's always liked it.'

No, Alba thinks. You're not having that. Helen said the silver looked beautiful against my hair. One of the few compliments she gave me. It's a small compensation, one I'm not letting go of. When I find it, I'll tuck it away, take it to school, leave it in my desk drawer – anything but lose it to you, brother.

By eleven o'clock, Alba's exhausted. Clive glows with energy. Leon comes back from the Rifleman's Arms, finds Alba in the kitchen, numb, far-away.

'What's he up to now?' Leon jerks his thumb in the direction of upstairs.

'God knows.'

'Wouldn't lose any sleep over it if I were you.'

'Well, I am.' She turns on him, darts of hate in her eyes.

'It's only *things*,' Leon says, trying to smooth her down. 'You don't need all that furniture and stuff. Look at me – I just live out of a suitcase. They're not even the kind of things you like, are they? Not worth getting into a ruck about. Let him think he's getting the bargain, eh?'

She can't do this. Clive mustn't get away with it. They must tussle over Helen's possessions, make it fifty-fifty, make sure neither has one hair on their mother's head more than the other. They're vying childishly for a dead woman's attention from whom there was precious little affection or love, and no understanding. They're fighting over her bones now, each object a talisman of success or failure. Helen's furniture is her only gift – a gift from the grave – she didn't care enough to give when she was alive. Helen's gifts – just empty boxes, gilded, ribboned, expensive, and inside . . . Nothing. Air. Hot damn air.

She goes to bed, doesn't undress completely, laying her jeans and top on the bedcovers in readiness to leap into them. As she drifts off, her mind wanders . . . Is there a fire . . . ? Are there burglars tonight . . . ? No, only Clive, with the fire of greed in his eyes, and large, large pockets. *He* won't sleep, she knows it. He's worrying through all the drawers, pots, and cupboards in the house. He's wearing a coat with big pockets, and trousers as voluminous as a clown's. He's got things up his sleeve, feather dusters and magic, strings of red handkerchiefs tied together – miles of them – pulling out of a red cavern in his pants. And he leans over Alba's bed, his mouth split in a wide white grin, his pig-eyes exaggerated with make-up, producing bouquet after bouquet of tattered paper flowers.

Saturday morning . . . Alba slept, but muscles stayed alert all night. She wakes like a board.

Clive's in the kitchen already, hunched, nursing a mug of coffee. He has the appearance of great guilt as he spoons in another sugar – Helen's sugar. It's wrong, he shouldn't even take it. He transfers the uneasiness about taking Helen's savings onto sweet stuff that makes him fat. Oh dear. Forget the stockpile of furniture he has planned, forget that. Sweat breaks out on his face and neck as he stirs the mug. He could be found out, he could be punished for stealing sugar.

Alba sidles round his bulk to get to the kettle. 'I think your idea of stickers is a good one,' she says lightly.

'Good.' The red sweater with random black squares on it turns to face her. Bullish clothes, on a man about to charge. 'Let's get down to it, then.' His eyes move quickly. They're shrunk this morning. They're pushed deeper in the dough. Deep inside his skull they move in league with the crafty workings of his mind. He'd need lead shutters over them to hide what's going on in there.

'I'd like to sort through the more personal items,' Alba says. 'Her diaries . . . that sort of thing. I'm not really looking forward to it but I'd rather get them out of the way first.'

Clive heaves his fatty shoulders up in a shrug. 'It's all the same to me,' he says, rinsing the cup over and over, scrubbing out the guilty evidence before going out.

Clive leaves his smell behind him. Alba sniffs. It's a rancid smell, like flowers going over, never so strong as now. It's his sweat chasing ahead of itself, his tension jumping out of every pore. Immediately she opens the window, goes to the front door, opening that, and fans in fresh air.

Clive stamps upstairs, goes into the living room, the

battleground. Alba follows. He was in the room last night, she knows it, but she can't see any extra items added to his labelled pile in the corner. Everything in the room, though, has been picked up and inspected underneath for craftsman's marks. The embroidery drawer has felt his quivering fingers slide among the linen runners . . . is there treasure there . . . ? His fingers have been right to the back, blind fingers, lifting each piece up, creeping to the back of the drawer, and coming out with fluff under the nails.

Yes, everything in the room bears Clive's touch, but it's all been put back in place. Funny how I know that, Alba thinks. Funny how all those fingerprints dabbed about are as obvious to me as though they were spots of black dye. How do I know these things? How do I know the children in my classroom have been looking through my desk-drawer, even though I can't remember the order of anything I put in there? I just know. Why? Well, wouldn't I do the same . . . ?

Alba kneels on the carpet and opens the doors of the mock-Jacobean court cupboard, and takes out the liqueurs and spirits, the stack of photograph albums, the 'fifties' teak fruit bowl with the bob-curl rim, the blue and white porcelain dinner service – never used – the crystal goblets likewise.

Clive saunters over from the windows where he has been standing in order not to look too eager, and casually picks up a large unopened bottle of Cointreau. He looks behind him, draws an imaginary line on the carpet with his eye, and puts the bottle down behind it. Refusing to kneel, he hovers over Alba as she pulls out more from the cupboard, swooping to pick up each full bottle as it arrives, adding every one to his cache behind the lines.

Alba says nothing. At first she pretends not to see what is going on. She tells herself she doesn't mind. Don't make a fuss – it's nothing. But she feels without power, shocked. She hadn't expected Clive to be like this. Always solicitous to Helen, always visiting with plants, chocolates, perfume, taking her out for meals, wooing her . . . She's been dead barely two weeks now, and all those funeral tears and that big show of emotion have been put aside as if Helen meant nothing at all. Perhaps he's like me, she thinks. Perhaps he got nothing from her either, despite all the crawling, and now he's grabbing all he can in an obsessive attempt to compensate. It could be so. He has a huge hole, a vacuum inside his torso.

But this doesn't mean I have to like him, she thinks.

Three porcelain plates in their tissue-lined box lay between them, each handpainted by a well-known wild-flower artist. Worth much. Three plates, two of them. Clive looks at them greedily and kneels down.

'These'll fetch something,' he says, sliding the boxes on the carpet to make a line in front of him.

Alba can remember when Helen bought them, how she'd met the artist, how they'd had tea on the lawn overlooking the sea. Alba was there that day. She'd seen Helen's cultural aspirations as quite poignant – Helen was happy and light. Alba had helped her choose. It was one of the few good . . . deluded . . . days.

She picks one up now. 'These have some meaning for me,' she says. 'Not much, but some.' She turns it round in her hands. ' "Autumn" is my favourite.' Autumn, her birth-time. A crescent of painted hips, ivy, brambles and a conker. The fruits of the year, the time of plenty, the sensual slightly-tattered leaves, the lazy let-down of summer. Fruit the end product, the purpose of it all. The prize.

As Alba moves the plate in its box to her side, Clive looks at her, his face twisted. 'You only want that one because it's worth more – it's got more paint on it,' he says, smouldering with fury.

Monday . . . Alba is the first to arrive at school. She goes straight to her classroom, sits at the desk, pulls a mirror out of the drawer and looks at her face. There's grey under her eyes, on her lids – to be expected after the stress of the weekend. Glasses will hide it well enough. They hide eyes which can see perfectly well without them all the time.

She takes a small paisley make-up bag from her briefcase and lays the contents in a row on the desk. Helen's make-up – expensive stuff. She twists a silver lipstick until the red colour comes up. The top is smoothed and flattened into a round, dulled with repeated applications. She looks at it closely, doesn't want to touch where Helen's lips had once been . . . Dead lips now. No lips now.

Twisting the whole lipstick out she carefully wipes it with a tissue to remove a thick layer, and then draws the new end over her own lips, over the discreet everyday pink already there. The effect is startling. She adds a red pencil liner to the edges of her mouth. Not the proper way to do it. Not like Helen. Helen always put on her lipstick like a 'fifties' film star, stretching and pouting in an almost obscene set of gestures. Alba will have to learn such techniques too, she thinks, if she wants to catch Kirkwood's attention. Blotting her mouth with the tissue, she gets up, walks around the classroom, tries a pout, runs her tongue slowly along the inner membrane of her mouth . . . like Marilyn, oh yes, just like Marilyn . . . !

And she does want to attract him. It's what's kept her going over the weekend. All that rummaging through Helen's clothes, all smelling of her still. The smell lost and searching for its owner, filling the room, swamping the air with the scent of jasmine. The jewellery, her thirteen silk slips, Clive bearing down on her, making the whole thing dirty, his lip curling as he holds up his mother's underwear, sneering with voyeurism.

Thoughts of Kirkwood come into this horrible reality like a blessed diversion. He's the diamond winking in all this shit, Alba thinks, recalling Dutch's words which take on a new meaning now. It's in the shit you'll find your diamonds, Dutch had said in one of his irritating homilies. Damn preacher!

She'd found the shit all right. And it wasn't inside herself either. Dutch had gone off and dumped her in a load of it . . . when he could have been there, supporting her through a bloody difficult time. But what a discovery she'd made. In the middle of this recent hell she'd found a gem from heaven – Keith. Perhaps it takes a dose of shit to highlight the brilliant facets that shine within it. All you have to do is scrape away, and there it is – a diamond, a huge diamond, smug, winking, brilliant. What a prize.

Impulsively Alba experiments with the rest of Helen's cosmetics. She's careful, she doesn't overdo it, but she's changing the note all right. And she can get away with it, too – one of the advantages of having a death in the family. Colleagues know she's lost her mother. They've seen the distraction, the quiet pain in her face. They know death brings massive changes. It shakes you up, makes you go off the rails. It brings out the hidden. Yes, pain does funny things. It bleeds through all the layers of the self, comes up right from the dark core. Trawls up what is there, what has never been lived . . .

Kirkwood notices her that morning. He's aware of the new note. At assembly the staff sit with their own form, one teacher at the end of each row in the block. Alba's half-way down the hall, but he can see her red lips from the podium

– startling lips in her geisha face. Red on white. Innocence and blood.

He walks into her as they pass in the corridor. 'I do apologize,' he says, and takes her arms. 'I wasn't looking where I was going . . . mind on other things . . .' he dashes a hand through his thick black hair, smiles his slow gap-toothed smile ' . . . too many things.' Still holding onto one arm he slides his hand down the sleeve of her blouse to let it drop at her wrist. 'I always think the beginning of term is mayhem and madness. Are you coping all right?' he adds.

Alba smiles, slightly self-conscious of her lips, and aware that the little *moue* is not lost on Keith. 'I think I shall have to move into school permanently,' she says. 'My brother and I are trying to sort the house out. It's hell.'

Keith makes a sympathetic noise. 'It must be quite a business.'

'He wants to sell up . . . right now.' Alba laughs. 'But I won't have that. I need time to find somewhere else to live. So things have become rather strained. I hope everything will resolve itself soon, though, otherwise I really will have to move into my classroom.'

He laughs, a quick laugh, much fire beneath it, much spring-fever.

Alba looks boldly into his eyes through her glasses, then takes them off, wipes them on her handkerchief, and looks at him again with the blue lenses. Not even this artifice can disguise what lies behind them . . .

'How would you like to come to Canterbury next week?'

'Canterbury?'

'On a dyslexic conference. I'm going. Deacon was coming along too, being the senior member of your department. But he's got a hospital appointment, and can't make it.' Kirkwood takes a breath, tugs at his collar, straightens his tie, assumes the old familiar velvet tone. 'It's a heads of department, head teachers, old boys affair,' he says quietly. 'But I think you'd get a lot out of it all the same. And there'll be plenty of time to look round the city between sessions.'

They walk slowly down the corridor together. Keith gives her a sidelong glance. 'Have you seen the cathedral?'

'No.'

'Something you shouldn't miss. I know it well. Canterbury's my neck of the woods . . . I went to Dover College.'

Alba nods, listens. 'It's supposed to be the king among cathedrals, isn't it?'

Keith opens the door for her into the entrance hall. He leans towards her, his face inscrutable, intense. Light floods in through the tall windows making her lips seem so very red, her skin so very white. He lets out a long wistful sigh, takes the cheroots from his jacket, and fondly taps the box back inside the pocket again.

'Alba . . .' he says, 'it is the most spiritual place I know.'

A movement in the air, a small caress of it on the cheek, can summon memories, alter life's course, still you where you are. You're on your way down the road, purposeful, the outing planned, and that little flurry, that stirring of the breeze, bounces gently on and off the fine hairs on your cheek. Antennae which read the invisible. And you've been boxed by a glove of thistledown.

Alba's on her way out of school in the late afternoon. She walks slowly to the car park, her briefcase and her free arm weighed down with exercise books. She gets the soft punch on the face as she stops by her car, and she looks up, looks for the arm that dealt the blow. A sudden craziness takes hold of her. She wants to toss the books high in the air, stamp on them when they fall, worry them in the dirt, and drive away. But as usual she bites the impulse back, and, opening the door, throws the lot on the centre of the back seat with practised aim. She gets into the car angrily, starts the engine. Her blood suddenly runs with grit, she knows the feeling well. She used to feel like this about Dutch. She stamps on the accelerator.

The old itch, the maddening challenge, the pull – that awful pull – comes back. With a heavy sigh she drives out of school, takes the single-track lane that avoids the town, and follows the bow-cambered road across the peat moors.

She can tell he's not living there any more. Even from a distance the cottage has a blank look. It sits, waits, everything held, everything in suspension until Dutch returns. The house lacks the heart, the hearth, the voice, noise, smell . . . him. Now it's like a clock with the inner workings taken away, its face robbed of a mind – a shell, a pretence.

She parks a little way off and walks slowly down the road towards it. On her left is the river, brilliant and blinding as the low rays of the sun ride on the water like a gold skin. The lush green on the riverbanks has over-reached itself. Stems have grown too tall – now they kink and fall over. Summer is on its way out. It's spent its desire, set seed, done. No point now. All the herbage sinks blowsily back to earth, each leaf pockmarked, shredded, holed, blistered, rolled and shrivelled by mindless, numberless insect mouths, and then dried to a skeleton by the desiccating sun. It's a nice way to go, a gentle rape, an inevitable rape – Alba thinks. It's the way of things.

She stops as the air shivers into a breeze which lifts the scent of the weedy river water to her nose. Helen is gone. Dutch is gone. She's alone. She feels it, allows it to cut its way through her. And she'll carry on. It's the way of things.

She has the key to unlock the door ready in her fingers. She hesitates. If she goes in she has the idea she'll disturb something – like treading on a hibernating animal by mistake. Would she get bitten, or would she destroy? She feels odd, standing there. She daren't look through the windows either – she walked straight past them, deliberately looking ahead. It would feel like trespassing. Moments of indecision pass. Leave now or go in . . . ? She jabs the key in the lock with a boldness she doesn't feel.

Dutch's cottage empty? No. Shock. The house isn't hibernating at all. She had it all wrong. It's alive.

Alba stands in the middle of the living room unable to go on. Immediately her eyes are fixed by a shape she can see through the glass-panes of the back door. Sitting on a post, backdropped by fields, watching her, is a bird of prey. Its yellow eyes gun into her own. She starts, claps her hand to her mouth. The bird lifts its great wings and flies off. She gives a little nervous laugh into the empty room.

But is the room, the house, empty? She looks around. It doesn't feel so. She calls Dutch's name, puzzled. She's sure he isn't here and yet, with equal weight, she feels he is.

Empty houses – they have this hollow feeling when you return to them from time away. Two days gone, and it's not so bad – you won't feel much when you come back. You'll just pick up the beginnings of a question mark forming in the air, a slow miffed resignation creeping into the atmosphere. The eyes droop, but they're not closed yet. But any longer – a week, or more – and you'll walk into a dead space where the eyes have shut and the air might be host to unfamiliar visitors.

Not so here. As Alba goes into each room she walks through something solid and lively. Dutch's belongings sit in a permanent state of anticipatory joy, despite his absence. She pokes her way into the lean-to, among the smashed clay pots, boots, tools and cardboard boxes. The only living thing among the dereliction are some large pots with iris tubers struggling in bone-dry soil, six inches of leaf above the rim. They can go no further, they'll die if they don't get something . . . water. She carries one pot into the kitchen. No water. Dutch has turned it off.

She takes a bucket, ties a long string to its handle, and goes out of the house and across the road to the river, where she leans over and lowers the pail into the water. The sound of a buzzard over the next field makes her look up and squint. Its cry so plaintive, so trust-me . . . so like a faintly-distressed babe, she thinks, from something so ready to dive and kill.

Canterbury next week, Alba smiles to herself as she takes the river water back into the house and pours it into the pots. The headmaster is taking me. What d'you think of that, Dutch? The air holds her thought, considers it. A small panic strikes her. If Dutch came back he'd be able to pluck that thought from the air and read it. She knows he could.

Slamming the front door, she leaves, tosses her head. 'You're not here, Dutch,' she says, 'and I'll do what I fancy, thank you very much.'

She walks past the kitchen window to check the side, and comes back. She's in a fever of thought now about Kirkwood. As she corners the building something catches her eye. A dark shape disappears behind the far wall of the house.

It's that woman again, Alba thinks, in sudden fury. I saw her much clearer this time. I saw the long black skirt stitched with mirrors, the loose black top, the black hair, the olive skin. I saw her, and she won't get away from me this time.

Unhooking the straps of her sling-backed shoes, she takes them off and leaves them in the road, running along it now in her stockinged feet to where the woman had gone. She reaches the corner . . . there's nothing but wood and junk stacked against the wall. Nowhere to run either, unless she was a fast climber. But she might be! Ignoring her feet, Alba climbs over the woodpile in a frenzy, her senses sharp, combing the air in front of her for the slightest sign. Nothing. Nothing at all. And the field, the only place where she could have gone, stretches away, empty.

Shaken, she walks back, sees her shoes side by side, incongruous in the grassy middle of the road. She picks them up, hurls them over the riverbank vegetation into the river. The splash makes her smile. Goodbye, schoolmarm shoes.

There's a warmth to the sun, a ripeness, and she doesn't want to leave. She does a little circle in the road, a lazy circle, a little dance in bare feet, and stops. Too gypsyish. Or, maybe not . . . Turning once, twice, faster, faster, she spins in a series of linking circles down the road's spine.

She can feel the skirt rise now, feel the weight of cloth as it pulls her out, yet keeps her steady in the middle. And she can almost see the flash of mirrors streaking the afternoon sun through the air. Mirrors stitched on black cloth. Laughing mirrors.

'What've you done with your shoes?' Leon stands on the patio watching Alba come up the path, a perplexed expression on his face.

'I threw them in the river.' Alba's voice has a sing to it.

He goes to laugh, then frowns. 'What did you do that for?'

'I didn't want them any more. They're too old-fashioned. Made me look like my mother.'

Leon nods. 'Oh, aye,' he says, not understanding at all. He scratches his head. 'Your brother rang.'

'Oh?' Alba becomes aware of her sore, bleeding feet.

'He's coming again next Tuesday, wants to sort out some more stuff. And he needs to discuss something with you.'

Alba tilts her head up. 'I won't be here. I'm going to Kent on Tuesday, to a conference with the headmaster. Can you keep an eye on Clive for me till I get back?'

Leon looks alarmed. 'Are you coming back Tuesday night?'

She shakes her head. 'Late Thursday.'

'So you'll be staying over with him?'

'Yes.'

'He's the geezer who came here with the wreath . . . who sent me out shopping for cakes?'

'Dr Kirkwood – yes.'

Leon's face grows dark. 'Watch him, Alba,' he says, suddenly serious. 'Flash git, if you ask me. Bit of a dark dangerous type. Reckon he fancies you.'

Alba laughs loudly. 'He's a married man, for heaven's sake. The head of a public school. Don't be so bloody daft.'

Leon takes a step towards her, hands on hips. 'I mean it. He's a real con man, he is. He'll steal your soul if he can, Alba, mark my words.'

Alba gives Leon a shove, half angry, half in jest. 'And what would you know of these things?' she says as she goes in, 'hmmm?'

13

Canterbury. Kirkwood. Another world . . .

Most of the journey goes by in silence. It's like driving to the edge of a cliff, going over, going down, down, mile after mile of abyss, everything vertical, shooting past, vanishing, falling . . . and Alba feels it. And as she goes down she's aware of change, loss, goodbyes. Fields, farms, buildings – she can't clutch at them as Keith speeds through. Falling . . . falling . . . and the details reach out to her like fingers of passing friends, touch her senses, wave farewell.

Imagine . . . One day, in a moment of lightness and despair, you take that jump off the bridge, the cliff, the tall building . . . and as you fall you know everything you see will be for the last time – you'll never see it again. Think how precious each object would be. How every grey brace and girder, pink thrift flower, mirrored window-face would have you marvelling . . . ah! – if you could have lived your whole life like this . . .

As Keith drives, Alba imagines herself inside the cavern of their descent. It's grey granite, dripping, ferned, soft and tactile, almost a womb. And although they drop free fall, Keith urges the car on. Does he know the abyss will not end . . . ? That they're safe, only free falling? Or is he waiting, has he been waiting all his life, for the crash?

His jaw is set, mouth shut in a tight line. He doesn't invite talk. Occasionally he jabs a cheroot in the car's cigarette lighter on the dashboard, puts it to his lips, ignoring Alba. Letting the car fill with smoke, waiting for Alba's distress before he'll open the window.

After lunch, when she'd come back to school with her small case, he'd been crisper than of late, but not unfriendly. And then within minutes of their departure they've left the road, are already inside the vortex, and there is nothing to say. Alba looks out at the world as it comes to meet and pass on through her. It is as if they have always travelled together, have read the same books, seen the same films. What is there to say of any relevance? When you're free falling *there are no words*.

Mid afternoon Keith stops for coffee. Here, among people, his smooth way comes back, his large frame moves easily through the cluster at the bar, the gap-toothed smile brings swift service. He talks to Alba about school trivia. They laugh over nothing. And then it's motorway again. Back to the falling.

After an hour Keith turns off, takes a road through the country, past oast houses, through that wistful Kent sobriety. He drives into a clearing in an old beech wood, and stops.

'I need to stretch my legs,' he says, as he gets out of the car.

Alba watches him walk away, pause, light a cheroot, and

walk on, his black hair swept by a breeze, his suit jacket flapping open. A hundred yards on where the trees begin, he turns, walking away backwards a few steps, and beckons to her.

She gets out. The wind catches her loose hair and blows it all over her face. She seizes it, tucks it inside the nape of her jacket, and walks towards him, self-conscious of the high-heels – every step needs her attention. Keith, his head on one side, considers her approach, and his mouth slowly widens in amusement.

'I like that,' he says.

Alba, near him now, raises her eyebrows, pretends dumb.

'Every step a conscious step – of necessity.' He laughs, poking fun at her, and saunters away under the trees. Last year's leaves crackle thinly and mast snaps under his tread. Alba slowly follows him, aware of her impediment. He sits down on a great arching beech root, brings his ankle up to rest on the other knee, and looks up into the tree. Leaves are already signing off, a few are falling.

'You women have a hard time, don't you?' he says softly, coming back to Alba. 'All these feminine contrivances – high-heels, skirts, stockings – all designed to fetter you.' He smiles at her, lowering the long, long lashes to look at the slender area just above her ankle. 'The world still belongs to men,' he says reflectively. 'What the feminine sphere is . . . remains a constant mystery to us. And yet we chase it all our lives.'

'That's very philosophical.'

He shakes his head, laughs, points a finger at her. 'You're right. It is.' He gets up, walks around the tree, comes back to her. 'This is the one place I've been back to that hasn't changed since my youth. I used to come here a lot.' He tilts his head, a smile coming and going. 'It was a favourite spot for the seduction of girls, I seem to recollect.'

Alba looks up at him, blushes, fights it away. 'You're lucky,' she says. 'I don't dare re-visit old haunts anymore. I've had some nasty surprises – woods chopped down and houses in their place, that sort of thing. Somehow going back totally ruins the memory of how it all used to be.'

Keith scuffs the russet at his feet. 'It's touching base,' he says softly. 'When you realize how you might have done things differently.'

'What would you have done differently?'

'The PhD took the stuffing out of me,' he says thoughtfully. 'Maybe I should have stopped before that.' He turns on the spot, following the sound of the wind in the trees, watching fresh waves of leaves spin down. 'Academics are one-sided people. Fêted for brilliance, sure, but our emotional lives never match up.' He brushes her arm briefly and sighs. 'Let's get back on the road.'

He walks back to the car with her, matching his pace with hers for once, head bent, hands clasped behind his back. As she stops at the car door, Alba hooks out the mass of hair from under her collar and lets it free. A gust catches it and white swirls about her face. Keith, his mouth slightly open, stares at her, his face suddenly full, blooded, sensual. Something is coming to fruit inside him.

Here she is – and Keith does not know what to do with her. What do you do at forty-eight, when the very something your innards have groaned for appears suddenly, without warning? She's like the comet in the night sky at the moment, he thinks. As big as the moon, a fuzzy ball, now silver, now white, now light, with a silver fish-tail that fans out behind it – like Alba's hair now, streaming back from her face.

And he, Keith, is the darkness all round her. And she . . . who crosses his path, comes into his lost, blind universe.

Yes she . . . she's come from nowhere, she's only passing through.

He must make her feel that the night is not dark, that it is made of moleskin, warms, gives safety, so she'll want to stay on. He can't jump on her – that would be like finding a rare Himalayan flower and crushing it under his boot. She's too delicate for that, too white. Angel, Mary, Mother of God . . . This whiteness, this purity . . .

He wants to scoop her hair into his hands, let it run through his fingers like silver, feeling the fine silk texture against his shaved cheek, his neck, in his mouth, obliterating everything in a crazy cloud of white. He'd take off her lipstick, wipe her lips back to their natural paleness, back to her blank-canvas face, before he made the decision what to do with her. And how would he kiss such lips? He would want to bite through them, make her bleed, force his tongue deep down inside her mouth to try and taste the nectar that was her especial food. How he could drown, how he could go under . . .

'Keith . . . ?'

'Ah . . . ? Nothing. Memories, that's all.'

Canterbury. Evening . . . The conference begins with a buffet and short session. There's no time to look at the city. But the cathedral close is lit. It tantalizes Alba. She wants to go there. Never mind the old cathedral at home – that's paltry. This is the big one, the linchpin. Kirkwood told her so. That makes it special.

Were it not for sitting next to Keith at the first meeting, Alba would have been overawed. It's all men – dark suits, dark voices, the cutting-edge of the public schools. But Keith's aura possesses her, wraps around her like flowing oil. Protected like this she can't be phased.

The evening passes slowly. Alba takes notes, listens, feels

mechanical. She can't unwind after travelling, after so much expectation . . . She barely has time to throw her case into her room when she's drawn out by Keith to mill with delegates, trying her best to look stately, not scared.

It's the same all day Wednesday. Alba wakes late, rushes breakfast, catches Keith's quizzical eyebrow, his critical eye. She keeps her head down, taking copious notes.

And then it's Keith speaking . . . she can't write any more, she puts the pen down and listens to him, worship growing inside her. A smooth diplomat at school, he is superb among his contemporaries. He doesn't just grasp language, he uses it, he rides it, directs it like a sinuous animal. When he's finished, there's spontaneous clapping. He sits down next to Alba, shuffles his papers, and gives her a wink, a flash of a smile. He enjoys the academic flurry, she thinks. The price? The life of the heart. It could never be otherwise.

So admired and respected by his colleagues, he's drawn away from her into groups in corners, to drink, smoke, discuss new rumours, to debate new appointments. Alba doesn't have time with him, she's shut out. There's nothing to do but resign herself to it all.

The evening comes. It's been an intense day. Dinner will be a long spell out, a reprieve. Although they'll still eat with the conference in the dining room, Kirkwood intimates to Alba this will be more of an occasion. She'll need to dress for dinner, take more trouble over herself.

'I'll call for you,' he says, going into his own room. 'I'm looking forward to some relaxation.'

Alba showers and dresses in black, one of the new dresses she's brought with her. It's startling against her skin. Can she take it? She sits down and begins to cover her pale cheeks, begins to hide the contrast.

Keith knocks, calls out to her. He must have ripped through dressing. No-one could be that fast, she thinks. She stays at the dressing table, considering her face in the mirror. 'Come in,' she calls back. She can't not.

He comes in, and immediately apologizes. But he doesn't retreat. He closes the door quietly behind him with great care, with a whisper.

The room is full of western sunlight. The windows suck it up, melt with it, and pass it through into the room onto Alba, like gold eyes. Unwitting, he's entered a shrine bathed in surreal light. The goddess sits at her dressing-table, in the middle of her make-up. God gave her a blank face so that she might craft the rest, make herself ready to visit humankind.

She has her box of tricks, her artifice, her paints, and she's about to wash in all the pink tones over her cheeks. But . . . she's doing it all wrong. The beige foundation is wrong. The rouge is wrong. Keith eyes her critically, searching her face in the dressing-table mirror.

The mirror has two side pieces which you can move to check the perfection of the make-up, not just from the front, but from the sides also. Without thinking, Keith leans forward and adjusts the side mirrors. When he stands back he can now see full three of her, a holy trinity of white.

'There,' he says. 'That's better for you.'

'You were quick,' she says, taking in the grey silk shirt, the open black waistcoat, the knife creases on his fine flannels.

He smiles disarmingly. 'Shall I come back in a while?'

Alba shakes her head. 'I'll only be a minute.'

'I shall be the voyeur, if you don't mind,' he says, with a short cracked laugh. 'I like seeing the way women do their faces – all these little feminine rituals. You don't see much of them these days.'

Alba's unnatural blue lenses look at him in the glass. She pushes the stool back. 'Excuse me,' she says. 'I'll have to take out my contact lenses. I've found all the cigar smoke very irritating.' And she gets up, goes to the bathroom, leaves him standing in front of the window bathed in the sun. On her return he swivels to look at her and his face freezes.

He looks into the silence, the nothingness of the deep lake – the open iris – all questions, all answers, submerged in their chilling clarity.

'God,' he says, almost leaping at her. 'You must take that stuff off your face,' he says in a way that no-one could refuse. 'Wipe it all off.' He picks up the tubes of foundation and rouge from the dressing-table. 'You don't need these, Alba. They spoil your complexion. Take the stuff off.'

There is something intensely compelling about Keith now. The teacher, the headmaster, has gone. Alba picks up the cotton-wool and lotion. She has no choice. Underneath academe, the man's voice bleeds.

And she doesn't want the onus to decide what to do right now. She wants that taken away. If Keith wanted to see the very inside of her . . . if right now he needed her soul to staunch his blood, she'd give it.

Keith stands directly behind her now, his hands squarely on her shoulders, arms straight, gaze flicking from one image of her to another in the triptych of mirrors.

'What is it?'

'I am fascinated by your . . . your translucence, your paleness.'

'Lots of people stare at me. I'm used to it. I can't sunbathe, I have to wear a hat, dark glasses, etcetera. People think I'm a freak.'

'No . . .' His hands press on her shoulders, an urgent smile comes and goes. 'No. You mustn't think that.' He looks at her triple reflections, his voice growing faint. 'No, you're simply a woman who hasn't touched earth . . . That was what Dutch saw in you, wasn't it . . . ? You don't have the taint.'

A dark streak sweeps over his face, a cloud-shadow running over the ground. The control gives all of a sudden, relieved of the compulsion to be out there, up-front, braving the bitter knocks of life. His clothes lose their life, they slacken off, hang flat and limp on his body. It's the sudden giving up, the resignation of the beggar who has nothing, but is still robbed, whose surprise is always underpinned by the faint hope that precedes all despair. Dutch has already had her – he saw the evidence of that in the Quiet Room.

Now he's aware of the falling, falling, of the unfamiliar out-of-reach on the chasm's edge. With a grey yearning he comes out from the place of pain, back to the innocent waiting white triple-goddess before him. In that moment he's caught, and the veil slips. It's time for confession.

He tells her about Maria. His marriage, his non-event. The excuse of her sick mother. The charade at school. The terrible frustration. The lack of sex. Oh, yes, especially the lack of sex . . .

Alba stays where she is on the stool, staring at herself in the mirror, the grace of the goddesses on her side. They make her calm. She listens, blinks, opens herself to his pain.

Keith takes his hands off her shoulders and paces the room, goes to the window, unknots the tie, letting it hang, sweeps the black hair back over and over, takes off the waistcoat and drops it on the bed, undoes his shirt buttons half way down his chest. He's a man gasping for air, unaccustomed to it being denied him. His clothes, his skin, are so hot he could tear them off his body. Anything – to be rid of the numberless darts that make their way from the very core of him up to the surface, piercing every part of him en route, firing him with pain.

And all the while he talks. He does not remember what he says. There's no thread, no direction. It all comes out . . .

. . . Keith. Six years old . . . left at boarding school, waving his mother goodbye, his father abroad already. Six . . . too young, the tender soul wounded irreversibly . . . the dark dormitory – how could it be so dark? . . . in his home even the shadows had been kind . . . now the iron beds stalked the cold barrack-like room. Six . . . beds advancing with their four-legged hungry gait . . . they'd eat little boys in the night but you'd never guess . . . in the morning all the children, they'd run about as usual, but they'd been eaten all right, their insides replaced by iron . . . six-year-olds with iron skeletons, iron innards, learning not to cry . . .

. . . Every night Keith had wrapped himself in his sheet, pulling it tight around him like a cocoon . . . a white starched sheet, yes, white again, warding off the hungry metal . . . white – his saviour. The years going by in a haze of kept-back tears, disappointment, hurts . . . mother visited but three times in six years . . . By puberty he'd wrap strips of white around him, jerk the cloth tight like a bandage . . . then, to stop the demons, he'd tie himself to his bed, sweating, the battle only on his side, as he waited for morning . . . His mother was told about the torn sheets by matron – she didn't understand, she'd mocked him.

An animal maimed does this – is the one thought which flits through Alba's blank receptiveness. It's not so badly injured it can give up to the pain and submit. It twists, turns, bites and snaps at itself and at anything near. It cannot know the calmness of submission. Its fierce crazed will lashes out, drains its energy. It cannot be helped. Could Keith give up the academic life, turn to the neglected heart? She doubts it.

Several times she wants to move, to interrupt him with her touch, but she can't. Keith isn't really speaking to her

– she's just the vehicle for his release. He talks to his twin self, his *mirror* image out there in front of him, dancing in thin air – the twin who looks back in wonder and pity at the hole in his guts, whose emptiness he had not touched until now.

And then he stops. The stillness thumps down. There's nothing but his breathing, the snatching of air.

Alba runs her finger over her pale lips. Seeing this, he returns to the present. The theatre of his face comes back with a heavy sigh, a quick rise of the eyebrows . . . a disownment.

'Well, that's that . . .' He puts his hands back on her shoulders again, hands that have been tied down in fire. 'Now what are we going to do with you?'

Me? Anything.

Alba looks down and then – very slowly – up, and meets his eyes in the mirror. Can he not feel her whole self slide around his body, eat his clothes, lick the smell of him from under his arms, his groin? He can't know what she offers him, or he would have taken it. It must be her eyes – they have no full-stop – he can't read anything in them. White-eyed people have no souls. Oh! for real eyes so he can sieve out what he needs!

'Do something for me, Alba.'

Name it.

'Paint your mouth . . . with this . . .' He leans over her, the smell of fresh sweat brushing her cheek, and picks up Helen's old red lipstick.

If he had wanted to dress himself up in women's clothes, Alba would scarce have found it more shocking. She expected to be stripped, flung on the bed, taken. Dutch had done it. He had opened the door for her there. He had put his mouth to her thighs, and she had burst open, singing.

*　*　*

The little shocks in life are not events foisted on us from outside. Instead they're a kink in our expectations. In our mind we have a film always running ahead of itself. The frames go snap-snap as the sequence maps itself out. And instead of staying where we are, we go there in a thoughtless rush, into never-never land. From now on life must match up to our celluloid creation.

Alba's little creation has suddenly jerked to a stop. The film's snapped. It lies in redundant coils on the cutting-room floor. She'd had her reaction all planned – now she has to abandon it. She's fallen into the gap. You can't think in a gap – you do what you're told.

Obediently she picks up the lipstick and brush. She's about to paint the middle of her mouth when Keith touches her wrist and stops her. He leans forward eagerly, his hands bearing down heavily through the thin dress on her shoulders.

'You do know how to do it, don't you?' he says, guiding her hand to her lips. 'There's a right way . . . and a wrong way . . .'

Alba falters. Keith takes his hand away but makes a movement with his fingers. 'Open your mouth a little . . . that's it . . . now, just draw a line,' he says, concentrating for her. 'That's it . . . just around the edge of your lips, so you get this perfect edge . . . Now fill in the corners . . . open slightly. Good girl.'

Alba strokes the brush up the corners of her upper lip and down the corners of the lower one. She does it with increasing confidence, a ritual slowness, with a consciousness from elsewhere. A dawning shivery sensation of power fizzes in her as she realizes the import of this commonplace feminine activity. For Keith it has powerful erotic meaning.

She looks at herself then, sees sly knowing dark eyes look back at her. Black hair, red lips, teeth filed sharp, the expression alive, animal. Her heart jolts. Shame warms her – shame, relief, the excitement of forbidden admiration. She'll catch up with the gypsy yet . . .

'Stop,' Keith gives a lengthy sigh, looks at her threefold mouth in the mirror. The middle of her lips is still bare and pale. 'OK . . .' He takes the brush from her fingers. She holds the lipstick up, offers it to him, knowing what he wants to do next. He worms the sable around in the little depression at the end of the lipstick until it is thick with red, red grease.

He crouches beside her – he's not the right height – and frowning, concentration drawn on his face, he gets up, seizes a small chair by the side of the dressing-table, and drags it over to her. The loaded brush is still poised in his other hand. He sits astride the chair, and pauses, looking at her unfinished mouth with weighty consideration, for the critical placement of the final strokes. The painting has taken years to come. He could so easily ruin it now, slip up. Then he touches her mouth with the brush, draws it across the middle of her bottom lip, holding his breath.

'Oh, my God,' he says, running his free hand through his black hair. 'Jesus.'

She looks into his dark brown eyes, sees wonder there . . . the wonder of being summoned to the marquee on Speech Day to be given the prize of prizes. She cannot understand it. The mystery of his compulsion excites her. But, like the Goddess, she doesn't show it.

Three reflections.

Three of Alba.

The triple prize.

Keith lets his breath go long and low, lays the brush down

reverently on the dressing-table, and stands up, moving around her, seeing her from every angle. White cheeks. Bowed lips. Obscene. Red. He shakes his head in disbelief, in awe, whistling silently under his breath. Grasping her hair, he scoops it in his hands, buries his face in it. Then he pulls it back.

His memory runs like ticker-tape . . . Her skin is the colour of lime-washed wood . . . the colour of panned-flat white suede . . . it's the strange diffuseness of moonlight on the garden when white objects are wan, bleached, familiar, but eerily not, with a lunar life of their own . . . it's white weatherboard on old beach huts, the temporary magic home by the sea of his childhood (childhood – did he ever have one?) . . . white . . . white talisman against the dark . . . and also a reminder of its fear . . . and it's all lost now. Past. Memories. Loss.

White, beautiful white. So hard to take. So hard to live up to. Better make your mark on it quick and break the tension. Only when you sacrifice the white on your canvas do the colours start to flow. White's the catalyst. You've got to move on, move away from it . . . that's written in white's script.

See the fine white cirrus, the ice-white in the sky, and you search around for the relief of eggshell blue at its edges. Imagine a sky all white – you'd be terrified. All that white, bearing down . . . like a shroud.

Keith focuses on her red lips, smiles to himself. What an insult to her innocent face, this whorish gash. How well the two go together.

'Geisha,' he says, excited, laughing aloud. 'Look at yourself, Alba. You were born to it. Look, that's what you are, eh?'

263

Hetaira . . .

He picks up the brush again, teasing it along her mouth. He grabs her hair, twisting it around his wrist, suddenly pulling her back with a jerk, before letting it slide loose through his fingers like silver sand.

Alba feels him press against her shoulder. She can smell him, she knows he's ripe. She half-turns on the stool, unzips him, hooks out his penis and takes it into her mouth, deep through her red, red lips.

It doesn't take long. As his fingers bruise into her upper arms, she tilts her head back and looks up into dark shattered split *angry* eyes. She pulls back, takes a tissue from the box on the dressing-table, and wipes the red grease on him away.

Moments later he has dressed himself, picked up the waistcoat from the bed, and walked out of the room. Alba is left with nothing but the taste of him inside her.

Half an hour goes by. Alba re-does her face, sits on the bed, hands in her lap. She can't hold what has happened, she's too close to it. Someone – Keith – must pick up the celluloid thread for her again. He knocks, and this time Keith waits for her to answer the door.

'Dinner?' he says, leaning against the door-frame, a slow gap-toothed smile coming.

Alba blinks, and rewinds the film. Nothing has happened. She can see it on his face. 'Fine,' she says evenly, content – he's got the end of the thread again now.

'I see you've re-done your mouth. Excellent.' The look is dark, lowered. The smile, still present, holds a demon in it. As they go downstairs to the dining-room Keith suddenly takes Alba's arm and twists it high up behind her back until a small sound of discomfort catches in her throat. Then he lets it drop. 'You're a little too forward for my taste,' he says, close to her ear. 'I shall have to take you more in hand.'

Alba's high-heels sound coarse, loud, irreverent in the cathedral. She wears them at Kirkwood's behest, with a skirt so tight it pinches her knees together and shows the outline of suspender buttons beneath. She's walking in another's footsteps – she knows it. She feels uneasy.

She'd seen Keith on home ground with his other companion once before. Now, faint shame begins to temper the excitement of holding onto his arm. She looks down, not up, at the architecture. She doesn't want people to look at her, at the face bare of make-up save for the red lips . . . red on bare white, at Keith's behest. She knows the way she's dressed excites him, but she no longer feels comfortable. Something is beginning to slip.

He's objectifying her. It's the lowest form of adoration, but adoration nevertheless. More of Alba, the flesh and blood woman, already the pale vanishing one, disappears. But that's women's lot, isn't it, Alba thinks. We're just pink shop dummies. Onto this plastic form we model clothes, make-up . . . not our own selves. Borrowed people, women. Always stealing, buying-in, allure. Our bottomless fear, not to be wanted for what we are . . . ? *No* . . . not to be wanted for what we daub on, for what we project.

Keith doesn't take Alba into the cathedral by the main door. Instead they enter by the chancel door near the choir. He wants to deny her the full treatment – the floating nave, the shock of it – until later. Until it suits him. He settles her hand on his arm, and falls into a slow promenade. When her heels skid on a brass tomb plate he winces, gives her a sharp irritated glance.

Keith looks about him, but not at the building. He offers a knowledgeable comment every now and then, but his interest is entirely feigned. He's got Alba on his arm, and he's watching people's reaction to her. It buoys him up to think he's responsible for their stares, their disapproval . . . their envy.

'Alba,' he says, nipping her ear with his mouth. 'I hope you're aware of the way people are looking at you – especially men.' Do your temple dance my little white houri, he thinks. Dance on your high-heels. Make them blush. Make them hold their breath.

Next to the altar where Thomas Becket was martyred, Keith stops and pushes Alba forward. She stands on the spot where the Archbishop was murdered.

'I wanted you to see this first,' he says, his face a smirk, a joke. 'It sets the scene for everything else.' He gives her a little shove. 'Becket was praying. Imagine that, Alba. The church was sanctuary. What were those men made of that they could so disregard it, hmmm?'

He comes directly behind her and, without warning, knees her hard in the back of the legs, behind her knees, pushing her down by the shoulders until she kneels on the floor. 'Imagine, Alba,' he says, 'Becket knelt as you do now, and was martyred. How does it feel, Alba?'

Alba's head is bowed. She feels the heat in the building, the fire under the vessel. Her insides start to jump about and quiver. Eyes are upon her, disrobing her, throwing her nakedness into the glass retort where all peer in with their devilish mediaeval eyes, poke at her, laugh at her, watch her limbs melt, her body go to mist, to steam, as she cooks, bakes.

The weight of Kirkwood, the air, the ghosts in the air, the bulk of the cathedral, all bear down on her.

'I want to get up.' She's shaking, in tears.

'How does it feel Alba?'

'Let me get up.'

'How does it feel, eh?'

She clambers to her feet, the heels scraping. She wipes her face with relief. After a pause she says, 'I didn't much care for that,' and her laugh is shivery. 'I felt I was being cracked open, forced open. As if I was a fly trapped inside a piece of amber, and something had nearly broken through.'

Keith laughs at her. 'It's almost tangible, isn't it?' He wipes the hair away from his forehead. 'There, now, Alba.' He draws her to him, presses her body tight against his. 'It's only my silly game,' he says into her hair. 'Don't get upset. There, there.'

'It's incredible,' she says, a shudder going through her. 'I've never felt anything like it. The cathedral near home leaves me stone cold. I always think I'm going to find something there one day, but I never do.'

Her voice becomes pensive. 'Dutch caught a hawk in there once, though. He whistled and it just came. I felt pretty weird then, too.'

Keith holds her away, stares at her, a flush of darkness going over his face and down his body, making him suddenly taut, making his grip on Alba's arms viciously painful. 'Did he? When was that?'

'In the summer some time . . . I think.'

'So you were seeing him again?'

Alba stops. 'No. Not like that, no.'

'So he gave you this marvellous experience, did he? Serenading stray birds. That was, I'm sure, only designed to impress you. The man was a falconer. It was probably one of his own birds.'

Alba looks down briefly. 'He said it wasn't.'

'You believe him?' Keith turns away, derisory sarcasm on his face.

Alba shrugs. 'I didn't know what to make of it.'

'You were too much under his spell,' Keith says shortly. 'You were a fool, Alba. He could show you nothing.'

As he speaks Keith takes her by the hand, and pulls her along through the choir to the small arch in the rood screen. From this tiny covered space she looks out onto the nave.

'What do you think of that?' he says.

The nave is vast . . . The pillars, a forest of stone, grow now! They're growing as she looks up. Giant trees pushing out of the earth, lusting after the sky. There's nothing but huge space here. It has no meaning, it disorients. The sky could end feet away, or go on forever, because the innards are only thin air. Spectacular air. Birth-air. Death-air. Wine-air. It is an alembic for the cooking of the human soul. Alba stands truly awed, forgets the uncomfortable moment with Keith, and leans against him, craning her neck up.

Empty nave. Yet, as she looks, not empty at all, but a mist, a mist that sweeps time past, present and future through it with a broom of breath. She looks into the mist and sees people moving through it: sees the peasant in green, the bishop in red silk, the King and the Joker, the man in the anorak, the woman with her pushchair and bright African bag slung over her shoulder. And they float, they are milled, turned to dust, to motes, to mist. And they dissolve, reform, laugh, shout. Their voices echo, ebb and flow like the tide in a huge cavern. She stands still and witnesses this life, this mist, appear and disappear.

Keith encircles her tightly with his arms, the length of his body pressed against her. But it doesn't stop what happens next.

There is Alba, her breath all gone, not on the earth at all, not feet on the stone cold floor, not numb toes in the pinching high heels, but there! above herself, looking down on them both, swimming in the giant air of the cathedral, with no boundaries at all. Now she feels herself laugh, touch fingers she does not know. It is the flying we have in dreams. She takes a breath, she's not afraid. She can come back in like pulling herself in on a line.

And it's all because Kirkwood is holding on to her. He will not let her go. He knows more than he reveals. He has control over these things.

Keith . . . his grip is the very devil, the brown-eyed devil, the one who keeps us here. She takes a small jittered breath and leans into his warmth, feels their individual heats mate. Without him she would have been so afraid. Without him, she would have been lost. She hears his breathing fast and shallow in her ear. So he has been there before, he has seen this – she knows it – and that is the reason he clasped her so tight, to let her be blown through.

Sex . . . with Keith, oh yes! When that comes, it will be the ultimate. Break the taboo. Yes. Yes. Break the taboo and screw the married headmaster. Laugh at Helen's secret. Laugh at her memory.

She'll have the man she deserves, even if she has to borrow him from his wife. She'll do it before any more empty years pass by. And she'll rub out both conscience and consequences. Oh, yes, this drug, sex, better found *now* than never . . . She'd stay firmly on the ground with Keith *and* she'd be able to let go, too . . . because he would have her thread wrapped firmly around his little finger.

When you experience the significance of something for the first time, it's like you're re-born. Consciousness suddenly comes into the hum-drum, the taken-for-granted, the asleep. At these times, when the lid's blown off your skull, the person you're with becomes the holder of the magic key. We don't like to go back again on our own . . . if we do we'll see merely the monochrome, and leave disappointed, lifeless, full of dismay.

Keith moves round to face her, his eyes like coals, a look of triumph on his face. Here it is – the real unzipper. Even the most unmoved stolid unfeeling individual would catch their breath. He does not know what she has seen. He does not care. All he knows is she was taken over by something immensely powerful . . . and that she will attribute the key to it to *him*.

'You knew that would happen. You've had the same experience yourself, haven't you?' Alba turns to him with wide, glassy eyes.

He smiles, looks down at her. 'Why do you think I brought you here, hmm?'

'What is it? What am I seeing?'

He shrugs. 'It is not for me to say.' A memory shoots in. He bites his words. He has seen that look on her face before: pain, transparency, ecstasy. In the Quiet Room after Dutch had . . . After Dutch had fucked her.

She walks slowly through the arch. 'I've felt something like this before,' she says quietly, more to herself than to him. 'When Dutch caught the hawk.'

And . . . in the Quiet Room . . . ? So *that* was what was going on. She looks up at Keith, thinking he hasn't heard her. But he has. A cold, dismissive stare spears shards into her new openness. She hugs her elbows, draws her arms into her chest, walks nicely on her heels again, follows him blind.

Keith walks away, mute from now on, with a cruel barely-a-pleasure feeling present. He's jerking an unseen lead, feeling her caught, running after him eager-eyed, wanting to please.

On the journey back, the same stop, the same woods, but the cavern sides sheer now, the falling faster . . .

Keith, silent, tense, his dark features pinched, gets out of the car. He lights a cheroot and walks out into the beech trees, looking into the canopy, seeing nothing. He'd had a girl up against one of these trees once, a long time ago. Which tree? Twisting on his heels he looks about, tries to translate the stuff of memory into the perspectives and distance that have changed with time, and now confound him. But he can remember the feeling of her soft body as he pushed her hard against the trunk.

Now these same trees mock him. They've grown so much in the thirty-odd years since that day. He knows the heartwood in the middle of the trunk will be of substantial girth now. It's one of nature's miracles. As tough and unmoving as a concrete core, it can nevertheless sway in a gale with wondrous uncanny flexibility. The heartwood can forget its rigidity, it can bend, stretch, give, survive. All these things it can do. He, Kirkwood, cannot. He cannot even forget the man he sacked. He cannot forget Dutch.

Alba watches him but does not get out of the car. She winds down the window and lets the cool early evening air blow in, faint with the sweet toasted smell of the changing season. Why has Keith been so tardy to take what she offers? Doesn't he want her? She's lost. She cannot begin to understand.

As he disappears into the beeches Alba gets out of the car. She's half-way to the edge of the wood when he suddenly reappears. He walks fast with intent towards her, dashing the cheroot end to earth behind him. She's seen him like this in school on rare occasions, when he's angry, when he's on his way to intimidate a group of troublemakers in the playground. He'll put his head down, bring his shoulders up, grow, fill out the suit, set his brow to charge.

'Give me some breathing space,' he shouts, blood

pumping dark in his face. 'Don't chase after me all the time. I can't have you do that – d'you understand?' Get thee hence, crucifying anima . . .

'I'm sorry— I wasn't—'

'You damn well are.' Her apparent innocence maddens him. He seizes her, pinching her skin, pulling her against his body.

The iron bars of his cage bow under the strain but they do not give. It is as if only his arms can reach through the bars, with hands that futilely grasp the air for sustenance – as prisoners do. It is as if his face is smashed against the small barred jail window, trying to steal the outside world into his humiliating cell life – but he cannot. All that remains is incredible frustration. Intense desire bound back, locked up, rattling the bars of the cage.

And she doesn't move. Here she is, unconditionally open, absorbing all of him at that moment, compelling him by her stillness, by her white body, by the eyes that thirty years ago he would gladly have risked all for, jumped into, and drowned. Loss and shame spin around the tortured axis of himself, crabbing back into his lived life gone, showing him the wrong paths taken, the price of academe, the future that in reality he has absolutely no control over, the future that's already been all wrapped up by his own treacherous hands.

He shakes Alba now, throws her away, pulls her back, squeezes her arms, forces her up till her feet skim the ground. He is the black python wound around her, she the fragile white meat. His mouth hits hers, he tries to draw her in, squeeze-suck through his lips all of her . . . her red mouth, her damn white skin, her form, her essence. His teeth pierce her bottom lip and meet. He tastes her blood, swallows the salt-purifying soul of her.

But she's still there, outside him still. Nothing she can

do will ever let him move through her skin and take up residence inside her. He can't have the white heart. He knows it.

Still gripping her with one hand, he rips the belt from his trousers, doubles it, twists her round, and brings the leather down with force on her skirted buttocks. Her body twists, arches in surprise under his restraining arm. He hears the mewing sound stuck in her throat, but it's not enough. He wants something to show for . . . all . . . this. The woman wears a black skirt: to belt her over that would be like kicking a black cat in the night – you wouldn't see the damage. He wants to see his vengeance wrought clear on her white skin. He wants to sully, he wants to mark her white skin, to laugh at it, to throw purple and red onto its mocking purity.

A few seconds of accelerated frenzy and he has taken hold of her skirt by the hem, and in three powerful jerks ripped it up to the waist. He flicks it aside. Underneath . . . her stockings, the oh-so-milk-white above them, and the underwear, the loose-legged lace . . . With one violent tug he pulls them off, catches her as she loses balance, drags her back.

The belt cuts into her delicate skin, the strokes flay her and . . . melt her. She has a mind that's become the empty sky, full of brightness, of tremor, where thought has ceased. All she knows is when he penetrates her, as he surely must this time, she will be an open kid-soft glove.

And what does Alba feel . . . ? The part of her present does feel, very much. While the other part floats on, looks down with judgement suspended.

She squirms, writhes her hips, tossed by pain. (The floating Alba tut-tuts.) One second: nothing, the huge waiting silent moment. The next: the vast, shrunk, narrowed screaming towards a measured mark that sends accelerated leaps of current jumping from nerve axon to axon. She can swallow up the gaps between blows. Caverns, cathedrals – nothing in them. Empty. Space. Nothingness. A twisted smile floats there. A voice thinly howls – it's wrong this way, it's wrong. But Alba is not her own any more.

Kirkwood lays stripes and bands, belt-wide, across her buttocks. He cares not for the noise, the frap! frap! in the silent woodland. He cares not for the possibility of being seen. He can't stop. There's a whip-handed demon in his fire that has to obliterate the white skin completely, to lay on this bruised red-purple instead, and deny the existence of white in the world.

He looks at the brown belt, the dark olive hands that wield it, and the feminine frailty he assaults, and he could leap in the air and whoop *Whoah! I am! I am!* All the frustration, the twisting angst, all the sense of his thirty-year long self-betrayal, and the reined-in lust comes out now with explosive force. It crackles through the air as his arm descends and rises, over and over.

And then suddenly it catches him. He's taken. Consumed. Split. Torn open, as a convulsion shoots out from his groin and shudders through his body. Gasping now, he doubles up, half falls on her, drops the belt, wrestles with air, grapples with tears.

With a sigh that plummets through him and howls in the empty wood, he turns away, butts his forehead against the cold trunk of the ancient beech, and steadies himself with arms outstretched, fingers mutely gripping the bark. It is finished . . .

Alba, still bent, slowly straightens herself. The torn skirt falls down on snagged stockings. She picks up the knickers and rolls them in a tight twist, clutches them in her hand. She makes a move towards the tree and his crucified form spread out against it, and stops. She does not know what has happened, but he is embraced by a sacred male space she knows she cannot enter. If she touched him now fissures would form and she'd see his large frame disconnect. She'd see him crumple. He will not take her now. She walks back through last year's leaves to the car.

Some time later Keith joins her, takes another cheroot from his jacket and lights it. His fingers are steady.

Alba slides her hand over his leg to his groin, her fingers widen and spread over the fine suiting. They touch the damp obvious patch, and curl back immediately, and she pulls her hand away, disappointment and smallness filling her.

The journey back is quiet. Dark falls. Keith, his jaw set tight, his head craned forward, takes on the road at speed. He stops once, for petrol. Alba changes her skirt. He does not comment, makes no remark about her stiff walk, the overly conscious way she lowers her bottom onto the passenger seat.

By the time they arrive at the school he has distanced himself from her. The old roles are back. Whatever happened was merely a detour. It has no meaning now, no need for remembrance.

Alba sinks into almost-tearful disillusionment as Keith glides into the empty car park and stops next to Alba's little Citroën. He glances across at her then, knows that look on her face, and reaches out to touch her chin, pulling her round to face him.

'What we did,' he says, blinking slowly with the long black lashes, 'I shall never forget. And there will be more . . . I hope?' He runs a finger over the bruise on her lip.

The question hangs in the air like a hook waits to draw the fish from the water. Alba blooms with heat at his touch, his come-back, and at the soft trip in his voice. She lets herself rise up, be netted, caught. More? Yes. This has only been promises.

14

Alba parks the car in front of Helen's garage, and sits for some time in the dark. She waits for the old Alba-face to drop in place – the one she hides behind – but it doesn't. Her skin no longer covers the same workings. Things have changed. In the street lamps' loom the driving mirror reflects a face drained of life. The red gash of her lips is still there but it's faded, lost its gloss. Now it's a wound in unsuccoured flesh, the geisha more ghost than human. She takes a tissue from her handbag, and rubs hard to remove what remains, but the red pigment is tenacious, the dye has sunken in. Her scrubbing makes it worse, smudges it so the red bleeds into the surrounding skin. She's nothing but a made-up corpse.

Lights are on in all the rooms. That's Leon. Lonely, he's fired a beacon against the night. Helen was always miserly – she'd rattle on about the price of electricity as though one forgotten light-switch would see them all in debt. When she was alive the house was always in gloom, the white-painted interior doing nothing to mitigate it.

Now the house is all naked windows, undrawn curtains – not inviting like this, either. Instead it's vaguely sinister, unfamiliar. The house has open eyes – cheap doll's-eyes, eyes with glassy stupidity, lacking all substance, with no-one at home.

She gets out of the car and dumps the case in the wet road. Like her clothes, it still smells of Kirkwood's cheroots. The soft rain falling frees the smokiness from the cloth and from her hair. The smell is not pleasant. It's the smell of the party's over, the return to jaundiced seriousness after the liberating thrill of drink. She trails up the path, ignoring the nets that shiver in the cottage behind her. Let them watch her back. She can shake off their disapproving stares.

The garden hasn't moved all summer. The plants never recovered from their spring butchery. The light from the house shines down now on stunted stems in great rectangular slabs. Like shrouds, she thinks, like shrouds.

Lit thus the house is ghoulish – a candle-lit pumpkin – there's no-one-inside, just nude light warding off witches and the evil outside . . . a whistling in the dark. Cut-out shapes in Jack O'Lanterns make you look over your shoulder . . . but it's only crude chunks cut out of an orange vegetable, picked, mature, rotting imperceptibly . . . mere compost-fodder. Why smile, yet shiver, at such a symbol? Because it says things aren't all right out there. The candlelight does nothing but reveal the hideous grin of the night.

Leon opens the door as Alba searches for her key. The hall light, full on with no shade on the bulb, throws his misshapen body into startlement. He's a small mad clown.

'Christ!' he says, shifting sailor-fashion from one foot to

the other in agitation. 'Things have been happening here. And Christ! What's been happening to you?' He skips about, the ground too hot for his feet to rest on.

Alba pushes past him into the hall. The bare bulb makes everything small, mean, falling inwards. Grimy. She notices cobwebs in the corners of the ceiling, opaque parabolas that must have been there for months.

In some houses you go in, take off your coat, and a lot more of you frees up too. You warm, expand, feel yourself truly inhabit the space, you feel the bright and the best of you surface. There's no expansiveness here at all. Her eyes try to get accustomed to being back, but it takes time to plump up the paltry. It's always been like this whenever Alba has been away on a school trip lasting more than a day. She's come home to taste impoverishment, to feel the building's fabric closing in on her.

Tea chests and furniture lie neatly packed against one wall. There are bright yellow stickers on each item – 'Clive's.'

She drops the case in dismay. 'What's all this?'

'He came back, didn't he,' Leon says, the foot-hopping getting intense. 'He's been packing all the stuff. A removal van is coming the day after tomorrow for it all. He left you a note – here.'

Leon hands her an envelope. It reads, *I've sold the house. You should be pleased. The view clinched it. It was a friend, a cash buyer. Robsons solicitors need your signature Friday.*

'Wonderful.' Alba screws up the note and throws it among the tea chests.

Leon clambers over the furniture, finds it again, unscrews it and pores over the words. 'Are you going to sign?'

Alba shrugs. 'What choice have I got? I'm just too tired to put up much more of a fight. I'll be glad to get out –

even though it couldn't come at a worse time. But I suppose the money will be useful.'

'What's going to happen? Where are you going to go?'

If there was just Alba, her clothes, a few personal items, she'd ask Kirkwood. He'd find her a room in one of the boarding houses, no problem. She could become an assistant house-parent for a while, be paid for it while she thought what to do next. Be nearer to Keith . . . But here is a house full of effects, and half of it belongs to her. She inspects Clive's cache more closely. Some of her possessions have been secreted amongst them. The silver-backed hairbrush has been hidden underneath carefully wrapped Japanese pots. No doubt there'll be more thievery. She goes upstairs. Sure enough, the few antiques and the finer pieces of furniture have spawned a rash of labels. Clive's been taking liberties while she was away.

'Leon!' she yells, finding her voice, the tiredness going.

He comes in after her, follows her from room to room. Paintings have been taken off the walls, leaving rectangles of a cleaner white behind. Drawers which contained collections of Helen's miscellaneous bits and pieces make too much din when they're opened – items are missing, and those that are left no longer fill the drawers, they have been spaced out one from another to make it look like nothing has been removed. But the shrunken contents shake and rattle when the drawers are opened. Dried bones clatter only in chests that are too big for them.

'He's not going to do this,' she says, banging her fist on Helen's dressing table, making an imprint in the dust. 'He's not going to take all he wants and leave me with the rubbish. We're going to move what I want out of here tomorrow. That gives us a whole day before he comes back. Damn his bloody stickers.'

'Where are you going to go?'

'That's not such a problem.'

'Aye, but where?'

Alba goes to the windows, looks out into the impenetrable dark. 'I've got a friend.' She looks down.

Dutch – a friend? Is he? Will he be . . . ?

'He's away at the moment. We can dump all the furniture and bits there, and then decide what to do with it later.'

'You'll need help, then,' Leon says, rubbing his rough hands together.

Late into the night Alba unpacks the tea chests in the hall, takes what she wants, and makes a little triumphant pile behind her. Leon sits cross-legged next to her, unwrapping what Clive has carefully parcelled, passing things to her, rewrapping and putting the discarded items back, padding the empty spaces in Clive's boxes with crumpled newspapers.

'How was the trip?'

'The trip?'

'Canterbury wasn't it? With the headmaster.'

'Oh . . . it was quite boring. Just a conference. A lot of talk, note-taking, that sort of thing.'

'Did anything happen?'

'What do you mean – happen? What could possibly happen? Nothing happens at these affairs. It's work. Work.'

Leon cocks his head on one side, a goblin, inquisitive, out of turn. 'Something did,' he says, smugly. 'There's less of you now than went away.'

Alba's laugh is loud, sharp, derisory. 'Ever heard of tiredness, philosopher?' she says.

Friday . . . The weather is mild, the rain holds off. Alba phones school, says she's sick. Kirkwood will know she's lying, but he won't want to see her anyway. He'll need the distance too. Like her, he'll need a few days to stitch a new mask in place.

She hires a van, and fills it with whatever she and Leon can move. A neighbour helps them with the larger pieces down the steep garden path.

She takes things she doesn't want. It's crazy, a compulsion, a blind desperation. Clive mustn't get it all. These things, they're Helen's affections that are being apportioned out. Whoever takes more, gets the lion's share of her. She drives Leon on in a panic – Clive might change his mind, come today. Leon might have heard it all wrong. She can't take any risks.

Dutch's cottage . . . The van bounces along the single-track road. The sodden peat beneath heaves like the sea under the weight of the over-laden van, and with Alba's uneven driving. So they're driving on water, it's only feet below.

The cottage comes into view as the land pans out flat. It's then that the impulsiveness of what she's doing hits her. But now there's no going back. She's stuck with a load of expensive junk. And she wants it. It's Helen's caress, her approval, her bestowed grace that her daughter is a worthy individual after all. But as she draws up outside the house, the madness falls away. A hollow self-ridicule takes its place.

'This is daft,' she says. 'I can't bring all this stuff here.'

Leon doesn't answer. He winds down the window and puts his head out to listen, to smell the air. There's a hazy mist – hard to tell if it rises from the fields, or hangs from the sky. It's very soft, very still. There's more life caught up in it than air can ever hold.

'Who is this bloke?'

'Dutch? A friend.'

'What kind of friend?'

Alba gets out, slams the door. She puts the key in the

lock, her jaw tight against his probing, against her having to look . . .

Leon walks in, thumbs in his belt loops, a swagger of admiration immediately evident in his walk. He turns to Alba. 'It's like a church in here,' he says. 'Would you believe it.'

Alba bristles. What rubbish the Idiot, the Joker, speaks. She snorts, moves away from him. Her face begins to fill up. Tears begin. She grinds them into her cheeks with an angry scour of her hand.

Leon looks about him with irritating awe. He looks at the ceiling, the walls, the Nain rugs hanging there, and the jesses and thin leather leashes behind the back door, as if it is all special, highly significant. 'Who is this friend of yours?' he says. 'He's quite a guy, isn't he?'

Alba watches Leon thinly. He's walked into a cave of jewels, like a deformed Aladdin come home. He knows what's here – instantly. He knows there's something here for him . . . She wishes she hadn't brought him. The delight on his sweaty red glistening face makes her feel small and ashamed. She's the one who's missed the obvious, whatever that is.

On the table one large pot of irises grow strongly, although the soil is as dry as desert sand. Alba, Leon, notice them at the same moment. Alba recoils, Leon almost jumps.

'What the hell are these?' He picks up the pot, turns it, looks closely at the backs of the strange leaves.

'I don't know.'

'Look at them—' He goes into the lean-to greenhouse and finds more pots in a similar stage of growth. 'I've never seen anything like it. The leaves are black – look here, Alba, underneath. On a copper beech, the tops are dark but underneath has to be green, so the tree can photo-syn-the-size—' he stumbles over the word. 'You've got to have some green in the leaf . . .' He rubs the surface of one with his thumbnail. 'Jesus – black all the way through.'

He comes back into the living room, picks up the one pot on the table, and hands it to Alba. She hesitates, then shoves it away in the dark of a cupboard under the sink. She can't go into the lean-to, to the strange black forest. There's import there for her, she feels it, but what it is she doesn't know. It's one of Dutch's meddlings . . . another one of his hawk-whistlings, his playing-about and denying he's doing anything out of the ordinary. 'Must be a freak,' she says, 'freak of nature.'

Leon shoots her an intense look. 'Like you and I, you mean?' he says slowly.

Mouth open, Alba turns to look at him, and rage rises in her like a black tide. Freak! Her? – How dare he! *She* is no freak. She's not black or twisted, she's . . . It's Leon who's out of synch with nature. Not her, not Alba.

She lunges towards him and clouts him hard across the face – the air between them suddenly red.

Leon claps his hand to his face, branded. Horror pushes out from every inch. He presses fingertips into his cheek-bones, trying to dam what is building up behind.

And then he's gone, he's flipped. He tosses in the air like a high-jumper, his limbs caught in an up-draft, no sense there, no grounding, all flung-up. He catches his skull between his hands, tries to squeeze it all back, but it doesn't work. Like a closed vessel coming to the boil, steam underneath pushes aggressively against the container, looking for the thin hairline crack. The unseen hands that perennially hover over him, waiting for their chance, pull him off the ground, smack his rear, toss him, let him fall on the floor. He lies gibbering, his eyes white, the pupils, the soul gone elsewhere . . . the face stretched so ugly she could kick it.

'You little bastard!' she screams, flinging her arms up, out, drawing in all the currents in the air to party with her anger. 'You bastard! How dare you put me through this! I don't know how to cope!' Other hands touch hers now, the malicious clown-hands that threw him up, and alien energy courses through her.

'You're a leper. Filth. The ugliest thing I've ever seen. You should have been put down at birth. I'd have suffocated you. I'd have stamped on your face. I'd have made sure no-one would have had to look at you and then have to look away. Oh, yes, I'd have mashed up your fat lips, dropped coals in your eyes, buried you alive, danced on your grave. You're all that stinks, crawls, and can't swim. The left-handed one, the club-foot idiot, the one thrown around the village, scorned. No-one wants you. No-one wants the deformed. What use are you? No bloody use. No bloody use at all. What do you do? Nothing but steal our air, steal our food. You take, and give nothing in return.'

Leon lies curled on the floor, grins rictus up at her. The demon is well in place. Alba rages at it, with it.

The fit goes on and on. Alba, her face a horrible red, snatches a blurred shaving mirror from the table, bends and shoves it in front of his face. 'Look at what you are,' she spits. She gets up, kicks him hard in his jerking thigh, cries out wild, slashes the air with her fingers then as everything falls, falls . . . falls down like a waterfall – cleaning, driving all to earth.

Words choke in her throat. Through tears, through tenderness, she kneels, runs her hand through his sparse red sweaty hair. 'Get up,' she says in a voice that sounds strange to her. 'I'm sorry . . . I . . . I . . . I need you, Leon.'

The room catches its breath.

In that moment Leon stops his hyena grin, ceases his jerking. He sits up, as if he's just been poked from sleep by intruders in the house . . . they've been stealing things, walking away with the goods. His face has none of its usual dragging pallor, bemusement, drunkenness. Instead, he's clear, in wonder, chirpy, at peace. He looks straight into Alba's eyes, at the tears now blotching her face. 'God,' he says, touching her with embarrassing reverence.

Alba throws her hands over her face. 'What have I done? What have I said?' she says, over and over.

Leon gets up briskly, as though the fit never happened. He laughs, touches Alba on the head, goes into the kitchen, takes the bottle of pills from his pocket and tips them down the sink.

Alba rushes after him. 'You can't do that. Are you mad?'

'We'll see, shan't we,' he says, singing to himself.

Alba leaves him poking tablets down the plughole, goes back to the living room, and sits down with a thump on the sofa. She looks up, looks around. The air is cautiously moving. The room is full of applause.

In silence Alba and Leon empty the van. Leon's silence is a dance. Alba's, one of deep troubled confused introspection.

They store the larger pieces of furniture in Dutch's sparse living room. Immediately it looks all wrong. No amount of rearranging will make them blend. The smaller items, together with Helen's few antiques, go upstairs in the spare room. Dutch's bedroom door stays shut. Alba goes up and down the stairs, goes in and out of the other room, but she can't touch that door, can't open it. She's invading the house, making waves in the ether. That's bad enough. The room where he slept, where they slept, mustn't be disturbed.

All day the van takes from Helen's house, and gives the unwanted, the fought-over, the shameless, to Dutch. Alba's feelings of misgiving are strong, but she can't reverse what they've done. Once you're on course you're caught up in the falling, falling . . .

If he came back now, Alba thinks, it would be the very end of her and Dutch. The thread would be cut, the flayed ends would wave like tentacles trying to grasp the ocean.

Alba's signed the documents, taken all she wants from the house, and left Clive with a vacuum to fill with his fury. And he will be mad when he comes to collect what he thinks is his. He'll find Alba and Leon gone, the key posted through the letterbox. No need for a note – he'll know what has happened. He'll be left with the shabby bin-ends, the kitchen to clear, the pale marks on the carpet where the furniture he'd wanted once stood.

'Where are we going to stay?' Leon asks, alarmed, as Alba shuts Helen's front door for the last time.

'Where d'you think?'

He coughs. 'Won't he mind, this friend of yours?'

'He said I could use the cottage while he was away.'

'But . . . like this?'

'It'll only be for a few days, won't it?'

'What about . . . me?'

'. . . You can stay too, if you want. He won't mind. Or you can go.'

'I'll stay, then.'

Dutch's house can't digest Helen's furniture. When they unload for the last time, Alba walks around, wringing her hands. She's a traitor. What would she do if he came back now . . . found this . . . She goes upstairs, trembles outside Dutch's bedroom, finally going in. Shutting the door quietly behind her, she reaches out, touches the edge of the bed, then slides her hand towards the middle, her body following.

The bedcovers are pulled back just as he left them when he went away. She sinks down on the bed, her face seeking the smell of him, but the smell is too old, too musty, faint.

Evening . . . Leon proudly makes sandwiches – the only food he can prepare – and goes upstairs, knocks on the bedroom door, tiptoes in when there's no response.

Alba is asleep on the bed, curled up, her fingers clutching the pillow and the slack of the sheet. He looks at her for a long while, then puts the plate down on the dresser and goes out.

That night the moon falls through the window onto Alba like pieces of milk-white paper all over the bed, over her pale face, sweeping over the white hair. It knows its own.

By Monday morning Alba's head is full with Kirkwood. She'd managed to keep him out over the weekend. There was the move, the cleaning, the rearranging. Anyway, Canterbury is a fantasy. It can't be real, not her – Alba – having an affair with the headmaster. It's not credible. You want someone too much, so you go into your own private other world about it. Real life gets pushed aside. Then the unreal takes over.

At times like these you can lose your conscience – anything's possible. There are no mistakes, no right-doings either. You're in the watery spin of Charybdis – you're part of the world, yet definitely not of it. Canterbury – that must be the other world.

As she dresses for school the thought of seeing Keith again, of smelling him, touching him . . . whips her blood into a froth. When she drives to school it's bubbling within, it's crazy, immolative. The addiction, all the sick longing of it, heats her up, makes her eyes bright, her movements

conscious, sinuous, especially for him. Skilfully she edits out
the scene in the woods on the journey back . . .

'Are you better now?' Keith comes into Alba's classroom
within minutes of her arrival. He startles her.

'Oh . . . yes,' she says, her voice a high breathy note.

'Is anything wrong?' He comes towards her, weaving
through a row of desks, lining up level the legs of all the
tucked-in chairs as he passes. To begin with he does not
look at her, while the air between them shifts, grows
accustomed to this meeting, the first since Canterbury. He's
been editing, too, but having more trouble with it.

'No. Nothing's wrong.'

'You can tell me, you know.' He looks up, pauses at the
front row, unnecessarily adjusting the lie of his shirt cuffs.

'I've moved out,' Alba says, and goes on to tell him about
the weekend, being careful not to say where she is now
staying. As she talks he walks behind her, brushes loose hair
back from her face, gathering it back in his hands. When
he bends, his mouth is at her ear. The cologne floods over
her as his smooth cheek touches hers.

'I've wanted you,' he says, cutting in to her irrelevant
chatter. 'All weekend I've thought of nothing else.'

Alba's chest caves in. She turns her head, feels his hot
fragrant skin on her cheek, and reaches out to clutch his
hand. He withdraws.

'Maria's come back from her mother's. So I'm afraid
things aren't going to be easy . . . for us.' He walks around
her, lifting the folds of her pleated skirt, inspecting her,
before allowing the cloth to fall back into place. 'But . . .
I'll think of something.' The winsome smile, the long, long
lashes, work on Alba. He looks at his watch, raises his
eyebrows, holds her there, tight, fast. 'I must be off.'

Alba can say or do nothing. She stares, netted again. How

his darkness glistens this morning, how it fascinates her. It's like the pristine beauty of a new slick of oil. Black, smooth, the flow of it . . . ah! . . . the sun runs over to slide across its surface, to be sucked, drawn down, smothered. Alba knows what entanglement with the stuff is like, she's not stupid. It spreads out everywhere, poisons seas, seeps through stone, taints skin. But at the same time it's a wrap, a black cape. She wants to lie in it, and crave its warm oiliness around her.

She watches his smile – a cut in the black, the contrast like her body against his, her psyche against his. And it is this contrast she must have.

What is a neutral? That won't move her, Alba. What is a beige, a taupe? A sensible colour that's been neutered. No juice there. As dead as a bank of sand. A wall of conformity, hankering after nothing, too boring, too bored to move. Mediocrity makes it content. It doesn't reach for the moon. It doesn't have that hunger.

White hungers now. White, coming right out of the closet, walking through ranks of mocking colour. It's white's turn now. Alba's turn.

White's always been shut in the dolly-box, it stayed sweet wearing a pinny. It stayed at home, the dutiful innocent white daughter, it never got its hands dirty, never went on the rut or the rampage, never went out to devour and plunder. It had flabby teeth that wouldn't, daren't, bite. It fell all over itself in its efforts to accommodate.

Now, white Alba has white hunger. The vessel froths over, the veils of white spill, crawl, along the floor. She needs black. She wants black. She'll eat iron-earth if she has to, to get it. She needs to feel its shape, its form, its taint. Its way of loving. Kirkwood.

'Keith – I want you too,' she blurts.

He's on his way out of the classroom. He stops, turns,

and comes back to her, lifts her from the desk, edges her into the tiny stockroom. There he flicks up her skirt, thrusts his hand up between her thighs, into the wet waiting centre, jabs his fingers up – a movement so sharp it is a stab – withdraws, and lets her skirt drop. Fingers and thumb rub together . . . he watches her white essence vanish into his pores. He smells, draws in deep, slips his fingers into his mouth, tastes her on his tongue. 'Yes . . . You do want me,' he says, 'don't you.'

And then there's noise outside the classroom. He nips out of the small room, his large body suddenly disorganized, jerky, limbs with a will of their own, the softness inside them having to harden – not wanting to. Pacing the room fast, he runs his hands through his thick black hair, as the mask stitches back in place.

'I must go.' He looks at her from behind shutters, the iris small, dark, intensified by frustration. He'd like to be able to take the kind of risk Dutch had done with Alba a year ago. Imagine – the headmaster secretly fucking on school premises, and getting away with it, every time. Yes, he'd like to do it now, with the noise of staff cars filling the car park on the other side of the hedge outside Alba's classroom windows. He'd push her against the books in the stockroom – books innocent hands would soon be using later in the day – and fuck her very, very slowly as colleagues talk and pass by. And . . . leave the door wide open . . . How would the white one deal with that . . . ?

Bitterly he knows he cannot do it. And Alba, she shouldn't make him want her the way he does. She demands too much. There are no half measures with her. She'll drag him into ruin. He undoes the jacket, digs at the knot in his tie. There's nowhere to run. He jerks the classroom door open, and shuts it with a bang behind him.

* * *

Fake lenses, tinted glasses, not even these can hide Alba's feelings now. She sees Keith, and her thighs crumple, the skin there crawls wet. She has to turn away, look at the sky, pay attention to children's chatter, try not to focus on him. They pass in school, and the breath from her lungs slams out. She's drowning, going under. She wants him between her thighs, pumping her full of darkness. She wants to feel the black seed of him arrow up through her body, make her utter black words.

And he too is boiling, spilling over, the sweat from him now like a tracer in the air as he goes about the daily business of school. He cannot have her? – what lack of judgement ever thought such a thing! Of course he can have her. He is the headmaster. He has courted power, tossed it about all his life. He is the man who can have cake . . . and cake.

Lust stamps out reason. Seeing her in school is like watching a white flag of surrender. But he can't go and claim her, take her over. He can't have her yet. And he's never had to wait before. He's not used to it now.

But the edge drives him on. He walks the sweet-sour blade, alive as never before, sharper, more acute. Challenges he has avoided, he now snaps up. School runs at an up-thrust pace. He has a raw energy that dismisses diplomacy, pushes him on, ignoring the chafe and grate he's causing among his staff. It's all in order to avoid her, to use up the restless force. To avoid her.

Whiteness shines in his face like a scrubbed-out sun. It gets worse, more intense, every day. He wants to pounce on her, rip, shred her, flay the tormenting skin, find his own whiteness beneath, his homecoming, his heart.

What about his career? It means so much to him. It means all to him, or so he would have had it, before Alba danced up out of the mist in front of his eyes. Now it's worthless, a wasted life, a prison built by his own hands.

In groups of four or five, Alba's last class of the day sits on Keith's private lawn outside his office. They look at the cedars in silence. It's a poetry class. Alba has already asked Keith if he would mind her taking the class outside his study windows. He didn't mind. How could he mind – every glimpse of her is a little bit of food.

The little groups stare, look at the sky, scribble, erase, and slowly commit their tree sonnets to their exercise books. The afternoon is warm, languorous, probably the last one before summer fades out. Alba feels it's so. She wants to taste it, wants the children to taste the poignancy of passage, of transition. Weep a little.

Dutch got them weeping. He knew how to open their hearts to pour poetry onto paper. He never taught it – he'd ask the children to move into that other land inside themselves, and he'd go there too. No me:them, no teacher:pupil. He'd drawn them a mapless ocean where he and they mingled, lost their form and structure. He showed them the way. Some still mourned his loss.

Keith goes to close the French windows soon after the class arrives, but changes his mind when he sees Alba. Instead he loiters in the doorway to watch her move among her pupils. Some of the girls are aware of Keith behind them. Dr Kirkwood has always been a lover in their innocent fantasies. They flick back their puberty-silk hair, and ply him with shy smiles. His face remains taut, the emotions passing over like clouds.

After a while he goes back to his desk, but turns the swivel-chair sideways, puts his feet up, and continues studying her from this position. He lights one cheroot, then another, filling the hole inside him with smoke. Instead of that empty cavern she should be there, curled up, for ever inside him, feeding his soul. He'll knit her into his psyche – one stitch a white-word, an Alba-word, the next one dark and masculine. One breath of perfume, one of after-shave. Soon, with practice, there won't be a join. She'll move with him, in him, like a white hand forced to follow the every move of a black glove.

Alba's long thin cotton skirt flaps gently against her pale legs. She's wearing stockings underneath, he knows that, and his eyes squint through the cheroot smoke, trying to make out the transition from soft grey to white at thigh height.

He puts his hand over his eyes. It hurts to look at her, to want her. She dresses modestly, she always has – apart from the flurry in Canterbury which so thrilled him. But now the subtlety has crept back, her make-up has returned to its schoolmarm delicacy. This veiling maddens him. She's scared, she's slipping, waiting, watching it fall away from her. She's trying to walk away while she can. He's going to lose her if he doesn't do something fast.

'Miss Farson?' he calls from his desk in the dim room.

Alba's at the bottom of the lawn where it slopes into the shrubbery. She looks up at his call, strolls through the quiet children, and stops outside the open doors, her way led by the smell of cheroot smoke.

'Can you spare a minute, Miss Farson?'

'Of course.'

'Your class are exceptionally well behaved.'

'They're always a good class.'

'Good. Excellent. Come in. I'd like a quick word.'

She walks smoothly past him, sits down on the proffered chair. Keith glances back at the children on the lawn. Not a sound. Not a murmur. Ah! – little innocents. Clasping his hands in front of him he looks at her, his expression serious, heavy, sensual. Blue flat eyes look back at him evenly, hiding feelings. He wants what is behind them.

'What are they writing about?'

'Trees . . . the cedars.' Alba puts her hand to her hair, smooths the pony-tail back from her shoulders. 'It's a legacy from Dutch . . .' she pauses, seeing his eyes flare. 'One of the good things he initiated, I suppose. And he certainly knew his poetry.'

'Dutch . . .' Kirkwood shoots back in the chair, and it rucks noisily over the carpet. His words come out with spitting contempt. 'The Poet. The man who wanted to be Yeats. Oh yes, I remember him well . . .'

Alba smiles, puts her head on one side. 'I hate to say this, but I think Dutch had quite a good measure of Yeats. I listened in to one of his classes. It was actually very good. Taught me a few things.'

'You're a bitch, Alba.'

Alba's voice dies.

'A bitch.' He says it slow, with relish, in a way that could make her do crazy things.

'I am?' she says simply, while her pulses jump and flutter.

Keith swivels in the chair, looks calmly over his shoulder at the intense concentration of the children on his lawn. Little innocents . . .

'You know Dutch will never get another job in education, don't you?'

Alba cocks her head on one side. 'Well, you sacked him after he . . .'

Keith smiles, widens his fingers into a span, and laces them together with step-by-step care. 'I took it upon myself to tell the police – not about you and him, but about my doubt around him . . . and the children,' he lies to her. 'That, my dear, is why he left you in the lurch so suddenly.'

Alba sits up. 'That can't be true,' she says, her anger up. 'He went months after you'd sacked him. You would have told the police straight away . . . Why are you telling me these lies?'

Keith leans towards her. His eyes pierce hers, his voice is low, bottomed out. 'I needed to be quite sure,' he says with a smirk. 'And . . . I'm a man who can wait a long time for the right moment. That moment came when I wanted him out of the way. He always had too much influence on you, Alba.'

'So you told a lie to get him into trouble. You saved it up.' She looks down. 'You knew he hadn't done anything wrong.'

'You'd been seeing him over the spring and summer. I watched you. It didn't take much to guess . . . I wanted him gone.' He lights another cheroot. The slight current of air through the open door blows the smoke in her face. 'Does that shock you?'

Does it shock her? If what Keith says had any truth in it then, yes, she's shocked — and something else. Keith had done this deed for her . . . it's shameful, but she's flattered.

'How does it make you feel, Alba, that I'm jeopardizing my whole career — over you.'

There is a long silence. Keith breaks it. 'I am,' he says, grimly. 'God only knows why, but I am.'

He mashes the cheroot in the ashtray and opens the middle drawer of the desk, taking out a small mirror on a stand, a silver brush, a lipstick. He edges them across the desktop to her. Without taking his eyes from her face he jabs the intercom to his secretary. 'No interruptions, please,' he says, and clicks off.

'You know, I loved the way you painted your mouth

before,' he says with a sly plead. 'Do it again. It turns me on.'

She's wriggling on the line – but she's still hooked, she's still jumping in the net. It's comfortable because there's a boundary. What does it matter if she can't breathe? Picking up the mirror she angles it, loads the brush with the new lipstick, one he has bought specially for her. Red, of course.

'Don't take any notice of the kids. They won't come in.'

'They might. Your secretary might . . . anyone could. Just what would they think?'

'I like the fact you're worried.' His laugh cracks. 'It makes this all the more exciting,' he says. 'Now, bloody do it.'

Before we break free, we have to carry out that last sin. It's almost a homage, an acknowledgement that sin demands. The boy tells of his stealing, says he will do it no more, and then he goes straight back to the shop for the final thievery, the last goodbye. The adulterer tells his wife the affair is over. He goes back to the other woman, intends to cut her off, to say that's it, we're finished you understand . . . and they screw, the best ever, one last time, for old times' sake. The final sad goodbye. Sin has a little fun in it. We hate to let it go.

Alba paints her mouth with Keith's choice of lipstick. She does it the best she can. The best ever. Her feelings . . . they've flown out of the window and gossip round the child-poets under the trees.

Keith sits close up to the desk, his hands in his lap, his face alight, his eyes full up. 'You're a bitch, Alba,' he says in short breaths. 'A cunt. I bet you've got a nice cunt, haven't you? I bet Dutch liked it. I bet he *used* it a lot. He liked to suck you dry, didn't he – remember, I saw you – in the

Quiet Room. What did you do, cream his mouth when he brought you off, eh? Make yourself all slippery for his dick, eh?

'I want to see your cunt, Alba. I want to see those white hairs – yes, they will be white, won't they . . .'

Children get up on the lawn, move about. Alba panics, the brush slips, the red goes awry.

'Ignore them,' Keith hisses.

'I . . .'

'Shut up. Keep going. That's it . . . good girl. God, you're just so-o beautiful when you do that. I want you to put some of that stuff on your cunt – not now, you silly bitch – later. Make it all red. Make it all greasy there.

'Tell me about your cunt, Alba. It's not white, is it? It's not innocent, oh-no, *fuck* that,' he laughs coarsely now. 'It's just a hole, isn't it? Dark on the inside. You're as dark as everyone else . . .'

Alba lowers the brush, sees the final jerk of his arm in his lap, watches his face cave in, and then she sees the small white shower of his semen land on the green leather of the desktop. White feebly aiming for white. Wanting to join, to reach her, to touch base . . . Never making it.

She gets up abruptly. Her insides lurch. 'How could you do that?' she says, genuinely shocked. 'There are children . . .' her voice rises. 'Children – oh, my God.' And she rushes past him out of the office onto the lawn, banging the windows shut after her.

The children look up, their mouths open, innocent curiosity on their faces. The bell rings for the end of lessons. She sighs with relief, dismisses the class. They file away, walk past Keith's windows quietly. Alba shoos them on, stands in front of the glass, her arms spread wide.

Minutes later she's in her car, the engine revving, her hands tense on the wheel. As she pulls out of school she notices Keith's grey BMW come out after her. She puts her foot down. She wants no more of the man. She keeps going, doesn't look back.

She drives too fast along the narrow peat-moor roads, needing every bit of concentration to avoid leaving the single track and going off into the rhyne. A fitting end, she thinks darkly.

At the sight of Dutch's cottage she cries out loud with relief. Sanctuary! Yes – sanctuary! Hasn't it always been so?

Pulling up, she rushes out, unlocks the front door, and throws herself into Dutch's living room. It never felt like this in any cathedral. Here the warmth, the acceptance, comes to greet her. Unseen fingers smooth her hair, brush her cheek, comfort her. She shouts for Leon . . . Silence. He's gone out.

Keith's car pulls up, flinging gravel to the sides of the road. She hears the quick snap of his shoes on the tarmac. He doesn't hesitate. The door opens and he stalks into the room. Air screams, the unseen dive for cover and tremble. He is trying to damp down, put the fire out . . .

'So . . . you're back here again,' he says.

Alba doesn't move, but steadies herself with one hand on the table. 'I don't live here,' she shouts defensively. 'I've got nowhere else to go. I'm just staying here. Dutch isn't here with me.'

'Is he not.' Kirkwood wrenches his tie undone. 'Is he not.' Shirt buttons fly across the room. He whips the tie from the collar, and drops it on a chair. He walks about, picking up vases, fingering the silk rugs on the walls, seeing it all, seeing nothing, breathing in short bursts through his mouth as if the room holds a smell he cannot stand.

'I came after you because I wanted to explain,' he says, not looking at her, his eyes taken up with seeking out all the objects that belong to Dutch. 'I wanted to say I couldn't help what I did. Things just got out of control.' He turns to her. 'Don't look at me that way, Alba. You mustn't – d'you hear me? You mustn't look at me with that disgust on your face.' His voice grows louder, trying to drown Dutch out, trying to appease the white goddess who's turning so nasty, who's darkening in front of his eyes.

Alba sways against the table, but doesn't move. The old abused rosewood puts its size between them. She doesn't speak.

Keith's eyes skate over the clutter on the table top. Her things . . . and *his* things . . . the trivia of living, the fluff of their lives rubbing easy shoulders, mingling like twin bloods.

'Did he fuck you on this table?' He steps forward. 'Did he? I have to know.' Filling in the white silence, he goes on, 'He did, didn't he? It's the sort of thing he'd do. Don't tell me. I know.'

'Keith . . . will you go . . . it doesn't help.'

'Give me a minute,' he says, turning his back to her.

A long silence. Alba moves away from the table to the open front door. If she can just get him out . . .

To her shock he swings round, grabs her upper arm. 'What the hell am I doing? Tell me, Alba.' His hands go to her shoulders, to her neck, curling around the white stalk, nearly squeezing, but not quite. Repeatedly he skims it, a farewell to the soft white skin invested with so much mystery. One hand slides down her arm and off.

Alba hisses.

He interprets the sound as mockery. He slaps her face hard, and her skin immediately reddens. The goddess must not judge him anymore.

'Was that not enough for you back there in school?' he says, very low, very quiet.

Alba twists free. 'Enough? You can't be serious. I hardly figured, did I? You might as well have had a magazine and masturbated over that,' she spits, her hand cradling the slapped cheek.

'I do. Often. That's what I do in my study when I'm alone. Shocks you, eh? Disgusts you.'

Alba looks down, brash in her mouth. She need say nothing in response.

'I do not have a sex life,' he says with bitter levity. 'Maria is not interested. But you . . . you want more from me . . . yes?'

'No. I don't. I want you to go.'

He nods. 'Of course. There has to be an end to this humiliating little dance, doesn't there.' He picks up the tie from the chair. 'But just one thing . . . Show me his room, Alba. The one where you and he slept together. Where he . . . where he screwed you. I . . . I have to see it to lay the ghost of you. It's the only way I can let you go.'

He's hustling her to the bottom of the stairs, pushing her on up ahead of him. His fingers on her arm again . . . too strong . . . a grip to squeeze water from stone, unnecessary, hard, the man who thinks only force controls . . . Yes, it zips through now, the first time she'd felt that grip. The week before summer term end . . . he'd seized her as she tripped under the cedars. He'd written on her skin a message she *wouldn't*, daren't understand. Now, the ghost of those fingerprints throb. It's the reckoning now, she feels it coming. Her fate . . . ? Surely not her fate . . . ?

They stop at the top of the stairs. The small square landing claustrophobic.

'Which room is his, Alba? Which one? Can I guess? I think I can.'

Alba gives Dutch's door the betraying look and he catches

it. Seconds drip . . . He throws himself against the door with unwarranted force, and it smashes open. 'So this is where you do it?' he says, shoving her inside. 'So this was your room.'

It's the slow calculation she'll never forget. No, years will pass, she'll never forget. There's no animal frenzy, but he's out of the cage all the same, no longer the civilized guardian of young souls . . .

'I want you to be quiet.'

Yes. Sir.

Quiet . . . You can't even hear the wind. This construct of silence around them, and him operating within it. His face – Helen's studious bridge face, the mind crafting out ahead its series of planned steps, concentrating, communing with himself.

Reaching down, Keith picks up the hem of Alba's long dress, and works from the bottom to the top, popping tiny mother-of-pearl buttons from the buttonholes, each move costed out, each step anticipated ahead. His breathing slow, under control, like a mantra. Every moment animal frenzy is born in his loins, and it bodily shakes him in its struggles to be released, but every moment he reins it in, holds it steady. Fire wrapped in water, neither consuming nor being drowned.

Alba react . . . ? She can't. There's almost nothing to react to. Where is the violence, the brutal taking? It doesn't exist in this silence. He's made another world in this room – his world. Here he is master. The script of the struggling outraged snarling woman, fighting for her chastity, is locked away in her box of shoulds. Rape? It can't be that. It's never like this, is it? Rape's something to resist. But women don't. Not wise to resist. Might get hurt. But what is worse? Guilt because you can do nothing, or scars? And silence . . . silence is seen as acquiescence, always . . . it's never viewed as a secret force, a clever weapon. It has no shout for that.

He works on, undressing her, neatly folding her clothes, draping them over the back of the chair. She looks into his eyes. A passionless hell awaits her behind the dark pupils. And she can look into them. She finds herself studying them, and finds no sign he's aware of the contact. She's looking into the eyes of a driven sleepwalker. He just carries on. The silence he's created is charmed.

When he has her naked, he steps back, blinking. Automatic fingers go to his neck to undo the tie which isn't there, which hangs out of his jacket pocket instead. He takes off his jacket and trousers, drapes them carefully over Alba's clothes. His eyes feed on her peculiar skin, study her with a frown of fascination. The shrug and slip of her shoulder, and the attempt to cross one leg in front of the other, remind him of Botticelli's Venus. Yes, she's just an artist's creation. His creation. She isn't real.

'Lie back on the bed. *His* bed . . .' He laughs then, the sound hurting the quiet.

On top of her, smothering her, his fingers snatch between her legs to open her. And she lies there, in the sunken middle of the bed where she used to roll with Dutch . . .

Deep down she entertains the get-out clause. So, this might not be how she wanted it to be, but maybe now, here in its throes, she can change, she can make herself *want* what he's doing to her. Make it not rape, but her choice. That way it'll be easier to get over.

But this isn't sex.

He's inside her. He barely moves. His thumb and middle finger explore all her flesh within reach. Up and down in methodical lines he goes, pinching her skin hard, hard enough for it to immediately bruise, colour, erase the white. Neat rows of butterfly-shaped bruises stain her arms. And he's covering her with them while he fucks her, ice cold, ever so slowly, in an arrested canter. His penis grinds against her insides like a knife sharpening itself on a whetstone. And she is dry, dry. Dry! No amount of willing can persuade her body that she wants . . . this . . .

He rears up now, looks down at the bruised handiwork on her breasts. He's urging himself to orgasm, face pained, sweated – but it won't come. Black hair flops over his forehead. Flinging it back, he sends drops of sweat over her face. Then his eyes look into hers almost pleading her for the key of release.

'Take out those bloody lenses,' he says, panting close to her face. 'I want to fuck *you*, not two bits of blue plastic. I want to look into you, right in . . .'

Alba goes very still. There's a marshalling in the room, a sound like birds rising from trees in a rush. Then, a whispering in her ear – you cannot give this away . . . don't do it . . . don't . . . do . . . it . . . don't . . . She listens to the voices, knows now, and her mind snaps back. Keith's eyes . . . the brown-eyed devil indeed. The one who keeps us here. She's on line to lose her soul . . .

'It'll take a few minutes to take them out. I'll have to go downstairs to the bathroom.' She holds her breath. The body is a mirage. Save the soul.

But Keith won't let her go. He insists she does it here – he's spotted the lens solution, the false-eye paint-box on the bedside table. She has no choice.

He watches the transition in awe. The lenses removed, the cage bars break. He knocks her flat, immediately, crudely, roughly piercing her. The fire makes steam. The steam is so much it douses. There are the pink-white eyes, the clear gel, the link with the other side of the universe.

Down below, between her thighs he moves in her dark innards. Yes, she's like everyone else. Dark, hot, like every other woman. It's a lonely triumph for him.

Helen read romantic novels. She'd brought Alba up under the pink sugar-vapour of a candy-floss cloud. It was cloaked biology, a nappa-leather shoe on the cloven hoof. One always had to be saving oneself for some man. Therefore men were never real, never could be.

As Kirkwood fucks her, Alba knows it was she, not he, who is at fault – if there are faults in this. It was she who had wooed Keith into her own romantic novel. But what about her soul? Her naked eyes have been plumbed by him. Whatever she is has been read, and now sullied.

She cannot stop the connection. For a moment it is as if they have swopped places. Yes, for a second Keith looks out from her white skull, she from his dark one.

Her body talks louder now. It won't countenance the subtle other. It doesn't want to know. It tightens, twists, dries on her. Every thrust is a nail of hate. As Keith shouts obscenities in her face, he slaps her again, scores her white already-bruised thighs, draws beads of blood.

'I've got her, Dutch,' he says, forcing his tongue in her mouth. Alba, the white corpse in glass has her arms behind her head. Her face, so empty, so receptive. The woman in the water.

He stops, looks at her face. Lost. He's lost.

He bends and – (why, oh why, does he do this?) – giving a great defeated sigh, he bends his head, and kisses her with genuine tenderness . . . and then sees this kiss of tenderness rip on through her, bring her back to life, to him . . . And he comes then, firing black sperm into her body, shooting it up, up, to her mouth. It's the devil's sperm, black, foul, ignorant. His wife had not wanted it. So it's been fermenting too long. It's become stale, sour. Too much for Alba to take.

But she takes it. She allows Keith to come home.

Black words spring in utter surprise from her lips. A shred of love is all it took – a mere shred. Her body runs ahead of her in its shameless role, and the tension splits. She, now pulsing with the dark one, goes under.

15

Betrayal . . . The house reeks. No amount of cleaning can remove the yellow-green taint from the air. The atmosphere holds all there ever was – all lies, every deceit, each invisible deed. The unseen clocks them all up, and they lie there, dissolved out, waiting for the man who can sniff the wind, free the trapped confessions, read the history from the scent of the crime.

Dutch can do this – Alba knows it. He will come back, and the house will chatter to him the moment he steps inside. Even at this very minute it is sending out a thrum on the airwaves, tickling his ears, making his mind turn south.

She's up early the next morning. She rips the sheets from Dutch's bed, screws them into a heap, not wanting to see the fatal stain which has dried there. They must be washed. Everything must be cleaned and hung out in the air. There might be a chance. Autumn air, so full of moisture, might suck it all up, absolve her. It'd all pan out, vanish in the vast moorland sky.

Leon hears her moving furniture, gets up from his bed on the sofa downstairs, and goes up to her. Alba backs out of the room with the linen.

'What's all this?' His sleepy face considers the sheets, his head turns this way and that. There is a faint script shivering all over them, the substance of a deed recorded. He can't read it, but he knows that the man whose house this is could decipher such things.

'I have a feeling Dutch is coming back. I thought I'd give everything a clean.'

Leon snorts, trying to catch her eye and failing. 'That's not true, Alba,' he says with the blurting of an innocent. 'Why are you making it up?'

'I'm not.' Still she can't look him in the eyes.

'I know a lie when I hear one.'

'It's not a lie.'

Leon steps in front of her, his hands on his hips, barring her way downstairs. 'I know a lot about lies,' he says. 'I'm a kind of expert. All my life people have told me lies. They said I was OK, that I wasn't an ugly bastard. Or that I was the salt of the earth instead – as if that made up for it. I've had nothing but crap since birth. People were afraid to be straight with me, so they just lied. This didn't make me feel any better towards them either. I felt worse.

'Even my epilepsy . . . they said it would get better as I got older. It didn't. I had these healer-geezers my mother sent me to once a week – they said I would have my last fit if they kept laying their sanctimonious hands on my head. None of it ever came true.

'When I had that fit here, I heard every word you said. And you know what, Alba, you were the only person who told me the truth. You made up for all the lies I'd been told. You named me fair and square. I knew I'd never have another fit – how many days have gone by now – no fits, no pills, eh? If I'd stopped taking them before, as I did once, years ago, I'd have had eight *grand mal* a day.' He pauses, licks his fat lips. 'So don't lie to me, Alba. It doesn't become you.'

She drops the bundle of sheets. 'The headmaster came here.'

Leon raises an eyebrow. 'I thought there was a bad smell when I came back yesterday. So what happened?'

'He made a pass at me, that's all.' She avoids his eyes while she sling-shots the part-lie. Her aim is good – it has to be.

There's a pause while Leon thinks, the process clearly visible on his face. 'Well, you were leading him on.'

'No. I don't think I was.'

Leon shrugs, puzzled, disappointed. There's more to it, but he'll say nothing. He makes his way back down the stairs, treading carefully. There's a waterfall of tears about to fall on him from behind.

She chokes. 'I've finished with that place . . . I've decided not to go back. It would be very difficult if I did.'

'Can you just do that? Walk out, I mean? That's a bit—'

'—Radical. Yes, it is.'

'Won't that make it hard for you to get another job?'

'It will.'

'Why not stay on till the end of term?'

'No . . .'

Pause. 'If he made a pass at you, can't you report it?'

'To whom?' Alba laughs, no mirth in it. 'No-one, I'm afraid, would believe me.'

She sits down at the rosewood table, and begins to write a letter of resignation. Of course she can't tell Leon the truth – and what business of his is it anyway? As she writes, deceit burns the white page. All the full stops, all the dots etch through to the other side, leaving tiny pinprick burns.

Leon delivers the letter in person. He offered to – he doesn't know why. His fits haven't returned. It's a debt he owes her. She might have passed it over, forgotten, but he hasn't.

In the school's main concourse he hovers, waiting to be acknowledged, pacing from foot to foot. Minutes pass. He feels so out of place, so stared-at. It's becoming a real debt-price all right. His own schooldays . . . those hated years, the dread of being picked on, scourged – nothing's changed. Now the girls become silent as they draw near him, only to explode into whispers and giggles once they're past. He wants to run. He's had it with being mocked.

And he does feel the difference between his kind and this. He too is vulnerable now – no more fits in which to escape. He will have to find another niche, grow a different skin. Find his own odd kin.

The secretary summons Kirkwood. Leon won't pass the letter over to her. He can't. It's welded to his hand, to his sweaty grip. He'd love to shove it under the office glass partition, hiding his face, but he has to put the envelope into the headmaster's own hand. It's been mapped out. He must see it through.

Keith comes out of his office and whips down the stairs. His dark face paler. Not a pallor of the skin alone, but something from a deeper place, a place of change, of grief. Eyes blankly connect with a world that's lost its spark. Eyes turned inward, voice turned inward, in the contemplation of loss. But the mask is well in place: the disdain, the faint irritation, the projection of his importance. It's something to fall back on, desperately so.

The ugly form of Leon stands awkward in the hall. Keith knows why he's come. There's relief and a cutting under his ribs. What a fine ambassador for Alba he is, Keith thinks with a smirk. He walks slowly over to Leon, adjusts his tie, and enjoys the embarrassed wriggling he can provoke simply with a dismissive look. He could make such sport with this dwarf, this circus-freak. He needs someone to boot right now.

Leon puts one hand up to shield his eyes from Kirkwood. He holds the envelope out in the other, at arms length . . . nearly does it . . . go on . . . take it . . . just . . . Keith slips his large smooth hands around the paper.

Leon shivers, a bolt of steel runs through him, slices through his guts, mercifully earthing at his feet. He looks down in amazement. He's sure that his shoes are steaming . . .

Leon feels the seeking grey hungry energy pass on through him like a dark sigh.

He was right to warn Alba about guarding her soul. But with Leon there's no meat – Leon knows it, and realizes his apparent stupidity is his saviour now. There's nothing for Kirkwood to suck out, nothing for him to get hold of. Nothing to attract, because there's no glamour. That's one quality those of his kind don't have – the power to attract. They're halfway to hell already, damned by the living and the dead. Who'd want to tarry with that?

The power of the small has needled Keith in the heart. Disturbed, he slowly takes the stairs back up to his office, tapping the envelope against his arm. He won't bother to open it. He knows what it is. It's the big white page, the few words writ large in black ink. Touching the envelope, some of his strength leaves him. He knows he will live in dull monochrome from now on. No black. No white. Grey.

He's a damaged man now. And he did it all to himself. A second's tenderness tripped him, started the painful bleaching process. Better to have been comfortable as he was, comfortable with the night, than feel the tiny flame of a white candle slowly eat him away.

Alba lies in the river opposite the cottage, her body only just submerged in the shallows. Stones beneath keep her anchored – the river flows fast here. The folds of her dress float wide around her like a tent. Underneath she opens her legs wide like a starfish, and the water flows into her, between her legs, cleaning her of the black sperm. The river runs through her, and on. It takes the black milt over the emerald weed, and then moves on, slower now, with a sullen step in the deeper reaches. The dead sperm are eaten and digested by minute mouths, minute scavengers. Nothing is wasted in this world. It all gives life to another. It all comes round again.

After the hot summer the water is warm. It drains from the surrounding peat fields where it has been held sponged, soaking, storing heat. The sun is shining today. There's a late spring buoyancy in its touch. Dutch was fond of lying in the river on hot days, Alba remembers. He'd said it was immersing himself in the tide of life. He'd said a lot of things like that on elderberry wine.

She sits up in the water. The air chills. Getting out, she makes her way up the bank to the house, the wet skirt sticking to her legs.

Leon arrives on his bike, sees the weed in her hair, her clothes wet, and goes into the kitchen to make tomato sandwiches. He doesn't know what's wrong with her. But that's not true. He does know. Fits once paid the madman, only he wasn't aware what happened during that process. He had a kind of craziness on the inside which broke free now and then. Alba's got craziness too, only she's not the kind to burst. She's got the poetic variety, as though a substance has been injected in her melancholy veins which drips away all day, all night.

Tears run down Alba's cheeks as she changes her clothes. Tears like the river, they go on and on silently, almost unconcerned, not really conscious of her at all, with a life all their own. She's been like this off and on since Keith left. There's no sound with these tears, no feelings of grief. After realizing they come and go of their own will, Alba lets them be.

Leon comes back with slabby sandwiches. 'What are you going to do now?'

Alba wipes the wet away from her face with her sleeve. 'Nothing.' She shrugs. 'Dutch always said he was happiest doing nothing.' The laugh is air-light, all used up. 'Now it's my turn.'

'Why did you leave him?' Leon squints at her, head on one side.

Alba starts. 'Who said I did?'

'I dunno.' He takes a large ungainly bite of his sandwich, stuffing more in his mouth than it will take. Tomato slices flap out between his lips like bloody tongues. He talks through the food. Alba can't make out all the words, and looks away.

'. . . He's all right, though, Alba. You won't get another one like him,' he ends.

Alba looks down at her pale hands. Her reply is barely audible. 'I know,' she says. 'I know.'

Leon sits up, slaps his big hand on the table between them. 'I think we should go out,' he says. 'I'd like to take you somewhere. Will you come with me? It'd be a bit of light relief. Take your mind off things . . .'

Nothing can take your mind from the fact you've sold a diamond for the price of spinach. Given your soul to the brown-eyed one. But she agrees. Something has to fill up the day, doesn't it? Something has to fill her up now she's running out, slipping away, like the sand flowing through the thin neck of the reaper's hourglass.

'Oh, no, not this place, Leon.' They walk across the grass to the west front, and some of Alba's spirit returns. She throws her hands up in the air, unbelieving exasperation in her voice. 'What d'you want to bring me here for? I hate the place.'

'Hate it . . . ?' He rubs his lips with the back of his hand, surprised at her reaction.

'Every time I've come here, something nasty has happened. God's got it in for me, I think. It must be because I don't have the right attitude,' she finishes cynically.

Leon scoffs. 'You don't need one,' he says. 'You just have to be yourself, don't you?'

'Here? Is that possible? Even desirable?' she mutters.

She thinks back to Dutch, strolling through the nave in his work clothes, his boots dropping mud, drunk, swearing . . .

'It's not that simple,' she says. 'It's my background – you should wear your best clothes, talk in whispers, feel some respect, some reverence. But I don't feel those things. I never have. I get more and more cynical as I get older. And what's in there anyway? Name me one single person whose met God in a cathedral . . . and it wasn't their imagination, or they weren't drunk.' She pulls a face. 'I don't know a soul.'

Leon smooths his rough hands back over his face and over his greased hair. He can remember as a young boy having to comb it before going into church. Old habits die hard. Old manacles have a rusty grip, a long memory.

Leon searches out the ordinary in the Cathedral. He's uncomfortable here, yet pretends he isn't. He doesn't know how to behave, is aware of etiquette he hasn't mastered and never shall. To him, visiting a church has always been an awkward privilege, like being a guest at a Royal Garden Party – more terror than fun. He doesn't pick up social messages. He can only seek out the small, the odd, the quirks in the making.

Clerics in their black gowns make him shrink back amongst the pillars, make him look the other way, wrestle with his hands, feel the sweat break out. Centuries ago his sort would have had to watch their tongues, even if they'd not uttered a single word. And Alba – he shoots her a look – she'd have been burnt for sure. Her white hair, the air of the unusual about her, would've sealed her fate without doubt. He can see them both now with a shudder in his mind's eye – Alba on one stake, him on another, fire at their feet, screaming to God who never listened, never answered.

The twisted, the maimed, the sick of mind . . . all were laughed at and jostled in those days. There was little pity. The Church was always on the look out for somewhere to plant its demons . . .

'If you were God, would you want to live here?' he says, looking up into the dull empty space of the nave.

Alba shakes her head, quoting Dutch. 'No – too many shoulds.'

Leon laughs as he understands. 'That's a relief, that is,' he says. 'You never know if you can be honest, and not have someone kick you for it. You've got to mind your p's and q's in these places, and it's such hard work.' His face takes on a new resolve. 'They'll have to take me as I am from now on.'

Alba shoots him a wry look. 'You and Dutch should get on,' she says.

Cavalier now, he strides towards the choir, looking about him expansively. Everything has fallen more comfortably to his level. Suddenly, by the side of the first row of stalls, he drops on all fours and crawls in between them. 'Look . . . you'll never guess what's down here,' he says, his voice muffled. 'Look, Alba, at the carving on these seats . . . goats, dragons, men with funny faces, some like me . . .'

Yes, Alba thinks, with tender surprise, the seats, as Leon calls them, are misericords. Misericords – acts of mercy.

Leon crawls along between the choir stalls, running his fingers over the carving in the dark. When he emerges at the other end, Alba asks him, 'How did you know all these were here?'

'I had a fit here, didn't I?' He gets to his feet. 'I fell into this lot. When I came to there was this man with donkey's ears looking at me.' He gives a lopsided grin. 'I thought – that's just how I feel when I'm coming round . . .'

Alba laughs. Leon belongs. When you least expect . . . you find what you are. He falls down in a fit . . . so out of control, he finds himself, he's recognized.

There are Leons everywhere in the cathedral. They look down from the capitals . . . men with toothache, the man carrying a goose, the packman with his sack over his shoulder, the man plucking a thorn from his foot, the thief stealing grapes . . .

'Everything's in here,' Leon says, in a kind of ordinary wonder. 'Everything in creation is all under this one big roof. Why else build such a large place? It's not for God, no. What do we need him for? It's to contain the whole of man, that's what.'

The profundity slips out. Leon's chin juts back as if he is looking at himself from the inside, and strange unlike-him words have been planted in his mouth. Still puzzled, he saunters out, leaving Alba behind.

'And where am I?' Alba says, under her breath. 'Nowhere in this place.' It's always hated the likes of me. I'm a woman, that's why. I deal with the mysteries of life every day. Periods – the bleeding that the body survives, month after month, year after year. Birth – the something coming from nothing – proof of being fucked by an invisible that needs *us* more than we need it.

On their way out, Leon, excitement ill-concealed on his face, makes her walk towards the south transept, to the dark contemplative shrine of votive candles. The metal tiers that hold the candles are all bare, except for one which burns right in the middle of the central tier. As she gets closer, she notices a pile of other candles, half burnt, snuffed out, badly hidden behind the offertory box, their wicks smoking. Leon rubs his hands.

'Is this your work?' she says.

He nods vigorously. 'I didn't want you to be left out.'

There's not much to do in the days, weeks, that follow. Leon is out at work. Alba lives in the vacuum of Dutch's cottage. Whatever strand her life will take, she can't seek it out until Dutch returns. There's an end to tie up before she moves on. Don't screw anyone in the house while I'm away, will you, he'd said. And Alba had got mad with him – the idea had been preposterous then. He'd said it to wind her up, but she remembers his face . . . the seriousness there, the sadness, as if he knew he was supping with Judas, knew what was to come.

No school now, no lessons to prepare, no marking, nothing. She's discarded the schoolmarm robe, and finds there's nothing underneath. She'd grown into that role too well. She hadn't realized it was an act, that it should have been just one of many.

Lovingly she cleans Helen's furniture now – the ill often clean. The soul wants to wipe away, wipe away, and has to learn the distress of the unchangeable, the unerasable, and eventually accept. Alba polishes the barometer, turns the carved slipper box upside down, the polishing cloth boring into every edge, her nails scraping out debris and fluff – the polish cleaning, the rag growing dirtier, Alba's satisfaction seeing the dirt removed. Helen's past comes to life now in a way it had never done when she was alive. Her possessions have become precious artifacts, inspected, patted, given attention, fingered, familiarized. Alba knows them like old friends.

Was Helen really that bad? A sugary, unreal vision of her mother supplants reality . . . Helen wasn't an awful mother, it was Alba's fault – she'd never appreciated her.

You can see pain coming well before it bites. It's like a ghost-rider on the horizon, hurtling towards you. You can sniff the flavour, the smell of it, well before it arrives. And if you watch, if you stay firm, you can watch the rider approach, you feel the pain hit like a wind that goes before him – you can feel the sound, the smell, the panic, the slicing hooves. Then it's on you, the hooves stamp on your head, mush your guts, turn you over and over. And then it's gone . . . but the debris remains, the dust in the air, the shrinking as it slips away to another horizon.

Appalling loneliness visits her as the year begins to die. It makes cells the colour of city skies, skies full up with rubbish. It comes out like the deadness of mercury from the core, settles, collects in a lead box under her ribs, indigestible. Nothing can etch it away. With Helen gone, Alba realizes why she needed her. Helen was merely a launch-pad for kicking feet, like the sides of a swimming-bath are to the swimmer. Without that hard boundary you don't ever make the first length . . .

After a long walk one lunchtime Alba comes back to the cottage and sees smoke, a thick column of it. She's been looking for flowers to strew on the river for Helen. The river has become an obsession. There's so much locked in it, like a moving book, but it goes too fast for her to read.

Now she runs along the road, her body melting with fear. Helen is in the house, burning to death. Alba must make it this time, rescue her, stop it happening. With no thought for danger she rushes in. The house is different. Furniture has been moved. There are empty gaps.

The back door is open. Outside, the field beyond is thick with smoke. She hears someone cough. She runs out.

The tall figure of Dutch stands upwind of a huge bonfire. She stares at the flames. It's a funeral pyre, loaded with Helen's things: smashed furniture, chair legs, old tapestries.

Dutch moves back, half-turns – he hasn't seen her yet. There's something fat on his crooked arm. Alba takes a step towards him, and the hawk lifts off and flies away from the leather glove. Dutch swivels round, meets Alba's eyes not with his own but with the cold all-seeing iris of the bird.

He's not the same man. He's lost weight, appears taller. He's shaved his beard – it stuns her – and the features exposed now are aquiline, severe, terrifying. He looks at her, through her, striking an ice-pick in her heart. And then he smiles, takes off the leather glove, and the severity of his features melts. The light and shade of six months away from her sweep across his face.

Leon pushes past her from behind. He's carrying a small japanned table and a dressing-table stool – Helen's. He sees Alba and carries on past her, his face rather blank, rather dutiful, and hands the furniture to Dutch. Dutch turns, tosses them onto the flames.

Alba shakes. She can't make her body move. She's like a child for whom massive disappointment, the final humiliation, has come. The promised birthday present that was never bought. How on earth do you react to that? You have to make excuses to save *their* face, don't you, not just your own.

She's rigid, stuffed with emotions too embarrassing for her to let out . . . her face twisting this way and that, a fake smile, then a grimace coming and going. Which emotion should she tag? And how should it come out? How?

For several minutes she stands staring at Dutch, her feet stupidly fidgeting in her shoes. Words which come up approximate nothing. She's lost her grip. Silent, seething, and a whole lot more besides, she looks at Dutch – maybe *he* will get her out of this – save her face, and his. But he has the audacity to smile – slowly – with brilliant confidence, full of amusement, tenderness. His little white . . . playing up again. Never understanding anything, always protesting. Christ! – but she's a challenge!

She turns her back to him and walks inside, stiff as wood.

He's cleared his bedroom of every trace of Helen's memory. The Victorian jewellery box with Helen's 'fifties' bangles – gone. The sewing-box – gone. The box of lavender-scented linen and tatting – gone. The three red-leather photograph albums . . . the only record of her childhood, her former life − gone. All her past − gone. Wiped out.

Alba flings open the wardrobe door. Most of her clothes are gone too, replaced by his. Joseph's coats, new, smart, bright, textured. The colours would suit him. Not the colours of a vagabond, of the middle-aged drop-out, the subverter of convention. No, these are clothes for a different purpose altogether. He's met up with the gypsy, she knows it − he wants to impress her, seduce her proper. Alba will kill him this time. Kill her this time.

Alba − her life gone. Dutch with a new one. Curse him. Damn him. Turn three times on the spot and banish him . . .

The door opens and he comes into the room. His presence is large and soothing − to the room, but not to her.

'Why did you do that? Why get Leon to help you? Why?' Her words are short, bottled, nipped by jagged edges. She's in a glass palace of the unreal.

'You think I want Helen's bits in my house?' He leans against the chest, preparing himself for the launch of her nails, the bite of her teeth . . .

'They were *my* bits.'

He shakes his head. 'No. They were a substitute for something else. Helen's bits and pieces. Her old garbage. You don't need them now. And I . . . I certainly don't.'

'It's move me out and get someone else in, is it?' Alba snarls. The gypsy must be waiting in the wings . . . at the local pub half a mile up the road . . . the dying bonfire is a signal for her to come after getting rid of every trace of Alba.

'What?' He throws back his head, laughs. 'I've already got one load of trouble in residence, *you*. I don't want any more.'

'I feel like screaming the place down.'

'Alba dear, don't. You're not the theatrical type. Don't –
unless it's with relief. What happened? Did you go crazy?
There was a house full of junk in here when I came back.
I found some incredible things . . . a commode – what d'you
want with that for Christ's sake? Bags of her clothes under
the bed. Pink girdles, corsets – the rubber all perishing –
stacks of bloomers. Half a ton of make-up, bottles of old
scent – Jesus – I even found a used bar of soap wrapped in
a silk handkerchief. What's been going on?'

Alba heaves her shoulders and looks away. The desire to
fly at him has gone. Something approaching relief takes its
place, though the last thing she'd want is for him to notice.

'Face it.' He's on his haunches in front of her. 'She was
your mother. That's all. You don't have an obligation to her.
You don't have to haul her garbage around for the rest of
your life to do penance for . . . hating her.'

'Hating her? I did? That sounds horrible.' She looks up,
wanting it different. 'Didn't I love her somewhere along the
line? Couldn't I have done?'

Dutch gets up. 'Maybe.' He shakes his head. 'I don't
know. Perhaps . . .' He sighs. Another thought threads in.
'What else has been going on? I couldn't get much out of
Leon. He was struck dumb the moment I came in the door.'

She sits up, looks him in the eyes. Fake blue. 'Nothing.
Nothing's happened. Helen died the week after you left. I
couldn't handle it. I cracked up, I guess. I gave in my notice.
I've been here ever since. I was . . . hoping to move out
before you got back.'

Sharp eyes pierce her for a second. 'Why are you wearing
your lenses, Alba? You're not at work. What are you
frightened I'll see?'

'I'm not. I've nothing to hide. Maybe I need a little
protection, something to hide behind for a while. A lot has
been happening to me.'

'I see. So you looked after my little cottage for me? Thank you very much. I am in your debt, aren't I?' He goes to the wardrobe, takes out the hangers with his clothes, and makes to go. His face is set. There's a huge disappointment on it. 'You can sleep here,' he says. 'I'll make use of the spare room.' And he goes out without a backward glance.

He's sniffed out the lie – Alba knows it. The peculiar honesty they've always had has been rent. Kirkwood's sword blindly cuts the air still, laughs, mocks. How delighted he would be if he knew . . .

And why can't she tell Dutch? Why has this thing grown so big? He'd been away, there must have been someone . . . others . . . Was it reasonable not to allow the same for herself? They didn't have an official relationship, either. Alba had walked out. Not even he could possibly know she'd spent the time apart wondering how to walk back.

She could tell him about Keith. Try and laugh it off. Say it was her dark birthday. But how can you tell your lover you met the devil, and knew what it was to make love to him . . . ?

Alba is November now – the dying, the emptying, the encroaching blackness. The process of decay goes on all around, slowly. Time to watch. Time to get intimate with the dissolving. Nothing else to do.

Dutch and Leon leave her alone. They've formed a silent alliance. They go out to The Duck in the evenings. They don't ask Alba to come. They shut her out. Leave her angry, hurt, on the far side of a desert, waving, hoping, but they take no notice. They won't come to her rescue.

The blackness outside her meets kin within. She can't pretend anymore. She's trying to cling on to this false inner whiteness. Alba the pure. Ha! ha! She no longer exists – if she ever did. She's grey, grey-black like the country, like

323

the weather now, caught somewhere she doesn't want to be. The uneasy mid-point on an unbalanced see-saw, the polarities hidden, in the non-light, the non-dark.

It's full moon. From the living room window she watches the two men as they walk along the road on their regular nightly visit to The Duck. Like black ghosts in a reversed landscape. Once, just once, Dutch looks back. Then he turns, sets his thick coat around his shoulders, moves on. It was not an invitation.

Not to be defeated, she wraps up and goes out too, waywardness in her heart.

The night air is built on charcoal, cordite, fog, moisture, blackened leaves. The fog of the womb. Every breath catches the throat with a cold rasp. Town air tonight will be caught with a faint snatch of acid.

She walks in the opposite direction to the two men, towards a line of willows, their bare twigs silver wire in the moonlight. The only density in the landscape is the broody shape of a holm oak. The evergreen leaves make a different noise as the wind blows through them. In summer this tree smoothed the air across its canopy. Now, the leaves are dry, still there, but crisper, almost in pain. The night air moves like dark sweeps from a painter's brush, currents talk, weave, play around her legs. It's scary out here tonight. Anything could happen – she knows it. And she doesn't care a whit.

The sky is dark, distant and wonderful, star-shot, out-brillianced by the moon. She could scratch the sky now, rip the cloth, see the bright lining of silver on the other side. Why not? Why not confront this God and tell him what a bastard he is. Tell him she's never believed, that the rawness of herself is the only thing she now has faith in. Yes, it'd be like tearing velvet, her nails like scimitars. She'd have God on the run. She'd be peeping through the mystery into his private house, robbing him of his power, the old patriarch.

Somewhere in the dark there's a chink — there's got to be, she thinks, her eyes searching. How else would the moon be full unless, at some magical place unknown to her, the velvet was drawn back a little for the light to stream through. The moon is God's Cyclopean eye. Can't be bothered to look through both eyes like the rest of the made-in-his-image creation. He only really sees at night. If you met God face to face you'd fry, that's what they say. But each month at full moon we taste a little of that ecstasy, and think we can have no more of it. We live under threat.

You can go crazy then, with that eye watching you, floating through the heavens, unblinking. At full moon the curtain's drawn back a little, and he looks down. Why just one eye? You don't need two if you're God — you can always have the other one shut. You can afford to sleep on the job. You can be downright lazy.

Full moon in November . . . Glory shines on trash, mould, soot-smell, clogged air, shards in the lungs. Even the air in the country has the pall of city taint. The fog of the womb.

November . . . despair. Dying is so very ugly. Plants hang there, sliming, going black. They don't go easy into the hard earth. There's no dignity here. A horrible fetid tongue licks the land, griming it with plague.

Alba lets out a long empty breath. She feels weighed down. Life? It's a sentence.

A white shape makes her look up. She's being watched from a post by a bird the colour of her hair, a barn owl. All eyes. All vicious claws too. She stops in sudden awe. And what are the night birds? They who defy the rules, who see clearly in the dark using the night as a great bowl of food.

Diclopean birds, faces borrowed from the moon, all eye, all eyes – God's night messengers – the coward.

Alba walks past the post, her skin prickling. The owl swivels its head to follow her with its eyes. It does not move. It's waiting to get her tonight.

The stars oh! in the black velvet. The turned inside-out innards of the familiar form of day. The smoothed pile of velvet gloves studded with inner workings, the odd fancy stitch. Sweat perhaps, the celestial droplets. Here the Plough . . . there the Pleiades . . . now Orion, just rising. Gems of sweat on the inside of a superior glove which can wink, glisten, go on forever.

Ponderous and light, Orion climbs the sky. He looks for toe-holds in this dark cup.

Cup of grey in day, Alba thinks as she walks on. I much prefer it now. The contast . . . oh! the brilliance . . . oh! the dazzling dark! The *Mother* dark.

So, stroke your hand, flick sweat from your glove, and let the fallen stars drop to earth. There they must live their temporary lives as they slowly evaporate and turn to mist. A mist appearing . . . and disappearing . . . *I am a fallen star . . . a fallen star . . .*

Alba claps her gloved hands. So much to us means the sky. It never changes in our short span. Man orders the sky, and God must laugh. How nice to be random, flippant, to fling sweat, stars, here . . . there . . . drops there, yes . . . and watch man measure the sky with instruments to create his frail, pitiable order. Live in the boundless, and do not label. The mind was meant for other things, for A to B, not to mechanize the mysteries.

She stops walking and goes to the riverbank, sits down by the edge. The surface of the black peat-water is silvered in the middle, shrouded at the far edge. She watches the cold boiling, the silver streaming, and it reaches out to her with its own black-gloved hands and takes her in . . .

The river flows in . . . through her and on. The moving book suddenly opens and allows itself to be read . . .

. . . Killing for entertainment . . . the children, innocents, piked on sticks . . . the squelch of a corpse's stomach under soldiers' boots . . . the rapes with knives, not bodies . . . the mines set to blow off limbs . . . the guns cocked to blow off faces. Red blood and gore, rivers of it now . . . white petals splashed with it . . . red flowers on the battlefield . . . the neighbour on fire behind her front door while youths laugh . . . the Inquisition . . . the abuse of magick . . . the rag-dolls of aborted babies . . . the easy destruction of Kirkwood's career with a lie – or with the truth . . . I could watch him be stripped, cast out.

Alba stares at the water as the images pass by. She's shaking, she's all used up. But there's more. What comes in as light . . . goes out reeking of putrefaction.

Keith floats by. His dark charm makes her sick with lust. Yes, the brown-eyed is an attractive catch. Always will be. He floats on the surface, an ungerminated seed. Something further on will eat him, acid will melt his coat. And he will come round again, in different guises – now the torturer – now the white lotus. He's on the circuit, same as her, on the never ending round-trip that's full of surprises.

Helen waves – she's on a pleasure boat, having fun, jollying up the company. She's white, angelic, the healer – what's *this*?!

And Dutch . . . what is this . . . ? He is the man in the tall black cape, the woman in the cape, and he, she, opens it wide to show the white inside. Magick. It's got to be magick . . . There, under his wing, safe inside the cape is Alba. His fledgling. His wilful white one who doesn't want to be, red eyes glaring at him, teeth biting his wrist, hating him, running away into middle-class convention the next time round . . . And she has been cast out, the wondrous wretch and weedless – as Dutch would say, quoting poems to her – to eat green herbs and be awakened and chastened by the rain's shower and winter's bitter weather . . . That's how the amber cracks . . . No wonder.

All this is me, she says. I am Murderer and Saint, Lover and Deceiver. Plenty of black here, under *my* ribs, beating in time with the universe. I am the fallen star meant to taste darkness. The woman all white. I wanted Keith's heart. I still do. I'll chase him for centuries, given half a chance . . . I want its soft moleskin deception, that caress, that brutality, its horrible beauty. And he – he wanted the white dove . . . Never inside me, but he saw it there and craved a black:white wedding. What thieves we were.

Alba clambers to her feet, bows to the river, the river of life, the Styx, the river of hell. She can remember nothing with her mind, but her body knows what to do. She watches herself as it flings off her clothes and leaps naked into the freezing black water. She watches, laughs as her white flesh goes under, drowns in blackness, is baptized. It's a phoenix burial in the water.

She goes to give the dark its due, and the moon becomes blurred by haze. The river is the black serpent, the oil-skinned rakshasa. It must have, it does have, its wicked sinful delightful initiatory way with her. She comes up. The moon comes out from behind the cloud with God-like modesty. So – God must be female. A man would have looked.

Alba leaps about in the road, runs on bare feet over the cold bitty gravel, rubs herself roughly dry with her shirt, and throws on her clothes. What madness! What delight! I am as black as shit! Ha! And I have diamonds . . . I've supped with the devil, from a short spoon, danced with him, fallen in love with him for ever, and it didn't kill me. I stuck my fingers in the black treacle pot and licked them, oh, yes . . . And I'm still here! Black Alba! I am! I am!

Running back along the road she sees Dutch and Leon coming towards her from The Duck. They're talking louder now, the drink bawling at the deaf world as they disappear into the house. Alba runs in after them. Dutch is examining the pot of black leaves Leon has just taken out of the cupboard and given to him. He had to. The room is filled with scent. It had seeped out from the closed cupboard and now, freed, bursts into the room, smothering everything with a sweet fragrance. The flowers are strange, as dark as the sky now, almost too much, a piece of the velvet glove . . . Whoever heard of a plant blooming inside a closed cupboard?

Dutch turns to Alba ashamed, aware of the alcohol veil. Her face is bright, sharp, alive. Little vixen. He can't focus on her. You set something up – you *think* you've set something up – and you think the moment of glory will be yours. But drink has always been that robber for him. It's a good stealer of ego, of miracles. Dumbly he hands her the pot, not knowing what to do with it now, not even able to remember what it once represented to him. She rushes out into the night air with it. Moments later he hears the crash as she drops it, smashes it perhaps, on the road. Leon shoots after her, a large box of fireworks in his hands.

Breathless she comes back in. 'You know what I did, don't you?' she says to Dutch. 'But I still have to tell you, don't I? Kirkwood and I . . . we fucked . . .'

He puts a finger to his lips.

'. . . and he is . . . and I knew . . .'

Dutch raises one eyebrow. 'Of course you did.'

'And . . . I enjoyed it.'

*   *   *

Outside Leon is letting off the fireworks. Alba runs away from him down the road to get a better look. Dutch comes outside too, standing bemused, wordless, out of the picture.

Alba's crazy, dancing, twirling in the moonlight. Cats appear from nowhere, yowl, wrap themselves around her legs. The moon yells, fireworks spit defiant light at the sky. Leon's a cat, a grin from ear to ear.

'How's this, Alba?' he yells, touching a match to the blue paper twists under each rocket. He stands up, leaps back, shields his eyes and the rockets shoot up, leave earth . . . fallen stars travelling home. The sky above explodes in fissions, fusions, orange sparks, flowers, bursts of orange motes. Bangs that make the velvet tremble.

Orion rises. They watch it climb, the arrogant giant stealing the sky, his belt beaded with sling-shots, his greedy limbs astride the heavens. He's fucking the sky, straddling it with virile limbs. He's already ripped the velvet cloth – he's the hunter, he has arrows – and he brings down the silver and gold now as Leon sets off candles, Vesuviuses, mortars, and Chinese crackers, to greet him. Dutch, too close, puts his fingers over his ears.

Suddenly silence . . . Alba in the moonlight, dancing . . .

Does she know, Dutch thinks, that her black skirt, the one with mirrors, rivals all the split-sky fire as she turns and catches the silver lining of the moon? Probably not. And she'd hate to be told.

Is she aware of her long black hair, the wild, feral face now, the incisor teeth, so carefully filed, out to get him – he shivers – once more? Probably not. Don't tell her.

And . . . he stops, holds his breath. Is she aware of the white owl coming from nowhere, hovering above her dancing form, descending like the Biblical dove, landing on her head? Of the red blood running down her white cheeks? Of the red blood running down her legs from inside her now, as she brings the red magick home? For God's sake, don't tell her that one.

Does she know of his great love, that she was the fledgling bird he had to let go of?

Probably not.

But she will.

The red-eyed, little white . . . W.i.t.c.h.